Also by Clinton McKinzie
POINT OF LAW

Coming soon
in hardcover
from Delacorte Press
TRIAL BY ICE AND FIRE

THE EDGE OF JUSTICE

Clinton McKinzie

A DELL BOOK

THE EDGE OF JUSTICE
A Dell Book

PUBLISHING HISTORY
Delacorte hardcover edition published June 2002
Dell mass market edition / April 2003

Published by
Bantam Dell
A Division of Random House, Inc.
New York, New York

Library of Congress Catalog Card Number: 2001052942
No part of this book may be reproduced or transmitted in any form or by
any means, electronic or mechanical, including photocopying, recording,
or by any information storage and retrieval system, without the written
permission of the publisher, except where permitted by law. For
information address: Delacorte Press, New York, New York.

Dell is a registered trademark of Random House, Inc., and the colophon
is a trademark of Random House, Inc.

ISBN 0-440-23723-8

Manufactured in the United States of America
Published simultaneously in Canada

OPM   10   9   8   7   6   5   4   3   2   1

In Memory of
Morgan Williams McKinzie
1970–1992
Thanks for teaching me to dream, bro.

ACKNOWLEDGMENTS

I WOULD NEVER have had the courage to write this novel if it hadn't been for the psychological support of my parents, Carl and Rena McKinzie, and my surviving brother, Wayne. The words on my dad's favorite ski hat urged me on—*No Guts, No Glory.* My brother, Morgan, taught me by example to fight for my dreams, even if it means taking horrible chances and getting kicked in the teeth.

My mother-in-law, Mary Memory, didn't call me a fool when I quit my job as a lawyer and deputy district attorney. She proved a great reader of early drafts. Thanks for believing in me, Momster.

My gentlemanly Rottweiler, Dempsey, had faith in me too. Not only did he spend years "spotting" me on climbs at Vedauwoo, but he also spotted me through the writing of this book. His faith was unflagging even when, on a so-called research trip, he broke his back in an icy fall. He didn't make a whimper as I crammed all one hundred pounds of his paralyzed body into a climbing pack and hoofed it out through miles of snow. The miracle workers at Colorado State University's Veterinary Teaching Hospital were somehow able to piece him together again.

John Talbot, my literary agent, was willing to take a

chance on this manuscript. Not only did he undertake its representation, but he marketed it with an enthusiasm that still astonishes me. Katie Hall and Danielle Perez, editors at Bantam Dell, made my dream a reality. And Deborah Dwyer, also at Bantam Dell, completed the monumental task of making the manuscript readable.

Thank you to all my friends who critiqued the early drafts and offered sage advice: Jon and Laura Mellberg, Scott Peterson, Detective Michael Jones, Ula Latimer, Mayor Richard Riordan, Matt Aminoff, Pam Dabela, William Ouchi, John Cooke, David Rone, Michael and Kelly Siegel, Beth Richmond McKinzie, Kevin and Tina Ellmann, Dan Forgey, and Louisa Craft.

And finally, thank you, Justine. You have safely belayed me through a trying time (even if you sometimes gave me a little "penalty slack"). Without you, this simply wouldn't be. Wild horses . . .

ONE

A DRY WIND BLOWS hard out of the Medicine Bow Mountains onto the high plateau of the Laramie River, just as it does every fall in the southeast part of the state. It's a steady pressure, as unrelenting as gravity, but also a force that seems to have a mischievous intent. The wind is regularly fed by the curses of the fifty thousand enduring souls who inhabit the high plains and mountains here. On this day its fuel is further charged by the oaths of people who have never before had the opportunity to feel its power. The multitudes of television reporters gathered outside on the courthouse lawn offer up foul maledictions. The wind is blowing their carefully brushed and stiffened hair out of place. Propelled by it, the occasional tumbleweed playfully interrupts their broadcasts as it bounces between the commentators and cameras. The few forlorn Klansmen isolated even amid the crowd across the street curse the wind too. It threatens to blow their pointed hoods right off their heads and reveal their true identities. Worse than that, it raises their robes like women's skirts, causing them to drop their placards and hold their arms straight down at their sides.

On the drive in this morning I'd been struck by just how much the prairie fauna surrounding Laramie is like my maternal grandfather's ranch in Argentina. There's the same sagebrush and chaparral bent by the wind toward the east, as if yearning for the sun to rise each dawn and exposing their backsides' naked roots to the fading night. There are the same surrounding high peaks capped with ice. But the town itself is nothing like my grandfather's nearest village, where idle gauchos squat on crooked, unpaved streets, and children play half-dressed in rags. This Wyoming town is even more exotic. Today Laramie probably appears strange to its longest-surviving residents. Over the past week strangers from across the nation have descended on the town with their cameras and microphones like a buzzing horde of bright-colored locusts.

Upon entering Laramie, I drive along past the courthouse with the other rubbernecking traffic and feel something on my face that has become unfamiliar—a smile lifting the corners of my lips. It isn't really a happy smile. It's more of a head-shaking *what the hell?* smirk. The thick torso of my mastiff-mix leans far out the backseat passenger-side window of the ancient Land Cruiser, and he seems to be grinning too. The crowd that's gathered on the sidewalk leans away from the approaching dog's head with his great yellow teeth and ropes of saliva that hang from black lips.

I'm lucky to find a parking spot five blocks from the courthouse despite the extraordinary traffic. There I roll up the windows just enough so the beast can't reach out and cause heart attacks by licking passersby. I dust the animal's dark hair from the white shirt and khaki pants that I wear for this occasion instead of my usual tired jeans, sandals, and untucked flannel shirts. Before walking away from the truck, I pull on a navy sport coat to hide the gun that's clipped to the belt at the back of my pants. I speak softly to the dog as I cinch the tie close around my throat.

"Stay, Oso. Watch the car."

I have never seen anything like the crowd that's swarming on the well-watered lawn outside Albany County's four-story sandstone courthouse. As I wind my way through the masses toward the low steps, I can't stop looking about and feeling that same sardonic turn of my lips. It seems that all the world is here in this small, usually quiet Wyoming city of only twenty-six thousand full-time residents. I have spent time in Laramie twice before: first as a child, more than two decades ago, when my father was assigned to the nearby Air Force base, and again as a cop, just two years ago, when I performed a brief investigation here. In both my recent and distant memories the town was as colorful as any university town but generally peaceful, nothing at all like the scene that affronts me today.

From around the country there are civil rights demonstrators, victims' groups representatives, the NAACP, print reporters, television journalists, ACLU protesters, church groups, titillated tourists, and members of the Ku Klux Klan and various other absurd militias. All are talking or shouting excitedly. I can see that someone has somehow partitioned them, as uniformed deputies allow some on the court side of the street and keep others across from it. Grand Avenue, which lies in between, is lined with double-parked media vans with dish-shaped antennas that extend from their roofs. They have all come for the excitement that can only be born of a true media sensation—the trial of Kimberly Lee's killers.

Two years ago the murderers of Matthew Shepard were spared the death penalty here in a trial that was broadcast around the globe. Just a year after the pair was sentenced to life in prison for the beating death of the gay university student, while the nation was still focused on the town and the horrors its youth could commit, a new bias-inspired murder swept the headlines like a whirlwind. Another minority student, this one Asian, was raped and strangled, and then further denigrated by racist words written in her own blood. The Shepard killing had seemed an anomaly, but the Lee murder had the national press wondering if something more sinister lurked behind the facade of the state's only liberal college town. The focus on Laramie couldn't be more intense if it were viewed from one of the University of Wyoming's high-powered microscopes.

Everyone is here, I guess, but the citizens of Laramie. I imagine them at home, hiding with their curtains drawn and their shotguns loaded, praying for the wind to blow this circus away across the plains.

A disorderly mob of spectators is queued from the courthouse doors at the top of the steps, down onto the sidewalk, and around the corner. Each one holds a slip of paper that I assume gives him or her a seating pass for the big event. More people gather around those lucky enough to have a place in the line, arguing and pleading for a spot. Amid the crowd at the top of the steps stands one of the largest men I've ever seen, even in a state like Wyoming that breeds big men.

His shaved ebony head rises well above the throng. Those near give him space in deference to both his size and the brown county sheriff's uniform he wears. With his face tilted slightly to one side as he speaks into the radio mounted on his broad shoulder, he watches my approach.

I jostle my way up the steps toward the deputy, pardoning and excusing myself among the turmoil, with one arm extended to guide my way through. The bodies before me give way grudgingly, moving aside only after giving my face a second look. With my courtroom clothes, all-American features, and longish hair, I could be just another pushy reporter cutting in line, or a young attorney or staff member of one of the parties. But my skin is a little too prematurely weathered, and there's the jagged white scar that runs from left eye to upper lip on my otherwise tan skin. They turn aside while speculating as to just what role I perform in this extravaganza.

"Special Agent Antonio Burns," the big man says when I'm near, enunciating each syllable of my title and name, "or should I call you QuickDraw? What are you doing here, man? You're just in time. Closing arguments start in fifteen minutes."

"I really hate being called that, Jones. If I see the columnist who made that up, I'm going to punch him in the nose."

He chuckles, not realizing I'm serious, and I pump the sweaty hand that swallows my own.

"Can you get me inside? I'm supposed to meet my boss, Ross McGee, in there."

The giant nods and then uses his bulk to part the crowd toward the courthouse doors. I'm pulled along in his wake. He beats his fist on the glass to draw the attention of the security officers within. When the door is cracked open by one, Jones barks, "Let him in. He's DCI." Then he grabs my arm and pushes me through.

I slip inside the building, away from the impassioned

crowd and into the quiet of the cleared hallway, where there
are only a few overwhelmed security guards standing anx-
iously by the metal detectors. I realize that these rent-a-cops
probably don't know what DCI means.

"Wyoming Division of Criminal Investigation," I explain to the nearest one and flash my gold shield as the detector registers my gun and shrieks in alarm.

"The courtroom's that way, sir," the guard says, pointing down the hall. I thank him and follow the point.

Inside the courtroom the bench and jury box are empty.
But the front of the courtroom is bustling with activity.
Where the single defense table should be there are two, one
for each of the Knapp brothers' legal teams. The prosecution has only one table, which is next to the jury box.
Because the County Attorney represents all the people of
the state and the jurors too, he is allowed to sit closest to
their box. And you don't want the defendants sitting anywhere near the men and women who will be judging them.

The courtroom itself is a surprisingly small venue for a
case that has people across the nation eagerly scanning
headlines and watching evening newscasts. There are only
about twelve rows of churchlike hard wooden pews for the
gallery. Simple white paint adorns the walls, and the only
decorations are an American flag and a Wyoming flag, one
on each side of the judge's bench, and the gold state seal
mounted before it. A short oak wall divides the gallery from
the participants.

Secretaries and paralegals gather around the lawyers in
the well like cheerleaders. It's easy for me to distinguish the
county's attorney from the defendants', even without the lo-
cation of the tables. The prosecutor is dressed in an expensive dark suit, while the defense attorneys, in the forlorn
hope of connecting with the working people on the jury,

wear khaki pants, ill-matched ties, and Western-cut sport coats.

My boss at DCI, Ross McGee, stands near the prosecution's table. He is also a lawyer but he's not one of the combatants in this trial. I've been told he's here simply to advise the County Attorney on the more complex legal issues that will doubtless be brought up on appeal, and at which time will become McGee's and the state's responsibility. The local police and prosecutor did not seek our assistance on this case; they wanted to keep the media attention for themselves.

Ross McGee is a striking man. He's very short and very thick, but his blue eyes blaze with the force of a far bigger man. Even without the harsh forward arc of his spine, he would barely reach five feet four inches in height. A white beard tinted the color of rust hangs all the way down to his hard little belly. His hairless scalp is the size and shape of a bowling ball, and it is marked with old scars and freckles. With a crimson Christmas hat, he would look a lot like an evil Santa Claus. Or with a horned helmet, a degenerate dwarf out of J.R.R. Tolkien's imagination. A former Army drill sergeant who had broken the spirits of thousands of boot camp recruits, there still emanates from him an aura of authority and potency despite his age, obesity, and poor health. His voice booms out above the murmurs from the front of the courtroom as he cracks a leg of the prosecution's table with his cane.

"Now don't you step in any shit, Karge," he tells the prosecutor. "I'm getting tired of cleaning your shoes."

The man he addresses smiles politely. I recognize him too. His austere image appears nightly on national newscasts as Nathan Karge, the current Albany County Attorney and likely the next governor of Wyoming. He has already won the primary in a decidedly one-party state. A former civil attorney who is known and respected throughout the Rocky Mountain region, he's finishing the term of the prior County Attorney, who had decided to take a breather after the Shepard trial.

Not wanting to interrupt, I lean against the wall in the back of the courtroom and watch the two men talk. From what I can hear, they are discussing the legal limitations of a closing argument.

McGee is the Deputy Attorney General of the Criminal Division, which is primarily responsible for handling the inevitable appeals to the state supreme court following criminal convictions. I work in an offshoot of that office that assists local police agencies in complex cases, investigates statewide drug distribution, spearheads multijurisdictional task forces, and sticks its nose into local corruption and conflicts of interest. McGee just yesterday ordered me down to this part of the state a week before I'm due at a civil hearing nearby in Cheyenne's federal courthouse. Along with the AG's office as a whole, I'm a defendant, accused of inflicting wrongful death upon three gang members there.

The order to come south a week early was delivered in the form of a phone message with McGee's usual labored breathing and terse, profane language. "Get your ass down to Laramie tomorrow! . . . Some girl, a cretin rock climber like yourself . . . she fell on her head and croaked. . . . The fucking governor wants us to look into it." Vintage McGee.

Two days earlier I'd read about the accident in the newspaper. The girl's name was Kate Danning and she fell off a cliff at a place called Vedauwoo during a late-night climbers' party.

After a few minutes I see the cane pointed my way.

"Get your hands out of your pockets," McGee barks across the courtroom. "You look like a goddamn pervert!"

I withdraw one hand to scratch my cheek with my middle finger extending toward him just as the courtroom's doors burst open. Spectators and reporters scramble for prime seats among the rows of wooden pews. I quickly drop into one near where I'd been standing at the rear of the chamber.

The journalists balance legal pads on their knees while clutching pens in their hands. Many are already taking notes, despite the fact that absolutely nothing is happening other than their own entrance. They gaze around them as they scribble, trying to catch and describe the atmosphere, I guess. I don't see Don Bradshaw, the *Cheyenne Observer* columnist who gave me my unfortunate nickname after the shoot-out with the gangbangers in Cheyenne, so I'm saved from giving the reporters an assault on one of their own to write about. The room had seemed cavernous to me just moments before, but now it feels like a pressure cooker. The faces around me are excited. They've come for a spectacle. People jostle one another for more room on the benches.

The pressure increases when the two defendants are led in by a handful of jailhouse deputies. The Knapp brothers look small and mean next to their Wyoming-size guards. They are clearly related, with the same slicked-back greasy blond hair, low foreheads, carefully tended wisps of facial hair, thin lips, and recessed chins. Their features and postures make them look like some less-evolved breed of humanity. Or maybe more evolved, the way things are going these days. Both wear cheap polyester suits, courtesy of the Public Defenders' Office. They walk stiffly in a sort of awkward shuffle, their knees slightly bent, and with exaggerated caution although neither wears shackles around his ankles.

The law dictates that they cannot appear before the jury in any sort of restraints until a verdict is reached. But I can see through their pants the sharp outlines of the bracelike device on each of their legs. Called a stilt, it consists of stiff Velcro cuffs above and below each knee connected with a hinged metal rod. The rods will snap straight if the wearer fully extends his legs by running, slowing him considerably and causing him to look ridiculous, like a man trying to trot while wearing stilts.

Once the brothers are seated with their attorneys, the deputies back off and slump in chairs strategically located for interception. Like nearly everyone else in the room, I look at the two defendants with contempt and disgust. From the televised reports of the case, I know the basic facts of the sadistic rape and murder they committed. And although they haven't yet been convicted, the evidence I heard about sounds overwhelming. I have no trouble myself finding them responsible for the killing. Innocent until proven guilty is only a concept for a jury to apply in a court of law; it has no application to the truth.

Every head in the place, except the defendants', turns and watches sympathetically as more deputies lead an Asian family to a cordoned-off row in the front of the courtroom. A bent old man who I assume is the victim's father, his spine apparently warped from months of sorrow and anger, leads the family. Behind him trails a woman who's crying quietly and three sullen-faced teenaged boys. At the front of the courtroom Nathan Karge, the County Attorney, stands like a solemn usher and bows his head to the family as they take their seats.

Within moments of the family's entrance, a bailiff scurries out of a concealed door behind the bench and shouts, "All rise!" A gavel cracks against wood as loud as a rifle shot. The scribbling and murmuring cease. The people in the room lurch to their feet.

Into the sudden silence, from a second, larger door, the judge emerges. I think she looks like a frail old woman being engulfed by her own black robes until I focus on her face. There's nothing frail about that face. Her lean jaw juts out like the brush guard mounted on the front of my truck. Thick gray hair is pulled severely into a tight bun. She glares out at the reporters crowding her courtroom and says not a word as the jury, a mix of twelve local men and women, is led into the court. All the jurors keep their eyes fixed on the floor as they take their seats. The enormity of the decision they will soon have to make seems to be a great weight upon their heads.

"Be seated," the judge tells the rest of the room once the jurors have found their chairs. She addresses them and says something I always appreciate hearing from a judge in a trial, before the defense makes their attempt to muddy the waters or spread a web of lies: "Let me remind you, ladies and gentlemen, that what you are about to hear is merely argument, not evidence." I only wish it were said right before the defense speaks, which I believe is really the point. But of course then it would be too obvious, too prejudicial, and too true for this truth-finding process. Without further preamble she announces, "Closing argument, Mr. Karge."

"Thank you," Karge says as he strides into the well.

He stands still before the jury members and moves his eyes across theirs, patiently waiting until he establishes contact with each man and woman in the box. Even all the way in the back of the courtroom, I can feel the charisma of the man. His face is earnest but tired, his eyes dark-rimmed from long nights of trial prep, and his rigid posture itself speaks of the anger he personally feels at the spectacular crime committed on his watch. Wearing a dark blue suit as his combat uniform, he looks like a courageous yet weary warrior fighting a losing battle on behalf of civilization. It's easy for me to believe he will be the next governor as the media is predicting.

When Karge begins to speak, even in this electric atmosphere, his words are soft and slow.

"Over the last four days you've heard about a killing," he tells the jury. "And all killings are terrible, but this kind of killing is worse beyond all others. A girl was raped. She was tortured. She was strangled. Then her body was mutilated. After a murder like this, we always ask ourselves why and try to understand. In this case, John and Dan Knapp made it quite easy for us. They spelled it out in Kimberly Lee's blood on the wall above her body. 'Chink bitch,' they wrote." Karge spits those two words out like pieces of bad meat. "That's why. Just because of the color of her skin, the shape of her eyes. And, ladies and gentlemen"—now his voice rises, and he turns and looks right at the two defendants—"*the evidence has shown beyond a reasonable doubt that these two men committed that most heinous of crimes, for the most wicked of reasons.*"

Karge starts describing the specifics of what those two animals did to Kimberly Lee, proving himself skillful at summoning up ghastly images in his audience's minds. As magnetic as the prosecutor's voice and words are, I don't want to listen as he begins a detailed analysis of the evidence as he'd presented it to the jury during the People's case. I try to shut it out by studying the rapt faces of the reporters around me. I'm not interested; my years as a state cop and the horrors I've seen have suppressed any morbid curiosity. Besides, I already know enough of the facts because the media has endlessly discussed them for months with the usual intent of titillation.

A young Chinese-American girl, a student at the university, was murdered in her rented house just south of town. Her naked, bound, and desecrated body was discovered by her Narcotics Anonymous counselor, who was also her boyfriend, at one in the morning when he stopped by to check on her. He had been worried about her, as she told him she was going to talk to the police about where and how she used to buy her drugs before getting clean.

When the Albany County sheriff's deputies came on the scene, they found racist slurs written on a wall, finger-painted in blood by a gloved hand. The blood came from where one of her breasts had been sliced off. At two in the morning the police went to the door of a trailer just a few hundred yards away to see if the residents had heard anything. Their knocks were answered by a shotgun blast. Two young men, the Knapp brothers, engaged in a brief, drunken firefight with the police before surrendering. Lightly wounded and handcuffed, one of the brothers slurred to the sheriff himself, "Bitch had it coming."

The evidence was quickly amassed. Inside the Knapp trailer was found a large quantity of methamphetamine, firearms, and racist propaganda. In the cab of their pickup was a bloody work glove along with the missing flesh of Kimberly Lee's breast. Both of the young men were known tweakers—users of crystal meth, also called crank—with lengthy criminal histories. A search of the crime scene in Kimberly Lee's home revealed a broken crank pipe with one of their fingerprints on it. The foul words written in blood on the wall were similar to the propaganda found in the Knapps' trailer. The evidence was irrefutable, according to the media and now the County Attorney.

In a town that had been sickened and vilified so recently by the homophobic murder of Matthew Shepard, this second killing must have stung like a slap in the face. Shepard's killers were not sentenced to death due only to a merciful plea by Shepard's own parents. But it's unlikely such clemency will be extended to the Knapps. Matthew Shepard's killers acted impetuously, in an act of supreme narcissism, while Kimberly Lee's violators were more outwardly motivated. The killers of Kimberly Lee wanted attention. They begged for it when they wrote those foul words upon her wall, above her corpse, in her own blood. It worked for Charlie Manson and it's working for the Knapps.

The citizens of Wyoming and the nation want their blood now. Only the death penalty, it's believed, will send a message to the town's youth that this butchery will not be tolerated and will proclaim to the nation that the people of Laramie will not condone it. So Nathan Karge has rushed this case to trial and valiantly fought off the Knapps' attorneys' pleas for continuances and venue changes. It has been less than a year since Kimberly Lee was placed in the ground under the scrutiny of television camera lenses from around the country.

There is one reporter who's not frantically scribbling like the rest. She sits across the room, four or five rows in front of me, not far behind where McGee slouches forward with his hands resting on the gold head of his cane. It isn't her spellbound attention that draws my stare, but something else and something obvious. Her long brown hair, her smooth white skin, her fashion model's profile. Her delicate beauty contrasts sharply with the images of rape, death, and hate that Nathan Karge is conjuring with his words. I watch her for a while, until she somehow senses my stare and irritably glances around her.

My attention is drawn back to Karge when I hear his voice again go low and angry like it did at the start. Cynical as I've become of attorneys, I can't help but be moved to vengeful thoughts by the man's words. I forget about that beautiful profile as I listen.

"Ladies and gentlemen, these two men you are about to judge have rights. This state and this nation give the defendants a right to a trial. They've got that. They have a right to be judged on the evidence. They've got that. They have a right to be judged by you, their peers. They've got that. They have a right to have their guilt proven beyond a reasonable doubt. They've got that." Then his voice again starts to rise. *"And just as they have these rights, Kimberly Lee and the rest of our community have rights too. The right to be vindicated. The right to be protected from cold-blooded animals. The right not to live in fear because of the color of your skin. Above all, the right to see justice done."*

His voice drops to almost a whisper. "And now, ladies and gentlemen, in Kimberly Lee's name, I ask that you enforce those rights. I stand before you seeking justice for her. And the community." He steps close to the Knapp brothers and points a steady finger at each in turn as he says, "I ask that you find John and Dan Knapp guilty of the terrible crimes they committed."

When he finishes, the only sound in the courtroom is that of his own footsteps on the pine floor as he walks back to his seat, his eyes fixed hypnotically on the jury the entire time. Even after Nathan Karge sits, a silence hangs clear and brilliant in the courtroom as if some great truth has been revealed. Finally the lead defense attorney comes to his senses. He scrapes back his chair and rises to face twelve angry pairs of eyes. They are no longer meek, those faces. It doesn't matter what the lawyer says, the verdict is all but delivered.

I look at the back of his clients' heads and wonder if they will regret what they did to that girl when they themselves are bound, not by thin cords like they bound her, but by the fear-scented heavy leather straps of a particular hospital gurney. When the worm-sized intravenous lines are inserted in each arm. It will probably take five years for them to reap what they've sown. Five years of endless appeals and crushed hopes. Five years of taunting by other inmates and guards. Five years of lockdown on death row. And at the final moment, when an unknown and unnamed executioner thumbs the plunger of a syringe and the poison begins its awesome surge toward their hearts, will they scream as Kimberly Lee surely did? Will they finally feel some empathy? I hope so. That scream as the solution of mortality is injected into their veins might make them human again.

At this moment, thinking these uncharitable thoughts in the back of the courtroom, I have no way of knowing that my investigation into a climber's death at Vedauwoo will lead me to discover the Knapps are innocent of Kimberly Lee's murder.

TWO

I NEVER GET A chance to speak with McGee. After the jury retires to deliberate, I swim forward against a strong, outgoing tide of reporters scrambling for telephones and their cameramen. I make it all the way to the front where McGee is leaving with the prosecution team. But before I can speak he whacks me hard on the ankle with his cane and barks, "Dinner at the First Story. Eight o'clock." Then he swaggers off while talking animatedly with Nathan Karge.

Outside, I find that the wind has waned a little and the sun is still relatively high over the twelve-thousand-foot summit of Medicine Bow Peak. I have nearly four hours to kill. With Oso panting excitedly from the rear seat, I drive fifteen miles east on Interstate 80 toward Cheyenne until I come to the soaring granite pillars, beaver ponds, and stands of pines and turning aspens of the region called Vedauwoo.

Heeding faint memories from my childhood, I weave the Land Cruiser through the narrow dirt roads far into the backcountry.

This place, so magical in my youth, has changed for the worse. Near the highway the state has installed toilets and fire pits in an attempt to tame the wild ground for tourists with motor homes. But they've been unable to destroy Vedauwoo's savage beauty. My father said Vedauwoo, pronounced Veed-a-voo, was the Arapaho word for earthborn spirit. And despite the man-made additions of picnic tables and the indecipherable graffiti on the rocks near the road, it still retains its primitive and untamed spirit, born of the earth. I stop close to the base of a granite formation that looks as though its towers were made by an infant god dripping wet sand.

I didn't come up here today to investigate. I haven't yet received the file on Kate Danning's accident, and I don't even know exactly where she fell. I came up for myself. This place is the reason I'd been almost happy when I received McGee's summons to return early to the southeast part of the state. It was here that my father held a rope in his strong, callused hands and taught my brother and me to climb vertical cliffs of stone. In my memory our mother, a descendant of poor Pampas Indios and Spanish aristocracy, looked on disapprovingly as she fried freshly caught trout over the dead wood she'd gathered. My brother Roberto and I were always laughing in those days, always competing on the rock and everywhere else.

In the years since we left Laramie our father had moved us all over the world, assigned to Air Force bases from Okinawa to Saudi Arabia. Each year he would take his entire vacation allotment of thirty days in one lump and drag us with him to even more exotic places that held a single attraction for the career officer—nearby alpine walls and peaks. And when I grew older, I traveled alone and with friends pursuing the passion he first taught us at Vedauwoo among the jagged peaks of the Tetons, the Sierras, the Bugaboos, the Alps, and the greater ranges of Alaska and Patagonia. But the memory of those early days at Vedauwoo remains on a special altar in my mind: the place where my passion was conceived.

I quit climbing following the shooting of the gang-bangers in Cheyenne. The events of that night, a year and a half ago, resulted in my being semipermanently posted, exiled really, all the way across the state from the place where I first learned the art of scaling stone. It was a form of penance, maybe, giving up the thing I loved the most. Somehow I thought it would be wrong for me to live too intensely, the way climbing caused you to do, when because of me others didn't have the chance to live at all. And I knew that I'd used up all my luck that night—the karmic consequences would be a bitch. But I never stopped training for it, believing someday I'd be able to rationalize that I've paid enough for the three lives I took. And today is the day. *Fuck it,* I've finally managed to convince myself, *they're dead and I'm not.*

There's something else too. Through eighteen months of adrenaline deprivation, a pressure has built in my chest like some overwhelming hunger. It's as strong as rage but not as angry. A sort of junkie's desperate need for a fix. If I don't feed it, I will surely die.

So my mood rides higher than it has in eighteen months as I hurriedly shed my court clothes and pull on worn canvas shorts while Oso sniffs and shambles among the trees. The clean mountain air is a salve for my soul. All sorts of old memories, good memories, spin through my head as I change, stashing my gun and badge under the seat. I can hear my brother's reckless laughter ringing off the rocks, the way it sounded before the drugs warped it, pitching it higher so that it always seemed in danger of shattering on the ground. Shirtless in the sun and tugging my climbing slippers onto bare feet, I feel the bittersweet excitement of coming home.

A half hour later the sticky rubber of my slippers is smeared on tiny crystals of quartz and my fingers are twisted, thumbs down, wedged only up to the knuckles in the vertical crack over my head. The ground is fifty feet below and strewn with jagged boulders. My breath is coming in rapid, shallow pants and I can taste the acidic flavor of fear in my mouth. Free-soloing without a belay, without a rope, I'm in way over my head. But it feels so good. It's been too long.

I chose this climb at random, my excitement overtaking my caution. Oso had followed me as I stalked up a short trail to the base of the nearest tower. It has an almost featureless seventy-foot face that overhangs slightly. The only irregularity on the rock wall is the thin seam of a crack that diagonals up it and broadens near the top. I swung my arms in circles a few times, dusted my fingers with chalk from the bag clipped to the back of my pants, and started up without looking for a gentler and wiser warm-up.

Now I torque my fingers deeper into the crack above me, then lean far back until my elbows are straight and the lactic acid that is screaming in my shoulders begins to dissipate. I force myself to take several slow, deep breaths. After a few lungfuls my heels stop their panicked quivering and my calm returns. With sweat stinging my eyes, I study the narrow crack that leads just twenty feet higher to the top of the cliff.

By contracting my biceps and the parallel bands of muscle that swell across the rear of my shoulders, I haul my chest back close to the granite. Releasing one hand, I shake it out beneath my hips, allowing the flow of blood to return, then place it higher in the crack where the fissure broadens. With relief I feel my whole hand slip in. I fold my thumb across my palm, flexing the fat muscles there, expanding my hand and letting it fill the crack. It's a solid jam. My other hand follows higher still. The sharp quartz crystals embedded in the granite bite through the protective tape I'd wrapped around my palms and knuckles. Hauling myself higher off the jams, I'm finally able to twist my toes deep into the fracture.

Soon I drag myself over the top, where I lie belly-down on the cool stone and pant like a tired dog. Everything that has gone wrong in my life over the past two years is momentarily forgotten: the imprisonment of my brother for manslaughter, then just six months later the deaths of the three young men I shot and the media uproar that resulted, the civil suit it sparked. My mind feels perfectly clean. The evening breeze blows over my bare, sweating back, seeming to sweep right through me.

I sit up and look around me as the adrenaline begins to subside and my lungs relax. Darkening towers of granite are all around me as far as I can see. They are purple in the twilight. Stars are just beginning to make themselves apparent in the still-bluish sky, and a sliver of a moon hangs over the scene to the east. For the first time in a long time, I feel content as I peel the bloody athletic tape from my hands.

Just when the goose bumps begin in earnest and I start to shiver, I crawl back to the edge and lean my head over. Oso sits amid the boulders below, loyally staring straight up at me just as he used to do when excursions like this were an everyday occurrence. I call to him.

"Thanks for the spot, Oso. I'll be down in a minute."

Then looking beyond the dog, where the boulders meet a screen of aspens, I see a blonde-haired girl with taped hands sitting very still, as if she's been watching for a while. Beside her is a small backpack with a pair of climbing slippers clipped on by a carabiner. Oso follows my gaze back at her and glances there for a moment in annoyance before again focusing his gold eyes on me. I wave at her and she grins back, giving me a thumbs-up. She's the second woman who has caught my attention in just hours. Maybe I am finally coming back to life.

I turn and head down the series of ledges that lead off the backside of the tower, feeling young and strong again. The reckless urge that sometimes overcomes me to scare myself silly and put it all on the line is sated for the first time in many months. *La llamada del salvaje,* the call of the wild, my mother describes it, taking the phrase from the Spanish translation of the Jack London story she read to us as children. It's a sort of genetic flaw that according to her descends from my father to my brother and me. It's a need that we learned to release, as our father had, by climbing rocks and ice and getting lethal amounts of air beneath our heels.

He taught us about moving in the vertical world just as he taught us a seemingly endless array of other strange sports and skills that were a part of his everyday life as an officer of the elite Pararescue Corps. Scuba diving, horseback riding, distance swimming, endurance running, skydiving, shooting, wilderness survival ... even the arcane arts of jujitsu and archery. But climbing was the only activity that received the passion and devotion of the family's men.

It has always been enough for me, but not enough for my brother. He eventually turned to the far riskier sports of cocaine, heroin, and methamphetamine. With that in mind, and after the shooting in Cheyenne, I resolved to ignore the Call altogether. But the Call's voice has proven too powerful. As I hop off a ledge on the tower's backside, then stem my way down the wide space in the middle of a giant broken boulder with a hand and foot smeared against the opposite sides, I feel like an eagle soaring far above the earth, gazing down on the granite, aspens, and pines before me, owning the whole place. My brother must feel something like this when the needle slams home.

Ten minutes later I find Oso in the growing dark, but the girl is gone. I look around for her as the heavy dog pushes his shoulder against my thigh and licks the blood from my fingers. I bend and rub the beast's chest, watching to see if she'll reappear. The only sound is the hum of the wind through the trees and me murmuring to Oso about what a good old fellow he is. I pull a sweatshirt over my head. I sit for a few minutes and drink half a quart of water, then slowly pour the rest for him while he slurps at the trickle. It's only then that I notice the woven necklace of alpine daisies entwined in Oso's collar. I'm surprised he would let a stranger that close.

Headlights, taillights, and neon signs reflect off my windshield as I move my truck with the evening traffic on Grand Avenue. Oso has his huge head out the passenger window, drooling again down the door and drawing smiles from the other drivers. The white petals from the flowers on his collar are blowing off in the wind and swirling around the truck's interior like victory-parade confetti.

Brightly flashing blue and red lights slow the traffic. Like the other drivers, I twist in my seat to see what's going on. A massive uniformed man who could only be Jefferson Jones is yelling orders to other deputies as they wave the traffic past. Curious, I pull in behind two patrol cars and get out, telling the dog to stay. I walk up to one of the uniformed officers, who immediately challenges me.

"Get back in your car and keep moving, sir," he snaps at me.

I ignore him as Jones approaches.

"You sure came back to Laramie on an exciting day, QuickDraw—I mean Anton," Jones says, rolling his dark eyes at my sensitivity to the nickname and waving at the uniform to let me across the invisible crime scene line.

"What's going on?"

"Just a little more freakiness. Icing on the cake, the way things have been going around here lately. Take a look for yourself—we've got a drunk Klansman in a tree."

I look down the residential street in the direction Jones points and see he's telling the truth. A few houses away there is a white-robed figure perched high up in a skinny oak that shades someone's front yard. It's an old man, with wisps of white hair streaming in the wind. The spotlights from more police cars illuminate him as if he's an acrobat about to perform a trick. Below him are three uniformed deputies yelling for him to get his ass down from there. A police dog, a lean German shepherd, stands on hind legs with its front paws planted on the trunk, growling upward.

"You're not kidding" is all I can say.

"C'mon, my man, check it out." Jones leads me down to the action. As we walk, Jones asks, "Where you been lately?"

"Up in Cody. My assignment in this end of the state didn't make me too popular around here."

"Lord, I know. Read about it. Still reading about it." The big man shakes his head and laughs. "You sure showed 'em that you DCI guys can shoot, though."

I ignore his comment, saying, "There's a hearing for summary judgment next week. My lawyer's hopeful it'll settle then."

When the hoodless Klansman spots Jones's approach, he begins to shout, "You get the fuck out of here, nigger! Go back to Africa, you big spade!" Then calmer, to the officers below, "I ain't coming down till the nigger's gone."

Jones chuckles and holds up his hands toward the tree in a gesture of surrender and begins to back off. He says to me, gesturing at my freshly torn hands, "Looks like you're still doing that Spiderman shit—why don't you go up and get him for us?"

Before I can respond there's a loud crack. We both jerk our heads up at the pathetic figure in the tree. The bough that was his perch has snapped and the old man is falling, crashing through more thin branches. He barely misses landing on the police dog, which lets out a startled yelp. In one swift motion the dog turns and bites the back of the old man's sheet.

The Klansman wails as the K9 officer drags the dog away. Laughter erupts from the deputies as they whoop and cheer the dog.

"Jesus Christ," Jones says, disgusted. "Someone call an ambulance."

The old man lies on the ground, crying and cursing, as two officers quickly pat him down and take a long folding knife from his pocket. Looking to Jones for approval, they don't bother to handcuff him. Their sergeant nods back at them. The old man is obviously drunk and fairly harmless, and it appears that in addition to having been bitten on the butt he's broken his arm as well. He holds it cradled against his chest. An ambulance rolls up within minutes and carts him off.

While Jones is orchestrating the old man's transport, another deputy approaches me. "What are you doing here, QuickDraw?" he asks without smiling.

"Hey, Bender. I can't say. You know, state business. But it's good to see you," I lie, looking up straight into Leroy Bender's wide moon-face. He's almost as tall as Jones, and nearly as heavy, but his bulk comes from fat rather than muscle. The uniform he wears is sloppy, one shirttail partially untucked and a white T-shirt showing between the straining buttons across his belly. He wears a cowboy's mustache like an upside-down horseshoe. It looks both absurd and menacing at the same time on his broad face. I know him as a suspect from an excessive force investigation two years ago, the last time I was in Laramie. The charges I filed against him were dismissed, I was told, for political reasons. I later learned that his uncle is the Albany County sheriff.

Now the deputy stands too close to me but I don't step back. He's rocking on his boot heels, his gloved hands on his waist with his thumbs hooked in his gun belt. The tight black leather gloves he wears are the universal sign of cops with too much testosterone; their sole purpose is to prevent splitting a knuckle on someone's head.

"Fuck you, Burns. That your rustbucket over there? If you know what's good for you, you'll get in it and out of my town."

I don't reply. I just keep my eyes on him.

"What went down in Cheyenne don't make you a hero. It just makes you a lucky piece of shit. QuickDraw my ass."

"You got lucky too, Leroy. You never got convicted."

The cop moves even closer. "Funny, I didn't feel so lucky with you pushin' those charges, and with that reprimand you had put in my file." He spits out a brown foam of tobacco waste and I feel its gentle tug at my pant leg.

I look away for a moment, down at my shoes, trying to will away the anger that's rising in me. But the hot pressure is too great. Just as I'm telling myself to do nothing, I shoot out one arm and plant my palm hard in Bender's solar plexus. "Stay away from me," I say as my hand presses into his soft flesh. He staggers back, more surprised than off-balance, and one boot heel catches on the grass. His gun belt clatters as he goes down. The deputies and other spectators around us freeze, watching.

Then Jones comes between us like a brick wall. "Cut it out," he says.

Bender's face is red and flared in the streetlights when he rolls to his feet. To Jones he says, "You got no rank on me, Jeff. Back off!"

"No, Leroy, but I got size."

It's a long moment before he turns and walks away. With a final hard look he says to me, "I take back what I said before—I hope you have a nice long visit in Laramie, you little fuck. I'll be seeing you. You can bet on that."

"Quite a town you live in," I say to Jones when he's gone.

Jones is frowning. "What the fuck you doing, Anton? You know better than to tangle with that peckerhead."

"I've got nothing to lose." It's true. My name and my reputation, once highly regarded in the state's small law enforcement community, have been sullied by the suspicions the Cheyenne shooting raised. For a while now I've sensed that my career as a cop is coming to an end.

"What about your badge? Shit, what about your life?" Jones finally smiles. "You sure made a lot of friends the last time you came to this part of the state. Most of the good cops think you've freaked out, they say you've become some kind of Dirty Harry rogue, while the bad cops love you. Excepting that scumbag Bender, of course." Then he laughs, adding, "And the sheriff."

I think for a minute. What have I done to offend the sheriff? Then I groan. "I'd forgotten about the sheriff."

Jones chuckles again. "I haven't. That was the funniest thing I ever saw. Anyway, I was hoping to catch up to you, Anton. Seeing you today, I figured you must be the super-secret agent on that Danning girl. I just love the way the state takes these things off our hands whenever there's a hint of a conflict."

"I don't really know anything about it yet. The office just told me to come down and see Ross McGee about it. I tried to talk to him at the courthouse, but he didn't have the time. I'm seeing him later tonight. Anything I should know?"

Jones looks at me for a fraction of a second too long before speaking. "Nope, I don't know anything about it either. It's the sheriff's deal. You ought to go on down and see him. I know he's working late tonight. Shit, we're all working late tonight. But go see him and get it over with." He flashes teeth that are brilliant against his dark skin and the night. "Y'all can talk about old times. And give me a call tomorrow. Let me know how it goes. We'll get a few beers while you're here, long as I'm not seen with you."

* * *

I take Grand Avenue to Third Street and then go south past the interstate to the Holiday Inn. Another NO VACANCY sign flashes brightly there just as one had from every motel I passed. Yesterday a secretary at DCI's main office in Cheyenne described the trouble she went through to get a room. Every hotel or motel had been booked for months, she said, for the Lee trial. The only way she finally reserved a space was by threatening to have the Department of Health pay a lengthy and determined visit. A reporter from a distant, small newspaper was apparently booted out and rendered homeless so I could have a place to sleep.

Despite the secretary's threat, the motel is actually Laramie's finest. It consists of a single sprawling brick building, two stories high, with a long wing of rooms that faces a grass courtyard and a partially covered swimming pool. There's a coffee shop and a bar just off the lobby, as well as a gift shop and some convention halls. The motel is at the very southern edge of town, where the land turns from tree-lined neighborhoods into scattered ranches and rolling plains.

After changing into a soft flannel shirt, jeans, and Tevas at the motel and feeding Oso, I leave him there and drive to the sheriff's office. The three-story building is next to the sandstone courthouse and houses the jail, the twenty-man Laramie Police Department, and the fire department in addition to being the headquarters of the Albany County Sheriff's Department. Inside the lobby I show my badge to the Explorer Scout who's manning the front desk and explain that I want to find the sheriff. The Scout takes my name and gives me an astonished look, probably having read my name in the papers or having heard some of the talk after the Cheyenne shooting. Then he makes a quick call and gives me directions before buzzing me through.

I vaguely remember the way down the maze of hallways to the sheriff's office although I've only been here once before. It was in more carefree days, two years ago, when one of the less notorious cases I investigated involved two deputies, Bender and another named Arnold, for the use of excessive force. The two officers had beaten a drunk Mexican farmhand outside a south-of-town bar, in front of a crowd of spectators. DCI, which is mandated by the state to investigate all allegations of official misconduct by city, county, or state officers, sent me to conduct the inquiry and to make a recommendation to the Attorney General's Office about the potential filing of charges against the officers.

I came to this very office to interview the sheriff. I was a little puzzled at just how helpful he acted in providing witness statements. Generally, the locals resent an outside agency poking around. But the sheriff gave me an animated demonstration of what the witnesses had said happened. First he braced his big belly and arms against his own desk, showing how the farmworker didn't cooperate in putting his hands on the hood of a car for a pat-down. Then he got on his hands and knees in front of me, facing me, to illustrate how the worker refused to lie flat when the two officers tried to take him down.

And it was at that moment that I made the mistake that earned me what is probably the sheriff's devoted animosity. I was standing in the doorway to his office with my hands on my hips, the sheriff on all fours before me, when I heard footsteps coming down the hallway. I glanced over my shoulder and saw Jefferson Jones, my roommate from the police academy four years before. How strange the situation must have looked to Jones: me blocking the doorway with my back and the sheriff barely visible beyond, on hands and knees. So I did it. I winked at Jones and with one hand made a short zipping motion in front of my pants.

Jones's short burst of laughter before he brought himself under control betrayed me. It caused the sheriff to look up from his demonstration and catch the gist of my unspoken but obscene joke. The sheriff threw me out of his building and filed a complaint with the Attorney General's Office.

At this time of night there is no one at the secretary's station outside the sheriff's office. I go right to the familiar open door and knock on the frame. Inside I can see Sheriff Willis not behind his desk, but slouching in a corner easy chair watching the news on a small TV propped on a bookshelf.

"Special Agent Antonio Burns, right?" he asks, taking a stubby cigar out of his mouth. I appreciate the sheriff's greeting, acting as if he barely remembers me. That makes things easier for both of us.

Without rising he gestures with the cigar toward another chair. The office walls are crowded with community service plaques and photos showing the sheriff with his arm around various local and state politicians. Cardboard boxes are scattered across the floor, some spilling their contents. With a glance I see they are pamphlets advertising Nathan Karge for governor. I remember hearing somewhere that the sheriff is Karge's campaign manager, and that he's expected to follow Karge to the capital after the election.

As I sit, I'm struck again by the wonder of how this fat, balding redneck can remain an elected official for so many years in a town like Laramie. The town today has as many Internet commuters and yuppies as it has ranchers. Probably more. In addition, it has a large and visible population of hippies. People in other parts of the state think of the town as Wyoming's version of Berkeley. Sheriff Daniel Willis is a throwback to a time when Laramie was a hard and dusty cow town, full of saloons and whorehouses, and where the western railway abruptly terminated not far from the peaks of the Snowy Range. He always seemed to me like the epitome of heavy-handed cowboy justice. Maybe a sheriff like him keeps Laramie's new citizens feeling as if they're in the midst of some rustic charm.

"I hear you're the one that's gonna look into that young gal's fall," he drawls. "Make sure it was an accident and that we're not covering nothing up. Should be pretty easy, I expect. Routine."

"I don't know anything about it yet, Sheriff. I haven't even seen the witness statements or the coroner's report."

"Coroner already made the determination, son. Accident. See what I mean about easy?" He's selling something and appears anxious that I buy.

I shrug. "I heard her boyfriend, one of the witnesses, is your County Attorney's son?"

"Yep. Brad Karge. I've known that boy all his life. His daddy too, who's going to be your next governor—you might want to keep that in mind. The boy's a pistol. Been in a little trouble, but nothing serious. He just messes around with those rock climbers and gets high a little. Still growing up." The sheriff pauses and studies me. "I heard somewheres you used to be a climber."

"I still am." I say it with unexpected pride, still feeling the euphoria of the afternoon's rededication to my passion.

Willis shakes his head, squinting through his pig eyes. "Sounds like a foolish hobby to me, son. Good way to get yourself killed. Anyhow, I'd appreciate it if you'd sign off on that girl's death right quick and move on. As you saw today, this town's got more important things going on. Put this accident to bed."

With a grunt the sheriff pulls himself out of his chair and picks up a thick manila file from his desk. "What little we've got is in there. Like I said, should be a piece of cake." With a quick toss that I barely catch as it hits my lap, he gives the file over to me and wishes me a good night.

THREE

THE RESTAURANT IS crowded and dark when I walk in a little after eight o'clock. Its air is perfumed with the fecund odor of portobello mushrooms steaming on a grill. I stand in the entrance with all the other locals and out-of-towners who are waiting for tables while my eyes adjust to the candlelit gloom. The reporters and tourists are easy to spot. They wear expensive new hiking boots and shiny Gore-Tex jackets, as if they expect to go backpacking after dinner. The angry looks on their faces lead me to suspect the locals are being seated first.

According to the garrulous clerk at the hotel's desk, The First Story restaurant is something the town is proud of. A former university professor bought the old building, which stands in the center of town. Like most of the other buildings in downtown Laramie, it had once been a brothel. The upstairs was divided into twenty or so small "cribs" where the working girls had plied their trade. The professor tore them out and installed a highbrow bookstore called The Second Story. She converted the lower level into this, The First Story, and hired a chef from one of San Francisco's finest restaurants to run it for her. Judging from the odor and the atmosphere alone, the place seems to be as much a part of the new Laramie as Sheriff Willis is a part of the old.

After a few minutes of peering into the darkness, I spot Ross McGee crouching like a troll over a small table in the far corner. There's a bottle of wine and a full glass before him. He has a hand clenched around each. Above the white beard his cheeks are flushed and his eyes shiny, indicating that maybe this is not his first bottle.

I pull out the other chair. "Sorry I'm late, Ross."

"Goddamn, you are sorry, lad," he growls.

"It's good to see you too. How's the old battle-ax?" I use one of McGee's own terms of endearment for his fragile and surprisingly beautiful wife.

"She's deliriously happy," he says, then pauses in his peculiar manner, sucking air into his emphysemic and overworked lungs, ". . . to see me out of town." His home is in Cheyenne, not far from the main office of DCI and the Attorney General.

Even though he has an exterior more prickly than a porcupine's, I like McGee as much as I like anyone. He takes shit from no one and routinely sends agents off on politically sensitive investigations with his mantra of "Do the right thing; don't fuck around." And when his agents get in trouble with the office for doing exactly that, McGee backs them up with the ferocity of an old hump-backed grizzly protecting her cubs. As a result he is feared, despised, and avoided by the state administration, from the Attorney General himself on down. My lower-level colleagues and I dread the inevitable day McGee will keel over from a heart attack.

He has an unexpected softer side too. He dotes on his wife's two miniature poodles with an obvious adoration that is completely out of character. When I once told him a story of my father's about a poodle, meant to be morbidly funny, McGee had been outraged.

In the early seventies, my father had been climbing near where two Frenchmen were putting up a new route on the great overhanging wall of El Capitan in Yosemite National Park. The route had been a nightmare—they'd run out of food and water on the fifth day and had done without for the remaining three. Near the edge of the broad summit, where an easy trail reaches from El Capitan's gentle back-side, the Frenchmen were congratulated by climbers, hikers, and tourists, all wanting to know what eight days of hanging by threads without a horizontal surface had been like. An elderly couple approached with a tiny toy poodle that wouldn't stop snapping at the Frenchmen's ankles. The couple indignantly refused to leash the pint-sized dog, insinuating that its aggressiveness must have something to do with the unwashed smell emanating from the climbers' bodies. To everyone's horror, one of the Frenchmen shrugged and nonchalantly punted the tiny dog over the edge.

When I told McGee that story, I expected to receive a rough chuckle. But instead tears came into his eyes. He reviled the French with language so hateful and vile that I noticed the office secretaries fleeing the room.

"Why are you late?" he demands.

"I stopped by to see the sheriff and get the file on the Danning girl. The sheriff and I had some patching up to do." I explain the mistake I'd made a year ago and McGee's satyr face is split by a smile. That's the sort of prank he enjoys.

"Good lad. I'd forgotten about that."

Then McGee's eyes brighten further as he focuses on someone behind my back. Turning my head, I see the reporter whose profile had so enticed me in the courtroom.

"Ross McGee," she says fondly.

"Aah, the lovely Miss Hersh." McGee gives her his most lecherous look, nearly smacking his lips.

She looks as if she's dressed for dining in Paris, New York, or Rome instead of Wyoming. She wears a long black dress that stretches across her thin hips, and a tight leather jacket. Clinging high up on her exposed neck is a string of pearls. She has mahogany eyes and her dark hair hangs limply almost to the tips of her breasts. The skin of her face and throat is a porcelain white, far different than the high-altitude tans of the girls I normally find myself attracted to. It's not easy to keep from staring.

"How are you, you old goat?"

"Fine, my dear. If I were two years younger...I'd be goring you tonight."

She laughs, and I like the confident sound. I think she can't be more than twenty-six or twenty-seven, nearly forty years his junior. Then McGee asks, "What brings you to this inhospitable state?"

"The newspaper sent me up to cover the trial, of course. Would you let me pick your brain with some legal questions?"

"You can pick me wherever you like....But first tell me how is your father...that ugly son of a bitch?"

She laughs again. "That's exactly how he refers to you—'that ugly son of a bitch.' At least when he's feeling generous. He told me to be sure and see you while I'm here."

McGee then speaks to me. "Don't get any ideas, lad.... This is Rebecca Hersh of the *Denver Post*....She's the daughter of an old enemy of mine...a limp-wristed professorial type....And this young ruffian is Special Agent Antonio Burns....You may have heard of him."

I rise to shake her hand, more than a little dazzled by her looks, as she assesses me in return. Her look is quizzical. "Aren't you the one who was in the news last year? That gang shooting?"

I feel the blood coming into my face and try not to wince. "I'm afraid so."

McGee is not the least bit sympathetic to my discomfort. He chuckles and coughs, saying, "They call him QuickDraw nowadays.... Will you eat with us?"

"I'm sorry, I can't. There are some others waiting for me. But I'd love to interview you sometime, Agent Burns."

"I'll think about it," I say. My face is hot.

She takes a card from her purse and puts it on the table in front of me. Then without pause she turns again to McGee.

"Let me ask you quickly, Ross, what did you think of the closing today?"

"In general...it was well done, lass."

"I saw you talking with the prosecutor. What was your role there?"

"Just to make sure the prosecution doesn't step in any shit...that'll make our shoes stink in the AG's Office... when the case comes up on appeal."

"Were any issues created?"

"Of course, my dear....There's always issues....And when there aren't...the Public Pretenders will make them up." He pauses to drag several ragged breaths into his lungs. "Nathan probably stepped in it a few times...in an appealable sense. But from what I saw...none are likely to stink enough...to get the case thrown out."

"When did he go too far?"

McGee counts off on his thick fingers. "When he talked about the community's right for justice and protection... when he called this the most horrible of all crimes...when he called the defendants cold-blooded animals...All of those are technically improper....There's some case law that says...the prosecutor can't inflame the passions of the jurors...or call the defendants names."

"But the defense lawyers called all the witnesses and police liars, and said that Karge was conducting a witchhunt for political gain."

McGee explains, "The prosecution does it, it's potentially reversible error....The defense does it, it doesn't fucking matter....You can't appeal an acquittal, lass. Only a conviction....Those are the rules of the game."

"I can't imagine the jury doing anything but finding them guilty of first-degree murder and imposing the death penalty. Can you comment at all, officially or not?"

"Unofficially and off the record...you never know what a jury will do...You understand, we're talking about your average...to below-average citizen-idiots here.... These are the same morons...who think reintroducing wolves is a federal plot to steal their land...and that Waco was an execution....And any time you try to get twelve people...to agree on anything, you're asking for trouble....All too often they'll focus on something...that's totally irrelevant....But the town's just as hot...to put the Knapps in the fryer as Karge is....People've been saying his predecessor was soft on Shepard's killers...letting the punks get away with their lives." McGee then starts into one of his stories, of which there seem to be thousands, while I signal the waitress for a drink stronger than wine. This one is about a domestic violence case he prosecuted where the victim was well known in the community and not very popular. The jury felt she got exactly what she had coming—a broken jaw courtesy of her drunken husband. They acquitted him. It was later revealed that one of the jurors had smuggled a bottle of whiskey into the deliberations. Instead of deliberating, the jury sat around drinking and talking about what they would have done to the bitch.

I've never seen my boss speak this much.

I'm crunching the ice from my drink by the time he's finished the story, unsure and uncaring of the point McGee is trying to make. But Rebecca Hersh has more courtesy. She is still standing by the table, looking attentive.

After a few other questions, she asks, "Nathan Karge looked tired to me. Everyone's talking about that too. Is it just the trial or has he been much affected by the death of that girl his son was dating?"

"I don't know... Nathan is a very private man when it comes to family.... He doesn't talk about his boy with me.... But it sure as hell was poor timing... having to deal with shit like that... in the middle of the trial of his career.... During a capital case like this... you don't want anything else on your mind.... Especially not with the fucking election coming up."

"Well, I've got to go find my friends. Can I call you tomorrow for some legal background?"

"Always, lass. I'm at the Holiday Inn."

"Great, I'm there too." Rebecca then gives me a slightly embarrassed look. "It was nice meeting you, Agent Burns. Will you think about doing an interview?"

As she leaves I can't help but turn in my seat and watch her walk away. When I face McGee again he fixes me with his bright blue eyes. "She's way out of your league, youth."

"Fuck you, Boss," I answer but feel it's probably true.

Back at the Holiday Inn, I'm both elevated from the climb—my hands still tingle with the feel of the warm rock—and embarrassed at how I handled my introduction to the reporter. The file I took from the sheriff sits unopened on the bed. I'm off duty and intend to stay that way until the morning. Oso's old bones are tired from the afternoon at Vedauwoo. Gorged with Purina, he snores contentedly, sprawled across the room's second double bed.

I find myself driving back through the breezy night again toward downtown Laramie, not knowing at first what I'm hoping to find. But images of Rebecca Hersh and the girl who gave my dog the wreath of daisies play inside my mind. I park and begin to walk.

I come across a place called the Fireside Bar. A neon sign flashes, "Dancin' and Drinkin'." Underneath, on the white wall in black marker, someone has added, "And Dyin'." I observe the souped-up pickups outside and see through the window throngs of young white men in tightly curled baseball caps. This was the bar from which Matthew Shepard had been lured by two yokels from the same nomadic trailer-park culture as the Knapp brothers. They'd cajoled the small college student outside, driven him onto the plains outside of town, tied him to a buck fence, and beat him to death with the butt of a pistol. They told the police they did it because he flirted with one of them and for the couple of dollars and credit cards he had in his wallet. The Fireside Bar had been a poor choice for the boy. And his murder brought Laramie the continuing fame the town never wanted and didn't deserve. I walk on.

Two blocks farther I come to the Altitude Brewery. It's a new place, large and open inside. The floor and fixtures are all bright pine. The customers are dressed in a mix of alpaca wool sweaters, fleece jackets, and tie-dyed T-shirts worn under open hemp shirts. Unlike the other places I passed, the banging rhythm vibrating out the door from this bar is secondary to the sound of voices. While that attracts me, what really draws me in is that through the front window I think I see the flower girl.

I walk in and sit on a varnished stump at the bar. The bartender, sporting a lip ring, a couple of nose rings, and viciously spiked hair, pours me an Easy Street Wheat from the tap. When he says, "You're welcome," I see that his tongue is also pierced with a silver stud. I stare toward the big-screen TV behind the bar, but I'm really watching the mirror below it—reflected there I see the girl sitting at a booth with three men, one ponytailed and older than the other two, and several more young men gathered around, gripping mugs of beer.

When she stands and walks toward the bathroom my eyes follow her. She's wearing threadbare jeans and a purple loose-weave vest. Her bare arms are tan and slender. There are thin cords of muscle running from her shoulders to her wrists. Her dirty blonde hair is mostly tucked behind her ears except for the few loose tendrils that sweep around her face. The young men around the table all steal glances after her as she bounces away. The only exception is the big, ponytailed one she'd been closest to. He looks at the others in challenge and annoyance.

I meet his eyes in the mirror for a moment and glance away. Then I look at my own. They seem to have recessed back in my head over the past year and a half, as if my with-drawal from the things I loved has withdrawn my ability to see the world. The sockets around them are tight and dark. People used to comment on my eyes, tell me what a surpris-ingly dark color they are, almost like coffee, against my lighter skin and hair. But no one's said that in a long time. Not since things started to go wrong.

A voice beside me says, "You climb solo and drink solo, huh?" She speaks with a Dead Head's lilt.

I turn and try to give her a smile. "Thanks for the flow-ers. My dog felt like a prince."

"I thought he'd either like it or eat me, man, when I put them around his neck. But he just ignored me the whole time."

"That's because he was busy, giving me a spot."

She laughs at that, her eyes wrinkling slightly at the cor-ners where, like mine, too much exposure to the sun and wind has prematurely carved thin lines. "He's big enough to spot. Falling on him wouldn't hurt either one of you much."

The mirror shows me that the ponytailed man from the booth is approaching. I can almost feel the air around us be-coming denser. He moves up close behind the girl and me, looming over us.

"I know you from somewhere, dude. Where's it at?" he asks.

I'm enormously tired of the infamy that resulted from the shooting. And just hours before, on the rock again at Vedauwoo, I'd thought that maybe I was finally learning to deal with it. With great reluctance I turn to look up at him and try to think of how to answer his question.

The man is huge in every way. He's at least several inches over six feet tall, nearly half a foot taller than me, and at a minimum of 220 pounds he outweighs me by 40. His powerful jaw muscles are barely contained by taut, tan skin. He wears his glossy black hair pulled back so tight that it looks like a helmet. Ropes of thick brawn bulge down his neck and disappear into his shirt. The hand he lays on the bar between the girl and me is scabbed and callused. It's also the size of a boxing glove. Seeing his paw, I realize that this guy, who I now recognize as an almost-famous climber, probably doesn't know me from that notorious Cheyenne event. The hands don't look like the type that regularly turn the pages of a newspaper.

"I don't know. But you're Billy Heller, right?" I hope that saying his name, establishing his identity, might make him forget about mine and appease his obvious hostility.

Heller's fame is limited to hard-core climbing circles. He was first noticed when he developed super-gymnastic routes at Tahquiz and Suicide. Then he spent a couple of decades as a wall rat in Yosemite before coming to Vedauwoo a few years ago in search of new material. I've heard he is the master of off-width cracks—the recesses in granite too wide to jam with a clenched fist and too narrow to crawl in and chimney with feet and hands on one side and one's back braced against the other. He developed intensely powerful techniques known as the arm bar, chicken wing, knee jam, and the kick-through. People say that he knows the physiology of musculature, joints, and bones better than a medical student. I've heard about how he can lead a rope up the blank roofs that jut sometimes more than fifty feet from cliff faces, roofs that contain only a single, wide fissure like a jagged earthquake fracture across a high-beamed ceiling. He will hang with his elbows and palms wedged in the crack and with his feet dangling over dead space, then fold his entire body like a jackknife to shove his feet into the tight space. And he will release his hands, so that he is suspended by just his feet jammed heel and toe into the crack, batlike and sometimes hundreds of feet off the ground, and do it all over again, inching along until he can pull himself over the lip.

The irritation emanating from him is probably due to the fact that his far younger girlfriend appears to be flirting with me, and maybe also because his recognition isn't more widespread. The multitalented, high-altitude climbers are the ones who receive the adoration of the broad population of armchair climbing enthusiasts. Like Messner, Beckey, Bridwell, and Viesturs. The specialists are largely ignored. And Heller, nearing forty, has to be in decline from the height of his powers.

The girl interrupts before he has a chance to answer. "Wait a sec—I've seen *you* somewhere—you're Something Burns, right? There was some article 'bout you in a climbing mag a few years back. Alaska?"

I smile, pathetically pleased myself to be recognized for something other than the deaths of three gang members. It was another life entirely and a good one. An article was published after I summitted an unclimbed alpine face with two close friends in Alaska. The trip was terrifying at the time, it seemed like an epic of ancient Greek proportions, but like most alpine trips it improved with time and hindsight. Whenever I look closely in the mirror I remember it. My cheekbone was smashed by a chunk of weather-loosened granite the size of a dinner plate, forever marking me with the pale scar that runs from under one eye to my upper lip. And a day later one of my friends took a long dive and broke his ankle when the rope finally caught him, slamming him against the wall. I rappelled off the mountain with him, cut two leg-holes in the bottom of my pack, and staggered out across the glacier with him on my back, his arms wrapped around my neck. It earned me minor hero status in the climbing community for a short time. The magazine expressed it as a self-sufficient contrast to the usual European tactic of calling for a rescue after the slightest injury, like a hangnail. The magazine published a feature article with photographs.

"My first name's Antonio, but everyone calls me Anton. For some reason Tony never stuck."

Heller sort of grins at me, his mouth twisting with what I guess is bitterness or envy, and says, "I remember that. Haven't heard about you doing anything new since then, though."

When I look at his face I see the jaw muscles still flexed under his tight skin. The words are too pointed to be friendly, the smile too mocking. I'm disconcerted by his apparent and immediate dislike for me; likability and a sense of cool are what have made me successful as an undercover investigator.

"I'm Lynn White," the girl says, squeezing my upper arm with her own small, tough hand. "And over at the table are Chris and Brad, and some other guys on a road trip through here."

I turn and give them a small wave. None of them gets up or acknowledges me with anything other than a brief look. The wiry one she pointed out as Brad resembles the County Attorney, Nathan Karge, although Brad wears blond dreadlocks. He has the same coldly handsome features. I figure he must be the son, the one who was with the girl four nights ago when she fell off the cliff and died. The funeral was just yesterday but it looks like he has finished mourning—I watch as he laughs and sprays beer from his mouth.

Lynn says to Billy, "Saw this guy up at Vedauwoo today. He was soloing on Crankenstine." Then to me, somewhat proudly, "Billy climbed that once with a broken ankle. Did the whole damned thing with just one foot."

I'm impressed and say so. "It scared the hell out of me today. With both feet."

Billy doesn't say anything, so Lynn goes on, "Billy's been here for just three years but he's already put up more than twenty routes that are 5.12 or harder."

I try again to be polite and say, "I think I'll stick to easier stuff unless I've got a top rope. You really got to be honed to lead up cracks like that."

Again, Billy doesn't reply. He just keeps his eyes on me, the challenge and the warning obvious. I read the message and look blankly back. Fuck him. I'm done with speaking the necessary platitudes to establish his dominance and reassure his ego.

Heller gives off a palpable sense of violence like an odor as we stare at one another. Unconsciously, I tense my legs on the rungs of the stool. Heller's bitterness seems so great that I wouldn't be surprised if he were to hit me without warning. For the second time in just a few hours, a juvenile urge warms my blood. I'm tempted to find out if I can take him. Machismo—my father says I inherited *that* from my mother's mestizo ancestors, even though it could just as easily be the result of the military upbringing he subjected our family to. I try to douse the fire with a long draw from my beer.

Lynn squeezes both our arms. "C'mon, guys. Cut the testosterone bullshit. Anton, you should come climbing with us sometime this week. We're out at the 'Voo pretty much every morning."

"I'd like that," I say, as much wanting to annoy Heller as wanting to spend time with her. "I don't know where anything is. I don't even have a guidebook."

"How about coming with us to smoke some blunts? We're going back to Billy's place."

Billy's eyes cut at her.

I shake my head and almost laugh. "No, I've got to sleep. I have to work tomorrow."

"What do you do?" Heller asks, finally speaking again.

"Pest control," I say quickly. "But I'll look for you guys up at Vedauwoo this week." In order to pay for my beer I have to open my wallet carefully so that my badge doesn't show.

FOUR

I WAKE UP EARLY and drive to a local park. There I find a set of monkey bars from which I can do my usual training: sets of pull-ups, push-ups, and leaps while wearing a pack weighted with climbing gear. It's a routine I have maintained even over the eighteen months of self-imposed exile from the rocks. Oso sniffs about the sand that surrounds the playground's equipment with his gray muzzle and shambling gait. For just a moment it makes me melancholy to see him looking so tired and old; when I'd first taken possession of him, he moved with the quick, explosive grace of a true carnivore.

The first time I saw him he was chained to the back porch of a house operating as a methamphetamine lab up in Rawlins. When I executed a no-knock warrant there with the local police, we found him half-starved and ferocious as a wounded bear. Patches of hair were missing from his pelt and raw sores blew with flies. Rather than just shoot him, we called in Animal Control officers. Only with great difficulty were they able to wrestle him into a cage using long poles with wire nooses looped at one end. There he tore at the bars until blood dripped from his teeth.

Animal Control said they would have to put him down. They laughed at the thought of anyone adopting him. I walked away to write my reports feeling sadder for this dog that had never had a chance than I did for the pathetic and violent young drug addicts I dealt with every day. After an hour I returned to the meth lab to find an officer poking him with a sharp-bladed shovel, seeing just how crazy he could make him before the Animal Control officers standing by put a bullet through his heavy, flat skull.

The charges against me for assaulting a fellow peace officer were deferred and later dropped. But on the spot I accepted a sentence that has now run five years by deciding to adopt the snarling creature as my own. I took him home.

Twenty-four stitches later and after two visits to the emergency room, I finally had him installed in my backyard, chained to an elm. It took six weeks of determined care and attention before he would even let me stroke him. After six months he was accompanying me nearly everywhere I went. In the places where dogs weren't allowed, he would sit hunched massively in the passenger seat of my rusty Land Cruiser and stare out the windshield until I returned, no matter how many hours it took. When I went away on climbing trips and left him in the care of friends, he would refuse to eat or drink until I returned. My love and devotion for the abused beast quenched his rage and mellowed him until the love was reflected back at me, magnified a hundred times. Instead of a raging brute he morphed into a gentle, playful giant. I named him after the animal he most resembled.

Between sets of pull-ups, I hang by my fingertips and watch a children's soccer game on a field nearby. The cold morning air, the laughter of the kids, the cheers of the parents, they all have me feeling so unusually good that for a moment I lose track of the beast. Just when I start looking around for him he appears. He barrels onto the soccer field moving faster than he's moved in years. A part of me admires that his creaking bones and ancient muscles can still carry him that fast; the rest of me begins running, calling his name.

Children scatter, their screams mixing with their parents' outraged shouts. Oso powers through them like they're a pile of leaves. With a youthful lunge he tackles the soccer ball, then crushes it in his jaws. I catch up to him and grab his collar just as he gives the ball a death-shake that flings drool into the sunlight. Angry fathers and mothers encircle me, yelling. I apologize repeatedly but to no avail. They aren't interested in anything but giving me a sound cursing.

"That's the most irresponsible . . ."

"A child could have been killed . . ."

"Keep that goddamn monster on a leash . . ."

"Someone should call the police . . ."

Finally I just drop a twenty-dollar bill on the deflated corpse of the ball and tug the dog across the field. We're almost past the chalked sideline when he squats his hind legs and defecates on the grass.

I try to berate him and drag him off but can't stop laughing. Coming back to Laramie and Vedauwoo is doing something to us both, making us younger and more carefree again. Every now and then, like on the rocks yesterday, I feel as if my emotional wounds are finally scabbing over.

Although the morning air is still cold, I eat my bagels with lox outside on the café's patio. Oso lies near my feet, relishing the occasional bite that I drop by his head.

The file that's open on the table before me is in disarray. I wonder if the sheriff did that on purpose. After carefully wiping my hands, I rearrange it in chronological order beginning with the reports of the responding officers and finishing with the county coroner's findings and opinions. The envelope that holds a stack of what I assume are eight-by-ten photographs of the scene, the body in situ, and the autopsy I leave unopened. Rather than risk upsetting the waitress who periodically checks on me, I save it for a more private viewing.

The initial report and investigation was done by Sergeant Leroy Bender, I'm unhappy to see. I read it skeptically and am not disappointed to conclude that it was a half-assed job. Despite handwriting that borders on a kindergartner's scrawl and numerous misspellings, I learn that Bender had been called into the station at nearly three in the morning to meet with Bradley Karge, who was reporting a climbing accident in a part of the Medicine Bow National Forest known as Vedauwoo. The Sheriff's Department apparently shares jurisdiction there with the federal government.

Bradley informed the sergeant that a girl named Kate Danning had fallen from a cliff during a late-night outdoor party and was believed to be dead. He gave the names of four other people who were present at the party on the rocks, and I'm interested to see Billy Heller's name among them. Lynn's name is not. Bender had called in another officer, named Knight, who is a certified Emergency Medical Technician, and the three drove up to the forest to, according to Bender's report, "investiget."

Once at Vedauwoo, Bradley Karge led the two officers with flashlights to the base of a cliff where a young female lay facedown on the rocks. Deputy Knight found no pulse and determined that she was in fact deceased. Sergeant Bender called for the county coroner's team to come and pick up the body.

Despite the circumstances, I can't help but smile as I read the last line of Bender's handwritten report: "There was no sign of fowl play."

Fortunately, the county's part-time coroner did a somewhat better job once he arrived near dawn with his staff of two local mortuary attendants. Probably because of the recent cross-examination he'd had to endure during the Lee trial, he had the good sense to photograph the body before it was moved to the morgue. Little else is contained in his initial report from the scene other than that he'd taken some photos, determined that the girl was dead, and that she had apparently fallen from a height of more than one hundred feet down a sheer cliff.

The next section of the file is the notes from the autopsy, which had been conducted that same afternoon. The deceased is described in them as a healthy nineteen-year-old Caucasian female, sixty-four inches in height and weighing 110 pounds. I only skim the descriptions of her injuries, which appear to be numerous contusions to the entire front of her body, burst organs, and broken bones from her face to her feet. There is a note of a preliminary blood test that revealed the presence of both methamphetamine and marijuana in her system.

I skip ahead to the coroner's determination of the "Cause of Death" at the bottom of the page and read that it was blunt-force trauma to the torso and head. The more interesting part of any coroner's report is the section entitled "Manner of Death," of which the coroner has only five choices: Homicide, Suicide, Accidental, Natural, and Undetermined—Pending Investigation. The sheriff had been correct in telling me that the coroner found Kate Danning's death to be accidental with no further need for any inquiry.

"More coffee, honey?" the waitress asks.

"Please." I smile at her and hold out my cup so as not to risk having any spill on the documents open before me.

"You or your dog need anything else?"

Oso raises his head and looks at her hopefully, but I tell her no.

"That guy's a monster. What kind of dog is he anyway?" she says, studying Oso's black coat, his flat, blunt head, and his enormous size.

"No one really knows exactly, but I think he's some sort of mastiff. They have dogs in Tibet that look a lot like him. My mother just calls him the Beast."

The waitress laughs as she leaves a check for me, then goes back inside.

I look back down at the page in front of me as I sip my coffee, my mind settling for a moment upon my parents' forced retirement to my grandfather's ranch in Argentina. My father had been on the verge of becoming a general when my brother was charged with manslaughter. Shortly after that I killed the three gangbangers in Cheyenne. My parents now lived in near-isolation on the ranch, wondering what they'd done to turn their boys into killers. Each in some quiet way blames the other, I know. My mother believes the games my father taught us as children and his career with its ever present possibility of violence nudged us in the wrong direction. My father worries it has something to do with our blood—the intermingling of three violent and warring cultures: Scots, Spaniards, and Pampas Indios. The last time I talked to them they were cool with each other, considering the prospect of divorce after nearly thirty-five years of marriage.

Willing myself back to work, I focus on the page again. My eyes fall upon the descriptions of the injuries sustained. The coroner had noted that there was a contusion to the rear of her head and a hairline fracture of her skull, again caused by blunt-force trauma. After that begins the description of the injuries to her face. I put down my coffee and flip back to Bender's report. He'd written that Kate Danning was found facedown. Then how did she get an injury to the back of her head? I wonder.

By the time I return to my room at the Holiday Inn, the day is already warming and even the perpetual wind off the glaciated peaks feels like an idle car's blower just starting to heat. I open the curtains to watch a few reporters sitting by the pool, some of them working on laptop computers and others talking on cell phones. I'm disappointed that Rebecca Hersh is not among them. At the small table by the bed I pull out the envelope of photographs.

During my six years as a state investigator I've seen a lot of bodies. Fresh corpses, old corpses, and worst of all, corpses during autopsies. Physically, the fresh ones aren't so bad. They're simply pieces of meat after they've lost their souls. The only really disturbing thing about them are the cloudy, sad eyes that always seem to be open. You can't help but think of the future that they'll miss seeing. Old corpses are certainly more disturbing, but it's a physical agitation rather than an emotional one. Bugs and animals enter first through the soft flesh of the eyes, mouth, and anus and drag out what belongs inside and unseen. Then there are the autopsies. They give me nightmares. There's something about a naked man, woman, or child being clinically cut apart on a stainless-steel table that is bad for the soul. The grinding of the electric saw on a skull, the crisp snap of bolt cutters on ribs. To me it's the ultimate desecration even though I understand the obvious necessity. I've never left one without immediately taking a long, hot shower and wanting several stiff drinks. But the shower and alcohol can only remove the taste and the stench, not the memory.

And so I feel an all-too-familiar reluctance when I slide the photographs from the stiff envelope. Working quickly and averting my eyes as much as possible, I sort out the pictures that document the autopsy from the stack and place them facedown on the bed. The unfocused glances at them alone bring the fresh-meat stink into my mind. I'm determined not to look at them at all unless it becomes necessary. Instead I study only the pictures of the girl as she'd been found.

The first photo of Kate Danning's corpse was taken from a short distance away. The photographer had stood high on something, probably a rock. It shows a young woman lying facedown on top of several large boulders. Part of the picture shows the base of the cliff just a few feet away from her. I don't quite recognize it although it appears somewhat familiar. Which isn't surprising as it has been almost twenty years since I've spent much time at Vedauwoo.

The girl wears tight black leggings and what looks like a heavy fleece jacket. Her legs are lean and athletic but one is sprawled at an impossible angle. Her brown hair is straight, just long enough to hide her ears. I'm relieved that there is no evident gore and that her eyes face the earth. The next photos were taken closer and show just the body as it was found. I hold the pictures close to my face and can see where her hair is slightly matted with blood on the back of her head.

Then there are more photos of the entire scene, this time taken from a greater distance and facing the cliff. The first of these shows the body and the base of the rock. A second focuses higher on the cliff and shows it in its entirety. The granite looks perfectly vertical and sheer. It's also vaguely familiar, but doesn't appear to be anywhere near where I soloed yesterday. The final photo from the scene was apparently taken from over the body, looking up the wall. I instinctively look for a way to climb it and see only a fist-size crack that leads almost all the way to the top. There are no photos of the top, where the party had taken place.

I call the hotel operator, who connects me to McGee's room.

"What?" His voice is thick with sleep and his general orneriness is conveyed in just that one word.

"It's me. I want to talk to you about this Danning thing, if you ever get your *gordo orto* out of bed."

"Impertinent youth. Don't speak to your betters that way.... Come over in fifteen minutes. Room 136...And bring some goddamn coffee."

* * *

I shower and shave, then knock on McGee's door at the appointed time. My boss answers the door wearing only an unbuckled pair of pants and with a thick cigar clenched between his teeth. His spine is bent by the small hump and the weight of his big, bald head like a branch supporting too much snow. Ash is sprinkled down his long white beard. The once-powerful torso shows the ravages of age, disease, and war. His bulging barrel of a belly displays a jagged scar caused by what I'd been told was Korean shrapnel. When he turns, I can see on his shoulder the puckered skin of where a bullet passed in and out. Beyond him in the room is a clutter of oxygen bottles. The man should definitely not be smoking.

"Frigging altitude," he explains, out of breath from the walk across the small room to answer the door.

Oso pushes his way into the room ahead of me and McGee leaps back from the door, moving with surprising agility for a man of his age and bulk.

"Jesus Christ, what is that? A fucking bear?"

Oso ignores him and collapses on the carpet. The murder of the children's soccer ball has left him exhausted.

"His name's Oso," I say. "But with his gray muzzle and big belly, he could be your twin."

"How the hell did you get him into the hotel? We had a hard enough time getting these rooms for the humans."

I slip my badge from my wallet and hang it on the dog's collar. "I told them he was a police dog. Then I got him to growl and they didn't argue. Smile, Oso."

The beast complies by halfheartedly lifting his lips and revealing his long, yellow-stained teeth. If it weren't for his tired and complacent eyes the effect would be terrifying.

McGee doesn't know him well enough to read the eyes

and says, "Goddamn!" and staggers back to the far side of the room.

When McGee goes back to dressing and while Oso pants, I explain the reports I'd read and the mention of an inconsistent head injury. I also tell him that the crowd she ran with is apparently into meth and dope. Giving me a foul-tempered look, he wonders aloud what is with drugs and climbers in this town.

Feeling defensive, I tell him that as a whole climbers are probably more law-abiding than any other class of athletes I can think of. The climbing community is largely made up of intensely devoted and responsible individuals. Their love of life and freedom, athleticism, respect for nature, and reliance on the teamwork of their partners for their very survival adds up to a sort of general social empathy.

But McGee appears to ignore my brief lecture—he growls out a litany of curses as he wrestles his bulk into a shirt then says, "If there was any hanky-panky up there... Karge's kid could cost him the damned election."

As I know he will, he agrees that further investigation is warranted and gives me his official blessing by saying, "Don't just stand there with your dick in your hand... do it."

At my urging, he picks up the phone and dials the Coroner's Office. The first—and possibly the only—thing I need to find out is whether there's a reasonable explanation for the injury to the back of Kate Danning's head. The coroner should be able to tell me that. But I suspect that if I were to call I would just get the runaround.

After McGee identifies himself as a Deputy Attorney General, he spars with the person on the other end. Finally he barks, "Three o'clock," and slams down the phone while muttering about "incompetent fucking vampires." Then

McGee leaves for court to assist Nathan Karge in arguing
the objections the defense had made during his closing. The
judge will rule on them while the jury continues to deliberate.

I sit on the bed with the window open, skimming distract-
edly through the reports one more time and wondering
where I should begin. Even in my room I can smell the dry
dust in the air, lifted off the chaparral plains by the wind as
it spins across the summer-baked earth. It reminds me again
of my grandfather's ranch, where on our visits there I wrestled in the dirt with my brother over who would have the
privilege of the first attempt on a new climbing problem
we'd discovered around the red cliffs near the main house.
Older and stronger, he always won. At that age it seemed I
only got to climb where others had been before. That was
something I strove to remedy in later years.

Starting an investigation is like spilling the pieces of a
jigsaw puzzle onto a broad table. Or like staring up at a
climb, trying to unravel the mysteries of the moves it will require to gain the summit. No matter how good you are at
putting them together, you're always a little unsure where to
begin. You hesitate and wonder if it's worth the risk and the
trouble. The sagebrush smell and the memory make me recall my father's often-repeated advice about starting a climb.
"Be prepared," he would say, "then be creative."

My father was once on an expedition in Pakistan when
he and his partner ran out of food while waiting for the
weather to clear. They were afraid to make the three-day
journey to the nearest village for supplies because a team of
Russian climbers had established a base camp close by and

were obviously eyeballing my father's intended route. So late one afternoon, while his partner guarded the line, my father hiked down into the valley where he remembered having seen a herd of sheep.

In the midst of stalking a young ewe, he realized he was being watched. A native herder sat beneath a rock's overhang just a hundred feet away, pointing an old muzzle-loading rifle at the poacher. Dad was creative: He grinned at the herder and gestured at the sheep while he pantomimed a lewd motion with his hands and his hips. The native had smiled back in comprehension, probably thinking that this was just another of those strange, lonely foreigners. Dad ended up trading a pair of binoculars for the ewe and receiving a wink and a slap on the back from the herder. Resupplied, he and his partner finished the route ahead of the Russians. When telling Roberto and me the story out of our mother's earshot, he'd concluded it with a wink of his own. "Be creative," he repeated.

Like climbing, the simplest way to start an investigation is from the bottom, talking to the initial witnesses. But in this case the witnesses are potential suspects, and I'm worried about how politics may have played a role in the Sheriff's Office's shoddy investigation. With the County Attorney's and future governor's son as the boyfriend of the deceased, and the sheriff as his campaign manager, I consider that the case may have been intentionally dogged. Before I talk to the partyers who were up there that night, I want to get a better feel for what is going on.

So I need to start with the officers on the scene and see what kinds of vibes I can pick up from them, but I'm more than a little reluctant to talk to Sergeant Bender due to our history. Deputy Knight will have to be my starting point. I call the Sheriff's Office and learn that both Knight and Bender work the swing shift; they are off duty until the evening. After I explain my need to speak with Deputy Knight, I wait for ten minutes while the duty sergeant verifies my credentials with the Attorney General's Office and calls the deputy with my number at the hotel. Outside my window, more reporters and tourists are starting to gather in the deck chairs by the pool as they hopefully await word of an early verdict. Rebecca Hersh is still not among them. I imagine that she's somewhere around town, ambitiously pursuing a human interest angle. Finally the phone rings.

"This is Knight. I'm not sure what I can do for you—" He speaks quickly, his words from the start conveying a defensiveness. It is a small hint that something's not right. He also sounds somewhat educated and young, which makes me happy. I'd dared to hope he wouldn't have the old-school, country attitudes of police officers like Bender and Sheriff Willis.

"I'm a special agent with DCI, Deputy Knight," I interrupt.

"I've heard of you."

Between the incident in Cheyenne, his sergeant, and the sheriff, it isn't likely he's heard anything good. His tone tells me that he is not one of the cops who thinks I'm a hero.

"Okay, now as you probably know, we look into all criminal matters where there's a potential conflict of interest with local law enforcement." I don't mention that it's generally in corruption cases. "We're taking a look at that Danning girl's death, and I just had a few questions. You were there early Sunday morning when her body was found, right?"

"Yes, sir. But excuse me—you said criminal matters. I don't understand what was criminal about it, a girl falling off a rock? The way it looked to me, she got stoned then probably tripped."

"We're just looking into it as a matter of policy. It was requested by the girl's parents through the governor's office. By the way, who told you she was high?"

"The boyfriend, you know, the County Attorney's son." I wonder why Bender didn't bother to put that in his report. Probably to avoid connecting the son to any embarrassing behavior. "Hey, um, do I need to clear it with the sheriff or anyone before I talk with you?"

"No, Sheriff Willis is the one who gave me the file."

"Okay, we've just been warned to be careful talking. You know, with all these reporters in town and all."

I try to move on quickly, not wanting him to give the sheriff a call. "Do you remember what Brad Karge said about her being wasted? What she was taking?"

"He said that she'd just been drinking. That they'd hauled a couple of bottles up there in the dark. Oh yeah, and there was a pipe in one of her jacket pockets. A metal one, you know. I found it when I was looking for her ID."

"Was the pipe used for pot or something heavier?"

"It wasn't for pot. I smelled it. It was for the heavy stuff. Meth."

That isn't in the report either. "Now you checked her pulse, right, and her pockets? Did you move her at all?"

"No, sir. I didn't even want to touch her in the first place, but Bender told me I had to."

"So was she facedown when you arrived, Deputy?"

"Yes, sir."

"Did you ask Bradley Karge if he'd moved her at all when he found her?"

"No, but he was pretty freaked out. Wouldn't go near the body."

"The autopsy showed that she had an injury to the back of her head, not just to her face. Any idea how she could have gotten it?"

"No, sir. The girl landed facedown, the way it looked to me. And stayed that way till the coroner's guys bagged her."

"Did you show the pipe to the kid or ask him about it? Or did Bender talk to him about it?"

The deputy sounds a little embarrassed. "No, they don't let me investigate deaths. I'm just a rookie, you know? I was just there as backup and 'cause I'm EMT certified. I didn't hear Bender ask him much. It didn't seem necessary."

"So I guess you didn't talk to any of the other witnesses who were supposed to have been at that party on the cliff?"

Now the deputy chuckles somewhat nervously. It's obvious not much of an investigation was conducted, and even as a rookie he knows it. "No, sir, sorry."

"All right. Well, thanks for calling me back, Knight. Good luck handling the crowds if a verdict comes back today."

The conversation leaves me with the feeling that either some incredibly sloppy police work had been performed or something more sinister is going on. I think about calling the duty sergeant again and having him call Bender, but I know the response I'll get from him. It will be either abusive or none at all.

Instead I get out the hotel's Laramie phone book and look for the names of the four other partyers whose names Bender had written in his report. Chris Braddock, Billy Heller, Cindy Topper, and Sierra Calloway. The only name that is listed in the White Pages with both a number and an address is Cindy Topper's. However, in the Yellow Pages I find a listing for Heller Carpentry. Construction and carpentry are the least offensive careers for full-time hard-core climbers, and I assume Billy Heller is no different. One can work a job for a few weeks, then spend a month or two traveling and climbing, living out of the back of one's truck. On a legal pad I copy down the numbers and addresses for Cindy and Heller Carpentry.

Then I make a call to DCI's main office in Cheyenne.

"DCI" is all the female voice on the other end says.

"Hi, Kristi, it's Anton."

"Hey, buddy." Her voice drops to a softer, concerned tone. As if she's speaking to a mourning friend or a dangerous psychotic. "How are you doing? Everyone around here's been talking about you, rooting that the case'll get settled or thrown out next Thursday."

"Keep your fingers crossed," I say. Then to forestall any further discussion of the wrongful death suit, I go right into the reason I called. I ask if she can run some criminal histories for me. DCI keeps the state's database and also has access to NCIC, the FBI's nationwide system. I give her all the names from Bender's report.

"Don't you have birth dates, Anton?"

"Sorry, but I can give you estimates. Heller should be in his late thirties to early forties. All the others should be between eighteen and, say, twenty-five."

It turns out there is only one Bradley Karge, age nineteen. Kristi tells me he's clean on the Wyoming computer. That means he has never been arrested in Wyoming, which isn't surprising since his dad is the chief law enforcement officer in the only county he's ever lived in. He has, however, been arrested and charged in both California and New Mexico for possession of narcotics. No disposition of the charges is shown on the computer, meaning that they were probably dismissed. His father's influence, I'm sure.

Billy Heller, a.k.a. William Heller, Jr., is no surprise

either. He has numerous Wyoming charges and some convictions. There are three convictions for misdemeanor third-degree assault, two of which were pleaded down from felonies, and a conviction for felony Possession of a Schedule II Controlled Substance, which usually means cocaine or methamphetamine. Kristi tells me that Heller is still on probation for the narcotics charge, although the charge is out of Teton County, not Laramie. She gives me the name of the probation officer and tells me she'll check around to find his number.

After a moment of further tapping of keys at her terminal, she tells me that he has just recently been charged with Possession with Intent to Manufacture and/or Distribute, but that the charge was dismissed only two days ago. But there is still an outstanding Petition to Revoke Probation based upon the new charge. I ask her whose name is down as the dismissing attorney and she says Nathan Karge. That is a surprise; I would have thought he'd have been too busy with the Lee trial and the election to deal with a commonplace drug crime.

Like Heller, Chris Braddock also is on probation for Possession with Intent to Distribute out of Teton County. The DOOs, date of offenses, are the same. That means they were doing a little dealing together. Sierra Calloway, if it's the same girl, had been charged with prostitution in Boulder, Colorado, but received a deferred judgment that's basically the same as a dismissal as long as she stays out of trouble. As for Cindy Topper, Kristi can find no criminal history for anyone with a similar name and within the scope of the birth dates I've given her.

I write down what she's told me and ask for the addresses given for Chris Braddock and Billy Heller in the probation paperwork. Not available by computer are the addresses for the out-of-state charges against Bradley Karge and Sierra Calloway, but Kristi promises to send out some faxes requesting them. I ask her to print out everything she has found and courier it to me at the Holiday Inn.

"I'll do better than that—since it's so slow around here I'll drive it out. Everyone is just sitting on their butts, glued to the television, waiting for a verdict in the Lee case. And it's just an hour from the office anyway." DCI's headquarters are in Cheyenne, Wyoming, just fifty miles over the low mountains to the east. "Besides, buddy, I haven't seen you in a while," she adds.

I tell her it isn't at all necessary, but thank her. I'm not thrilled with the idea of her coming. I'd just barely escaped having a relationship with her when I was assigned to the main office in Cheyenne. At a party we both drank too much and she clung to me the entire evening, demonstrating her availability by lifting her shirt to show me the faint ridges of gym-earned muscles on her stomach and the lower edges of her black lace bra. Only with great difficulty had I managed to elude the temptation that night and go home alone. Now, eighteen months later and emotionally damaged, I don't know if I'll have the will to ward off a second assault.

There's no answer at the number I had gotten out of the phone book for Cindy Topper. On the map at the front of the directory I find the street where she lives, mark it, and tear out the page. While I'm at it I look up the address of a local mountaineering shop. I will need a climbing guidebook in order to figure out directions to the rock from which Kate Danning fell.

Outside my window the reporters are beginning to frolic in the pool. When Oso and I go out the door, I feel the wind, warmer and stronger still, heated and gathering speed from its short journey across the dry plains on the way to Laramie. I wonder if I'll have time today to return to Vedauwoo and climb shirtless again with the sun on my back. The thought is too hopeful for the trouble the wind is blowing my way.

FIVE

TIM'S OUTDOOR STORE is just a half block off
Third Street on Grand Avenue, almost directly across
the street from the sandstone courthouse. Activists, protesters, and the curious are already gathered there on the lawn.
Curious myself, I glance at the crowd to see if the Klansmen
are back before going into the store. They aren't; apparently
one of their numbers had embarrassed the Klan enough the
night before. The fact that they can be humiliated restores a
little of my faith in humanity.

Inside, amid crowded racks of clothes, bikes, packs,
and gear, I recognize the small, slender figure sorting climbing shoes and hiking boots against one wall. Lynn. She's
wearing a pair of khaki shorts and a too-large V-necked
shirt. Her small feet are bare beneath thin brown ankles. I
smile at another girl behind the counter as I walk toward the

shoes. It's the third time I've come across Lynn in just two days. Maybe my luck is changing.

She looks up and sees me as I wander over, and smiles. "Hey, Anton. You stalking me or what?"

"You're the stalker. You watched me climb, gave my dog a lei, even came up to me in the bar last night. Now you show up when I go shopping."

She laughs and says, "Well, don't become a stalker then, I already got one." The corners of her lips drop a quarter inch or so.

"What's that about?"

She looks back at the shoes she's arranging and doesn't answer my question. "So what are you doing here?"

"Shopping for a Vedauwoo guidebook. You work here?"

"Yeah, man, I run this place."

"Do you give discounts to climbing partners?"

"You're not a partner."

"Maybe I will be soon."

She looks back up at me, amused and speculating.

"How soon, Anton? You want to meet my friends and me up at the 'Voo? Like tomorrow morning, early?"

"I'd like that. You guys can show me the good stuff. Top-rope me up the hard ones. But I think I'd want to have you holding the rope, not your pal Heller. He didn't seem too friendly, and I'm a little out of shape."

"You didn't look it the other day when you were soloing." She blushes a little as she says it, then looks around again and sees the girl behind the counter watching us intently. Lynn stops smiling and stares at the girl until she looks away and pretends to busy herself with the magazines stacked there.

"How 'bout meeting us at Reynold's Complex, like at eight o'clock?"

"Sell me a guide so I can find it and I'll be there."

She leads me over to a rack of guidebooks and hands me one called *Heel and Toe—Climbs of Greater Vedauwoo.*

"How come they call it *Heel and Toe?*"

"After you do a few fat cracks up there you'll find out, man. They should call it *Bloody Knees and Elbows* or *Gnarly Fucked-up Off-Widths.*"

I groan. "Off-widths." Climbing off-widths means sticking in just one elbow and a knee, wedging them tight, then wiggling up sideways. There is no more physical, feared, or painful type of crack climbing. Vedauwoo is famous for them.

Lynn rings the guidebook up on the register while the girl who'd been standing there keeps sneaking mirthful looks at the two of us. I notice Lynn takes twenty percent off the listed price. I guess I'm now a partner.

"I'll see you in the morning, Anton," she says, her brown eyes smiling.

From there I drive to a pet store at the south end of town not far from the hotel to get a new bag of food for Oso. After parking outside on the street, I stand enjoying the sun and the wind for a moment while I flip through the pictures in the guidebook with it propped open on the hood. Just when I think I've found a picture that matches the coroner's, I hear a voice behind me.

"Hey, *cabrón.*"

The word raises the hair on my arms with a gentle sting. I turn and look at the four Hispanic youths who've gathered around me on the sidewalk. Oso thrusts his head through the window, a low growl vibrating from his throat. One stands before the loose half-circle of the other three with his hands clenched at his sides. I can see the homemade gang tattoos across his knuckles. All of them wear too-large red-checked plaid shirts with only the top buttoned and baggy pants. Above the shirts they each have an ornate "13" tattooed on the skin of their throats. I recognize a couple of them only vaguely as junior members of the gang I'd investigated in Cheyenne eighteen months before, but can't remember any names.

I toss the book through the open window beside Oso's head. I give the kid a puzzled look but don't say a word.

"I said hey, *cabrón*. Fucking *joto*."

Oso growls louder at the words. The youth looks at the beast in the truck's window and perhaps sees that the dog is too big to get through it. But he may not even notice or care. I can see that his pupils are just pinpricks. He's on something strong. His jaw is locked and beads of sweat run down his face. Behind him a middle-aged woman inside the store is watching the scene through the plate-glass window and punching numbers into a telephone.

"Remember me, motherfucking Burns?"

"No."

"Remember *mi hermano,* Dominic, *quebrachon*?"

I blink slowly with an inward wince. I'd put a bullet through his brother's head. And through the flesh of the two other Sureno 13 gang leaders with him. Last year in the shoot-out north of Cheyenne.

I become aware of my gun's warm metal on my skin where it's clipped inside the back of my pants but don't touch it as the boy turns slightly and holds his hand out to one of the others behind him. One steps forward and holds his own hand open, exposing his palm. A concealed two-foot length of pipe slides down from his baggy sleeve. The one who's been talking, Dominic's little brother, snatches it from him and faces me again.

That sunlight seems as brilliant as a spotlight from where I stand. All sound disappears—the cars moving on the street, the birds in the trees, my big dog's growl. Time and the wind slow until they don't exist. Images are reeling up in my mind and I'm powerless to choke them back down. Then the boy slaps the pipe against his palm. One of the others behind him shouts something I can't make out.

Struggling to concentrate, I see the boys' heads turn to where a police car is pulling up to the curb. The light reflecting off the windshield conceals the driver. Instead of dropping the pipe and running, the boy's tiny pupils turn again to me, unconcerned with the new presence, but the others begin to back away.

The boy raises the pipe and snarls again, *"Chupatame, año!"* then swings high and hard, two-handed.

I watch the pipe coming toward the side of my head as if it's something happening to someone else far away. The memory of another young man's face, Dominic's, floods my vision. The face is grinning, holding the glinting barrel of a shotgun out just below the chin. And then the face jerks back as a hole appears through the bridge of his nose and red mist erupts in the air. With only that year-and-a-half-old blood in my vision, I finally duck, more to escape the red spray in my mind than anything else, and hear the pipe sweep the air above me.

My eyes and mind clear as I stagger back away from the boy. The deputy has gotten out of the car and is holding his pistol braced on the roof, shouting. Oso is rocking the Land Cruiser on its axles as he roars and throws himself against the too-small window. The boy has his back against the store window, the pipe raised again, but now his rage seems to explode. He begins shouting back at the street cop. Screaming really, madly and for revenge. I can almost feel the drugs pumping through him, upping the volume. As he screams he whips the pipe through the air in short, savage swings.

The three others are long gone as more police cars arrive. Soon a number of officers are on the sidewalk surrounding the boy, just ten or so feet away, their guns drawn and pointed. I stand behind them telling them to wait, just wait, the kid will put down the pipe.

"Go ahead, fuckers! I kill you all!"

The officers are all yelling for him to drop the pipe. Their fingers are on the triggers. Safeties off. You don't touch the trigger unless you're going to shoot. That was the first rule we'd all learned in the police academy. The boy's neck with its "13" tattoo is swollen with rage.

The tall, thick form of Sergeant Bender suddenly enters the fray, gun in one hand and a charge of pepper spray in the other. He steps between two officers and fires a chemical blast. The kid swings wildly but is too far away to strike anyone, howling obscenities. Miraculously, no one pulls a trigger. I hear myself shouting, "Don't shoot, don't shoot!"

As the pipe comes around in a full swing I launch myself forward, springing hard with all the power in my hips. My shoulder hits the boy's middle like an ax, cutting him in half, and the two of us slam into the storefront window. The glass bursts under the pressure and we topple over the low wall into the pet store.

A heavy hail of glass shards rain on my back as I fight to pin the boy while my shoulders take the blows from the end of the pipe. I head-butt him in the face just as the other officers manage to holster their weapons and move into the fray.

When I'm able to step back and collect my senses, the

boy is kneeling on the broken glass with tears streaming from his wild eyes, blood running down his still-snarling mouth, and a tooth hanging, over his lower lip, that's held only by a stringy root. I can see the backs of his fingers reaching up over his shoulders from behind where the deputies have them pinned.

I feel a hand grip my shoulder. I turn and Sergeant Bender leans toward me to whisper, "You fucking pussy. You should have shot him. For a second I thought I could get away with shooting you."

I stare into his eyes, only inches away. Then I knock his hand off my shoulder hard enough to fling it into the air and walk back to the truck to calm Oso.

Bender laughs and says louder, "Gee, I wonder how they knew you're in town? You got a lot of friends, Agent. Keep it up."

SIX

IT'S AFTER NOON before I finish answering questions and writing out my witness statement. When McGee comes in from court I'm sitting alone on a table in an empty interview room, eating a slice of cold pizza I can't even taste. But it has the texture of rubber. The small, depressing room consists of cinderblock walls with peeling paint, a steel door, and the ever present one-way mirror. For furniture there are only three wooden chairs and the scarred table on which I sit. I've been thinking about the night I shot Dominic "Dice" Torres and two others. That night eighteen months ago has haunted me ever since. It has left me in a daze that just yesterday I thought I was finally shaking off. Then this morning the ghosts came to life. My hands are trembling when I lift the pizza to my mouth for another bite.

I remember nearly every word of the four-hour deposition I gave about that night. For some reason it seems more real than the actual event. With my back straight in the chair and cold tears of sweat running down my flanks beneath a hot wool suit, I was questioned by a flamboyant attorney named Morris Cash, who was unfortunately but appropriately known as Mo Cash, and two of his associates. Cash makes a good living suing police officers and police departments in federal courts all across the western states. It's a good enough living for him to drive a Mercedes SUV and wear ostrich-skin boots with his Armani suits. According to Ross McGee, Cash pursued the families of the men I'd killed as if they were "shitting dollars."

I'm not at all confident that the attorney assigned to defend me and the office, a rookie Assistant Attorney General fresh out of law school, is up to the task of taking on Cash and his minions. I've learned through friends in the office that it will be his first solo trial. That means either that someone senior in the AG's Office has determined that the case is very one-sided, for or against me, or that no one with any experience wants to taint himself politically by defending the killer of three Hispanic men. My attorney, Clayton Wells, is a skinny, prematurely balding young man whose eyes constantly slide away from mine whenever we speak. He is scared, I can see. Of me, of the case, of the attention it has garnered. I know the judge and jury will be sure to pick up on that fear.

Mo Cash was friendly with me during the deposition I gave, laughing easily and attempting to establish some sort of camaraderie. But I've been around defense lawyers long enough to understand that he will be far different in court. With the jury looking on, there in the actual courtroom, he will treat me with disgust, as if I really am the cold-blooded killer that his filings in the case claim.

After the court reporter had me swear to tell the truth, I

explained to Cash and his associates that at the time, as I was a relatively new agent with a face that was still unrecognized in Wyoming drug circles, I was assigned to infiltrate a Cheyenne-based gang that had been dealing methamphetamine throughout the state. They supplemented their income with half-baked extortion schemes, pawnshop snatch-and-grabs, and the occasional violent home invasion. My "vehicle" into the gang was a confidential informant named Jimmy Hernandez. Although a twice-convicted felon, he was, I believed, a criminal by unfortunate circumstance rather than as the result of an immoral calling. I actually liked him, although I didn't say that at the deposition. The AG's Office had him cold on some distribution charges that would make for his third strike, meaning he would be going away until he was an old man. For a generous plea bargain from the AG's Office, he'd agreed to risk his life and introduce me into Sureno 13.

Things went well for a long time. I was actively working my way into the gang's inner circle and getting the names of suppliers in three states and buyers across Wyoming. The fact that I wasn't more noticeably Hispanic didn't hurt my association with the gang. Unlike big-city gangs, Wyoming's have a more liberal race policy. They will accept anyone they think is sufficiently cool. And I was likable. I could talk the talk and wear the right clothes. It was something I'd learned from a military childhood of attending different schools almost every year, always being the outsider, always trying to charm my way to acceptance. Early on I became skillful at ingratiating myself with all types of people, from the jocks to the nerds to the skateboarding hippies. My graduating yearbook lists me as having been voted "Most Likable." With the Surenos, it also didn't hurt that I was fluent in Spanish, thanks to my mother's mestizo heritage.

Jimmy had introduced me as his ex–brother-in-law, recently released from prison in California after serving a stretch for bank robbery. At first I just hung out with him and the other gang leaders, laughing and joking with them, pretending to smoke their marijuana, drinking cheap beer. After a few weeks they asked me if I wanted to take the position of one of their dealers who'd been shot by an irate customer. I refused, telling them I wasn't going to risk going back to the can to make a few bucks slinging crack. But I was always willing to help out in other ways, like working on cars or helping someone move. Soon I was invited to make some money by just protecting the deals, standing by as muscle in case something went wrong. That was a job I accepted.

The gang members themselves were not that bad individually. I even liked some of them the way I liked Jimmy. But something about their upbringing, whether it was the modern media's celebration of violence or something simpler like poverty and broken homes, I don't know, but something caused them as a whole to lack simple human empathy. They were entirely self-centered. They could not comprehend that hurting another or taking something they didn't own was wrong when it brought them what they wanted, whether it was power or control or money or more drugs.

Late one night I'd gotten a frantic call from Jimmy. He was crying into the phone, almost incoherent. Eventually I got the story out of him. Some of the gang leaders had picked him up from his mother's house and insisted that he come along on what was meant to be the burglary of a local family's residence. It had ended up badly though—the family was home.

They tied up the man, his wife, and his two daughters.

Then they held a gun to Jimmy's head and made him have sex with the eight-year-old. "This is a test," they told him. Another gun was pressed between his buttocks as he complied. Afterward, Jimmy was dropped off back at his mother's house. He said the others were in the hills, celebrating in Dominic Torres's ranch house, where I'd been several times before to meet drug suppliers and provide security during the deals. "I didn't burn you," Jimmy told me through sobs. "But they *know*!"

Hurriedly dressing in my gang-persona clothes, I verified with the local Cheyenne police that there had in fact been a home invasion and rape, perpetrators unknown. According to them the family was too terrified to talk. I got in my truck and drove by the DCI office to be wired before going out to the ranch. It was arranged for two other agents to follow me out as backup but remain hidden in the sagebrush a few miles away.

The whole drive out there I breathed deep and fast, trying to empty my mind of Jimmy's sobs and what had surely been a little girl's screams. What had been going through her parents' minds as they'd been forced to watch I couldn't imagine.

I stood in the dirt outside the small ranch house for a long time before going in. The winter wind blew in gusts across the frozen chaparral. I knew something was wrong but my judgment was warped by outrage. There were three parked cars, but no lights, no music, no voices. The place looked about as inviting as a steel trap. But I was determined to gather evidence that would convict them no matter the risk. I finally walked in by gently pushing open the unlocked front door.

Dominic "Dice" Torres stood alone in a band of moonlight that ran across the filthy living room from a window.

He held a sawed-off shotgun in one hand, flat against his leg. Then two others stepped out from an interior doorway. Luis "Flaco" Gallegos and another I knew only as Smiley. They both had small, cheap pistols down at their sides. True to form, Smiley's teeth flashed in the half-light.

"*Oye, ese. Qué pasa?*" Dominic said as he raised the shotgun to just under his chin. My hand snaked down under my jacket and gripped the plastic butt of my 9mm Glock as I stared into the twin voids of the shotgun's barrels. The room erupted with flashes and explosions like lightning and thunder across the plains.

It would turn out that, inexplicably, Dominic still had the safety on. Only one of the other two even got off a shot, which buried itself in a wall of ruined stucco. Dominic went down with a 9mm hollow-point bullet through the bridge of his nose. Luis got one in the shoulder and another in the chest. Smiley took his through the teeth. Somehow I wasn't touched. Besides the bullets and bodies, all there was in the way of physical evidence when my backup arrived was the tape from the wire I wore with Dominic's innocuous words: "*Oye, ese. Qué pasa?*"

During the deposition, Mo Cash was at first attentive and polite. He pointed out some inconsistencies. Why would I go in there alone when I knew that my cover had been burned? Why were there no accusations on the tape but simply a harmless greeting? Why would Dominic Torres have the safety on when he raised the gun to kill me? How could I possibly have managed to shoot dead three armed men who already had their guns drawn, who had the drop on me?

Later, Cash's questions became a little harder, like, "Isn't it true, Agent Burns, that the three men were un-armed, that you in fact planted the guns on them after they

were dead?" He would wink at me sometimes when he'd
ask these things, since there was no jury present, saying in
subtext, *No hard feelings—it's just my job, pal.* And I had to
answer as my almost prepubescent attorney instructed me,
"No sir, that is not true. I did not plant guns on anyone," instead of responding the way I wanted, which was something
like a simple "Fuck you."

The plaintiffs' theory of the case is that I went to the
ranch house with the single-minded intention of murdering
the three "friends" there. That I walked in, murdered
Dominic Torres and his friends in cold blood, then retrieved
some stolen weapons out of my truck to plant on them. The
complaint states that I was motivated by frustration. According to it, I was discouraged because over the entire period of a three-month undercover investigation, I had failed
to obtain reliable evidence of any criminal activity by
Sureno 13. That is simply untrue. There are hours of tape
and other evidence that could conclusively prove numerous
criminal acts by Torres and the other two. But Clayton
Wells, my attorney, warned me that we might not be able to
go into any of that during the trial. The judge could rule it
irrelevant to the central question of whether or not I had
acted wrongfully in causing the deaths of the three men.
When I snapped at him—*"I thought the purpose of a trial
was to find the truth"*—his eyes just slid away once again. I
should know better than to make such stupid statements.
Without that evidence, my defense will hinge upon just two
things: my testimony and that of Jimmy Hernandez, who
can tell the jury that I'd been burned. And Mo Cash will ask
the jury if they can believe me, when it's my money and the
office's at stake, and whether they can believe Jimmy, a
twice-convicted felon. I expect to lose the trust account my

grandfather left me as well as whatever's left of my professional reputation.

"You don't look so good, Burns. You look frigging beat.... We should call you Deadeye instead of QuickDraw," McGee says, studying me as he comes into the interview room.

"I'd rather we just forget about the nicknames," I say. I chew slowly on the pizza and concentrate on swallowing.

McGee sits heavily in a plastic chair. "Can't say I blame you, lad. What happened?"

I give him a shrug and explain the run-in with the seventeen-year-old gang member. "I didn't recognize the others, but the one we hooked is Dominic Torres's little brother. They're going to send him to Evanston for a psych eval."

"It seems a little strange. That he'd just run across you like that.... I would have expected him to have stalked you instead.... Something like a shot through a window...or a bullet in your back.... Or just take all your money in that civil suit.... They say revenge is a dish best eaten cold."

"Well, he wasn't. He was pretty damn hot, stoked up on crank, I guess. Anyway, the local cops don't think he was over here looking for me. They say it was just coincidence. His gang, Sureno 13, is out of Cheyenne and Casper. They just come to Laramie to stir up trouble with the cowboys and hippies and look for girls at the university. The cops are out trying to find his buddies. How they knew I'd be here, I don't know. I wouldn't put it past my pal Bender to tip them off, though."

What was Bender doing there in uniform just hours after the duty sergeant told me he worked nights? I take this to mean something's definitely fishy with the Danning case. Am I paranoid or could this thing with the Surenos have been a setup to get me out of action?

McGee doesn't respond to my accusation. Instead he says, "I got a call from the sheriff. He wants you out of town.... He said he didn't want any more trouble...with the gangs. I guess I don't have to tell you to watch your ass, lad....Especially when you go to Cheyenne...next week for the hearing. Wear a friggin' vest."

I toss the crust back in the pizza box and pick up another piece.

McGee watches me chew and I look down at the floor. Ever since the shooting, every time I've seen him, I can feel him studying me, as if he can weigh what's in my heart and in my head. McGee has been my sole support among the brass at the AG's Office, but I think his endorsement is somewhat reluctant. Like everyone else, he has questions of his own about that night. The administration had wanted to charge me criminally and see where it led. That would have been good politics for people such as the then–Attorney General, who was running for national office at the time. It would have sent a message that Wyoming will not whitewash the police-related deaths of their minorities, that they take such things as seriously as Los Angeles or New York. I suspect it was McGee and the fact that I'm something of a minority myself that saved me from an indictment. But they can still file a case at any time. There's no statute of limitations for murder.

The cheap carpet on the interview room floor is stained with vomit and urine. I stare at it and realize the healing I've felt since my return to Laramie the day before is totally gone.

"You want off this investigation? If you can't hack it

here...let me know now. I'll get you back up north. You'll only have to come back...for the hearing next week." McGee's voice is uncommonly soft.

I shake my head angrily and feel tiny pieces of glass fall on the bare skin of my arms. "Fuck that, Ross. I'll finish this." I'm glaring at him and I realize he wanted to make me mad. So I smile and say, "Everyone tells me this Danning thing is supposed to be routine anyway."

McGee gives me a nod with a rare and crooked grin, displaying two decades of military dentistry.

SEVEN

A T T H R E E O ' C L O C K we drive out to the county coroner's office in the basement of Ivinson Memorial Hospital. The coroner himself, Dr. Jim Gustavson, meets us in the narrow lobby. Apparently the job in a small town like Laramie doesn't require a receptionist. Nor does it require a full-time coroner—on the way over, McGee told me that Gustavson works part-time as a mortician. He is a small, bald man with the sort of pasty complexion you would expect from someone whose professional life is spent among the dead. The white hospital smock he wears is stained with dried blood and other unidentifiable bits of gore. There is a nauseating chemical smell about him. He introduces himself to me without offering a hand and hellos McGee in a casual way. They've apparently met before. It sounds to me as if they are professional acquaintances rather than friends.

"Come on around, gentlemen. I'm finishing up a little project in back."

I follow them past the unmanned counter and through a pair of metal doors into a room with a single stainless-steel table. The air in it is cold. It stinks of death. Cluttered shelves line the walls above long counters except for one side, where the entire wall is taken up by large, square doors, each about the size of a coffin. It looks like some sort of enormous filing cabinet. McGee had warned me that the coroner would want to talk in the cutting room. "The prick likes to keep you off-balance... when you question his incompetence.... A typical friggin' ghoul's ploy."

A twisted corpse lies naked on the table. I look away from it quickly, but McGee limps right up and examines it with a critical eye.

"Car accident?" he asks, puffing hard from the short walk.

"Right. The boy was sixteen. He lost control of his car out on 287—driving far too fast, of course. He was sideways across the highway when the eighteen-wheeler caught him. See the bumper imprints where it came through the top of the door and crushed his chest? You can read the license-plate number there. His parents will never have to ask if anyone got the number of the truck that hit him." The coroner chuckles as he makes the feeble joke. Neither McGee nor I join in.

I spot a counter along the wall that doesn't look as if it has any body parts or blood spatters on it and place my briefcase there. Opening it, I take out the file on Kate Danning and spread it on the counter. I don't want to be in the same room with the corpse any longer than I have to, so I interrupt McGee and the coroner as they study the body.

"Dr. Gustavson, I'm hoping you can answer a couple of

questions about Kate Danning's autopsy. You did the cut on her Monday, right?"

"Oh yes, just three days ago. She was a pretty girl, at least before she landed on those rocks. I actually know her parents."

"As Sheriff Willis probably told you, I'm looking into it as a routine inquiry. There's a potential conflict of interest because the County Attorney's son is the primary witness. Do you know him?"

Gustavson chuckles. "Who, the County Attorney? I see him almost every day."

I suppress the urge to roll my eyes. I can already tell this guy's going to jerk me around. "The kid, Dr. Gustavson."

"Sure, I've met the boy several times over the years. Nice young man. I saw him just the other day at the funeral. He looked devastated."

That doesn't quite match with how I'd seen him at the bar. I remember him ignoring my wave when Lynn pointed him out. He was with the other climbers at the table, laughing and spraying beer from his mouth, just one day after his girlfriend's funeral.

"I just wanted to ask you about the injury to the back of her skull. Do you know what caused it?"

The coroner looks at me as if I'm dim-witted, and then looks at McGee and smiles. "She fell off a cliff, Agent Burns."

I'm not in the mood to put up with any shit, but I try to ignore his tone. "The reports and pictures I saw indicate that she landed on her face. What I'd like to know is how did she crack the back of her skull?"

"Let me see my report." The coroner takes the pages from my slim file. I grimace inwardly. He hadn't washed his hands after touching the corpse during his discussion with

McGee. I stand at his side and point out the mention of the injury to the rear of her head. The doctor grunts, then shakes the autopsy photographs out of the envelope. In them the thin girl is naked on the same steel table, posed in sad postures for the camera. Sure enough, one of the photos shows the vivid yellow bruise and jagged tear of parted skin at the back of Kate Danning's freshly shaved scalp. I also point out to him the picture of her at the base of the cliff and the small bit of matted hair visible on the back of her head.

"It looks to me like she struck it on the way down. There's your explanation, Agent. She bounced on the cliff." He's smiling again.

In my already fragile emotional state, the pictures have affected me strongly; I want to wipe the smile off his face with my knuckles.

I show him the eight-by-ten of the sheer cliff, vertical to overhanging, as well as the picture of it I'd found in the Vedauwoo guidebook. Trying to control the aggressiveness I'm feeling but not doing a very good job, I say, "Show me what she bounced off of, Doctor."

The coroner remains adamant. "Well, young man, that's the only way she could have gotten that. Maybe you should go up there and jump off yourself—see what pops you in the head."

"How about we go up there together and I throw you off?"

His spine jerks straight and he glares at me. I glare back. I expect a rebuke from McGee, but it doesn't come. He's shuffling through the autopsy photos. I'd offered to show them to him before, in the hotel, but he'd declined.

"Gustavson," he suddenly barks, "what the hell's that?" He holds up a shot of the crushed face and chest. With a thick finger he draws a line across the girl's throat. There is an angry red mark there. The coroner takes the photo from him and looks at it closely.

"Oh yes, I remember that. She was wearing a necklace of some sort. A piece of colored string, if I remember correctly. I couldn't untie it and had to cut it off. It must have caught on something, probably when she hit the back of her head."

"You keep the goddamn necklace?"

"No, I put it in the incinerator. It was inexpensive and not very glamorous, for a girl with such wealthy parents."

I glance at McGee and see that he looks as worked up as I feel. His labored breaths are increasing rather than diminishing. His fierce blue eyes blaze above his beard. Heat and blood are brightening his face. "You did the cut on Lee, right? She was strangled.... With a narrow pink cord...I've seen the fucking pictures....And she was using meth. Just like Danning...or at least had been....Are you catching my drift, Gustavson?" He says the doctor's name as if it's an insult.

Gustavson turns away. "Coincidence." He slides all the photos back into the envelope and tosses it rudely on top of my other papers on the counter.

"Christ!" McGee continues. "Did you check for binding marks on Danning?" He steps closer to the coroner. I can see the doctor wince at the smell of McGee's cigar-flavored breath.

"No, Mr. McGee. There was no need—that girl fell off a cliff, damn it."

McGee moves even closer and Gustavson steps back, looking cornered. "Landed facedown? And got a fractured skull in back?...Never looked into a strangle mark...on her neck? Christ, you better not...have fucked this one up too."

"I hope you at least did a rape kit," I say.

"I was told it wasn't necessary."

"Who the fuck told you that!" McGee swings his cane in a low, agitated arc. With a sharp crack it strikes the steel table upon which lies the boy's body. I half expect the corpse to jump off the table and run. There's something particularly profane about our anger in a room where the crumpled and naked body lies partially cut open.

The coroner is now glaring back at McGee, red-faced. "The sheriff did! And he was passing the message on from Karge!" We both stare at him, stunned. "So if you want to shout at someone, go shout at them. Listen, I did what I'm supposed to do. I cut them up and tell you how they died. And she fell off a cliff, so don't go making this kind of stuff up! I've suffered enough with this Lee trial!"

McGee speaks slowly. "If you're looking for sympathy, look it up in the dictionary.... It's between shit and syphilis."

Gustavson regains some of his composure. "Please leave. I've got to finish this one." He motions at the boy's corpse. "And you're chasing your tail if you think anything except that the girl fell off a cliff."

I gather the papers and photos back into my briefcase. On our way out the door, McGee turns and again growls at the coroner. "Where is she? Buried or cremated?"

"Buried Tuesday," Gustavson says, as he stands unmoving over the boy's twisted corpse. Then he adds, uselessly, "Closed casket, of course."

Outside in the heat and the wind I walk slowly with McGee to his office-assigned Ford sedan that we're driving. The vinyl seats are hot and the car reeks of his cigars. McGee had earlier declined to drag his bulk high up into the Land Cruiser and have the beast drool down his neck. So I'd left Oso at the hotel with a Do Not Disturb sign on the door to save an unwary maid from a surprise.

"What's this about the Lee?"

"Possible clusterfuck.... She was strangled by a thin cord too.... But all the way."

"The Knapp brothers were in custody when Kate Danning died, right?" I say, thinking out loud. "It happened in the middle of their trial. Another young, dead girl involved in the local drug scene, possibly strangled, at least partly. So I guess we have a problem with the good doctor's coincidence theory."

"Coincidence doesn't get a trial, lad.... I presume it guilty until proven innocent."

"What are you thinking, then? Someone else did Kimberly Lee? Not the brothers? I thought that case was about as solid as they get."

McGee jams a fresh cigar in his mouth and paws at the car's cigarette lighter. He doesn't answer me but curses some more around the fat roll of dried leaves.

"What about the rape kit on Lee? I don't remember hearing about that. What did it show?"

McGee tears the cigar out of his mouth, his eyes as bright as its hot cherry. "That's what the little shit was talking about.... That's why the defense raked him over the fucking coals.... He didn't bother to do one on Lee ... since everyone knew who killed her. The incompetent prick!"

I'm amazed. On the same day he was burned for not doing a rape kit in the Lee trial, he doesn't bother to do one on Kate Danning. You would think he'd learn from his mistakes. And why would Karge not want one done? Even if his son's semen or pubic hair were found on her, why would it matter, as everyone knew he was her boyfriend? It's too late now—Kate Danning's body is in the earth and even if we dig her up, she'll have been washed by the mortician, probably Gustavson himself, before the funeral.

Then McGee's cell phone rings. He wrestles it out of his suit pants pocket and stabs the button. "McGee."

Without a word he presses the button again. He stares straight through the windshield, straight into the hot sun, as he growls, "Goddamn. Verdict's in."

EIGHT

I'M SITTING UP front next to McGee when the reporters once again burst into the courtroom. Twenty minutes earlier the deputies and security guards outside the building took note of the badges we displayed and let us through the agitated crowd that was massed by the courthouse's entrance like runners at a starting line. Behind us now, they nudge one another and argue for more room on the hard pews.

I feel uncomfortable with the media staring at the back of my head. Once or twice I think I hear my name among the whisperings, followed by the sardonic nickname "QuickDraw." Then I feel even more uncomfortable when the Lee family is led in to take their seats directly behind us. An apology is on my lips, for exactly what I don't know, but I don't turn around. The five of them sit silently except for the occasional sniffle that I assume is the result of Mrs. Lee's ever present and well-deserved tears.

On the ride over and then in the courtroom, when it was still empty and quiet, McGee had growled out the forensic details of the Lee case.

Kimberly Lee was beaten and raped before she was strangled by a nylon-sheathed cord three millimeters in diameter. Cord of the same color and diameter also had been used to bind her hands behind her back. The strangulation had been carried out by the use of some sort of slipknot rather than simply having been held in two hands like a garrote. When she was found the pink cord flecked with purple was still biting into her flaccid skin. There were several different abrasions on her neck caused by the cord, indicating she'd struggled bravely before the lack of blood flow to her brain and the resulting lack of oxygen caused her to lose consciousness forever.

The bright, thin cord was unusual. It was dissimilar to the cords sold in both the town's mountaineering stores as well as in all of Laramie's hardware stores. One of the few high points in the defendants' case was that no more of it was found among the brothers' belongings. The prosecution was unable to explain where the Knapps had purchased it.

A second point for the defense was the fact that no rape kit was ever performed on the victim's body. The good Dr. Gustavson's autopsy was cursory at best, unlike the exacting procedures the state's examiners would have used.

Generally, the state's superior resources are taken advantage of by local law enforcement in all serious or complex cases. But DCI was not invited to participate in the Lee investigation. With the believed killers so quickly and easily apprehended, both Nathan Karge and Sheriff Willis, his campaign manager, apparently felt the state's assistance was not needed. Or, more likely, they wanted to do this case on their own and not have to share any credit. They wanted to show Wyoming and the nation that they were diligent and effective; that in the wake of Matthew Shepard's murder the town and its elected officials were perfectly capable of handling this all by themselves. In the midst of the campaign, Karge and Willis needed to be the heroes. They jealously guarded the limelight.

I remember a part of the closing arguments I saw the day before. The defense argued to the jury that a reasonable doubt exists for two reasons. First, because no rape kit was performed, there was no DNA evidence tying the Knapps to the scene—only the single fingerprint on the broken crank pipe, which could have gotten there a number of ways. Second, the prosecution had been unable to associate the cord to the defendants. These two facts, their lawyers said, raised a reasonable doubt as to whether the Knapps really raped and murdered Kimberly Lee. It was a rush to judgment based on shoddy evidence and political ambitions.

The defense also tried to explain the Knapps' peculiar way of answering the door as a drunken mistake, the result of several years of "unfortunate" encounters with the local police.

Karge responded in his rebuttal that no case was perfect, there are always unanswered questions, and there are always a few things that can't be explained, but that this sort of speculation did not amount to a reasonable doubt. He pointed out the weighty evidence that proved the Knapps' guilt: that Kimberly Lee was planning on telling the police where she used to get her drugs; one of the Knapps' fingerprints on the crank pipe near the victim's body; the hacked-off piece of Kimberly Lee's breast along with the work glove found in the bed of their pickup; the way the Knapps answered the deputies' knock on their trailer with a shotgun blast as if they expected the police; the racist propaganda found inside; and, most damning of all, the slurred statement one of the Knapps made to Sheriff Willis—"Bitch had it coming."

Now I find myself staring at the two defendants as the deputies lead them shuffling into the courtroom. The Knapps walk cautiously, limping a little from the leg braces hidden by their public-defender standard-issue cheap polyester suits. I'm thinking about another dead girl with abrasions on her neck and the casually discarded "necklace," wondering if this entire circus could be a mistake.

The bailiff slams down the gavel and shouts, "All rise!" Everyone in the courtroom leaps to their feet on the old wooden floor but the defendants and their parents. The mother and father sit grim-faced and angry behind their sons, sure like everyone else that their children are about to be found guilty. I take the opportunity to look around for Rebecca Hersh, and spot her thick dark hair and alabaster skin near the rear of the chamber. I wonder what she would write if she knew about the things McGee and I learned in the coroner's cutting room.

When the judge comes in, she gives the family and the public defender's staff who sit among them a brief glare before she tells the courtroom to be seated.

"Mr. Karge, Mr. Crane, Mr. Schneider," she says to each of the attorneys, "I'm told we have a verdict. Are you prepared to receive it?"

Each answers with a solemn nod. Most of the room gets to their feet a second time as the jury is led into the box. The men and women look uncomfortable, knowing that every eye in the room is searching their faces for some clue. They keep their eyes in neutral places—the floor, the flags, the judge. Once the jury is seated the gallery is told to take their seats again. It's almost like a game of Simon Says.

"Members of the jury, have you reached a verdict?" the judge asks them. The foreman stands with a dip of his head and holds out a piece of paper to the bailiff, who carries it to the judge. She glances at it without expression and sends it back to the foreman.

Never before having observed a capital trial, I watch impressed by the speed of such a consequential proceeding. As soon as the slip of paper is back to the jury, the judge asks the defendants to rise and the foreman to read the verdict. The defendants' attorneys and family members now stand with them. I've never heard anything so quiet as that room, packed with one hundred and fifty people. It's more hushed than a moment of silence at a funeral.

The foreman reads the first charge, Wyoming Statute 6–2–101, Murder in the First Degree, in an almost serene voice. It sounds suspiciously to me like the soft hiss of a fuse being lit. The room holds its collective breath as the foreman pauses and looks directly and bravely at the defendants. His voice is gentle as he pronounces a single word: "Guilty." But that one word causes the courtroom to explode.

Before the spectators even have a chance to exhale, one of the brothers shouts, "Bullshit!" He flips the table in front of him into the well of the court. There's an audible pop as the restraining devices concealed beneath his pant legs snap open. He balances awkwardly as he begins to rave. The two deputies, seated in folding chairs behind the defense table, spring toward him. The other brother sweeps his own table clear of his attorney's books, legal pads, and laptop computers.

He too is screaming at the jurors, males and females alike, "You bitches! You fucking bitches!"

The two deputies struggle with the brother who's flipped the table, while the other is held by his own attorneys. Everyone in the room is on their feet and the chamber roars with noise. I'm among them, considering a leap over the short wall that divides the pews from the court's well.

Before I can, a door near the jury's box bangs open. Jones strides out followed by another two deputies. The heat goes out of the brothers' curses at the sight of the enormous man moving coolly toward them. Coming at them is something they hold in utter contempt—a black man—with the courtroom lights reflecting off his shaved skull like a halo. Even worse, it's a black man wearing the uniform of authority with a badge on his chest and a gun at his hip. Their shouts turn to mutters as Jones efficiently handcuffs the one held by his attorneys while four deputies take care of the other. Jerking slightly against their captors, as if a brief trickle of potassium chloride is already entering their veins, both brothers are led out of the courtroom.

At a nod from the judge, Jones walks to the rear of the chamber and positions himself against the main doors. He folds his arms across his wide chest. The message on his face is clear: No one is getting out until the judge dismisses them.

I look around the room and watch as the reporters assess their chances of getting past Jones, then resort to scribbling and talking among themselves. The defendants' mother is openly sobbing while her husband sits red-faced in what is either shame or fury. Behind me, the Lees are not exulting in the one verdict they've heard. They sit stone-faced. No public condemnation or punishment of the animals who killed their daughter will bring her back. The defense attorneys and their staff right the overturned table and recover their scattered belongings.

The judge beats the bench with her gavel to silence the room. "Mr. Foreman," she says, "you may continue reading the verdict."

"Objection!" the lead attorney yelps from where he's crouched, picking up his computer. "Your honor, I move for a mistrial!"

"On what grounds, Mr. Smith?"

"This jury has clearly been prejudiced by what they've just seen."

Karge speaks up. "It doesn't matter, they've already reached verdicts."

"But—"

"No more argument, please, Mr. Smith. Motion for a mistrial denied. You'll have an opportunity to poll the jury after the verdicts are read. Continue, Mr. Foreman."

The defense attorney interrupts again. "Objection as to the absence of my clients from the courtroom."

"They've made themselves quite unavailable. You may inform them of the jury's verdicts once this proceeding is finished. Now be quiet and save your objections," the judge snaps at him.

The foreman maintains his composure except for a small quaver in his voice as he reads each count and the jury's finding of guilty. By the end of his reading, the entire courtroom is again buzzing with murmurs. The reporters are visibly anxious to get to their phones and cameras, but the judge keeps them in their seats with a harsh glare. "Frigging ants in their pants," McGee stage-whispers to me.

After the judge allows the defense to despondently poll each of the jurors as to whether the verdict to each charge was their individual verdict and the unanimous verdict of the jury, she tells the attorneys they can take up posttrial motions the next morning. She sets a sentencing date in eight days—next Friday at nine o'clock.

Karge objects to that. "Your honor, the State is prepared to proceed with sentencing immediately."

"I'm sure you are, Mr. Karge," the judge snaps at him now. "But I'm going to give the jurors a few days off. Surely you don't want the jury to vote on whether to impose the death penalty with *this* scene fresh in their minds."

Karge wants exactly that. He waits a moment before sitting again, as if he's considering whether he should argue the point further, until the judge's glare burns his legs out from under him. He does a strange thing when he sits—quickly turning in his seat, he gives McGee and me the briefest of glances before turning back to the papers on his table.

I wait for the reporters and spectators to flee from the room before I follow. Moments earlier McGee trailed Karge out through a side door after the County Attorney gravely shook the hand of Mr. Lee and received a low bow from both him and the victim's mother. In the hallway I spot Jones standing by a window, watching the exodus of spectators and the agitated crowd on the grass outside. While disparate portions of the crowd chant different slogans, either in victory or in anguish, or for even some stranger passion, the television commentators talk excitedly at their cameras.

The big man gives me a familiar roll of his eyes when he notices me coming toward him. "Never seen anything like this, QuickDraw. Hope never to again, but I know next week could be worse. The sentencing, you know. At least I finally get a day off tomorrow."

"Your guys did a good job getting ahold of them."

"Next week those boys are sure as shit going to be wearing shock belts. One false move and zap!" He pushes an imaginary button with his finger. "We once put it on a young deputy and shocked him. Guy peed his pants."

Feeling talkative from the day's events, I recall one of McGee's many stories and tell it to Jones. During a robbery trial McGee prosecuted, the defendant hadn't liked the way the case was going. So he grabbed the bag of the state's evidence and took off running out of the courtroom. The jury convicted him anyway, in absentia, and without a good deal of the evidence. When he was finally caught weeks later and brought in for sentencing, the pissed-off judge gave him the max—twelve years. McGee said the guy appealed, arguing that he was convicted without sufficient evidence, and the Supreme Court overturned his conviction, setting him free pending a new trial. Of course the stolen evidence was never recovered. And in the second trial he was acquitted.

Jones says with a laugh, "Justice, huh?" Then he in turn tells me his own story about a courtroom uproar. It was a rape trial he saw Nathan Karge prosecute. During his closing argument, Karge was interrupted by the sound of small shrieks and running feet. He'd been graphically describing to the jury how the perp forced his penis between the victim's lips and shoved it again and again in her mouth, bruising the back of her throat. A troop of Girl Scouts had just wandered in to see justice at work, and their den mothers were chasing them back out the courtroom's door.

"What do you think for the Knapp brothers? Life or death?" I ask.

"It's a foregone conclusion, my friend. Those suckers

are gonna die. And fast, with that new expedited appeals process. I give 'em three years and they're toast. I'm not feeling too sad about it. Crime's been way down in this town since we've had those two locked up."

"You get the feeling there's anything strange about the case Willis and Karge put together?"

Jones won't answer that. He just says, "Wasn't my case, bro."

So I drop it for now and ask, "You still want to get together? How about me teaching you to climb tomorrow? I've got to go out to Vedauwoo on this Danning thing."

Jones laughs. "Oh yeah, my wife would love that. I was thinking more along the lines of getting a few beers." Then he looks thoughtful for a minute, and says, "But I guess it would beat lifting weights in the gym with those redneck peckerheads. You serious?"

"I am."

"Okay then, I'll give it a shot. If you break any of my precious bones, she'll rip your head off. And both the sheriff and the judge will run you out of town if I can't do the security for the sentencing."

I arrange to meet him up at Vedauwoo late the next morning after I've climbed with Lynn and her friends.

NINE

OUTSIDE NEAR THE courthouse's large glass doors, Kristi, the DCI secretary, is waiting for me. She carries an oversize purse on a strap across one shoulder. From the top of it pokes a manila envelope that I assume contains the printouts I'd requested. She wears a short navy skirt without stockings, and a man's white shirt. Her blonde hair, curly and piled high, does not quite match her skin. Her tan is too dark. It's the deep bronze of someone who spends her weekends oiled by the pool instead of on the granite. When I worked out of the Cheyenne office her breasts had been the subject of intense scrutiny and much speculation. Real or fake, everyone wondered. I know that if I'm not careful I'll find out.

She sees me and bounces up the steps. Her eyes crinkle when she smiles as she pecks me on the cheek. Her hug includes the warm press of her hips. From these things I have no doubt she's more than willing to stay the night. She probably carries a change of underwear in her purse.

"Hi, Anton," she breathes against my neck.

When I manage to politely disengage myself I say hello.

"We all heard about what happened today. What a terrible thing! Are you all right?"

I nod uneasily. "It wasn't that big a deal. Did you bring the printouts?"

"Ha! You won't get them that easy. Making me drive them over is going to cost you at least a dinner." She says it with a wink and a twist of her hips.

I don't mention that she volunteered to bring them, and don't ask what "at least dinner" means. I'm simply glad McGee isn't here to poke fun. I wonder if right now he's ruining Karge's moment of glory by telling him about our conversation with the coroner.

Kristi drives me to the hotel and on the way I have to fill her in on every detail of what happened in court. In my room, she sits on the bed rubbing Oso's flanks while the big dog groans with pleasure. "A girl doesn't get to make a guy feel this good very often," she comments.

I pour water for us both into the plastic bottles I use when I climb. I mistrust hotel glasses in general—I've never noticed clean ones on the maids' carts and suspect they simply wipe them off using the same rag they swab on the toilets and sinks.

Picking up the phone, I dial an endless series of numbers: credit card, access code, etc., to check the messages at my small office-of-exile in Cody. The first two are from local police officers wanting my assistance. Then there is one from the County Attorney up there requesting my presence at an evidentiary hearing. The fourth is from a potential snitch I'm courting. The fifth is from the lawyer, Clayton

Wells, who is representing me in the civil suit. He wants to talk to me before next week's hearing for summary judgment. He wants to talk about settling, he says. I suppress a grimace and erase that one as quickly as I'd saved the others.

I almost drop my bottle of water when I recognize the voice of the sixth caller.

"Hey, bro," it says. "Bet you're surprised to hear from me. I want you to come down and see me. I guess you know where I'm at, and I'm not going anywhere at the moment. Can't tell you how to get here though—I came by bus." He chuckles. "Don't bother to RSVP, you're on the visitors' list. *Hasta luego,* Ant."

The message ends but I don't hang up. This is the first time I've heard from him since he went to prison two years ago. He's refused my calls, refused my visits, refused to even talk with our parents. Roberto doesn't want us to see him locked in a cage. After a moment the mechanized voice that manages the messaging system is threatening to disconnect me if I don't press a button. I let her hang up on me.

To avoid having to explain the shock that is probably evident on my face, I dial one of the numbers Kristi brought me. It's the direct line of Heller's probation officer for his possession conviction in Teton County. I smiled when I first saw the number among the papers she gave me, and that she also had put down the PO's home number. Kristi is known as being very resourceful, among other things.

I don't expect to get a live voice, as POs are notorious for screening their calls. I'm not sure if this is due to being overworked or if they simply come to dread meeting with the criminals whose lives they are supposed to manage. So I'm surprised that a real voice answers, but predictably it sounds harried. I look at my watch and realize that the PO is probably getting ready to leave for the night.

"Jim Deagle. What do you need?"

I introduce myself quickly, slurring over my name, and ask about Billy Heller.

"That guy," Deagle says. He sighs and sounds irritated. "His case was transferred to me three months ago. And I haven't seen him yet except for in the climbing magazines. He's something of a rock-climbing star, and I do a little of that too."

I'm not at all disappointed that the PO didn't pick up on my name. My brief fame in the climbing community was years ago and never very large. I'm worn out from my long day and don't feel like a discussion about climbing. And I'm even happier he doesn't seem to recognize my name from the Cheyenne shooting.

"Is that why you filed a revo on him? No-shows?"

"That too, but mainly because he picked up a new charge. It's irrelevant now—I filed to withdraw the petition today."

"Why?"

"Our now-famous County Attorney down in Laramie left me a voicemail saying he's dismissed the distribution charge. And we let our guys get away with five no-shows before we nail 'em."

"How come you let them get away with not showing up so many times?"

"It's procedure, Agent. We're understaffed and underfunded here, just like everywhere else. We can't go to court every time someone doesn't show or drops a hot UA," he says, meaning a drug-tainted urine analysis.

"Can you tell me anything about this guy?"

"Well, his file shows a bunch of charges and some

convictions for assault. But he's never done any real time, just overnighters. I got a copy of the police report for the most recent charge—the one that was dumped—and it says he was caught driving around with a couple of cases of Sudafed. Guy must've had a bad cold! Anyway, they charged him for attempt to manufacture meth, but Karge let it slide just the other day. Most of what I know about him is from reading those climbing magazines my wife got me a subscription to last Christmas. He's getting on in years, but is still a great athlete. To tell you the truth, Billy Heller's sort of a hero of mine, except for the brawling and druggy stuff, of course."

I take Kristi to a Mexican restaurant called Café Ole that's just a few blocks from the Holiday Inn, on the other side of the interstate. All the reporters must be busy writing their stories or commenting in front of their cameras, as the restaurant is nearly empty when we enter. We sit at a small table in the center of a large room crowded with linoleum tables. A waitress brings us both Coronas with wedges of lime shoved down through their necks. Kristi giggles when the young waitress asks me for my ID, and then laughs outright when she's asked for hers. After we place an order and drink a second beer she has a question for me.

"People are saying you might be leaving DCI. Maybe police work altogether. Is there any truth in that?"

"Who's saying that?" It really is an impressive conjecture, I think. I hadn't discussed my plans with anyone.

"Pretty much everyone. They're saying that the shooting and lawsuit last year really screwed you up."

Made to smile by her directness, I ask, "Is this conversation just between us or will it be added to the rumor mill?"

"Just us. Cross my heart." She traces with her fingertips from chin to stomach, then across her breasts.

I take a long pull on the Corona while looking at her. "I guess you could say that I'm a little disillusioned."

"With carrying a badge and gun, honey?"

"Yeah. And all the legal, political bullshit."

When I started I just wanted to go after the bad guys. Especially the drug dealers, the greedy, careless men who hooked my brother like a hungry trout. I wanted to catch them and help the prosecutors punish them. But in my six years as a state cop I've learned it isn't quite that simple. Catching them is fun; it's the easy part. But once you do, they don't follow the rules. They pull guns and shoot at you. And even when you finally take them down, a fast-talking lawyer, a friend of the judge, springs them on a low bond within hours. They're back to selling it the next night, threatening the witnesses against them. And months later, when they finally come to court, if they come to court at all, the lawyers scream about how you had no reasonable suspicion to investigate. No probable cause to make the arrest. That you never read them their rights. Even when everyone in the courtroom knows it's a lie. When I discovered early on that law enforcement is just a game with rules more complex than cricket, I studied the game and learned to play like an all-star. But it doesn't do any good.

The law says that when someone is guilty of selling meth, it's a four-to-ten-year sentence in prison. But I've learned that the game is one-sided; the rules are enforced against the police but not against the accused. I've yet to see someone get four-to-ten for the crime. The cases are pleaded to lesser charges with short sentences and useless probation. Or the prosecutor is scared or lazy and just lets it slip away. Or, the times I've bullied the deputy county attorneys into taking a case to trial, even when the conviction enters, the judge will simply reduce the sentence on his own. And even if they eventually go to prison, they're paroled to a halfway house after serving a quarter of their sentence. It's really a lousy game. It shouldn't be a game at all. And I'm tired of playing.

But more recently I've also seen it from the other side, when I was so close to being charged with three counts of murder myself. I was truly lucky that McGee had blustered the office into withholding the charges and waiting to see how the civil suit shakes out. But I wonder, my own self-interest aside, is that justice?

An evening crowd is flowing into the restaurant. They are the same reporters and commentators I saw earlier lounging by the pool. Many of them stare at me quite frankly. I guess that word has gotten around about who I am and what I did. The attention makes me feel uncomfortable. And I'm feeling both wired and stressed from the day's events.

Kristi folds her hands under her chin with her elbows on the table and doesn't say anything for a while. Her eyes probe mine, then I see them cut along the scar that runs down to my lips.

"I know about your brother," she suddenly tells me.

I say nothing, just stare at her.

"He called the office yesterday, wanting your number. Uh-oh, I shouldn't have mentioned him. I can see it on your face. Now you're mad. Listen, I was just curious about you, so I borrowed your file. I didn't mean anything by it. I just know he's in jail, for manslaughter."

I keep on staring, so she shuts up. Just as my brother

wants no one to see him in a cage, I can't stand the thought of him being there. It's something that I don't speak about, that I don't think about. He has always had enough energy for ten ordinary mortals. When he was climbing, it took the biggest faces in the mountains to dissipate it and make his energy safe. When he was using drugs, it took enormous quantities to satisfy and calm him. The thought of all that explosive energy contained in a small steel cell makes me feel both claustrophobic and sick. But the cop in me knows that a cell is exactly where my brother belongs.

After a few minutes of silence, I wave the waitress over to ask for the bill and a take-home box for Oso.

It's just a short drive back to the Holiday Inn, but it's made long by the silence. In the lot I turn off my engine next to her car.

When I start to open my door, she says, "I'm sorry, Anton. I shouldn't have brought that up. I'm really sorry!"

"Are you okay to drive back to Cheyenne?"

"I think so. I only had two beers."

For a moment longer we remain in the Land Cruiser, each of us with a hand on the door releases. Her other hand plays with the hem of her skirt a few inches above her knees. Between us hangs Oso's massive head. He is gazing down at the Styrofoam box on the seat between the secretary and me, drooling. She looks at him, the box, then out the windshield, and says, "But I wouldn't mind staying either."

I take a deep breath and with my elbow push Oso's head back into the rear seat. "I think you're a kind and beautiful woman, Kristi. And probably just what I need tonight. But it may not be what I need tomorrow, because I really don't know what I'm doing right now."

She kisses my cheek. Then she kisses the dog's and pulls on the door handle.

* * *

After she drives away, I remember that I'd never picked up the dog food. So when I start the engine again, Oso is concerned. He's ready to get at what's in the box. He doesn't have the foresight to see that he'll be hungry again come morning and I'm unable to explain. Driving north on Third Street, I stop at an all-night convenience store. There's a patrol car in the lot. I consider driving away and finding another store, but through the window I see that it isn't Bender chatting with the girl at the counter above the racks of cigarettes and candy. So I park and go in.

I lift a twenty-pound bag of lamb and rice kibble to my shoulder and walk to the counter. The young officer there politely steps aside while I pay. The officer gives me a closer look when he catches the flash of the badge in my wallet, and I turn to acknowledge him with a smile before leaving. Then I see the name Knight stenciled on the silver plate pinned to the patrolman's chest.

"Deputy Knight. Hi, I'm Antonio Burns, Special Agent with DCI. We spoke earlier today."

The rookie seems startled to see me. I guess that Knight has heard all about what happened earlier in the day. Maybe he was even one of the officers there outside the pet store—I hadn't been paying attention. After a moment we shake hands.

"Call me Dave," he says.

"Actually, Dave, I thought of another question or two. Do you mind talking for a minute?"

Knight looks like he doesn't want to, but says, "Sure, but just for a minute. I'm supposed to be on duty right now." To the girl behind the counter he says, "Be right back."

We walk outside and I drop the bag of dog chow on the hood of the Land Cruiser. "I forgot to ask if there was a rope hanging off that wall."

"Wall?"

"You know, the cliff above the girl."

"Uh, no. I really can't remember. It was still dark when I was there. Like I told you before, I was just there to see if there was anything medical I could do."

"What about that guy who was supposed to be up there partying with Brad Karge and Kate Danning, name of Billy Heller. Do you know him?"

"The climber. Yeah, I've seen him around but never arrested him, if that's what you mean. Just chased him off a couple of times."

"Chased him off from what?"

"Uh, nothing really. He just sometimes cruises for young girls. He's got a rep for that sort of thing. You know, getting them boozed or stoned or whatever, then taking them home. The word is that sometimes he's a little rough, and sometimes they're a little young." Knight looks around the parking lot, then glances at his watch.

"How about Bradley Karge, the County Attorney's son? Do you know him?"

"Just seen him around, on the street, sometimes with his dad."

"Do you know Chris Braddock?"

"I can't…No, sorry. Look, I really have to go before I get in trouble."

I study him for a minute. Then I ask on a hunch, "Did someone tell you not to talk to me?"

"Uh, no." The rookie looks me right in the eye as he says it, and then quickly glances away. "I gotta go. It was good meeting you, Agent Burns." He walks to his car and gets in without going back into the store to finish his conversation with the girl behind the counter. I watch him all the way until his taillights disappear down Third Street.

When I get back in my truck Oso is lying on the backseat, strangely subdued. His usual position for waiting is to be crouched awkwardly in the too-small passenger seat where he can better keep an eye on me through the windshield. Something is wrong but I can't think what it is. Then the smell of the Mexican food reaches me and I see that the box is missing. I remember leaving it between the front seats. When I look into the backseat where the beast sprawls innocently, there are pieces of white Styrofoam scattered throughout the back of the truck. All appear to have been licked clean. "There sure seems to be a lot of crime and intrigue in this town," I tell him as I reach out an arm to gently knuckle his broad head. "But I never thought you'd be a part of it too."

TEN

LYNN DRIVES THE rutted road too fast, her old pickup truck banging over the holes and washes. Her dirty blonde hair is being sucked out the open window by the wind as she slows and looks for me at potential spots. The pickup accelerates when she sees me parked in a rocky turnout on a hill surrounded by pines. I'm sitting on my open tailgate, swinging my legs and enjoying the clean morning air. The wind still has a chilly bite to it as it blows right through my battered canvas climbing pants and old wool jacket. I've pulled a red balaclava just over the top of my ears so that the rest of the ski mask hangs limply at the back of my neck. I signal at her with a slow, circular wave.

She skids to a stop next to my ancient Land Cruiser and I hear the rip of the emergency brake being pulled. As she steps into the dirt, Oso huffs out of the woods. His shaggy fur is bristling with brambles. He goes right toward her to check her out. She's fairly short, only four inches or so over five feet, and when he sniffs her his nose is level with where her belly button is exposed beneath her sports bra and open jacket. She flinches and laughs when he follows up the cold-nosed sniff with a single rough lick before he lumbers off. She zips up her short fleece.

"Hey," she calls to me.

"Hey yourself."

"Just what kind of dog is that?"

"I don't really know for sure. He looks like some Tibetan mastiffs I once saw." Then I ask where her friends are.

"They hopped out to Glenwood Canyon. Billy has some business up in Casper later. So it's just you and me, man. And I hope you brought a rack—those fuckers took mine without even asking." She means a set of chocks, cams, and carabiners to be used for placing protection. They're devices set in the rock and connected to the rope in order to catch a fall.

Oso takes another swing by her and she grabs the thick fur on the sides of his face, kneading it. "He looks like a bear. That's what his name means, right? So what do you want to climb?"

"Right. You're the local. You choose it. Just make it a crack. I hate sport climbs."

Lynn looks thoughtful as she pulls her long hair back into a ponytail and ties it off with a rubber band from around her wrist. With her arms behind her head, her jacket lifts, revealing her tan, flat stomach. She catches my eyes lingering there for a moment until I consciously focus on her face.

With a grin, she says, "How about 'Hung Like a Horse'?"

I flip through the guidebook I'm holding and find the climb. Rated 5.11c, it's at the upper end of the difficulty scale. Especially for cracks. And especially at a place like Vedauwoo that's famous for sandbagging, or dangerously underrating climbs. It's described as a finger crack that widens to thin hands and then off-width. I look at her small, hard hands and know she'll have the advantage. I nod and say, "Okay."

"Grab your rack and follow me," she says and swings her own pack on her shoulders. Oso and I follow her up and over a steep slope.

She moves easily up the rocky trail, like this place is her backyard. Maybe, I think to myself, feeling so clean and fresh it has to be a dream, she is one of the earthborn spirits this place was named for. A pixie that dances across granite. A spirit born of this place, Vedauwoo.

We skip on small rocks across a stream, and she laughs as Oso simply plows through and shakes icy water on us. Beyond the stream is a meadow with grass and small white flowers that rise as high as my chest. I pause, breathing easy, and watch the wind make patterns across it. It smells faintly of a sweet perfume. Past the meadow, we hike a faint game track through the trees and between boulders until we come to an eighty-foot-high rock face that looms over us with an angle far beyond vertical. Here she drops her pack at the base of a narrow crack that splits the face.

She watches me eye it critically from the bottom on up. Even in my prime I would feel threatened by a climb like this. "Looks thin," I say. "You lead."

"So you're not one of those macho assholes who always has to be first up, huh?"

"I'd just embarrass myself if I were."

We sit at the base and tape our hands while we talk about other Vedauwoo climbs I'd done many years ago with my father and brother. They'd been easy climbs compared to something as technical as this. But they were plenty exciting for me when I was ten years old. She picks through the gear that I spill from my pack and selects an assortment of chocks, camming devices, and a long, tied-off piece of cord to build an anchor at the top. Clipping all of these things to a runner she wears over her shoulder, she shimmies into her harness.

She ties one end of the rope to her harness with a double figure-eight knot. I place her on belay by taking a bight of the rope close to her knot and shoving it through a locking device on my own harness after I find a comfortable rock to sit on. I'll pay out the rope as she climbs the rock and places cams or chocks in the crack every ten feet or so. If she falls, and if the protection is well placed and correctly clipped to the rope that trails from her harness to me, I'll be able to catch a fall by locking the rope in my belay tube.

Feeling the warming sunlight radiating off the rock and preparing for the exertions ahead, Lynn slips out of her fleece jacket and stands clad only in a brief athletic bra and tights. She studies the crack for a minute, knowing that I'm admiring her exposed slim and strong body. Ready, she dusts chalk on her hands, then slips them into the crack. She takes a few deep breaths, releasing any thought but of hanging on and getting up into the sky.

Twenty minutes later she's slick with sweat and panting like Oso after a hard run. I'm awestruck that she made it up without falling or even hang-dogging on the rope. It's the hardest crack I've ever seen climbed by a woman who's not in the magazines. But then I haven't been reading them lately. Near the top, where the crack broadens and flares and the entire wall overhangs several degrees, she had supported herself by just a jammed knee, a pasted hand, and an incredible display of abdominal strength while she placed my biggest cam and clipped the rope to it. She ties into the anchor she's built at the top and lets out a shout that ricochets off the towers. I lower her gently back to earth.

"Nice going."

"I've done it a few times before."

I look at my hands, still scabbed and sore from my solo two days ago. "I'm wishing for smaller hands right now."

"You used to be a superstar. Don't disappoint me, man."

I laugh and she does too. She keeps her eyes on me as I pull off my jacket and shirt and swing my arms in circles. It's only a matter of time, I think, as I watch her watching me. I can't get over how good the cool, pine-and-flower-scented wind feels on my bare skin.

I climb the crack too fast and recklessly, but I'm safe from cratering onto the forest floor as the rope tied to me now runs over the anchor at the top and down into Lynn's belay device. Because of my bigger hands, on the lower part where the crack is only an inch and a half wide I'm forced to use what is a painful technique compared to the straight thumbs-up method of jamming she'd been able to employ. I wiggle my fingers in over my head, thumbs pointed at the ground, and then torque my wrists straight down. Only in this way do I have the jamming power to stay in the slot. I look down at her once and she's smiling. I guess I'm living up to my former glory.

She takes me to another climb where she allows me to lead as we continue talking about climbs we'd both done in the Tetons and the Winds and the Bugaboos.

"Have I earned the title of Partner?" I ask at one point.

"Oh yeah."

"And a discount on a new rope?"

"As long as you keep climbing with me, dude."

"What about your friends? They didn't seem to like me too much."

"They're tough to know, but you'll get to like them. And them you, man. It'll all come out in the wash, you know? But Billy's going to be real fucking jealous for a while. We split not too long ago."

"I've heard about him."

"He's a wild man, that's for sure. Dude is absolutely primal." She looks past me as she talks about him, her eyes shining. "He just likes to run things a little too much for me. Controlling, you know? He likes being the King of Vedauwoo." Then she looks right at me, weighing and sizing. "But you might give him a run for his money."

"What about the others, Brad and those other guys that were in the bar?"

"Peons, man. They're just his fucking belay slaves. Billy's always got a crowd of kids around him. Like he's a god or something."

"Did you know that girl who fell up here a couple of weeks ago? Kate something?" I don't know why I haven't yet told her that I'm a state cop investigating Kate Danning's death. Maybe it's because she hasn't asked, and I don't know how she will react. Or maybe it's just my undercover instincts to try and see what information I can get before I reveal myself. If that's it, it doesn't work. I don't get much.

"Yeah, she was kind of a friend of mine. Let's not talk about her."

And I'm having so much fun that I don't push it.

"I promised someone I'd meet them up here for a quick climbing lesson. I've got to hang around for a little bit." We're back at our cars.

"Another chick, huh?" Lynn asks teasingly, but a small shadow passes over her face.

"No, it's a guy I work with that I promised to teach."

I walk Lynn to her truck and throw her pack on the torn passenger seat. She hasn't gotten in yet, so I walk around and open the door for her. Metal creaks from a rusted dent in the door. She hesitates before sliding in behind the wheel, looking at me in a way that is strangely shy for a woman who doesn't seem very timid.

I shut the door and she spins the window down. "You're something else, man. Can't you tell what a girl wants?" She smiles earnestly, showing her small, white teeth as I bend down to the open window, resting my taped hands on the frame. I look into her eyes for a long moment. Then I put my lips against hers, moving them back and forth slowly. She slides her pointed tongue past my lips and traces my teeth. I can feel the heat of her body even though only our mouths touch. The electricity radiating off her almost makes me shiver.

After a minute I pull away. She growls at me convincingly, then says, "You know where to find me, dude." She starts the engine, puts the car in gear, and drives away at a much slower pace through the pines but still leaving a trail of dust. The wind sweeps it to the east.

As I watch I feel a stirring within me, but it's not what you would expect. It's more a sensation of danger. Like looking up at an alpine wall alive with falling ice and rock and comprehending both the glory and the death that resides there.

ELEVEN

FOR A HALF hour I sun shirtless on a flat boulder and chew a PowerBar while Oso pants in the shade of an overhang. Every few bites, I tear off a small piece with my teeth and throw it to the beast. He snatches it out of the air with a wet flash of yellowed fangs, beating his stump of a tail in the dust.

A black sports car comes carefully nosing over the ruts in the dirt road. When it's close enough for the sound of the souped-up engine to reach me, I roll off the rock and stand by my truck. More than once I hear the oil pan slowly scrape over the rim of a hole. When the car comes to a stop, Jones unfolds his massive frame from behind the tinted windows. He's dressed in track pants that read "University of Wyoming" down the legs and a black T-shirt that's stretched tight across his torso.

"Shit, QuickDraw, I knew this was a bad idea. I just had

this thing washed." He looks unhappily at the layer of dust that's settling on the Corvette.

"That's a hell of a car to have in a place like Wyoming, Sergeant Jones," I say. "A regular pimpmobile. All you need is a purple felt hat."

"You never know when you'll need the speed, my man. So what's up? I got a feeling you didn't invite me up here just to teach me 'bout climbing. Don't think I got the build for it." While watching me he holds up one arm, then curls his fist toward his face. The bicep that juts out is nearly as big as my head. "Gotta be a wiry sucker like you. Right?"

"Put that thing away before you scare the ladies," I say. "And yeah, you're right. I need someone to help me out here and be a witness. But the few local climbers I know are involved, and all the other cops seem to hate my guts. So it's gotta be you, my friend."

"When I told my wife I was going climbing she nearly brained me with a golf club. Said she ought to be the one who gets to kill me, not my secret agent friends or some damn rocks. Hey, is that Oso hiding under those rocks like some big, ugly troll? Come on out here, dog. Remember me? I damned well hope so. Don't eat me now. Boy, you've sure put on some weight."

"I had him neutered last year—plus he's getting old. The vet said he was showing signs of prostate cancer."

"Now that's a shame," Jones says to the dog, lifting the beast's thick tail and looking. "You used to have some big *cojones,* as your grandmama's people would say."

I laugh and tell Jones about the get-well package my father sent from Argentina after the surgery. It contained several dried pig's ears and a catalog that advertised prosthetics for dogs. "None of them looked large enough," I say proudly, "not even the ones for Great Danes."

"You got the machismo of your mother's people, all right," Jones says, chuckling.

While Oso presses against his thighs and groans as Jones thumps him on the hips, I take out from the mess of crates in the rear of my truck a separate pack that holds a camera and evidence bags. I hand the pack to Jones, explaining what's in it and asking him to be careful with it. I checked it out of the office in Cody on a hunch and will have to pay for it if it's damaged.

Jones fumbles with the pack playfully before he follows me down a trail through aspens that are just starting to turn. The leaves are yellow and gold and their smooth bark is as white as the crosses in a cemetery against the bright blue sky. Every time I look back to see if Oso is with us, I catch Jones staring around him as if he's in another world. There's a small smile taking the place of his usual scowl. Vedauwoo is working its magic on him. As we walk I explain what a half-assed investigation Bender had done. Jones grunts noncommittally but doesn't look surprised.

After a few minutes of walking I realize we're on the wrong trail. I sit down on a log and consult the guidebook while Jones rolls his eyes.

"Great," he says. "It's not a fall that's gonna kill me. We're going to starve to death in this fucking wilderness."

I find the proper path in the book and tell him so. He's looking up at a predatory silhouette that's gliding effortlessly across the sky.

"I got to bring my wife up here sometime. She digs this nature shit. What is that—an eagle?"

"Vulture," I say.

We reverse our tracks back past the cars and I get us started on the correct path. "Tell me, what's going on in the

Sheriff's Office? Are you going to be top dog when Sheriff Willis follows Karge to the capital?"

I don't really expect an answer from him. Jones isn't the type to complain about his colleagues. Team loyalty is something that has been ingrained in him from years as a football player—two years as a pro. I've always known that he is ambitious too, and will not say anything that might denigrate his career or office. He once told me when we were in the law enforcement academy together that he wanted to be Wyoming's first black sheriff. That would probably make him Wyoming's first black elected official. He came to the Cowboy State on a scholarship from the hopeless despair of Compton and somehow fell in love with the place. He is something of an exotic here, amid the yuppies, hippies, and rednecks.

So I'm surprised when he answers my question with anything other than a platitude.

"The place sucks, man. Between you and me, they're a bunch of scumbags from Willis on down."

"Why's that?"

"Your buddy Bender is getting the nod from Willis, who'll go up with Karge when he's elected governor. Bender told me that just a few days ago...after the sheriff didn't bother to let me know. And in Laramie, the resigning sheriff's endorsement is as good as an election. Jesus Christ, that cracker Bender is a nasty, dumb redneck fuck. You know he's Willis's nephew, don't you? And he's going to be the Man, protecting and serving the citizens of Albany County," he says angrily. "And by the way, thanks for not filing those charges on him last year when he kicked the crap out of that Mexican guy. That would have been the only way of taking him out."

I stop walking and turn to face him. My fingers are

curled into my palms. "You don't know what you're talking about, Jones," I say quietly, looking up into his face. "I recommended he be charged with felony assault. I pushed it all the way. But Karge went screaming to the AG about it and they cut a deal. The best I could do was to get him an official reprimand."

Jones holds up his hands, "Whoa there, QuickDraw. Okay, I didn't know that. Anyway, to answer your question, the place is fucked. Willis's only interest is to get Karge elected governor, then ride his coattails to the mansion in Cheyenne and wherever he goes from there. Bender is going to be the next sheriff, at least until the next election, but by then he'll be established and it'll be too late. And me, I'm thinking about splitting. I've got applications in with the feds. DEA, DOD, and FBI—any old acronym will do."

Things must really be bad if Jones is going to desert the career he has put so much time and effort into.

After a while I ask, "How well do you know that rookie Knight? He was up here that night with Bender when they found the body."

"Don't know too much about him, 'cept that I was his field training officer for his first month. He's a good kid, coming along well. From what I hear he's a serious biker."

"What, like on a Harley? I can't picture that. Too clean-cut. He looks about sixteen."

"Naw, QuickDraw, biker as in pedaling. The guy rides in races. You'll see him out training on the empty blacktop north of town, on that road that goes up toward Roger's Canyon."

I ask if he knows Billy Heller, Brad Karge, and their crowd. He says no, but that he's heard Heller has a reputation for roughing up underage girls. And that he knows Brad has been a big headache to his dad, that the group as a whole is known to use a lot of drugs. "Lunatic climbers," he adds.

"How about a girl named Lynn White? You know her?"

"Is this an official question or is it personal?" he says with a smile.

"I don't know yet."

"Well, I don't know the chick, carnally or otherwise."

"Good. Keep it that way."

We twist our way through ever larger rocks toward the foot of a wall. When we are close I pause and reach up to unzip a pocket on the pack Jones wears. I take out the fat envelope of the coroner's pictures. I shuffle through them while Jones looks over my shoulder and lets out a low sad whistle as I flip past the autopsy photos. I compare the photos of Kate Danning's body at the scene with the steep granite before me. With a glance I find the place where she landed, but don't look too long at the congealed black gunk that still remains pooled in the boulders' pockets. I dump my pack on the ground while Jones sets his own down gently.

"Suddenly this doesn't seem like such a good idea," he says. "So this is where she bit it, huh?"

He's staring at the dried blood that no rain had come along to wash away. It's as if nature is conspiring to leave it exposed for as long as possible, in the hope that someone will notice that an outrage was committed here.

"This is it."

"So how come DCI's looking into this? From what I heard, coroner said it was an accident. What's up?"

"Who'd you hear that from?"

"Your buddy Bender's been talking about it to anyone who'd listen. He's pissed about it, doesn't like someone checking out his work. Especially you. So how come you're doing it?"

"Her family's connected somehow with the governor. They can't accept that she got stoned and fell."

Jones looks empathetic, his scowl gone and his eyes soft. "Accidents are the worst. No one for the parents to blame, no one to take it out on. So all that grief just wells up. Shit, I know what that's like." At the academy I'd learned that his mother died of stomach cancer and that his sister was killed in a car wreck.

"Crazy climbers," he goes on. "Why do you expose yourself like that? It's like painting a target on your ass and bending over so God can have a good look, take his best shot."

"I'll show you in a minute."

He rolls his eyes, their whiteness bright against his dark skin.

"Anyway, I'm not so sure it was an accident. She had some bruises and a fracture to the rear of her skull, but she fell on her face. Also there was some ligature marks on her neck that the coroner was eager to discount."

"I hadn't heard about that."

"It wasn't noticed by Sergeant Leroy Bender either, Laramie's own Sherlock Holmes."

"So what are you looking for?"

"I'm not exactly sure," I admit. I point up at the cliff. "But one thing I'd like to check out is whether there's anything she could've banged her head on when she was coming down."

Jones studies the cliff. From above the sticky black pool it's almost dead vertical to where the sky begins a hundred feet over our heads. The granite is pockmarked like bad skin, full of small ridges, crystal nubs, and tiny pockets.

What looks like a fist-size crack splits the upper part of the face.

"Doesn't look like it from here," he says. "You fall, you aren't gonna touch anything till the ground."

I spill the gear and rope from my pack, then begin a brief lesson on the complexities of belaying and the use of the ATC.

Running his hands over the small, slotted device, Jones asks, "What's ATC stand for?"

"Air Traffic Controller. That's what you'll be if I come off."

"Appropriate," Jones reasons, again studying the wall that I intend to scale.

I go on, "Now when I yell 'Off belay,' you pop the rope out of the ATC like this. I'll pull up all the slack to where you're tied in. Then you start climbing. Don't worry about falling—you won't go anywhere. I'll have you on tight from above."

"You'd better." He looks like he's feeling dubious about this whole project.

I start to lead up the face. The only features on the first twenty feet are small, lateral edges. I pull myself upward on pockets in the rock so small I'm lucky to get much more than a fingertip in. Jones can handle it, I hope, but I prefer a solid crack any day. Then I reach a fist-size fissure that continues straight up and feel relief as I shove my hands in, curling my fingers tight, and feeling the bite of the rock against the outside of my palm and the soft meat of the back of my hand between the thumb and first finger. My relief intensifies as I hang off one fist and bury a mechanical cam deep in the crack, then clip the rope to it.

"Hey, QuickDraw, I forgot to ask. How we getting down?" Jones yells when I'm near the top.

I'm too out of breath to attempt an explanation of rappelling. So I just shout, "We fly!"

"Yeah, just like that girl," I hear him mutter.

I pull myself over the top onto a broad ledge. At the back of the ledge, where the pillar once again soars upward, there's a small, dark hole. In the reflected sunlight reaching into it I can see the uneven floor and distant darkness of a cave beyond the hole. On the ledge is a pair of ordinary bolts with steel hangers near the edge of the cliff. With green spray paint someone has sloppily printed "No Trespassing" on the rock just below the hangers. Climbers are becoming as territorial as surfers and gangbangers. I clip a carabiner to one of the hangers, then freeze. The click of metal on metal didn't sound right. There's something about the way the metals touched that has the hair on my arms standing up.

I leave the carabiner dangling on the hanger and move on up and over the bolts onto the ledge. Standing up, I notice a second pair of bolted hangers concealed in a crevice off to one side. I ignore these too and instead begin building my own anchor. I place three pieces of gear in a crack and tie them together with a thin cord, making a solid, backed-up central placement. I clip myself to it with enough slack so that I can lean out over the cliff and help Jones with the climb.

Then I go back to the suspect bolts on the ledge's edge. I take a sling of webbing from over my shoulder and slip a loop through the carabiner I had placed on the hanger. I tug hard. The hanger comes free from the rock, popping me hard in the forehead. With a low curse I look at the rock from which the hanger came free—there's no bolt. The hanger swings free at the end of the sling. On it there's some sort of residue that looks and smells like Krazy Glue. I curse again, amazed. It takes me a couple of minutes to realize the horror of what someone has done here.

After warily double-checking my self-built anchor, I yell, "Off belay!" I lean out over the edge and watch as Jones jerks the rope out of the ATC. I pull up the slack. Locking the rope through my own belay device, I shout, "On belay!" as I promised him I would and tug the rope twice, causing it to snap at Jones's harness. Jones studies the face above him for a long time, shaking his head and presumably swearing.

He moves slowly once he starts up the cliff. He is sweating and gasping for air just ten feet off the deck, hauling himself skyward with his massive arms alone, gripping the edges with all his formidable strength. Oso sits up and watches curiously. "Put some weight on your legs. You aren't a cripple," I yell down, trying to be helpful.

"Fuck you!" is the reply.

"It'll be easier—I swear."

"Bite me!"

"Okay, so I take it you don't want any advice?"

"Shut up and keep that rope tight!"

I make a whistling sound. "Poor sportsmanship. Penalty: ten feet of slack." I loosen the rope to tease him, then pull it tight again.

He looks up, truly terrified now. "Don't do that!"

Thirty feet off the ground, Jones comes to the first piece of gear: a cam with the rope running through it. As Jones starts to climb above it, I tell him to pull the cam's trigger and take it out. Jones complies without comment, apparently breathing too hard for further profanity. From above I watch his calves beginning to tremble with the onset of the dreaded sewing-machine leg. When Jones raises his head for the next hold there's white all the way around his eyeballs.

I pull the rope as tight as I can and tell Jones to let go of the rock and lean back, to just sit in the harness and rest. "You won't fall, I swear. I've got you tight." Jones grudgingly and desperately does as I recommend, but instead of resting his arms he grips the rope as if he's going to strangle it. I hold my tongue and don't offer any further advice, but cannot refrain from pulling the camera out of my pack with my free hand and snapping a quick picture of Jones grimly hang-dogging. Fortunately, Jones doesn't notice.

Finally, he's up. He rolls over onto the wide ledge and appears to hug the horizontal rock with great passion as he blows and sucks the high, clean air. When he looks up at me he is grinning.

"You are one crazy motherfucker!" he says, laughing. "But I think I could get into this climbing shit!"

I explain what I'm doing as I tie Jones in to the anchor on a long line just in case he stumbles. Jones is still smiling and gazing out over the aspens and pines and onto the plain below and beyond.

I show Jones the hanger that had been glued to the rock and explain how I'd jerked it right off.

"Why would someone put that there?"

"I guess someone didn't want anyone else coming up here. Anyone who clipped those hangers and trusted them as an anchor would be dead."

Before going into the cave, I study the natural platform. It is roughly ten feet by ten feet and sticks out from the cave entrance like an unrailed balcony. The edge at the end of the balcony is smooth. There is nothing for Kate Danning to have hit her head on, and there is nothing that could have caught at her necklace and caused the abrasion in the photos. Above the platform and the cave entrance the pillar reaches another fifty feet higher. Telling Jones to wait here, I untie myself from the rope and gingerly follow a narrow, broken ledge that leads around to the other side of the pillar. On that side is an even bigger ledge, populated by several stubby pine trees growing directly out of the rock. Branches are broken off—probably used as firewood for parties in the cave. Boulders and more ledges lead in what appears to be an easy scramble up to the summit.

I ease back around on the narrow ledge to where Jones waits on the balcony, still staring happily out over Vedauwoo. He blanches as much as a dark black man can when he notices that I'm unroped. "Hope you know what you're doing, bro."

I fish a headlamp out of the second pack and put it on. "Let's check this cave out."

From the police reports and photographs there is no indication that anyone ever bothered to climb the pillar from which she fell to see where the climbers' party took place. But then if the investigating cops had not been so lazy, there would almost certainly have been a dead cop when he hung from the bolts. For a moment I'm almost sad that Sergeant Bender isn't a climber.

I pause for a long time at the cave's entrance, carefully studying the interior. What I see in the glow of my headlamp is that the cave appears to consist of a single large and irregular room. Empty beer cans and broken glass clutter the floor. There are some ratty old sleeping bags piled by the back wall. The floor is a mess of burnt-out roaches and cigarette butts. The ceiling is only three feet high near the rear, but slopes nearly ten feet high just inside the entrance. I brace myself on one arm and twist all the way around to look up at the ceiling. I spot a narrow chimney that rises straight up toward the pillar's summit until it disappears in darkness. Then I duck inside the cave, followed by Jones.

We both move around in it, looking without touching at empty cans cut in half for inhaling drugs, cigarette butts, and other debris. Reluctantly, I tug on some surgical gloves and unroll the dirty sleeping bags. I find nothing inside but used condoms. I make a face and roll them up again.

"Well, I don't see any signed confession written in blood," Jones says.

I keep prowling around for a few more minutes, but soon I'm reaching the same conclusion. This is going to be a short investigation, I think; all that is left to do is interview the partyers. Maybe the head injury and ligature mark were simply random, unexplainable injuries after all.

Jones, still tethered to the safety line, goes back out into the sunlight and I start to follow him. But on a whim I stop and look again at the ceiling.

The narrow chimney is really a long, smoke-darkened hole, maybe three feet by eighteen inches. Just wide enough for a body to fit through. With my headlamp's help I discover small foot- and handholds, then begin to pull myself up into the narrow recess. Jones sticks his head back in to watch as my head, shoulders, then torso are swallowed by the rock.

In up to my butt, I can't find any more holds. I worm higher by bracing my shoes against the cool wall behind me and my knees against the front, creating a wedge. I do the same with my hands and elbows and work myself higher. Ten feet in to the mouth of rock it begins to widen. Turning my head, in the headlamp's glow, I can see another chamber opening up.

It opens into a wide room even bigger than the one below. A broad Carolina hammock is strung between two chocks sunk in cracks on opposite walls. A shotgun is propped in a recessed corner near an old Coleman lantern.

A half-empty case of Yukon Jack lies on the ground. And there are tins of food, a stove, pots, and two twenty-gallon bags of water. There's a fire pit too, near the vertical entry hole that continues on up but grows too small for me to climb higher. Something shiny flashes in the reflected light of my headlamp near the floor of the chamber. Into a small recess someone has shoved an empty bottle of whiskey. I withdraw it using one of the surgical gloves I'm still wearing.

The bottle's bottom corner is crusted with blood and there are several strands of blonde hair stuck to it. Why would someone hide and keep an incriminating piece of evidence like that? I wonder. It doesn't make any sense, unless there's more than one killer and one is trying to keep something over the other. I bag the bottle using the evidence envelopes in the pack, and then photograph the chamber.

Back down in the cave, I show Jones the bottle through the clear plastic bag and point out the bits of dried blood and hair on its base. "Holy shit," he says. "Holy fucking shit."

"You never know," I speculate. "Maybe that's from some long-ago fight. Maybe this bottle's been up there for years."

Jones looks at me with a cool, level, sergeantlike gaze. He is back to being a cop and the day is no longer a lark. "And I'm the tooth fairy. That's no coincidence, Anton." For once he doesn't bother with the nickname. "Looks like you've got a murder investigation, bro. Now how the hell do we get down?"

TWELVE

MCGEE IS WAITING for me on the courthouse steps. He's perched like a gargoyle, one that's wearing a sloppy business suit, on a short wall adjacent to the steps with cigar smoke curling from his beard. The steps and the courthouse lawn are relatively quiet. On the street a lone media van from a TV station in Cheyenne, hopeful for some new development, rests out of the sun in the shade of a cottonwood's turning leaves. I park in front of the van. Flashing McGee a thumbs-up, I crack the windows and then lock Oso inside.

"It was a productive morning," I say as I approach him.

"Wish I could say the same. Damned constipation is killing me."

I ignore that. "I was up at Vedauwoo this morning," I tell him, explaining the cave and finding the incriminating bottle that could have caused the injury to the back of Kate

Danning's head. "It doesn't look like the bottle was wiped—there's still some blood and hair on it. If it matches the girl's, we've got a murder for sure. And hopefully the killer's prints."

McGee grunts and says nothing at first, just sucks on his cigar. After a moment he spins his cane's gold head with a thick, gnarled hand while holding the length of mahogany wood in his other. The eagle's head comes off in his hand. I smile when I see the cork stopper that is hidden beneath it. McGee lifts the top of the dissected cane to his lips and tilts it back, then wipes his mouth with the back of a hand. He holds the cane out to me but I gesture no thanks.

"Know what this fucking means?" he says after a second pull at the flask, the whiskey making him sputter and cough.

"It means we're looking at the County Attorney's son as a killer."

He nods. "Not just that. The drugs and the ligature abrasions . . . all the similarities to the Lee girl. Climbers with raps for dealing meth . . . they could be the scumbags Lee was going to turn in. Not the Knapp brothers . . . Motive and some evidence. Might mean nothing, but we have to look and give it over to the defense . . . it's exculpatory fucking evidence," he says, coughing again and spraying saliva. "Evidence the Knapps have a right to."

I don't want to do that. I don't want to give up anything to anyone until I know all the facts. "Why now, when we don't know if it's exculpatory or not? We can pass it on later if it's germane. They've already been convicted. The jury said they're guilty beyond a reasonable doubt. Why tell them anything before we know for sure?"

"The conviction hasn't yet entered. Not on the record. Not until the sentencing. . . . We're still bound by the rules of discovery. We have to turn over to them . . . any evidence, no matter how unlikely . . . or risk taking it up the ass on appeal . . . when it's my goddamned case, not Karge's." He moves a hand over his scarred scalp and growls, "Christ, what a bloody mess. At some point I'll have to talk to Nathan. . . . See how he wants to handle it. If the media were to get wind of this . . ."

"You're the lawyer." I think about what he means. Just based on the nature of the crime, the case is already a media circus. If it comes out that the prosecutor's own son is a potential alternative suspect the defense could have used as a tool to pry some doubt into the juror's minds, the case will explode in Karge's face. As will his political ambitions.

"So while he's preparing for the biggest sentencing of his life," I conjecture out loud, "one that the papers say will make him the next governor, and maybe even take him higher after that, we're going to tell him we're investigating his son for a murder and maybe screw his conviction?"

"Just so."

"What will the judge do?" I ask.

"She could throw out the verdicts. Reopen the defense's case. Or she could declare a mistrial. . . . Karge would have to start all over. Either way, his political stock . . . won't be worth a sack of shit."

That's really not so bad, I think. I've always hated the way politics and justice are married. The two have no business together. I know that firsthand, after the incident in Cheyenne.

"What if we do nothing, or the judge does nothing?"

"Then those two shitheads, the Knapps . . . they're going to die on a gurney. No one's going to turn this thing over on appeal. . . . Certainly not the governor, who'll be Karge by then...not the state Supreme Court. It'd make them look like pussies...after all the Shepard stink.

"So keep it quiet for now. Run the prints on that bottle, pronto.... Tell the lazy pricks in the lab it's priority. That's from me.... And get the DNA checked too. But that'll take a few weeks.... If the prints come back as young Bradley's, then I'll go have a talk with Nathan...see how he wants it handled. You'll need a day or two to run the prints.... You just keep doing what you're doing. Find out if Kate Danning was killed. Find out if there's any other links to Lee.... And for God's sake do it quietly. We've got less than a week before the sentencing to make the call."

Using the address I had found for Cindy Topper in the Laramie phone book, I drive to a small apartment building just a few blocks from the University of Wyoming campus. The building is neatly maintained with five apartments facing the street on the lower level and five apartments above. Cindy Topper's is on the upper level.

Knowing the crowd she hangs out with, when the door opens I'm expecting to see tie-dyed curtains and scattered drug paraphernalia. But when Cindy answers the door at three o'clock in the afternoon, behind her is a clean, plant-filled room heavy with the odor of burning incense rather than marijuana. Green leaves and flowers rise off of every surface. The plants' earthy odor combines with the sweet incense and gives the air a tropical flavor and humidity.

I introduce myself and she giggles when she sees my badge. There's no time anymore for me to screw around, playing undercover. "Oh my God, you're the one Lynn told me about. You don't look like a cop," she tells me. Then, "Holy shit, does Lynn know you're a cop?"

"I don't know—we haven't talked about our jobs. Look, can I come in and talk to you for a minute?"

"Sure, I'm just starting to get ready for class but it's not till four o'clock. A climbing cop!" The idea seems to really amuse her.

She waves me in and curls up on the couch while I sit in an easy chair opposite her. After she tucks her long hair behind her ears, I ask what she's studying. Massage therapy, she replies. There are not many men in the world who would object to having her hands on their skin. She is a very pretty girl and, even though it's late in the afternoon, she wears only a short white silk robe as far as I can tell. As we talk she pushes the robe down between her legs and brings her bare feet up so that her thighs are curled against her chest. Each of her toenails is painted different colors like a bright arrangement of flowers.

To keep from staring at her bare legs, I look around the room. Tarot cards are spread on the low coffee table between us near what looks like a crystal ball. Aside from the plants, there are framed Rousseau and Gauguin prints on the walls. These too have a tropical feel. A small poster on one wall, strikingly out of place, is of Billy Heller powering an overhanging lateral crack on red sandstone. Fluorescent slings of webbing hang from his bulging shoulders. The poster is encased in a large wooden frame that has been hand-painted. The bright frame and its prominence in the room suggest almost an altar to me. In one corner of the room is a backpack with a pair of climbing slippers and a chalk bag clipped to it.

"Want some herbal tea?" she asks, picking up a steaming clay mug from the table. "I just brewed it. We can share."

"Thanks, I'm all right. I want to talk to you about Kate. How well did you know her?"

"I thought you'd want to talk to me about Lynn," she says, laughing. "Kate's dead, you know."

This isn't the reaction I expected. I explain that I've been assigned to look into Kate Danning's death and that there are some things about it that don't look like an accident. Cindy doesn't seem to care one way or another. She seems utterly detached from it, as if her friend has merely taken a vacation.

"I met her when I took an Outward Bound course up in Lander before starting school, like two years ago. She was an assistant instructor or something. We became friends there."

"Was she a good climber?"

"She was great. Maybe not as good as Lynn on cracks, but next to her she was the best around. I just do sport climbs. Cracks hurt too much." She shakes her hands and pretends to wince.

"Tell me about Kate. What was she like?"

"She was, like, a pretty free spirit, you know? You could tell she had a good soul. Real positive energy. And she was real together when I knew her back in Lander. Then she came out here with Brad and she got a little weird."

"What happened?"

"Look, I can only tell you some stuff if you promise not to tell anyone."

"I promise," I say, knowing that it's probably a lie.

"Kate met Brad up in Lander too, where she'd started hanging with him and Billy. That was kind of strange, 'cause most people are immediately attracted to Billy more than Brad. The dude's like a magnet. But I think she was scared of him. Billy's a real primitive-type man, like a great big grizzly bear or something. You've heard of Billy Heller, right? He's Lynn's ex, so watch out. But anyway, Kate took a test and found out she was pregnant. That really freaked her out at first. She cut out the dope and all that, you know, really cleaned up her act, and she and Brad talked about it all the time. Like how they would name it Vedauwoo or Laramie. Then Kate miscarried after a big fall two or three months later and it freaked her out even more. In a real negative way. Like it was her fault, and the bad karma was going to stick with her."

From the rest of the story she tells me, I learn that after the miscarriage, Kate became severely depressed and was again using a lot of drugs right up until the time of her death. I try to get her to tell me if Kate was mad at Brad or was about to leave him, but all Cindy will say is that she doesn't know about any of that. I have a feeling that she does, though. And that's what I need most—a motive. Each time she tells me she doesn't know something, she looks right into my eyes and grins a little, like she's enjoying keeping a secret. As we talk the robe slips on her legs where they're still folded against her, bare heels against her butt, so that the only part of her lower body the robe covers is a portion of her crotch. Something about her makes me think she knows about that too, and is enjoying it.

"Tell me about that night when Kate fell."

She looks me right in the eyes again and the corners of her mouth rise in a tiny grin. But then she wraps her arms around her slim legs as if distressed at the recollection. "I don't remember a whole lot about that night. Don't bust me, but I was drinking and smoking some too that night."

"What time did you get up there?"

"I went with Sierra, the others already up there—"

"Sierra Calloway?" I interrupt, remembering the name from Bradley Karge's witness statement.

"Yeah, right. She's sort of a friend of mine, dates Chris sometimes. Anyway, we'd go up that pillar to party a lot with those guys. There was this real wild energy up there at night."

She explains that they went up there a little past dark. A rope had been left hanging for them, along with a pair of etriers and mechanical aids for ascending the rope rather than the rock. Sierra jugged up the rope first, and then the rope and etriers were lowered back down for Cindy. The group on top poured beer on her as she ascended the line, laughing and sputtering. At the top were Sierra, Lynn, Kate, Chris, Brad, and Billy.

Lynn? I ask myself. Her name hadn't been in the report. I push the thought away.

"Were you Billy's date for the party?"

She laughs again, releases her knees, and sips at her mug of tea. "Everybody's Billy's date, man. We're all real healthy and open up there. See, sometimes I'm his date, but not that night, he was playing it cool with me." I think she looks a little annoyed. "So I left after a while. With Sierra. Chris was kind of being a dick too. And he's usually such a nice guy."

"Did Lynn leave with you?"

Her face flushes a little. "I don't remember when Lynn left."

"What was everyone doing before you and Sierra left?"

"You know, just shit. Drinking and smoking. Partying."

"How were Chris and Billy being dicks?"

"Messing with . . ." I have a feeling she's about to say Kate, but she stops herself and looks me straight in the eyes again, turning up the corners of her mouth. She shrugs and the robe rises a little but I keep my eyes on hers, willing myself not to look. That's what she wants; it will give her some sort of power over me. And I find it isn't that difficult to keep my eyes on her face now. Down below the surface she is harder than she first appeared. I'm beginning to see that. After another sip of tea, she continues. "They were just like being macho jerks, screwing around. It was a bummer. So Sierra and I split. It was early still. We'd only been there an hour or so." Then she adds, "I think Lynn left before us."

I want to believe that. "What did you do after that?"

That smiling look again. "I don't remember. Went home I guess. We didn't hear about Kate until the next day."

I'm about out of questions. At least until I learn something that will give me the leverage to pry at what's been behind her direct looks and smiles. I ask if she knows how I can get ahold of Sierra so I can see if she remembers anything else.

"She lives north of town, in a trailer with a bunch of dogs in the middle of nowhere. No phone or anything, like total isolation. When she needs one she uses mine."

"Can you tell me how to get to her place?"

"Ha! I've been there maybe a hundred times and I probably still couldn't find it. Every time I've been I've followed her truck. It's just some random dirt road just east of Buford. But I haven't seen her at all since Kate's funeral. She works at some motel, cleaning rooms." Cindy smirks unpleasantly as she says that.

"If you do see her, please tell her I'd like to talk to her." I put my card with the phone number in Cody on the coffee table. "Thanks for talking to me." She rises too as I get up, exposing more of herself, but I turn away toward the door.

"Hey, you want to climb with me sometime? Lynn

knows how to share." I wonder what she means by that but a part of me doesn't want to know.

"I won't be climbing much for a few days," I say, but also tell her that maybe I'll give her a call sometime after I sort all this out. We both know I won't.

At the door she smiles up into my eyes and bends a little to shake my hand. Her other hand holds the folds of her robe together down near her waist. The top of it falls open, revealing one perfect white breast with a rose tattoo around the nipple. I don't hear her close the door right away as I walk back down the stairs to my truck at the curb.

I find the old ranch house far out on the west side of town across the railroad tracks that divide Laramie. The division is economic and aesthetic as well as geographic. On the east side is the small downtown area of rustic brick buildings and the tree-lined streets and nicer homes around the university. But here to the west there are fields with horses and cows that separate the homes. The streets are unpaved and without traffic signs, and the homes are made of cinderblocks and worn wood with blue tarps that sag out over patios. There is a strong odor of manure in the air. Oso intently watches the cows from the backseat, swishing his tail at my head.

In the police reports, Brad had listed this house as his address. It's also the business address of Heller Carpentry. There is a yard at the end of a dirt driveway with three cars in it. One is an abandoned-looking pickup without wheels and resting on its axles, another is an aging Jeep with stickers from climbing companies covering the back windows, and the third is a nearly new Ford van with oversize wheels. I get out behind the van and feel the strong west wind blow up and through my untucked flannel shirt. I have to hold the tail with one hand to keep my gun concealed.

The two-story house is almost as dilapidated as the wheel-less pickup in the yard. The paint has long since worn off the wooden siding, and the porch seems to dip and roll as if it's being lifted by waves. A green glass bong stands in plain sight by a camp chair. Not seeing a doorbell, I bang on the door with my fist. I can hear a phone's insistent ringing beyond it.

A few moments later the door is opened by Bradley Karge. He looks both sleepy and stoned. His blond dreadlocks are in disarray, snaking out in all directions. He stares at me without recognition. "What's up?"

"I met you the other night. At the bar, with Lynn. My name's Anton Burns."

"Oh yeah, man, I remember. Guy who'd put up some routes in Alaska or something. Billy'd heard about you." His eyes are glazed and shot with red. "You goin' climbing, or what?"

"I just want to talk to you for a minute. Actually, I'm a cop and want to ask you some stuff about Kate." As I speak I give him a flash of my badge.

Brad's mouth drops open for an instant, then he whips his head toward the house's interior. He starts to close the door. "Shit, I can't talk about that right now. You better get the fuck out of here, man." The way he says it makes me think he's more afraid than threatening.

"I'm not here to hassle you about dope or anything," I say quickly, "I just want to talk about her and what happened that night."

I can hear a phone slam down and heavier steps fast approaching the door, booming on the worn pine floors. Had Cindy called to warn them that I'm a police officer and asking questions? The door is jerked back open and Billy Heller pushes past Brad. He towers shirtless in the doorway, his blunt jaw pushing toward my face. I take an involuntary step back. His shoulders are the size of bowling balls and beneath them his lats stand out like the edges of some meaty fan. The skin on his chest and face is entirely hairless. Looking into the bigger man's eyes, I see the pupils are tiny dark holes. He's tweaking on something. Hard.

"Get the fuck off my property, cop. Get the fuck off now."

"I want to talk—"

"You don't start running, I'm going to throw your ass off."

He comes through the doorway until his chin is almost jutting against my forehead and I step back again. I feel the boil of blood start in my chest, a familiar roaring in my ears. Time slows as my concentration focuses on only the man, with the rest of the world beginning to disappear. Something about this guy really pisses me off. And despite his immense size, I have no fear. I was only scared for a brief moment. Then the thrill, the risk, it pushes through the fear. It's the same wild rush and concentration that soloing gives me, that drugs give my brother. *La llamada del salvaje,* as my mother would say. Or a call to the grave with someone as strong and crazy as Heller.

"You touch me and I'm going to throw you down for obstruction," I tell him, my voice distant and low to even my own ears as I stare up into the red eyes above the sweating face. I can see that his synapses are firing contradictory instructions. I watch a decision being weighed in a mind that is artificially scrambled. I wait for his conclusion to attack, ready to cut him to the floor with a turning kick at his knees. Thinking ahead, I see myself pulling my Glock out from the small of my back and ramming it into his nostrils. Then a small gleam of reality penetrates the roaring in my head. Amped from the drugs, it will take a bullet in the brain to stop him once it begins. And my gun isn't loaded—it hasn't been for eighteen months. Not since Cheyenne. So I step back again, hating it, and begin moving almost sideways down the steps and toward my truck, keeping watch on the big man in case he decides to make a move.

"We'll be talking," I say to Brad, "and you and I too," I say to Billy. "Whether you want to or not."

"I'll jack you up if you come back on my land, cop," Heller yells with triumph in his voice at my retreat. "I'll shoot you like a trespasser, motherfucker. You stay the fuck away from me and Brad. *And you stay the fuck away from Lynn.*"

I keep my eyes locked on Heller's as I get in my truck and slam the door. Oso is rumbling like a train from where he squats on the passenger seat with his snout pressed hard against the glass. I only break my gaze from Billy to back down the drive, but Oso's fierce amber eyes never waver. Billy stays on the porch, grinning now as he watches me pull away.

THIRTEEN

"FIRST OF ALL, I want to know why you're willing to talk to me. I asked around and heard you've always refused to give interviews," Rebecca Hersh says. I can tell that she's trying to lock me into talking about the shooting with her, as if I'd made a promise. But all I agreed to was coffee.

I first came across her on my way back to the room at the Holiday Inn. She was sitting by the pool with some other reporters in the shade of an umbrella that the wind was threatening to launch into the air. Her pale skin glistened from exercise, and her cheeks were tinged pink just below her eyes. She was dressed in a pair of Lycra shorts and a tank top. A pair of running shoes was at her side and her feet looked cool where she dipped them in the chlorinated water. I waved to her as I went by. She surprised me by walking over and asking if I would get cookies and caffeine with her at a shop by the railroad tracks called Coal Creek Coffee. She was waiting for me there, showered and dressed, when I walked into the café a little later.

She's changed into brown silk slacks and a black shirt with a Chinese collar. Her leather jacket is hung over the back of her chair. As I order a cup of pesticide-free Chilean roast and an oatmeal muffin, she studies me with mahogany eyes framed by dark hair. Once again, she takes my breath away.

Sitting across the table from her, I try to quit staring and focus on her question. Am I willing to talk with her just because she attracts me so much? That's really pathetic, I think, but it may be true. Among the other psychological injuries it inflicted, the shooting robbed me of my confidence, and I realize I'm desperate for positive attention. And lately I seem to be letting pretty girls manipulate me. But just as my spirits have been rejuvenating since my return to this part of the state, I hope to rediscover the confidence that was taken from me. For too long I've been replacing it with a bitter depression. I want to talk to her and let out the poison that still flares within me.

But I don't tell her that. Instead I just say, "I'm tired of toeing the office line, saying 'No comment.' That just gives you reporters the chance to take the other side all the way—there's nothing to balance it with."

She thinks about that for a minute and nods, understanding.

"So, I hear you used to live in Laramie," she begins.

I can't help laughing. "Interrogation 101," I say, replying to her quizzical look. "They must teach you the same things at journalism school that they do at the police academy. You know, first lock the subject into talking with you, then make him comfortable by starting with comfortable subjects. Their background and all that . . . I'm surprised you didn't bring along a partner to play the bad cop."

She blushes a little, then laughs too. I'm pleased to see her professional journalist's mask slip a little. So I go ahead and talk to her about growing up at all the far-flung military bases my father was stationed at. About my maternal grandfather's ranch in Argentina, which from rare visits there was the only permanent home I had ever known. About my mother, who is Spanish and Pampas Indio, and my father, whose parents came to the States from Scotland. About college at Berkeley and my master's degree in criminal justice from the University of Colorado at Boulder. Her technique is flawless; she reels it all out of me as easily as coiling a rope. Every now and then she fits in details about her own past as we talk. Her father became a professor of economics after he served with Ross McGee in Korea. She went to college at Smith and then journalism school at Columbia. She tells me she is an avid distance runner and asks about the risks of alpine climbing.

I explain to her that climbing isn't as deadly a sport as people think. In all of North America, only about fifty climbers died in the last year. Over the two decades of my own climbing career, I know just a half-score of friends and acquaintances who've cratered. But just because death by climbing is somewhat rare doesn't mean it's unknown or even unfamiliar. Cheating Death is the very essence of the sport; Death is always watching you when you're on the rock.

"I don't get it," she says, repeating Jones's question from the morning. "Why risk anything at all? Why not accept the slow, easy pleasure of a long run or something like fishing?"

A hundred books and articles have been written on the

subject, like Mallory's famous quote: If you have to ask the question, you won't understand the answer. The best I can do is to tell her, "Because you have to. Once you do it, once you experience the thrill of putting it all on the line with all that air beneath your heels, you can't stop. It's an addiction, really. It becomes like a hunger in your stomach." I tell her about my mother's theory, *la llamada del salvaje.*

"I think I'll stick to running. Did you become a cop for the excitement too?"

"That, and the usual cop's need for justice and order. A therapist I was made to see after the thing in Cheyenne said there's been so much disruption in my life that I have an urge to control those around me. And there's the competitiveness—I can't stand the thought of someone getting away with something, you know, hurting someone and then just walking away. I have a hard time letting it go, but that's something I'm working on." I have never come to terms with a system based on the principle that it is better to let a hundred guilty people go free rather than wrongfully convict one innocent person. It's okay for people to be victimized again and again as long as no one is mistakenly locked up.

As we talk her hands are on the table, one holding the pen as she scribbles the occasional note, the other securing the pad. Her quick fingers look strong for such a slender woman, the nails unvarnished. "I bet some of the same things made you want to be a reporter," I tell her. "Maybe you should try climbing."

When she laughs she slowly shakes her head and her hair drifts back and forth across her cheeks.

After our coffee and snacks are delivered, she begins questioning me about that night eighteen months ago, and I feel the bitterness I'd forgotten over the last few minutes rising up again. She does it in a sympathetic tone, with a pretense of total understanding. We both know I'm being played, but I let it happen. I tell her everything that happened, from my confidential informant's sobs to the final gunplay itself. She murmurs, "You must have been terrified" and "How awful" at all the appropriate times.

When I have told her all I can about that night, she asks, "Will you get in trouble for talking with me?"

I shrug. "Maybe. But I guess I don't care all that much. McGee might be mad, but then again, he seems to like you." I can still imagine him, though, roaring, "You what!" when I tell him I've given a complete interview. Then he'll chastise me, about how what I say to anyone can be used against me when I testify. I know it's good advice; these are the things my lawyer should tell me but is too inexperienced and afraid of me to say.

"I had the *Post* e-mail me all the clippings. I read that there was some talk of charging you."

"Yeah, a few people in the AG's Office wanted to prosecute me criminally. Still do. A lot of politician types and community activists too. For murder or at least manslaughter. It would be good politics—get the minority vote, you know? If it'd happened in any other state, any state with a larger minority population, they'd have hung me out to dry from the start. Ross McGee saved my ass by refusing to do it. He even threatened to resign if the office pursued it. And thank God my mom's Hispanic."

"So tell me about the civil suit. How did that come about?"

I tell her that I doubt it was the idea of the Torreses or the other families. They knew those three would die either from a bullet or in prison. Sure, they want revenge, especially the surviving sons and the other gang members whom I'd betrayed. But they want a more primal vengeance than just dollars. They want me six feet under and they want it to take a while. She already knows about the attack from the little brother yesterday. I tell her the suit came about as most of them do—a shark of an attorney, Mo Cash, saw an opportunity and went to the parents with it. His take will be forty percent of whatever is recovered.

Initially I hadn't cared about the money, as they were seeking it only from the office, believing a lowly state employee like me couldn't have much. I was more worried that a civil verdict against me would result in the murder charges being filed. And about the damage it would do to my professional reputation. Of course, after all the media attention there wasn't a whole lot left of it to degrade. And then Cash and his associates discovered the trust fund my grandfather had left me, and now I could lose it all. Everything, really. My job, my inheritance, and my freedom.

"In the clippings I read, it seems there's one columnist in particular who has it out for you—Don Bradshaw of the *Cheyenne Observer*. He's the one who called you all those names."

"Yeah," I say, "rogue cop, QuickDraw, and all that. I really hate that guy. You know I once arrested his son for selling ecstasy to schoolkids? He went out and hired Mo Cash to try and get him off. And Cash got him a good deal too, a deferred judgment, thanks to all his connections and despite my screaming and moaning. Keep that in mind when you read Bradshaw's stuff. Tell me if you see him around—I'd like to say hello." The asshole had even printed in one column that my brother was in prison for manslaughter, and that my father, as a Special Forces soldier, undoubtedly had taken lives himself. He'd called us a family of killers. But I suspect politeness overcomes Rebecca's journalistic, predatory instincts for a good quote and she doesn't mention my brother.

I tell her about the summary judgment hearing next week and my unrealistic hope that the whole thing will be thrown out then. My lawyer isn't promoting that hope. For a motion for summary judgment to be granted, dismissing the case, there must be no material facts in dispute. And the question of self-defense versus murder is a large one.

After a few more minutes it seems like the interview is over. She snaps the cap back on her pen and puts away her legal pad. I'm disappointed but try not to show it. I realize how much I've been enjoying her company. Although I've been through a number of women over the past eighteen months, I can't recall a single conversation. I'd used their flesh, not their minds. So I decide to give Rebecca Hersh a gift.

"In the spirit of cleansing my soul here," I tell her, "I'll give you what might be a scoop on the Knapp brothers if you promise not to print or speak a word of it until McGee clears it."

She promises, "Absolutely off the record," and holds up three fingers in a Girl Scout's salute.

So I tell her about the methamphetamine connection, the bottle, and the ligature abrasions on Kate Danning. Her eyes light up like she has a fever.

Through the café's big windows I see it's thoroughly dark outside. The caffeine causes a rumble in my stomach and I ask her if she will have dinner with me. She comes back to earth with a startled look at her watch. She tells me no, she's late for a preplanned dinner with friends. For a moment, unjustifiably, I picture her telling them about how she had coffee with a murderer, one who even had the moxie to ask her for a date. But then I try to persuade myself that I see some reluctance in her eyes as she pulls on her leather coat. Before she leaves she asks if she can have a rain check.

It's Friday night. I have nowhere to go, nothing to do. For a moment I consider calling Kristi in Cheyenne, seeing what she's up to and if she would like to drive over. But I push that urge away. I like her too much.

On the way back to the motel I buy a bottle of tequila and another of lime juice from one of Wyoming's drive-thru liquor stores, then a large cheese and pepperoni from Grand Avenue Pizza. I fill a water bottle with the hotel's ice and mix in the Herradura and juice. Oso gets the pizza crusts but I don't share the rough margarita. I feel like I need the release of the liquor tonight before I drive down to see my brother tomorrow. I need to deaden my anxiety, and I know from too much experience over the last eighteen months that a tequila hangover will do that for me—put a hazy buffer between reality and me. A cowboy movie is playing on the TV but I ignore it while making notes on my laptop computer of the day's findings.

I'm well into my second quart-size bottle and the pizza is half gone when there's a hammering on the door. My face is numb from the tequila, and I have to glance down to make sure I'm still dressed. Looking through the peephole at first I can't see anyone. But then at the bottom of the wide-angled circle there is Lynn, her dirty blonde hair across her face in the evening wind. She looks angry.

When I pull the door open she shoves me hard in the chest with both hands. I hope Rebecca Hersh or her friends aren't around to see this.

"You're a fucking cop!" she says, coming in after me. "A goddamn narc!"

With a lucky snatch through the tequila haze, I grab her wrists as she raises them to push me again, and twist her onto the bed. She fights it, bringing up a sharp knee that's viciously aimed at my crotch. I turn one hip to the side just in time.

"Wait a minute, wait a minute, hang on, let me explain." I try to calm her. Her breath is hot on my face. She squirms her small, strong limbs beneath me in an effort to get free.

Finally she stops struggling and I feel safe enough to get up and sit in the chair. I know the "But you never asked" explanation doesn't stand a chance. So I tell her the truth—that I climbed with her because I wanted to, not as part of any investigation. And I prove it with the evidence that I hadn't pressed her to talk about Kate. And until this afternoon, I go on, I didn't even know she'd been up there that night. There was no mention of her presence in the police reports. There's still anger in her eyes but she seems to accept what I say. "Look, I don't care if you smoke a little pot, just don't do it around me. As long as you aren't selling it, I don't care. You're an adult. I'm not going to arrest you."

Suddenly she laughs. "You're drunk," she says. "You reek of tequila."

I laugh too, realizing I've had a stupid, drunken grin on my face even while we wrestled. "Make you one?"

"Do it, man."

I take a spare quart water bottle and fill it with ice, then half tequila and half lime juice. As I make it she turns off my western movie and turns on and up what must be MTV. The wail of John Popper's harmonica fills the room. "So what the fuck's going on?" she asks.

"First, I need to know what you were doing up there that night," I answer, trying to concentrate on the questions I should be asking her.

She scrunches her face either because of my question or the sip she's taken of the drink. "We go up there to party, man. All the time when it's warm. Anyway, Cindy and Sierra and me split early that night. It was just the guys and Kate who stayed."

I can't tell if she's lying. My receptors are definitely impaired. "Did you leave with Cindy and Sierra?"

"No way. I don't hang out with those two whores much. I had my own ride, my truck." She also tells me that she didn't run around with Kate all that much either. She more or less keeps to herself.

I try to question her more about what was going on that night, but all she'll tell me is that it was a usual party for them—smoking dope and drinking. I ask who was tweaking on meth but she says not her, that she didn't know anyone up there was, at least not that night. Despite my impairment, I'm pretty sure she's lying about that. I ask why Brad didn't tell the police about her being up there and all she can tell me is that maybe he forgot, or maybe Billy told him not to, to keep her out of it.

Lynn finishes the quart I gave her and I make two more. My eyes keep catching on her thin lips, her sharp teeth, and her pointed tongue when she licks her lips. Then my eyes drop to the open buttons at the top of her shirt. It takes a staggering amount of effort to lift them back to her face. We're talking about other things now, and I realize I've become somewhat desperate for her company. Any company. My emotions have been bouncing like a yo-yo for the last two days.

Coffee with Rebecca had boosted my libido, as had the

renewal of my climbing career. The tequila just fueled the fire and added to eighteen months of depression and loneliness. Things are getting dangerously out of control. I know it but can't stop it.

While we talk she gets her embroidered cloth bag from where she'd dropped it by the door in the midst of pushing me.

"Before I got pissed at you, I found this and wanted to show it to you." Then she laughs and adds, "Shit, before I got pissed I even shaved my legs!"

She hands me an old, well-thumbed issue of *Rock and Ice* magazine. It's the issue that featured me and the climb I did with my friends in Alaska's Ruth Gorge. Lynn takes it back and opens it to the full-page picture of me hanging from the colossal, three-thousand-foot wall, as high as three Empire State Buildings stacked one on top of the other.

Pointing at it, she's swaying slightly on her feet. I can't tell if she is dancing to the music from the TV or just feeling the effects of the drink. "Now that's feeding the Rat," she says.

"Feeding the what?" I haven't heard the term in years and my tequila-fogged brain has a hard time recalling what it means.

"The Rat, man. You know, it's something climbers got in their bellies. It claws around in there, begging for and feeding on the stupid shit we do. Like getting a fix. It's something Billy's always talking about."

I hold the magazine open and look at the picture with her. The friend who took it was above me, looking down. He took it just a few minutes after the dinner-plate-size flake of rock had come whistling out of the sky. I'd looked up at the sound, thinking maybe I could dodge to the side, but wasn't quick enough. The picture shows me hanging suspended from a rope, gazing up at the camera. Beneath me is simply a universe of space and then a jumbled glacier far below it. I'm grinning at the camera but the smile isn't genuine. A smear of bright red blood is running from my left eye, across my mouth, down my neck, and splashes across my yellow jacket. The cheekbone from which the blood has erupted is already swelling grotesquely. My helmet too is streaked with four smeared lines of red from where I'd felt it for holes with my fingertips. Even more than the blood, the most arresting part of the photograph is my eyes. They are round with terror despite the grin. The Rat was feasting.

I remember the bite of the antiseptic that Hal had splashed on my face before pinching the skin back together with Krazy Glue from the repair kit. I'd been taking hard pulls on a plastic flask of Yukon Jack at the time, the taste and the pain bringing tears to my eyes that stung when they mixed with the flayed skin of my cheek.

"That's how you got that, right?" she asks as she stands close and traces the scar on my cheek with her fingers.

I nod, unable to take my eyes off the photo.

Tequila-scented and still swaying, she moves behind me and puts her arms around my chest, pressing herself against my back. Her hands move over my muscles, then trace the ridges of my ribs and stomach. For a moment I think, irrationally and drunkenly, that it's Rebecca behind me. I almost say her name. I feel her face between my shoulder blades as she blows hotly through my shirt and wet on my skin. Rising up on her toes, she touches my neck with her lips. I drop the magazine on the bed and reach behind me, holding her to me. Then I turn to her.

* * *

I finally lie still, spent and exhilarated and wary. I've never known a girl to be so strong and wild. My wariness comes from that roughness, the way she shouted those words in my ear and impaled her body upon me with such force. "Fuck me!" she'd demanded, again and again. "Harder!" Although I am by no means inexperienced, this was a whole other world. Past girls had proved agile and limber but nothing like this. This was something else altogether.

Lynn's face is buried against my chest. Her breath is still blowing as hot and fast as mine. Again without intending to, I imagine that her blonde hair, where it sweeps across the muscles of my stomach, is darker and richer, like Rebecca's. Turning my head, I can see Oso's yellow eyes watching from his prone position in the corner. His ears are forward; his amber eyes concerned. I feel that he's trying to send me a message that he himself doesn't quite understand or know how to express. A hint of danger. A warning.

"Holy shit," she says, rearing up over me with her voice a purr and her eyes glassy, "that was good. Give me a minute, man—then let's do that again."

FOURTEEN

I'M UP EARLY the next morning despite a headache and a slightly sick feeling down low in my gut. The sight of the bed torn apart and the empty tequila bottle on the dresser turns a worm within me. Outside, as I hurry through my morning training, Oso watches balefully from where he's preemptively tied to a tree as another soccer game is taking place.

Back at the hotel I shower, shave, and take two bagels and a paper cup of tea from the hotel's coffee shop. The mountain-born wind hasn't warmed yet so I pull on my wool coat and call for Oso to "load up" into the truck. Once on Interstate 80, we head east past Vedauwoo, where the granite is orange in the morning light. In Cheyenne I stop by the unoccupied lab at DCI's headquarters to drop off the bottle I'd recovered from the cave. I had already called the chief tech and conveyed the need for urgency along with McGee's endorsement. I was told to expect results the next day, Sunday. Then Oso and I turn south on I-25 and cross the state border into Colorado and the flatland of the eastern plains.

Five hours later the sun is high and the road has turned hot. I pass the signs for Canon City and follow directions to the Colorado Bureau of Prisons. It's a sprawling series of concrete buildings ringed with chain-link fencing, concertina wire, and warning signs. Parking at the far end of the asphalt lot under the shade of some dusty elms, I let Oso out to water the trees before locking him back in the truck with the windows partway down. Distracted, I forget to tell him the usual, "Stay, Oso, I'll be back," and the dog gives his impolite master a hurt look as I stride away toward the building.

He looks harder than ever, I think, staring at a face that is very much like my own through the bulletproof glass. We have the same slightly hooked nose, full lips, and dark hair that come from our mother's Indio ancestors. We have the same heavy brows and protruding jaws from the Celts whose blood runs in our father's veins. But my features lack both the cruelty and beauty of my brother's. His cheekbones are higher, his eye sockets more slanted, and the eyes themselves convey a mercilessness that mine do not. They are a pale, cold, and startling shade of blue. His skin used to be tan like mine from too much sun, but confinement has turned it a faint shade of olive, almost translucent. And the man behind the glass wears his hair long and unkempt. He could be a movie star playing swashbuckling leading men if he weren't an adrenaline junkie whose fix comes from the dangers of both heights and chemicals. And if he weren't a convicted killer.

At a bar in Durango one night three years ago, when thunder roared across the sky and Roberto had stabbed a syringe into his arm like a bolt of lightning, mainlining meth, a cowboy was scoping the girl my brother was with. The cowboy left his friends, who were chuckling and elbowing each other in a cracked leather booth, and approached Roberto's girl. The cowboy came between them like a driven wedge. "Take off, spic," he said as he shouldered Roberto out of the way. Then he reached a hand up beneath the girl's skirt and grabbed at her crotch. Almost casually, my brother smashed his mug of beer against the bar's brass rail so that he was palming the mug's base, the broken upper half like an open mouth with teeth of jagged glass. When the cowboy turned at the sound, Roberto slammed it into the cowboy's face while the man's friends looked on. Then he took him to the floor and beat him to death before a bar full of witnesses. They said my brother was laughing.

"Hey, bro. What's up?" he says, grinning into the telephone receiver, his eyes exuding some weird demonic energy.

" 'Berto. You doing okay?"

"Gettin' by."

There's a long pause as we simply look at one another. His smile turns surprisingly gentle.

"How come you called?" I ask. "It got me worried about you." He's never called before. He's never written. He's never wanted me or anyone else in the family to see him like this.

And I can understand that. Seeing my brother this way

is the last thing I want to do. It's hard to imagine him confined. Even as a child Roberto was always like a cougar, utterly wild and uncontrollable. The rest of the family was a little scared of him and a little awed—he seemed to have too much energy for this world. Yet here he is, kept in a cage, snapping at the bars. I can see in his hard blue eyes that the past two years since he began serving his sentence have certainly not tamed him. His eyes look frenzied and maniacal. In a way, I'm glad to see a spark still in him. Only it doesn't look like just a spark. It looks like an inferno.

"*Che,* I've been thinking a lot 'bout you. I got you in my mind, you know?" He taps his index finger between his eyes. "I could feel it when you were on the rock, when you were shooting those fuckers I read about, when you were mopin' after. Now you're back in the saddle, right?"

"Yeah, 'Berto, I am." I try to laugh. "Don't get too weird on me, okay?"

For the first time since sitting down behind the glass, my brother closes his eyes and stops the family's signature staring. "Tell me what you've been climbing, Ant."

I describe in detail the few big climbs I did in the Tetons and the Winds that summer before the shooting in Cheyenne. There was a brief trip to the pink granite of the Bugaboos when I used up some vacation days. I don't explain my year-and-a-half absence from the stone. My brother keeps his eyes shut as I talk, interrupting only to ask for more detail. Then I tell him I've been at Vedauwoo the last week and he smiles, remembering the cracks our father had first taught us on.

"*Veed-a-voo,*" he almost hums without opening his eyes. "That's a magic word. That's the first place I'm heading to when I get out of here."

When I've finally caught him up on the intimacies of

the climbs, Roberto opens those mad eyes and says, "Now tell me what you've been fucking."

"Not much," I lie, "but I've got prospects. How about you?"

He laughs so hard he pounds the phone on the counter in front of him. A guard steps up behind him but Roberto waves him off. "Real comedian, *che*. Very fucking funny. But I've been getting in shape for both." I can see it's true. His jaw is swollen with muscle, as is his throat. Under the V-neck of his blue jailhouse shirt, I can see a deep line that intersects his pectoral muscles. Each of his forearms is as thick as the striking end of a baseball bat. I've never seen him stronger or crazier.

"Starting your training a little early, aren't you? You got a few years left before you want to peak."

"It won't be that long, bro. I guarantee it. And I've already peaked."

I don't like the way he says that. I don't like the sudden heat I feel radiating through the phone in my hand. I speak carefully, slowly. " 'Berto, do your time and come out clean. Don't screw it up."

He waves my concerns away and I try to let it go. "That's all there is for me to do here. Train. Pull-ups and shit all day long. I've got some maps in my cell that Mom sent me. Topos of the Cerro Torre, Punta Herro, Cerro Standhardt and Torre Egger, all that stuff near the ranch. Some photos too. I think there's some new routes to be done, bro, and I think some old ones can go free."

"The Rat's getting hungry," I say without thinking, repeating the expression Lynn had reminded me of.

He knows exactly what I mean. "Fucking starving, bro. Fucking *e-mac-i-at-ed*."

"Mom's writing you?"

"Uh-huh. Can you believe she's encouraging me to do more climbing when I get out? She used to freak when Dad took us, then when we got older and started going on our own. Guess she's decided it's better than other rushes." He winks. "Speaking of rushes, how you liking carrying that gun and shield these days? Still hookin' and bookin'? Shot any more of those nasty drug dealers lately?"

So I tell him that I'm thinking of quitting, about next week's hearing, and what I'm doing down in Laramie. He frowns when I mention Billy Heller's name and turns serious.

"I know that old freak," he says. "Stay away from him, little bro. He's even crazier than me."

"That's hard to believe."

He laughs. "You still got that dog? He doin' okay?"

Oso was far younger the last few times I saw my brother, when Roberto was living and using in the mountains of southern Colorado. The visits were infrequent because I couldn't stand seeing Roberto on the edge of combustion. My brother and I were opposites then, I believed, with me a rookie cop with a master's degree and him cooking off his brain cells as fast as he could. But there was an immediate bond between the beast and him. I think Oso recognized Roberto as a kindred wild spirit, a canine soul before the days of domestication. The two of them would wrestle like wolf cubs for hours on the carpet while growling ferociously and gently gnawing at each other's throat.

I tell him Oso is all right, just old, and repeat the story about the soccer ball, which has Roberto hooting.

Even as he laughs, I feel overwhelmingly sad about so many things. About my faithful dog who won't be at my side much longer. About my brother burning himself up in jail.

About two other brothers who may unjustly get a fatal ride on a hospital gurney. About an unsolved climber's murder in Vedauwoo. About the lives I took in Cheyenne. About the upcoming hearing that may result in my being criminally charged and publicly humiliated. And about the end of the career I once thought was my calling. I feel as if I'm trying to ascend a thin, worn rope with an impossible weight strapped to my back. I'm ready to leave—I desperately want to get back on the rock, where the only thing I have to worry about is falling.

"So how come you called for me to come down here?" I finally ask him.

"I wanted you to see this, see me here. And I want you to know you'll never see me in a fucking hole like this again."

"What do you mean? I'll come down and see you here any time you want."

"You'll never see me here again, Ant," he repeats, smiling and looking right through me. "But don't worry, I'll still be looking after you." Then he slowly hangs up the phone. I see his lips purse in what must be a whistle to the guard. I bang my own phone against the glass but he doesn't turn around.

From Canon City I drive north back toward Wyoming. I nearly swoon with the need to feel an enormous void beneath my heels. The short climbs I've done in the past few days have set the hook firmly back in my mouth. And the visit to my brother has only jerked it deeper. Just past Denver I suddenly cut across three lanes of traffic and leave the interstate highway, going through Boulder on the way to Estes and Rocky Mountain National Park. As I drop into the valley there, I feel the old thrill that the sight of the craggy peaks always gives me. The glaciers high above Estes sparkle violet in the sunset, and above the snow and ice the granite of the peaks are a deep purple.

I drop off Oso under the porch light at the small house of a graduate school roommate. And I politely refuse my friend's offer to climb with me while his wife entertains Oso. I want to climb alone, solo. I drive a little farther through the night toward the Glacier Gorge trailhead and try to forget about the incriminating look the dog gave me as I pulled away.

At the parking lot I fill two water bottles that still hold the sickly odor of tequila. I feed into my pack a rope, a jacket, a small rack of gear, two ice tools, and my crampons. All I take in the way of food is a couple of PowerBars.

Near midnight I'm breathing lightly, wet with sweat, when I come up out of the trees and low mountains and reach the dark wall that is the base of McHenrys Peak. My crampons scrape and squeak up a long pitch of easy rock before I gain a couloir of ice that has hardened to glass under the months of summer sun. It shatters into broken circles the size of dinner plates with each swing of my ax, but I'm immune to the peril. My mind is heavy with my brother's last words. I wonder if he's feeling me in his mind right now, feeling the vast black space beneath my boots.

On the summit I sit under the stars and let the cold wind dry my clothes. When I begin shivering in earnest I put on my down jacket and pull my pack up over my legs. Through the chattering of my teeth the concerns that clog my head mutely rattle out of me until my mind begins to clear. I lie that way until the dawn lifts away the darkness, and I resolve to do nothing about what my brother said. Telling the prison officials would do nothing but get him hurt or make him angrier. It's his life. The Rat is buckled in the driver's seat and will take Roberto wherever he wants with the accelerator jammed to the floor.

FIFTEEN

AT A LITTLE past noon on Sunday, Oso and I are back in Wyoming. We speed into the capital city of Cheyenne, which is really just a dusty little cow town squatting on the plains. I park in the nearly empty lot outside the office building that houses the AG's Office and DCI's headquarters. As I open the back door for Oso, we both watch a tumbleweed race erratically through the lot and across one of the town's busiest streets. There is no traffic to slow the weed on its frenzied errand.

The beast's gaze follows it, but he doesn't give chase. I'm not sure if it's another sign of his advancing age or if he's just trying to be well behaved, thinking that if he's good I won't leave him behind on my next climb. "A few years ago you wouldn't have let that 'weed get away," I chastise him. "I guess you used it all up on that soccer ball the other day."

I unlock a side door to the building with an electronic

card, and Oso comes in behind me. At a bank of elevators, Oso eyes an open door suspiciously before I can coax him in. When the elevator starts with a jerk, he spreads his legs wide and lowers himself a few inches. We ride down into the basement that houses DCI's laboratories. Again I use the card to let us into the Forensics Department, which is where all physical and trace evidence is analyzed.

Behind the receptionist's station in the windowless office, Dave Ruddick, the chief forensic technician of DCI, leans back in a chair smoking a cigarette and reading a *People* magazine. His excessively long legs are propped on the desk in front of him. I have never seen him sit without his legs propped up on something—they take up a good portion of his six feet and seven inches and will scarcely fit under a desk. Looking up at me, he grins with teeth that are equally overlarge and casually tosses the magazine on the desk. He starts to drawl out, "Howdy," but it turns into a yelp of fright when he sees Oso. It comes out something like, "Howdiiii!" He leaps to his feet. "Jesus, I've heard about that monster!"

"Thanks for working the weekend, Dave."

"No problem," he says, watching Oso in the same cautious way the dog had looked at the elevator, holding out a trembling hand to be sniffed. "Gets me away from the wife and the kids, you know. Is that thing safe?"

"Oh yeah. He's a cupcake."

Oso, still on his best behavior, licks Dave's hand.

"So how's that case going in Laramie? We heard you had a run-in with some of the younger Surenos."

"Yeah, those guys don't like me much. As for the Danning investigation, it was supposed to be easy, just make sure the locals weren't covering up anything, with the County Attorney's kid being there when the Danning girl fell and all. But it's looking more and more like they're hiding something. In the words of the immortal Ross McGee, it's a clusterfuck."

Dave laughs. "The bosses are real happy to have that old degenerate out of town for a while. For two weeks now they haven't had to worry about the secretaries filing a class-action sexual harassment suit." McGee's grotesque but harmless flirting is a source of intense concern for the AG and his immediate staff. At one point they even hired a feminist to give us, and more pointedly Ross McGee, a mandatory lecture on the subject of appropriate office behavior. He'd limped in a half hour late smelling of tobacco and whiskey, patted the speaker on the rear with his hoary hand, and said something like, "Sorry, darling...I got caught up in a *Penthouse* while sitting on the crapper." Dave and I and all McGee's other disciples live in fear that they will one day use it as an excuse to fire him. But so far they haven't had the balls.

Dave waves me back toward his office and says, "It's an interesting bottle you brought me. So who's covering up what in Danning?"

I follow him down the hall and into the wide laboratory that is his office. The room is large and cluttered with metal tables, scales, refrigerators, gyroscopes, and an assortment of stranger scientific instruments. His desk is at the front of the room, facing it, like a teacher's. Taped to the wall behind it and the filing cabinets that surround it are finger paintings that Dave's children have made. I pause and admire them as I explain about the suspect injury to the back of Kate Danning's skull, the positive drug tests, the unexplained abrasion to her neck, the shoddy initial investigation, and Karge's request to the coroner that no rape kit be performed. I don't mention the similarities to the murder of Kimberly Lee.

"What did you find?" I ask, pointing at the whiskey bottle that sits on the desk, enclosed in clear plastic. The bottle itself is covered with grayish dust. Next to it rests a Magic Eight Ball, which is the source of great amusement for all the staff. When I was working cases out of this building we would regularly consult it.

Dave sits behind his desk and once again props up his feet. "A lot of smudges and partials, a couple of complete prints, and that the tip of the neck, where the threads are, was wiped with a cotton cloth of some sort. Probably a T-shirt."

"I didn't wipe it. I picked it up with rubber gloves."

"I figured you knew what you were doing. Anyway, some of the prints came back as unknowns. Two I got matched up with one of the names you gave me. Bradley Karge, the County Attorney's son. We got his prints off the fed's computer from when he was arrested in New Mexico or someplace."

I sink into a chair and Oso drops at my feet. "Wow. That's what Ross and I were afraid of."

"You know, if the media gets ahold of this..."

I don't let him finish. "I know, I know. The sentencing's going to be in less than a week. This Friday. Right when the county's attention is focused on Nathan Karge. If it comes out that his son could be a killer himself, Karge is as good as gone. There's no way he'll make governor. Not if he raised a murderer, or even a suspected murderer."

Dave looks uncomfortably stern. "From what I've seen of the man on TV, that'll be a shame. That man should be governor. Or senator. Or even president. He's the kind of guy that makes Wyoming look good. I hope you know what you're doing, going after his boy and all. Especially right now."

I scratch Oso's ears. "They gave me the investigation and I'm investigating it. Let the chips fall where they may."

Dave shakes his head. "Sometimes that doesn't mean it's the right thing to do. There's such a thing as discretion."

I stop scratching Oso. "That's interesting, Dave. So you're saying maybe I should let the next governor's son slide on a potential homicide, but when I righteously shoot three dealers and rapists who were drawing on me, it's okay for the office to discipline me, exile me across the state, make me out as some kind of dangerous rogue, then assign some rookie to defend me, when you and everyone else here knows it's just politics."

Dave holds up his hands. "Hey, hey. I'm not saying that at all. And you did get screwed. That was bullshit, no one's denying it. Forget I said anything. This place is getting to me...." He passes me a sheet of paper with fingerprints in squares on it. "Look, there's the partials from the bottles on the left. On the right are Bradley Karge's prints from when he was booked on that drug charge in New Mexico."

I examine it. And I decide to cut Dave some slack, both because of what he's just said about me getting screwed and the fact that he was willing to come in on the weekend and look at the bottle. Besides, I like him and he's very good at his job. And one can't help but be influenced by the political intrigue that sweeps through this office like the Chinook.

"I can never read these things. But you say they match?"

"They match."

I check to make sure that Dave's name and signature are on the paper, making him an official witness now.

"What about the other prints? The unknowns?"

"Nothing came up on the crime computer. I can't match them to anybody. They're not Brad Karge's, and they're not Heller's or any of the other names you gave me."

I'm disappointed to hear that. I would like nothing better than to arrest them both. Heller's behavior at the bar and at his house has earned my sincere antipathy. As has his reputation as an abuser and corrupter of young girls. It would be a community service to break up his little cult. For a moment I feel uncomfortable about my night with Lynn, a prominent member of that very group. I should have had better judgment, more self-control.

"What about the blood and hair? And what about saliva from where someone would have drunk out of it?"

"All in the works, pard. Those things will take some time to check out the DNA. I need the sample from the dead girl, if you think it's her stuff. I already put in a request with the Albany County Coroner. At least the blood type matches the girl's, for a start. You might want to have McGee lean some of his weight on the coroner, get him to rush me the sample. From my phone conversation with him I got the feeling he might drag his feet a little."

It will be a pleasure to pay another visit to Dr. Gustavson with Ross. And it's time to bring in Bradley Karge for some official questioning. There is not yet quite enough evidence to charge him with Kate Danning's murder, but it is getting very close. Before I borrow a phone and call McGee at the hotel in Laramie, I take the Magic Eight Ball off Dave's desk and give it a shake. "All signs point to yes," it reads.

McGee has scheduled an appointment for us to meet with Nathan Karge this afternoon. A roving security guard at the courthouse, a big, sunburnt man with a mullet haircut, unlocks the door after McGee knocks on the glass with the gold head of his cane. The rent-a-cop recognizes McGee and is fawningly polite to him, probably realizing that a bad word from head of the state's law enforcement division could keep him from ever getting a job on any police force in Wyoming. I smile, smirk really, watching the guard say "Good afternoon, sir," and "How are you?" in his redneck drawl. There are few things more awkward than a cracker kissing ass. McGee merely grunts at him, and the guard in turn pretends I am invisible when I try to show him my badge. I wonder if he is a relative of Bender and Willis—he has the same big, sloppy, corn-fed build.

McGee looks worse than I have ever seen him. His skin is almost gray above his long white beard. His breaths are rapid and shallow, as if it is costing him an enormous effort to keep his lungs inflated. McGee sounds like Oso after a long run on a hot summer day, but with the addition of a new wheeze that makes me think my boss's throat is constricting. Leaning heavily on his cane as we climb the stairs, he shoots me a truly malevolent look when I move to take his free arm. I jerk away from him, a little stung by his glare. And saddened by his condition.

At the top of the stairs we finally come to the County Attorney's Office. I shake the double glass doors but find that they are locked. McGee again raps on the glass with the head of his cane. After a wait of a few minutes that is silent except for my boss's ragged respiration, it is Nathan Karge himself who appears on the other side.

He doesn't smile at the sight of the two of us outside his office's door. He looks tired but fierce. His tie is loose at the neck and his shirtsleeves are rolled above the elbow. Out of habit I notice his hands. He has surprisingly muscular forearms for a lawyer and there is a scribbling of tiny white scars across the backs of his hands. It causes me to examine the prosecutor more closely, wondering if he'd ever been a climber. On each side of his long, sharp-edged nose are faint black crescents beneath his eyes that indicate too many sleepless nights. He gazes at us through the glass as if evaluating whether to invite us in or not and rubs a hand across his jaw. I can almost hear the sandpaper rasp of his two-day-old beard.

"Still trying to ruin my life, eh, Ross?" he asks bitterly, finally unlocking the door. As he speaks the words he looks embarrassed that they have come from his own lips. "Sorry, I've been working late. Or early, I guess. I don't know anymore. Come on in."

We follow him through the office lobby to a warren of hallways and smaller rooms. Karge's own office is all the way in back, in one corner of the courthouse. It is as austere as the man himself except for the stacks of notebooks and folders on his desk. There's an American flag and a Wyoming flag, and not much else but a picture of a young Bradley Karge with his mother, who I was told died of breast cancer a decade earlier. The windows face the south and west. I look out past his desk and can see the icy twelve-thousand-foot summits of Medicine Bow Peak and Old Main just forty miles distant. The sun is just starting its arcing descent toward them.

McGee collapses in a chair. Karge doesn't ask him if he's all right. He doesn't offer him a drink. I don't say anything either, but that is only because I know better. I resent that Karge acts unaware of McGee's condition, though, and find myself beginning to dislike the man.

McGee says, "Nathan...this is Agent Burns...with DCI....He's the one...been looking into Kate Danning."

Automatically, I start to step forward to shake the County Attorney's hand, but stop and return to my position by the door when the man merely nods at me.

"Your reputation precedes you, Agent."

I can't tell what he means by that, so I say nothing. From the look he gives me I have a feeling that Karge is not one of those people in law enforcement that thinks I have done the state a favor by shooting three bangers. Besides, it wouldn't be good politics for a man with national ambitions to become friendly with someone who was involved in the disputed deaths of three minority citizens.

"Well, Nathan...our lad here...he has some problems...with the coroner's findings."

Karge leans back in the chair behind his desk and raises one hand to the edge of his nose, which he pinches with his thumb and forefingers as he shuts his eyes. From my experience in reading body language it is apparent he's trying to have patience with an unimportant and disagreeable topic. When he opens them he says to us both, "I heard that you talked to Dr. Gustavson. He said you made a reference to the Kimberly Lee case. I want you to know that I don't appreciate you looking into a case that doesn't involve you or your office, except possibly Mr. McGee as a legal advisor."

McGee is diplomatic. "This is about Kate Danning.... Agent Burns found some...inconsistent injuries....Injuries that don't appear...to have come from a fall...but happened before she died....And he found a weapon up there...on top of the cliff....It's got some blood and hair on it...which might be Kate Danning's...the results aren't in yet." He pauses for several breaths, then says, "I'm sorry, Nathan."

The County Attorney drops his hand and stares at me. After a long while he asks softly, "What kind of weapon?"

"A bottle, Mr. Karge. A whiskey bottle," I answer. I don't mention that I know it is Danning's blood, or at least her blood type, or that Brad's prints are on the bottle. I am afraid that if I tell him that he will never let us talk to his son.

Karge shuts his eyes again, then opens them and continues staring at me. They are red-rimmed and weary and the black smudges beneath seem to have grown twice as dark and heavy in the last few minutes. "Why would you think Brad would hurt her? She was his girlfriend. He'd even introduced her to me. That was very unusual for him, and we haven't been getting along too well lately."

I feel some sympathy for him. He is a man who has devoted his life to the law, at least until he decided to pursue a career in politics. And now his ambitions could be ruined by his son, just as my father's ambitions to become a general were spoiled when Roberto was arrested and convicted. How painful it must be to watch your son self-destruct and at the same time ruin your own career as well.

"I don't know yet. There were others up there too. A couple of locals named Billy Heller and Chris Braddock," I say to soften the impact and give him hope that his son is not the only suspect.

"That's right. Brad told me there were others up there that night."

I ask, "Did he tell you who they were? I'm not sure if the list of names in the sheriff's report is complete." I'm wondering about Lynn and if she'd told me the truth about leaving early.

"You'll have to ask him, Agent. I can't recall and I haven't even seen the report. I've been rather busy."

I think that is a strange answer. I remember Sheriff Willis telling me that Karge had borrowed and read the report. But with the campaign and the Lee trial it's understandable that he would have a lapse in memory.

"So what are you going to do now, Agent Burns? Have you talked to my son already?"

"No, he won't talk to me. I was hoping that you could help."

Karge looks at me sharply, then at McGee. "You're asking me to advise my son to talk to you, when you want to implicate him in a murder?"

McGee answers before I can. "There's a reason, Nathan.... A reason Agent Burns is asking.... Maybe Brad was involved...and maybe he wasn't.... But Burns found a few things...that may be possible links...to the Lee killing.... The exculpatory kind."

Karge's face turns red, his tragic composure slipping, and he explodes. "That's ridiculous, Ross. What the hell are you trying to do? Is this some kind of political crap? Trying to keep me out of the governor's race?"

McGee stays calm, evidently having expected this sort of reaction. "Look, Nathan...we've known each other...a lot of years...I think you know I'm a straight shooter.... Now do you want to hear...what Burns—"

But Karge isn't listening. He turns to me. "And who do you think you are? I know all about you, young man, and I know you have no credibility at all! You kill three men in cold blood, then come here to implicate my son and destroy my career?"

I feel myself getting hot, but I hold up my hands and step toward his desk. I want to explain that I hate politics, that I simply investigate and act on my findings, but both pity and anger trip the words on my tongue. Before I can say much, Karge stands up abruptly and slaps his palms on the desk, leaning forward. He shouts at me, "Get out of my office!"

And that's what I do. I leave without a word. I go out to the courthouse steps, where I wait for McGee in the sunlight and breathe slow and deep to let the anger out.

It is just ten minutes later that McGee comes out, shaking his head and leaning hard on his cane. He looks like the inevitable coronary could come any minute. Karge's rage has burned off the last of his energy. It's the second time I see him unscrew the eagle's head and take a pull from the hidden flask. A good portion of the whiskey runs down his beard and onto his already stained tie. Sagging down onto the low sandstone wall, he ignores me for a few minutes while he struggles to catch his breath.

I finally say, "I can't say I feel all that sorry for that guy right now."

"Come on, lad . . . how would you feel . . . if you learned your son . . . was being investigated for murder . . . and the case that's the fucking pinnacle . . . of your career may be . . . a bunch of horseshit. . . . Goddamn, have a little sympathy."

I think about repeating McGee's often-quoted phrase about exactly where in the dictionary sympathy can be found, but say nothing.

"I told him . . . if he didn't get the boy to talk . . . you're going to get a warrant. . . . Then it's a matter . . . of public record. . . . The media and all that."

"So he'll get Brad to talk to me?"

"He's going to go . . . get him . . . and bring him . . . to the hotel."

"Don't you think it's interesting, McGee, that by doing so he's saying his career's more important than the potential consequences to his son?"

"Or maybe he's certain...his son will be vindicated....
Maybe he just wants...to do the right thing."

"I don't think his son's going to convince us of his innocence."

"Nor do I, lad...nor do I," McGee says sadly.

SIXTEEN

AN HOUR LATER we are still waiting back at McGee's small suite at the Holiday Inn. Ross has chosen to conduct the interview in his room so that Oso cannot terrorize either of the Karges. We had argued briefly about that—I have found in the past that Oso is useful in keeping people honest. There is something about his size and yellow eyes and teeth that brings out the truth. McGee thought it would be unnecessarily coercive. But then he has never met Brad Karge and doesn't know the trouble I expect to have in getting answers from him.

While we wait I make notes on my laptop computer, then check the batteries on the microcassette recorder. I have heard about too many times where the batteries failed during an interrogation, losing that part of the interview. If a case like that ever goes to court, the defense attorney will accuse the officer of intentionally discarding it and argue to the jury that it contained evidence that would have exonerated his client.

Finally there is a knock at the door. McGee sits up on the bed and pulls off the oxygen mask he has been wearing. We haven't spoken much during our wait, as I think he hates having me see him sick and vulnerable like this. Out of the deep affection and respect I feel for him, I scarcely look his way.

After giving McGee a moment to catch his wind, I open the door and wave Bradley and Nathan Karge into the room.

Brad's face looks sullen beneath the tangle of blond dreadlocks. He tugs at the sparse goatee on his chin and glares at me. A tight tank top shows off his sun-bronzed skin and lean, youthful muscles. Other than that, he wears baggy shorts and leather sandals.

Behind him, Nathan Karge's face is neutral. He doesn't even look my way as he introduces his son. He simply says, "This is Brad," and walks to the bar sink to pour himself a glass of water.

I ask Brad if he wants anything to drink.

"Fuck that," he says.

"All right then. Sit down if you want," I say, indicating the other chair at the small table. "I'm going to turn on this recorder. This is Special Agent Antonio Burns of the Wyoming Division of Criminal Investigation. Today is September 17, the year two thousand, at about four o'clock in the afternoon. I'm in Deputy Attorney General Ross McGee's hotel suite at the Holiday Inn in Laramie, Wyoming. Also present are Ross McGee, Nathan Karge, and Bradley Karge. Now, Brad, I'd like to ask you some questions regarding the fatal climbing fall suffered by Kate Danning. But first I want to advise you of your legal rights—"

Nathan Karge spins away from the bar and says, "What is this? What are you reading him his rights for? Is he in custody?"

"No, Mr. Karge. I'm simply doing it as a precaution. There are three law enforcement officers in the room, including yourself who brought him here, and I do this as a matter of practice even in consensual interviews such as this."

While Karge thinks about that, McGee speaks up. "We all know he's not . . . in custody, Nathan . . . but let's entertain Agent Burns." He intends it to sound like a reprimand but I know it is not sincere.

"I don't give a fuck anyway. I didn't do anything," Brad says.

I explain his rights to him and at first am only able to get him to grunt noncommittally when I ask if he understands his rights. With some coaxing I get him to answer "Yeah" to each of the rights I state. Out of the corner of my eye I see the County Attorney shaking his head, angry.

I begin by asking Brad about how he met Kate, and what the nature of their relationship was. Brad states that they met when he was climbing in the Tetons and that they started dating right away. He admits that they were intimate on the first night they met. He perks up a little as he talks about that, and looks directly at his father when answering. I glance at Nathan Karge, trying to guess at why the son seems to be taking such pleasure at saying this in front of his father. His white face is streaked with red splotches beneath the tired eyes.

After ten minutes or so of outlining the nature of Brad

and Kate's relationship, I move on to what they were doing the night she died.

"We partied up there sometimes. There's a cave. It's where we kick in the summer."

"Who glued the bolts to the rock?"

Brad smirks. "You found those, huh? I don't know who put them there. Probably Billy. Dude's got a sick sense of humor," he says admiringly.

"Who was up there that night?"

"Me, Kate, Chris, Billy, some other chicks."

"Who were the other girls?"

Brad appears to think about it for a while. "Cindy. Sierra." Then, after a pause, "And Lynn. You know Lynn, right?" He smirks again.

"Can you tell me their last names?"

"Cindy Topper. Sierra . . . , I don't know. Lynn White."

"Did everyone get there at the same time?"

"Naw, dude. Me, Billy, Chris, and Kate were up there early. We'd been climbing around there all day. The other chicks came up after dark and jugged up a rope we left for them. They left early too, before Kate fell."

"What were you doing?"

"Drinking. Smoking some pot." Brad again looks at his dad, who turns away, back to the bar.

"Was anyone taking any other drugs?"

"Don't think so. You know, I don't remember."

"Did you have sex with Kate up there, during this party?"

"Yeah. Me and Billy both did." He is looking at his dad again. I wonder if the County Attorney knew this embarrassing fact—if this was why he asked the coroner not to do a rape kit on Kate Danning's corpse.

"Both of you?" What had Billy brought all these kids up

there for? I remember Lynn calling him the King of Vedauwoo, and Deputies Jones and Knight telling me how those kids worshipped him. At Vedauwoo, no one could touch him. Apparently they were all his supplicants.

The father turns around to say something, then stops and goes back to the bar. The red splotches on his face are darker, the skin around them whiter.

"Where were the others while this was going on?"

"They were around, you know. Hanging out."

"Did anyone leave before she fell?"

"Like I already said, the girls did. First Cindy and Sierra. Then Lynn. She was a little pissed, if you know what I mean."

"Do you know what time Cindy and Sierra left?"

"No, dude. I was wasted. I wasn't wearing a watch."

"Can you even guess?"

"It was night. It was fucking dark."

"How long after they left did Lynn leave?"

"Don't know. Ask Billy." His grin is almost sly when he says it. God, I think. Had Lynn been up there when Kate fell or was pushed?

"How did everyone get down?"

"We rapped off, man. There's a pretty easy climb off the back side but I won't do that when I'm shit-faced."

I think about that for a minute. That means after Kate was smashed on the boulders at the bottom of the cliff, they rappelled down to almost on top of her. And someone pulled the rope and coiled it while standing over the body. To me that indicated no one was too upset with her death— this was quite a cavalier group of friends.

"So only you, Billy, and Chris were there when Kate fell?"

"S'right." He is watching his father again. And I see that Karge is staring back at his son.

"Where were each of you when she fell?"

"In the cave. We had a fire going, I had a bottle. Billy and Chris had some beer. Billy doesn't touch the hard stuff, so Chris won't either."

"What was Kate doing?"

"She was outside the cave, on the ledge. Dancing or something."

"Did you have any music?"

"No, she was dancing to the tunes in her head, I guess."

"How did she fall?"

"Don't know. None of us saw it. We just looked over and she was gone. When we couldn't find her, we rapped down the ropes. There she was, at the bottom. We went into town and I called the cops. That's it."

I look at McGee before asking the next questions. McGee has been sitting on the bed, leaning with bearded chin on his cane in his usual gargoyle pose with his eyes closed. Now I see a flicker of blue beneath his shaggy white eyebrows when he opens them to determine the reason for my pause. Then he gives me an almost imperceptible nod.

"Why'd you hit her with the bottle, Brad?"

"I never hit—"

Karge surges forward from the bar, toward me. "That's it! He said he didn't hit her with the bottle. That's it! He doesn't have to answer those sorts of questions anymore! Let's go, Brad."

I don't move and ignore Karge's interruption. "Your fingerprints are on the bottle, Brad. That bottle has her blood and hair on it. Why did you hit her?"

Karge is shouting, now at McGee, as he tugs on his

son's arm and pulls him up out of his chair, "This is entrapment, McGee! No one ever said anything about any prints! This is a witch-hunt!"

McGee speaks for the first time since I started asking questions. "Let him answer the question, Nathan. This is a homicide investigation."

But Karge has the hotel door open and is trying to drag his son out through it. Brad jerks his arm from his father's grasp, turns to me and gives one final smirk, then walks out the door. Nathan is yelling, "This is not a homicide! It was an accident! What this is is politics, a political persecution, and I'll have you both out on the street! Go to hell, McGee!"

I can't help myself. I say, "You're a long ways from the governor's office right now, Mr. Karge," as the County Attorney storms down the hallway.

"What now?" I ask McGee as I snap off the tape recorder. "I didn't even get to ask him about the ligature marks and the connections to Kimberly Lee. I was looking forward to springing that."

I expect McGee to be wound up, but he just looks wearier and more haggard than ever. Even though he has barely moved in the last ninety minutes, he is almost gasping without the oxygen bottle. "I can either try to speak... with Nathan again in... the hope of getting some cooperation"—he sees me shaking my head at him—"or we can go the other route... play hardball, get warrants."

I nod. "We need to do something soon, Ross. That sentencing is just days away now. And I don't think I have enough to pull off an arrest warrant yet. All I've got is a dead girl who the coroner says fell, a bottle and some prints, but there's no DNA match yet with the blood and hair to Kate Danning. And I need some sort of a motive to explain to a judge, to tie it all together."

McGee doesn't want to or can't talk much anymore. "Keep digging," he tells me. "Fast. Quietly."

Back in my own room I make notes on the laptop about the interview with Brad Karge and a list of the things I need to do while awaiting the DNA results on the bottle's blood and hair. The first order of business is to talk to Chris Braddock and Sierra Calloway. And at some point I need to confront Billy Heller and see what he has to say. I will take Jones or another cop with me as additional muscle for that. Finding Chris is the most important. Unlike Sierra, he was still up at Vedauwoo when Kate Danning fell. Hopefully he won't be quite as hostile as Heller.

In the stack of printouts Kristi gave me I find his number and address. I think about driving over there but decide to call first. The phone is answered on the eighth ring by an adult voice that could be his father's. He's not there, the man tells me. As far as he knows, Chris is out, maybe at his friend Billy's. I am not ready to go out there yet, not until I learn more and have some backup with me. I leave my name and my office's phone number with the man.

Next I try calling the climbing shop, which is the only number I have for Lynn. The phone rings and rings until I realize it is already Sunday evening, that the shop is closed. In a way I am relieved—I'm not looking forward to talking with her after that drunken night. But I need to talk to her soon. I need to know if she was lying about having left early.

I decide to concentrate on finding Sierra Calloway. Again using the phone book, I begin to call all the hotels and motels in Laramie, identifying myself and asking if she's an employee there. I don't have much luck until my last call, when the only number I need is a "0." The operator at the Holiday Inn transfers me to the on-duty manager, who checks the books and tells me that Sierra Calloway has worked there for the past few weeks, but that all the maids have long since gone home for the day. He doesn't have a phone number for her and doesn't think she has a phone, but he describes her for me. I tell him not to bother leaving her a message—I'll find her in the morning.

When I put down the phone I notice for the first time that the message light is blinking. Following the hotel's instructions, I retrieve the message. It's Lynn. Her voice is soft and slurred; she sounds stoned. She asks where I've been, how come I haven't been by the shop to see her. She hangs up after telling me to call her soon but I guess is too high to remember I don't have her number or address. It is not in the phone book—I will have to ask Kristi to call the phone company or the department of motor vehicles in order to get it.

Frustrated, I check the voice-mail system at my office up in Cody. Clayton Wells, my lawyer, has called again telling me we should talk settlement before Thursday's hearing. Rebecca too has called. She is all business and addresses me as Agent Burns, not Anton. She says she has some follow-up questions she would like to discuss. The fact that she called my office in Cody instead of reaching me at the hotel makes me think perhaps she is not interested in seeing me face-to-face again. Because of that, the drunken episode with Lynn, and the fact that I have really learned little else but that the fingerprints on the bottle were Brad's, I'm reluctant to return her call.

At a loss, I scratch Oso's head while I pick up the old is-sue of *Rock and Ice* that Lynn left in my room. Feeling some-what vain but needing a confidence boost, I reread the article about the climb my friends and I did in Alaska and study the pictures.

Flipping through the magazine, one photo obviously from an even older era catches my eye. It is of a climber ascending a crack while wearing dated clothes—a rugby shirt and painter's pants. The lean body and face are familiar, but younger. The short article that accompanies the photo is titled "Where Are They Now?" And it's about Nathan Karge.

For some reason I am not all that surprised to find out Karge had once been a climber himself and a good one. I had noticed the muscles of his forearms and the scars on his hands. Apparently he pioneered some early routes in Vedauwoo and at Devil's Tower. There is an impressive list of first ascents he made. The article talks about that and then how he went off to law school, purposely ending his climbing career. The subtext of the article is snidely clear. Traitor. Nathan Karge gave up climbing to become an attor-ney and a square. It also mentions that his teenage son is showing signs of picking up the torch and carrying on the climbing tradition.

Reading it twice, I begin to understand what some of the tension is between father and son, other than the son's rebel-lious use of drugs and extremely casual sex. Nathan Karge gave up climbing to become a provider and a better role model for Brad. He gave up passion for money and security. But if my mother's theory is true and such things are genetic, the son in-herited *la llamada del salvaje,* the Rat, or whatever else it is called. And his son turned to the warped and messianic Billy

Heller as a father figure he better identified with, one who represented everything Nathan Karge gave up.

I read the article a final time, not knowing what to make of the fact that the County Attorney himself used to be a climber. I wonder if there's a Rat still rattling around in his rib cage.

SEVENTEEN

AFTER MY DAILY training I sit on the hotel bed, freshly dressed, holding a toothbrush in my hand. I am staring at the television as a Monday morning national news show gives an update on the long-awaited sentencing of the Lee defendants. Video clips from last week are played of the chanting throngs outside the courthouse. The anchor's voice sounds excited, as if tickled by blood lust, when he says that prosecutor Nathan Karge will seek the death penalty during the sentencing arguments to the jury on Friday.

A knock on the door causes Oso to jerk up his head, preparing to give his usual bellow. I hold up a hand with my palm out to silence the beast and then go to the door in my bare feet.

Through the peephole I see a cleaning cart and a brown-haired girl wearing a loose gray work blouse and a pair of baggy shorts so large they resemble a khaki skirt. She matches the description the hotel manager gave me. I open the door and tell her to come on in and not to mind the dog—he's harmless and we'll be leaving soon.

The maid approaches Oso with an unusual lack of caution. She pats his thick head as he sniffs at her hand.

"Hey there. Aren't you a big fella."

I sit on the unmade bed and begin pulling on my sandals, keeping my eyes on the TV. The maid giggles as Oso slowly rolls over on his side and offers his belly to scratch. I see it out of the corner of my vision and snort to myself.

"Some tough dog he is," I say, "letting someone he just met have their way with him."

"Dogs dig me. I've got seven myself."

"Seven dogs? That sounds like a busy house."

"It's a friggin' nightmare," she says, laughing. "What's worse is when I get them all in the car with me. They tear around like cats, chasing each another. Doing crazy stuff like humping in the backseat and hanging out the windows. It's so bad that I hate to drive with them anymore. But I'm a sucker for dogs. Every time I find a homeless one I take it in. Plus the animal shelter knows what a sucker I am—sometimes when they can't find a home for a nice one they use me as a sort of foster home till some other sucker comes along. But by that time I've fallen in love and won't give 'em up. Seven dogs. God, if my landlord knew, I'd be out on my ass."

She squats with ease as she rubs Oso's tummy. The girl's appearance is something like a cross between a ballerina and a junkie. Her bare shoulders and arms are thin and limber like the branches on a young tree. The khaki shorts balloon out over her equally thin legs. Slightly swollen and lined not by age but by hard use, her face looks as if it belongs on a heavier body. When she puts her head down, close to the dog's, her hair parts across the back of her neck. A tattoo of a grinning skull with a halo of roses is revealed there.

"I like the tattoo," I tell her.

She looks up at me, her green eyes sparkling mischievously. "Oh yeah? That one's old, couple of years." She stops scratching and stands up, much to Oso's disappointment. "I got a new one just a few weeks ago. Check it out." She hoists one leg of the baggy shorts high on her hip and turns to the side, displaying her entire bony thigh.

The tattoo starts just below the bottom line of her white underwear where its thin band comes around her side. The top of the tattoo is an outstretched hand reaching upward, toward the strap of white cotton. The hand rises from the depiction of a long female climber's body, the lower foot of which is nearly down to her knee.

"Wow," I remark. "That's one of the biggest tattoos I've ever seen. At least on a girl. You a rock climber?"

"Sometimes, when I get around to it." She drops the leg of her shorts and squats again to Oso. "You look like you climb." She nods her head toward my backpack in the corner. It has a rope lashed to its top.

"Like you, I guess. When I get around to it."

"What are you doing in Laramie? Climbing at the 'Voo?"

"A little. I'm here for the trial, like everyone else."

"Oh yeah?" She asks, "You one of those 'investigative reporters'?"

"Something like that."

The maid stands up. "I should get to cleaning. Got to get through a full hotel again today." She nudges Oso's belly with a tennis shoe worn sockless. "You need anything besides the cleaning? Anything special?" She stands before me and puts her hands on her cocked hips where a braided belt holds the oversize shorts low on her waist.

I look at her for a few seconds. "I think I know what you mean," I tell her.

"You do, huh?" she asks, and giggles in a way that sounds both silly and contrived. "'Cause even a good-looking guy like you sometimes needs something special."

"How much does something special cost?"

"Depends what you want."

I reach into the back pocket of my pants and bring out my wallet. She laughs again expectantly, anticipating cash, but her laugh is abruptly cut off when I flip open the wallet and she catches sight of my badge.

"Oh shit. I didn't mean anything, I was just fooling around."

Her voice isn't girlish anymore. It sounds low and scared.

"Actually, there is something special I need. But not that."

"What?"

"You know a lot of the climbers around here?"

Her face is confused, her jaw slack and her eyes wide. She is sullen when she answers. "Yeah, I know some."

"Do you know Billy Heller, Brad Karge, Chris Braddock—those guys?"

"I've seen them around is all."

I put away my wallet and give her a long look.

"I've been looking for you, Sierra. You've been busted before, right? In Boulder?"

She nods.

"You're on probation?"

She nods again, then clenches her fists at her sides and

looks as though she might cry. I finish putting on my sandals.

"Look, I'm not out to bust you," I finally say, and then make a threat. "I don't want to take you away from your dogs. Just be straight with me and answer some questions, then that's it. Okay?"

She unballs her hands and tears begin to roll down her cheeks as my words sink in. "Oh God. Whatever you want." I motion her to the chair at the small table where she sits down primly and wipes her cheeks.

"Do you hang out with them?"

"Yeah, sometimes. Not as much as I used to, but yeah. I know them."

"Do they sell drugs to you?"

"No, I don't . . ." But then she catches my look and stops.

"What's the name of your PO?" I ask. "Or should I call the courthouse in Boulder and have them look it up?"

"Okay, yeah, they sell me stuff sometimes. They sell it to all their friends. Pot and crank, nothing heavy." She keeps her eyes on the floor. Oso rolls back onto his chest and looks at her almost sadly.

"Crank's pretty heavy," I tell her. "What sort of quantities do they sell?"

"Just little bits, just to friends. Climbers. That's all I've seen. But I hear they make the stuff. The crank, I mean. Those three, they always have a lot of it. I hear they sell bigger stuff, to real dealers in Cheyenne and Casper."

"They sell to the Sureno 13?"

She nods. "I think so. I've seen them with some of those guys."

Suddenly I'm back at that night eighteen months ago, my informant's terrified voice telling me I'd been burned, then driving out to the old ranch house on the cold, dark plain. I wonder again how I was burned—who had told the Surenos that I was an undercover police officer.

"Tell me about them. What do you know about Heller and Brad?"

She wipes at her cheeks again, takes a deep breath and lets it out. "Heller's an asshole. He's a fucking lunatic. And Brad's just like him, but, like, his sidekick. They do everything together. They make me do stuff before they'll give over. You know, like tie me up and take pictures. They hit too. That kind of shit. They do it to a lot of girls around here. Like a couple of fucking rapists, those two." Her voice is getting harder, changing from scared to angry. She looks up at me. "You know Brad's dad is the County Attorney?"

I nod.

"See, nobody messes with them. And people look up to Billy like he's a fucking god or something. Everybody worships him."

"So they're not scared of getting busted?"

"Not much. Or at least they didn't used to be. But the two of them are getting worse. Last time I saw Billy, at Kate's funeral, he was walking around saying nobody can touch him, that he owns the cops and the prosecutors."

"Do you know what he meant by that?"

"Naw. Probably just that he's got something heavy on Brad, something he can take to his daddy. Maybe about that night that Kate fell. But he always had that anyway. They're real assholes, those two. But Chris isn't that bad a guy. He's just a kid. He just hangs around with them. We used to call him Mini Me 'cause for a while he had a ponytail and dyed it black to look like Billy."

"How about Kate Danning? How well did you know her?"

"Not real well. She was Brad's special piece of ass, but I think Billy was nailing her too. He's like that. Like he wants to own every young thing in town. And the younger the better. He needs to know he's the boss."

"How about Cindy and Lynn?"

"Cindy's like me, only she's got folks who give her money, so she don't got to do the things I do. Lynn is Billy's special piece. He's like the King of the Fairies in that play I read in school, *Midsummer Night's Dream.* He's that guy Oberon, and she's the queen, Titania. They both screw with each other by fucking other people. Those two deserve each other."

I listen to this without expression. I am thinking back to my night with Lynn, trying to fit the information with what I'd seen, heard, and felt. At first it doesn't wear quite right, but then in a way it does.

"So what happened up there last week, when Kate fell?"

"I dunno. I left before that happened, with Cindy. There was some bad vibes up there that night. See, Lynn was pissed 'cause Billy and Brad were getting Kate wasted. I think they were going to screw around with her, you know, the way they've done with me. It was a bad scene, so Cindy and I rapped off and split after just an hour or so."

"Did Billy or Brad have a reason to mess with Kate? Were they mad at her?"

"I heard she was getting some pressure from her parents—they'd had an intervention or something—trying to get her into Narcotics Anonymous."

I make a mental note to try to get ahold of a counselor at NA. A vague recollection of the closing arguments in Kimberly Lee's trial comes to me—it was her NA counselor, also her boyfriend, who found her. He had been worried about her because she was thinking of talking to the police about where she'd gotten her drugs.

"Okay, Sierra, thanks for talking to me. I may want to talk to you again."

"That's it? You're letting me go?"

"I told you I'd be straight with you, so yeah, that's it."

She starts to cry again and I pass her the box of Kleenex from the bedside table. Sierra blows her nose loudly and stands up. She straightens her blouse.

"If they find out I told you that stuff they'll come after me."

"Then let's both of us forget we talked, okay? And my room's clean enough; just leave me some fresh towels. Get some new friends and a new job, Sierra. You won't even outlive your dogs if you keep this up."

I pick up the phone and dial the number to McGee's room. I let the phone ring until the hotel's answering service comes on before hanging up. Then I try the climbing shop where Lynn works, and a recorded message tells me the store doesn't open until ten. Again there is no answer at the phone number I have for Chris Braddock.

Finally I reach a real human being when I call Kristi at DCI.

"Did you get the message I left you?"

"The one where you proposed?" she asks. "Wait a minute, I guess that was a dream, buddy. Yeah, I got your message. And I found the stuff you needed."

"You're fantastic, Kristi. Maybe I should propose."

"Not if you're going to keep asking me to get young ladies' addresses and phone numbers. Anyway, here it is."

After I copied the information down, Kristi says, "You

know, buddy, if you're thinking about trying to get a date, I'd skip it. This Lynn White is a messed-up chick."

"What do you mean?"

"I ran a check on her—just two years ago she's listed as a reporting party and victim of a sexual assault. From what I can tell, she went to the hospital in Laramie and reported that a guy raped her. William Heller, Jr., who's one of those guys on the printouts I gave you a few weeks ago. Anyway, she made a complaint, then withdrew it just hours later. So this Heller was never picked up or charged. Sounds like damaged goods, buddy. You'd be better off with me."

Not knowing what else to do and needing to kill some time, I snap the short leash to Oso's collar, tell him to heel, and we walk out past the maid's cart and the lonely swimming pool to the truck.

Right at nine o'clock I walk into the courthouse and badge my way past the security guards at the metal detector. The whole place, open for business, seems eerily normal after last week's circus. There are no reporters and no protesters. Instead there are just regular people going about their business. Lawyers, defendants, clerks, and local citizens getting their driver's licenses and plates.

I speak to one of the security guards, asking where juvenile court is being held. The guard gives me directions to a courtroom on the floor above. I want to see Dominic Torres's little brother get arraigned, see if the shrinks have found him fit to be formally charged. A part of me is furious at all the Surenos and the families that are suing me, and another part of me feels sorry for this boy who is so full of drugs and rage. And I am thinking that if he is deemed fit, when he's assigned a lawyer, I'll talk to the lawyer about getting the charges dropped if the kid's willing to talk about Heller's connection with the Surenos.

Up the wide stairs and into another hall, near Nathan Karge's office and the sheriff's holding cells for prisoners who must appear in court, I find the courtroom the guard had described. I push through the two sets of double doors that lead into it. The doors are padded along the edges and make a sharp *shhh* as they swing closed behind me. The first thing I see inside the chamber is the back of Rebecca Hersh's head. Those long, tangled auburn curls are hard to miss. Her face appears over one shoulder at the sound of the doors whisking shut. She smiles at me.

I am embarrassed that I have dressed only in a T-shirt and jeans. And the T-shirt is not even a new one—it's a little ragged around the neck and reads "Exum Mountaineering" on one side of the chest and again in big letters on the back. I know I must look unprofessional. Then I see her glance at where the short sleeves of the shirt are stretched tight over my arms. I feel better about it, but in a way even more foolish. Vain. Like a meathead jock, and it is easy to see that's not her type. I briefly wonder how a simple glance and smile from her can make me feel so self-conscious. It seems like a very long time since I cared.

It is the hissings and murmurings that make me look away from her smile. I notice for the first time that there are other people in the room. And quite a lot of people for such a small courtroom. They are all looking at me and whispering to one another. The impression isn't welcoming. Many of the younger ones, in their late teens or early twenties, wear their dark shirts buttoned to the neck over white T-shirts. Some wear baseball caps backward and others wear tight-fitting ski hats stretched low on their foreheads, almost covering their eyes. Those ski hats are referred to by cops as "condoms for dickheads." They are an essential part of a gangbanger's wardrobe. All the spectators, with the exception of Rebecca, are Hispanic or mixed. They are undoubtedly the family and gang relations of the Torres boy who tried to brain me with the pipe.

There is no judge on the bench and no clerks or deputies in the room. The prisoner hasn't yet been brought in from the holding cell after his mental health evaluation at the state hospital in Evanston. I think about leaving and am sure it would be the wise option, but then I sit on the pew in back of Rebecca's instead. Twenty or thirty pairs of eyes remain on me, and colorful expressions are muttered in Spanish, like *puta* and *maricon*.

"What are you doing here?" I ask her.

"I'm sick and tired of doing 'local color' and interviewing people about what they think of the Lee case. So I thought I'd just hang around the courthouse and hope for some excitement." She smiles again at me, then says, "And I've been thinking about how to do an article about you and your hearing on Thursday. I'm just not sure of my angle. It could be on gangs in Wyoming...or maybe civil rights enforcement in Wyoming. What do you think?"

I am disconcerted by her smile. Just last night, when I got her phone message, she seemed impossibly distant. Instead of answering her question, I wonder about what she thinks of me. Then out of the corner of my eye I see a girl, shirt buttoned to the collar and wearing the de rigueur cap pulled low, stand up and walk toward me. Several of the youths around her snicker in anticipation. I turn to watch her approach, my face neutral.

She walks right up to me and hesitates. Then she spits in my face. I see it coming but can't move in time to stop it. Rebecca gasps in front of me. I slowly rise to my feet and wipe the spittle from my cheek. The girl raises her hand to slap me. I catch her wrist in midair. Gently, still holding her wrist, I turn her around and push her hand up behind her back in a come-along. I nudge her to the aisle and toward the doors that lead into the hallway.

The spectators in the courtroom jump to their feet. The hissing and expletives begin again after a moment's silence, louder now. They are loudest of all from the girl I hold. Just as we reach the swinging doors, the girl's free hand shoots back and grasps at my crotch. I catch this wrist too and pin both her hands behind her as I push her through the doors chest-first. Her friends follow and spill into the hallway behind us. I push her cautiously and quickly, feeling as if I'm walking on some narrow ledge.

The door ahead of us in the hallway reads "Sheriff's Office—Holding Cells. Authorized Personnel Only." The girl sees where we are headed and begins to swing her body back and forth as she curses. She kicks at my legs.

The twin doors to the Sheriff's Office are single sheets of bulletproof glass divided in the center. Through the glass I see two uniformed officers studying a newspaper on the counter, their backs to the door, unaware of the tension in the hallway. I urge the door with my foot but it barely moves. It's locked. There is a button on the wall on the opposite side of the door that operates the electronic lock. The crowd is encircling me from behind. Their curses are coming faster and louder.

I kick the glass door with the toe of my sandal. It makes the glass slam against the electronic lock but it doesn't move more than a fraction of an inch. Inside, the two uniformed deputies whip their heads around. Bender and Knight. Shit. They stare at the girl's face that's pressed against the glass and my face behind her as I mouth the words "Open it."

Bender's eyes move from mine to the crowd gathering behind me. I turn myself and look at the wall of young gang members and older family members that's forming in the hallway. Then I look again through the glass and watch as Knight moves toward the door, his hand on his baton. Bender says something sharp to the rookie and Knight freezes. His eyes stay on mine until he turns away from me, away from the button and the door. Then Bender also turns and they both lean on the counter to study the paper just like before.

After a few seconds, Bender shoots me a look over his shoulder, grins, and then goes back to the paper, shaking his head.

The girl stops trying to pull her wrists from my grasp. She stops too with her Spanish obscenities. In realization and delight she calls to the crowd gathered behind us, "They're not helping him! They're not helping him!"

I feel as if I'm in a dream where everything is going wrong, where everyone is not what they seem, and where everybody is against me. The bangers close in until I can feel the vibrations of their angry curses on my back. I beat the glass door with the forefoot of my sandal, rocking it in its steel frame. The glass rebounds back and forth in its limited range of motion. Small chips of plaster snow down from the ceiling. A spray of profanities and spittle from the crowd in the hall raises the hair on the back of my exposed neck. I begin to shout, "Open it! Goddamn it, open it!" The deputies inside don't turn. Then I feel the first blow to my skull.

It rocks my head sideways and I taste iron as I bite my tongue. But I keep my hands locked on the girl's wrists. She is shrieking now, incomprehensible words, almost keening in exultation. I pull her back from the glass a few inches. I raise my whole leg, folding it, knee high against my chest and to the side of the girl. I slam my heel against the glass. It crashes again against the lock but doesn't yield. More plaster, bigger pieces, come off the ceiling. I feel a hand grasping at the small of my back and the cold touch of my own pistol as it slides out from its hidden holster. A second blow blasts at my skull. Then a third.

The last thing I hear as my knees give way and I collapse to the ground is what sounds like the voice of Rebecca Hersh, panicked and screaming, "Help him!"

EIGHTEEN

I FEEL AS IF I am rising up out of a dark pit. It's like when I wormed my way into the mouth of that chimney from the cave below, where Jones had grumbled and watched. In the distance I think I hear Oso barking rhythmically, the way he does when he trees a squirrel. I stem with my knees and elbows braced against the cold stone, its irregularities cutting into my back and ribs, and pull myself higher and higher toward the sunlit chamber above as my senses begin to return. And then, before I even open my eyes, I know where I am. Oso's barks turn into the amplified beats of my pulse. I can smell the antiseptic odor in the air. I can feel the touch of thin, worn cotton on my skin. Then the hurting starts and it feels as if the chimney is full of sharp-edged granite, cutting my flesh.

The sound of a turning page comes through the mist of pain that is on the verge of dropping me back into the dark chimney. I wait a little while before attempting to open my eyes. When I finally do, the fluorescent light stabs into my brain, causing me to quickly close them. A few minutes later I try again and it's not quite as bad. I move my head when I hear another turning page, and see Rebecca Hersh in a chair in the corner.

She comes slowly into focus. A ray of light from the window cuts across the room and illuminates her pale skin. Her eyes are puffy and red and there is a slight blue bruise on her forehead where her thick hair is swept back. She looks up and sees me staring.

"Anton..." is all she says at first. She comes up out of her chair, letting the magazine slide to the linoleum floor, and kneels beside the bed. Both of her hands reach up under the sheet and I feel their warmth on one of my own. After studying my face for a few moments, she says, "How do you feel?"

"Probably about how I look," I manage. My lips and face feel swollen. I am tempted to tease her, to ask her why reporters always pose that question when they talk to accident victims, bereaved widows, and newly orphaned children, because the answer is so obvious. Bad. Very bad. But I don't ask. The effort of getting the words together would be too great.

Instead I try to recall how I got into this hospital bed and how my body became so battered. A vague recollection of a shouting, kicking mass of angry people is as far as I can get. I remember though what she had said to me in the courtroom—that she was looking for some excitement— and almost smile. "What happened?"

An angry look replaces the concern in her eyes. "Those bastards," she says. "Those cops. They saw what was happening and didn't do anything. When they did, they sauntered out of that office. They sauntered! They only came when I started screaming!"

I want to know the details but there is a wind roaring at me, its noise surrounding me. My vision begins to blur at the edges. I taste salt in my mouth and want to spit but can't. The roaring and blurring swirls around me like a tornado, sucking me back into the chimney. Rebecca lifts her head and I try to focus on the shining reflection of myself in her eyes.

I see her lips open. "I called Ross McGee in Cheyenne. He's coming. He's on his way."

What's he doing back in Cheyenne? I wonder as I let the wind take me and drag me back down into that black chimney. I'm falling. I don't bother to claw at the rock with my fingers and toes; the wind is too powerful and I don't have the strength to fight it.

Waking up the second time is easier. If it weren't for the throbbing in my skull and the aching along my back and legs, it would be like coming out of a deep sleep. When I open my eyes I again feel the deep stab of the fluorescent bulbs into my brain. Like before, I wince and squeeze them shut. There is a different noise than the beeps this time. It sounds like the whir of an electric motor.

"Sorry 'bout that," an unfamiliar voice says.

"QuickDraw, you waking up? You coming back to us, Anton?" It is Jones's bass. "Hey, did he just open his eyes?"

The unfamiliar voice says, "I dunno. I thought so, just when the flash went off."

I speak through swollen, dry lips. "Jefferson Jones, what the hell are you doing to me?"

Jones laughs in relief. "You are back! And ornery as ever too! Welcome back to the light, my friend."

The light isn't welcoming. I squint around the room from where I lie in the hospital bed. Jones's immense bulk hovers over me as he squeezes my arm. Another man stands beside him wearing a wrinkled shirt and jacket with a bolo tie and holding a camera. The man's face is as disheveled as his suit. Hair sprouts randomly across it in a pathetic attempt at a goatee. He looks ridiculously small and skinny next to Jones.

"This is Kevin, our crime scene tech. We were trying to get some beauty shots for your obituary, but seeing as how you're still alive, maybe we'll use 'em as evidence to nail those kids who did this to you."

Beaten up by a bunch of kids. And in the courthouse too. I'm embarrassed.

I nod at the man who looks eager to take more pictures. Then I spot a cup of water along with a pitcher next to the bed and reach for it. My ribs ache when I stretch out an arm but not enough to indicate a fracture. After I take a couple of gulps, draining the cup, I ask, "What's the damage?"

"Concussion, bruises, et cetera. Nothing broke. Wouldn't be that big a deal if you weren't such a little guy." Everyone is small compared to Jones.

"Tell me what happened. Last thing I remember I was trying to take in a girl at the courthouse—she spit in my face—as a mob formed and your pals—"

"Whoa there, easy fella," Jones says. He turns to Kevin and asks him to wait outside for a few minutes. After Kevin leaves the room, he tells me, "That guy's in tight with those rednecks. Sheriff's wife's nephew, and probably somehow related to Bender too. Incestuous bunch of crackers. Wants to be a cop, but he's too scrawny to make it through the academy. Anyway, Bender and Knight apparently broke up some mob that was beating your ass in the court hallway.

The way they tell it, three or four of those Sureno 13 punks were kicking and knuckling you, with others cheering them on. But then there's that girl reporter, a nice-looking thing by the way, who keeps telling me the two police officers wouldn't let you into the holding cells, that they just laughed as the bangers took it to you. Oh yeah, one of those kids got your gun and brained you with it. Which brings me to another bit of strangeness. It was a good thing there were no bullets, but why the fuck you carrying your piece unloaded? The state don't supply you agents with lead or something?"

"Forget that," I tell him. The gun hadn't been loaded in eighteen months. Not since Cheyenne. "I remember seeing those two clowns laughing as I went down. I'm going to burn them for that."

"Easy, cowboy. I get first shot at them. Officially. Your cute little reporter friend already's talking 'bout filing a complaint with the office. Maybe the state'll send another one of you agents down to investigate that! Anyway, Bender and Knight are saying they heard a commotion, saw you go down, then saved your ass. Bender is boasting that it's the second time in a week. And he says the reporter's full of shit."

"Where is she? She was in the hallway when I was jumped. Then I thought I saw her here earlier with a bruised face."

"She's around, but I kicked her out when we came in to take the pictures. Caught an elbow during the ruckus is all. She's acting like she's your personal watchdog now. Says she knows you through Ross McGee. She your girlfriend or something?"

"I wish. Speaking of watchdogs, where's Oso?"

Jones laughs. "We've been trying to take your Land

Cruiser to the impound lot for safekeeping. Got the keys out of your pocket. But that damned monster wouldn't let anyone near it, even when we tried to give him a Big Mac through the window. Finally that reporter girl gave it a try, and damn if he didn't let her in. I thought she was dead meat when she opened that door. I thought there'd be blood on the roof for sure. But she just started it right up and followed a marked car to the lot, even let the dog out for a piss. He wouldn't leave the truck though, hopped right back in, so we locked him in there with the cheeseburger."

"What about the Surenos who pounded on me?"

"Those boys and girls are filling all our cells, partying and laughing about giving it to you. If the public defender doesn't get some of them bonded out soon, they'll take over the place. Bender and Knight, with the help of some of those security guys, arrested the whole lot of them."

Jones calls Kevin the photographer back in to finish taking pictures. After a few of my face, they have me roll onto my front to get photographs of the bruising to my back and legs. Jones jerks loose the tie on the back of the hospital smock and whistles through his teeth when he sees the exposed skin that's turning black and blue. "You look like a piñata after the party's over," he comments. "Cute ass, though."

"Fuck you, Jones."

As Kevin is finishing up with the pictures, the door bangs open and McGee shuffles in. He is out of breath as usual. His face is set in stone and his blue eyes blaze. But he looks better than he had the day before, as if anger has burned up some of the sickness. "Goddamn it, Anton... can't you keep out of trouble?" he bellows. "You look like a bull's been tap dancing on your hide." Then he whacks Jones's ankle with his cane and huffs, "And you, what kind of town do you have here...letting those kids take advantage of one of my limp-wristed agents?"

Rebecca eases into the room behind McGee without making a sound. I quickly roll back over and pull the sheets up to my chest as she looks at me and smiles. McGee continues to rave. There is a swollen purple bruise on her forehead and her cheeks are red and flushed. Seeing her earlier hadn't been a dream. In my head I can hear her shouting for help when everyone else had turned their backs. I give her a small nod, smiling back, unable to communicate the gratitude I feel toward her with words, but hoping my eyes pass along the message.

After McGee finishes deriding the Sheriff's Office, his own agents' ineffectiveness in a fight, the citizens of southeast Wyoming, and the human population in general, Jones excuses himself from the room and takes Kevin with him. McGee and Rebecca pull both of the room's two chairs close to the bed, where McGee hesitates before lowering his bulk. Instead of sitting, McGee examines a sore spot on my cheek that has swollen up under my eye. "Looks like Nikes," he remarks. "We'll hold all their shoes as evidence...just to screw with 'em. Reminds me of a case a few years back. Four bangers opened a can of whoop-ass...on one of their friends. Someone nearly finished him off...with a kick to the head....We couldn't figure out who did the coup de grace...until we matched up the tread patterns on their boots...to the marks on the vic's face. It turned out they beat him...because he'd played a little prank on one of the others...who'd passed out drunk the night before. You see, the vic had smeared the banger's privates...with peanut butter, then called for his dog...to clean it up while he took pictures."

"Thanks for the story, Ross. Is there a point?"

"Nay, lad, just an observation. So tell me what happened to you. The sheriff told me . . . his men's version, and sweet Rebecca Hersh . . . told me another. Give me the gospel according to QuickDraw Burns."

I repeat what I can remember. McGee sits through my short narrative twisting his cane in his hands and remaining largely silent, only occasionally asking a question for clarification. He says nothing when I finish, but the blue eyes are brighter than ever. Rebecca adds how the morning had ended—with police officers and security guards dragging the gang members away as they kicked at the head and back of my prostrate form. One of them even unzipped his pants to urinate on my face, but Rebecca's shouts left him unable to make the necessary water. "That's where I got this," she says, pointing to her forehead. "When the police came in after all hell broke loose, the one who wouldn't let you in the door hit me with his elbow. I think he did it on purpose."

Bender, I think. After a pause I say to McGee, "I want them burned."

"Sure, lad. But what would we charge them with? And how would we prove it? It looks like they did . . . save your hide from worse."

"Fuck," I say.

After a few minutes of glowering at the wall and barely tolerating the pounding ache in my head and the cutting sensation that I feel across my ribs with each breath, I put that question to rest for a while.

"What were you doing in Cheyenne this morning?" I ask.

"The AG wanted to see me . . . wants you to back off this Danning thing . . . Karge has been making complaints . . . making threats. I told him to go fuck himself." I wouldn't have been surprised if McGee did so in exactly those words. No wonder he wasn't popular with the administration.

"Do you want to hear the latest on Danning?" I pointedly look from McGee, to whom the question is addressed, to Rebecca, wondering if he will ask her to leave the room.

McGee looks at her too. "Let's have it. And I want her to hear it too. She's earned the right . . . after trying to save your sorry butt. In addition, we may need some help . . . from the media on this. Otherwise everyone's urge . . . will be to bury it. But I want it understood, lass . . . that all this is off the record . . . you cannot write one word about it . . . without my permission. Do I have your word?"

She gives it, prudently not mentioning that I have told her some of it already, and McGee quickly fills her in on our concern that Kate Danning did not fall off the cliff. He summarizes the evidence for her like the veteran prosecutor he was before his diminishing health and increasing vulgarity made him no longer fit for addressing juries: the unexplained bruise to the rear of her head, the ligature mark on her neck, the bottle with what was probably her blood and hair on it, Brad Karge's fingerprints, the unproductive interview, and the admission that both Brad and Billy had sex with her that night.

I add what I learned from the hotel maid, Sierra Calloway, that morning. I don't mention my evening with Lynn. I can't bring myself to admit what I did while I was drunk, both because of Rebecca's presence in the room and the ridicule McGee would rightly subject me to for having slept with a potential witness.

"It sounds as if the weak link . . . is obviously this youth Chris. Have you talked to him?"

"No. That was number one on my to-do list before I got

jumped. And it still is number one. I'll do it as soon as I get out of here."

Rebecca hasn't said a word during our summaries. Now she asks, "What I don't understand is why. Why would those climbers push the girl off the cliff?"

I think about that. "I don't know much yet about Brad Karge, other than that he seems to be doped up most of the time. Heller though, he's a control freak. According to everyone I talk to, all those kids worship him. And he takes advantage of them, particularly the young girls, and keeps them all well supplied with crank. Maybe Kate Danning had threatened to turn him in. Or maybe he was just having fun. But we know Brad hit her with a bottle because of the fingerprints—we just need the DNA and a witness to confirm it."

McGee says, "Which brings us to Kimberly Lee again. We know she was at least an amateur climber . . . may have run around with this Heller cult. According to her boyfriend . . . the NA counselor . . . she was planning on telling the Sheriff's Office . . . where she'd gotten her drugs. Maybe the Danning girl was thinking . . . about doing the same thing. And maybe the Knapps . . . weren't Lee's dealers after all."

"Or maybe Heller's just found a new way to feed the Rat," I say.

"The what?" Rebecca asks.

I explain that Heller's getting older without ever having achieved the fame he probably deserved. His climbing skills are diminishing and he's losing his grip on the group of kids who are his supplicants. Maybe this is a new way to control them, while at the same time finding some new avenue of pursuing thrills. I can picture him enjoying the rough sex, corrupting the youths around him and the youth that had betrayed him, while as a side benefit protecting his drug-selling income. He could easily have killed Lee and set the Knapp brothers up for it. It would have been simple, especially with the County Attorney's son as his accomplice. The locals would have eagerly ignored them as suspects.

"But those climbers couldn't have killed Kimberly Lee," Rebecca says. "Remember, the Knapps confessed. And what about the evidence found in their pickup? What about the pipe in her house with one of the Knapps' fingerprints on it?"

I look at McGee. "Anyone could have dropped the glove and skin in the pickup. Who did they confess to? Who found the pipe?"

McGee says, "Sheriff Willis. Sergeant Bender."

I don't say a word and McGee nods at me that I don't need to. We are in agreement that the Sheriff's Office is suspect. The fact that there was a brief gunfight with the police when the Knapps' door was first knocked on at two in the morning could simply be the brothers' standard procedure, considering their pseudo-militaristic leanings and the liquor and drugs they had been consuming.

"Nathan Karge's campaign manager and his nephew," Rebecca says to herself, gently touching the bruise on her forehead. "But I can't believe Nathan Karge would go this far to protect his son. My God, the man's going to be the next governor!"

"The sentencing's on Friday morning," McGee reminds us. I have to struggle to remember that today is Monday.

They both leave to get dinner on their way back to the hotel soon after a nurse brings me a tasteless hunk of chicken with green beans and Jell-O. The doctor stops by to check the size of my pupils. He tells me that although I am basically just bruised, I have a concussion and they want to keep me in bed and awake to prevent me from slipping into a coma. I ask him what will be done if I do go into a coma. He shrugs and gives a long explanation that amounts to: not much.

Despite the doctor's order that I remain overnight for observation, I resolve not to spend another minute there. Both the rubbery meal and the thought of Oso alone and worried in the truck gets me to my feet. I wince when I stand, and want to wince even as I breathe, but am able to slip the hospital gown off my shoulders. At the foot of the bed I find a plastic bag with my clothes neatly folded inside. The shirt smells vaguely of floor polish and shoe leather. I am able to slowly pull on my jeans and T-shirt but leave the sandals unstrapped. It hurts too much when I bend over.

In the hallway outside there is a uniformed deputy reading the sports section. I'm relieved not to recognize him. He is large-boned but frail—too old for patrol duty. His face looks more like that of a retired farmer than a cop, with close-set, friendly eyes and an upturn to his lips that appears permanent. The fingers that grip the paper are nicotine-stained. An enormous and ancient revolver is strapped to his gun belt.

"Hey, Agent," he rasps, "you ain't supposed to be going nowhere."

"I'm not under arrest, am I?"

The cop scratches his head. "Nope. You leaving?"

"That's my plan."

"Mind if I call it in real quick? I'm supposed to keep an eye on you."

He says it innocently enough, as if he is there simply to protect me from a further attack by Sureno 13. And that might be all he has been told to do, but I look at him suspiciously, wondering if he too is some distant relation of Sheriff Willis or Nathan Karge. And it doesn't look like he would be much protection; even his gun looks as if it's on its last legs. I let it go. I'm more worried about my dog than whether and why the locals are watching me.

"Not at all, Deputy. Actually, I could use a ride too. I need to go to the impound lot, where they've got my car. I don't know where I am."

NINETEEN

OSO IS DELIGHTED to see me when I get my truck from the Sheriff's Impound Lot. He makes a strange sound in his throat, like an affectionate growl, and thumps his head into my chest when I open the door. I wince again and rub his flanks, feeling choked up by his obvious concern for me. And McGee's and Rebecca's and Kristi's. For the first time since the shooting in Cheyenne, I realize that people care about me. Oso explores the bruises on my face with his rough tongue. I take him back to the hotel to feed and water him.

From among the crates of climbing gear in the back of my truck I find an old bottle of prescription pain pills. Codeine and Tylenol. I take three before going to sleep, another three in the middle of the night, and by morning I feel stronger but a little fuzzy. The shower still stings the places where my skin has been abraded.

Sometime during the night the phone rang. I had ignored it, too sore and emotional and drugged to hold a conversation. Now I listen to the message that was left on the hotel's answering system. It was Lynn, who again sounded stoned. And angry.

"Fuck you, Anton. Really, fuck you. I know you're there—I drove by and saw your truck in the lot. I just wanted to say thanks a lot for calling me after you balled me the other night."

"I didn't have the number until yesterday," I say aloud to the telephone before erasing the message. I feel guilty and stupid. And not ready to call her back.

After giving Oso an early-morning walk, I go into the hotel's coffee shop for breakfast. My damaged face causes every head in the nearly full café to turn to me. I pull a *Denver Post* and the *Laramie Boomerang* off a counter and find a table for four that is uninhabited although still full of stained coffee mugs and half-eaten meals. Pushing the mess aside, I sit and open the *Post*.

"You're the DCI agent, right? The one that was assaulted yesterday at the courthouse?"

I turn to see a middle-aged man in slacks and a polo shirt instead of the waiter I had hoped for.

"I am, unfortunately."

He introduces himself and says he works for the *Rocky Mountain News*. Then he moves to sit down across from me, but I raise a hand and say, "Look, I'm not going to talk about it. Let me get some breakfast in peace."

The man hesitates. "I'd really like to ask you some questions."

"I'm sorry, friend, but I'm not going to answer them. Get the police report—it's all there. You can get it from the Sheriff's Office." I turn back to the paper.

"You should read the *News,* not that rag," the man says before putting his card on top of my paper and walking off.

Reporters approach me two more times before I am even able to place my order. Neither one of them is the *Cheyenne Observer* columnist whose nose I want to punch, which is fine with me because I don't feel strong enough to do the damage I intend. Between interruptions I skim the *Post*'s "Denver and the West" section and see a brief blurb with Rebecca Hersh's byline. "State Agent Attacked in Laramie's Courthouse." The article is only two paragraphs long, just five quick sentences, but in that short space she summarizes my beating by a group of juveniles and refers to my past history with the Sureno 13 gang. I don't sound like much of a hero—just a state cop who's being sued by the families of three men he shot and who got his ass kicked by a mob of angry kids. It's accurate, but a little humiliating. It doesn't mention the role of the deputy sheriffs in failing to respond. In the local Laramie paper there is an even briefer article about the incident under the "Lights and Sirens" department.

Just as the old dishes are carted away and my eggs and toast are delivered, Rebecca herself appears, distantly followed by McGee, who is leaning heavily on his cane. She looks good and fresh; the bruise on her forehead has already faded a little. Her hair is pulled back in a tangled ponytail. There isn't a trace of makeup on her face, but her cheeks are flushed as if she has been running. She wears a long-sleeved T-shirt and her lean legs are encased in Lycra running tights. A memory of Kate Danning's splayed body and tights flashes unbidden in my head.

"Hi, Anton," she says, sitting down at my table. "How are you feeling? And what are you doing out of the hospital?"

"I feel like I've been run over by a train," I tell her. "I checked out last night."

"I hope the doctor approved that," she says doubtfully.

I don't reply and she doesn't pursue it. Beyond her McGee is working his way through the reporters, with whom he appears surprisingly popular. They are hanging on his every rasped word, laughing.

Rebecca looks around the café for the waiter. "Why's everyone giving me the stink-eye?" she asks after tentatively waving to some of her reporter friends and not receiving any response.

"Because they've been trying to talk to me all through breakfast, and now I'm talking to you."

She smiles. "How come you're talking to me?"

"You weren't polite enough to ask before sitting down."

She laughs and McGee finally arrives and also sits down unasked. He clutches three or four newspapers of his own. No wonder the reporters appear to like him; he makes a show of reading all their articles.

"You look worse than some corpses I've seen," he growls to me.

"You don't look so hot yourself," I say.

"Frigging altitude."

"Or those cigars you smoke and all the whiskey you drink. It looks like I made the papers, Boss. Again."

"I sold you out to Rebecca Hersh . . . that intrepid reporter. She wants to do . . . a feature on you now."

It is Rebecca's turn to blush. I say, "I hope it's not more about me getting beat up by a bunch of kids."

"I haven't worked it all out yet," she explains, suddenly very professional, after the waiter comes back to fill my coffee and take orders from the new customers, "but I want it to be about police officers who have to use the guns they carry. And how it always ends in lawsuits. A sort of comment on the state of the law these days. I'd also talk to Morris Cash and the federal judge who's involved." After the waiter leaves I suggest she use the various recent examples from New York or Los Angeles instead of my case in Cheyenne. I have had quite enough publicity.

"The *Post*'s readers aren't concerned with those places. They want to hear about something closer to home. So you're my man."

I wish.

Rebecca says she has some questions for us both about the Lee trial. McGee waves a fat hand at the café full of reporters around us and replies that she can ask them later. So instead she tells us about the two antelope and the badger she saw while running on a trail through the foothills that morning. "This is an amazing place," she says. "You've got gangs, murderers, cowboys, corrupt cops, hippies, and incredible wildlife all in the same town."

I remember the times when my brother and I, as kids, hiked into the low hills and canyons just east of town. A badger lived just off the overgrown road. If we ran around a turn and came quickly enough into view, we would catch the badger out of his hole and get to watch him scurry for it, muttering in annoyance. We even had a name for him—we called him Nixon because he reminded us of a picture of the president. Then one day just as we came around the corner there was a long series of staccato gunshots followed by laughter. Three university students were gathered over the corpse of the badger they had just shot. They laughed and fired into it some more until all that was left of Nixon was a blown-apart pulp of hair and blood. I remember crying silently in the bushes while Roberto crept up to their truck, took out his pocketknife, and slashed all four tires. It was the same general area where Matthew Shepard was tied to a buck fence and pistol-whipped to death, the same area where Rebecca witnessed such beauty today. Wyoming is a strange place, I think.

Once I finish my own meal, I put a ten-dollar bill on the table and reluctantly leave, explaining that I have some calls to make and reports to write.

Back in my room, I again try Chris Braddock's phone number. It is answered by the same mature male voice I had spoken to on Sunday evening.

"Is Chris there?"

"No, he's not. Want me to take down a message for him?"

"No, that's all right. But I really need to get in touch with him. Is he at work or something?"

The voice laughs. "Chris doesn't exactly work. He's gone on a climbing trip. Some of his hippie friends came by and carted him off on Sunday night."

"Listen, my name is Antonio Burns. I'm a Special Agent with the Attorney General's Office. It's important that I find Chris and ask him some questions. Who am I talking to?"

"This is Chris's landlord. I own this house and rent out rooms to college kids, mostly. Chris isn't in any trouble, is he, Agent?"

"I don't think he's in any trouble. I just have a couple of questions for him."

"He's not a bad kid, you know. Just smokes a little dope in the backyard where he thinks I won't notice and hangs out with a strange crowd. I wouldn't want to see him go to jail or anything."

"Who came and got him on Sunday?"

"They were the same ones he always hangs out with. An older guy named Billy who looks like a professional wrestler and a younger guy who never washes his hair. The guy with the hair's name is Brad Karge. He's the County Attorney's son."

"Do you know where they were going?"

"Only because they were arguing about it so loud in the room next to where I was trying to watch the Rockies game. See, Chris didn't want to go anywhere. He kept telling those two that he was tired and had things to do. But they weren't having any of it. They kept on arguing with him. I walked in to ask them to keep it down and saw that those two were packing his gear, with Chris just sitting there like a kid who didn't want to go to church. The big guy gave me a nasty look, so I ended up just turning up the TV."

"Did they say where they were going?"

"They kept talking about someplace called Cloud Peak. They were acting weird, like they usually do. Telling him something like that's where the angels fly."

I hang up the phone and sit still on the bed for a long time. Despite the old codeine I took after breakfast, my head, back, and legs still ache. The stuff is probably too old to be fully effective. Or worse, maybe it has developed some side effect like hallucinations. I try to remember when I was last injured and got the prescription. Two years ago? Three? After a few minutes I get up to stare at myself in the mirror. My eyes are set deeper than ever, pushed back by the swelling of the bruises on my cheeks. The tennis shoe tread is still plainly visible on top of the old scar that runs down my face.

"Shit," I say to my reflection. The visage there looks as bad as I feel. I really don't feel up to taking a trip.

When I get my car keys from the top of the dresser, their jangle causes Oso to lift his heavy head. The beast follows me outside, past the pool and the curious stares from the tanning journalists. In the parking lot I unlock the truck and drag a large storage crate from the rear. I carry it into my room and then make a second trip for the other.

Back in the room I open them up and pull out some of my camping and climbing gear. Within minutes the room looks like an outdoor store that has been bombed. Everything smells slightly of dirt and sweat and gasoline. Oso recognizes those odors and is familiar with the packing process. He watches intently, in anticipation, as he always does when a trip is being planned. He knows we are going out into the mountains, and there is nothing he likes better. And I usually feel the same.

There is a knock at the door and I call for whoever it is to come in. I expect the maid or McGee, but it is Rebecca. She steps into the room and over the mess to sit on the bed while I wrestle my sleeping bag into the tiny stuff sack. The effort makes my ribs ache.

"Going somewhere, or are you just a slob?" I'm pleased she is back to being casual with me.

"An impromptu camping trip. That witness I wanted to talk to, Chris Braddock, was apparently coerced off into the mountains Sunday night by Heller and Brad Karge. I want to talk to him, and I'm a little worried they know it. I don't want him to have a climbing accident up there."

"So what are you going to do? Try and stop them from climbing? By yourself?"

I shake my head as I fill water bottles at the sink. "No, just try to talk to them. But mainly make an appearance in the hopes that it'll keep the other two from doing Chris any harm up there."

"Great. I want to come."

I turn off the sink and wipe the bottle on a towel before tossing it in the open pack. "Sorry, but I don't think that's a very good idea."

"Why not?"

"Look, they're up in the Big Horns, in Johnson County. It's easily a four-hour drive up there. And where they're climbing is a place way back in the wilderness—a long, long hike. It's cold, there's bears, and I may have to do some climbing myself. But I promise to give you a full report when I get back."

She crosses her arms in front of her like a petulant, beautiful child. "I still want to go. Like I told you yesterday, you seem to be where all the excitement in this town is, at least until the sentencing. And do you realize that if the Knapp brothers didn't kill Kimberly Lee, that this could be the biggest story I'll ever see?"

Instead of replying, I shake the fuel bottle to see how much gas it holds.

"Maybe you don't think I can keep up. Well, I ran six miles this morning. You may have once been some semifamous athlete, but I can easily keep up with you, especially the way you look right now. And I may not know how to climb, but I grew up camping all over the country with my dad."

"Sorry, but also there's the fact that these are not three of the nicest guys."

She looks at me, her smile gone. I know what she is thinking, and wonder if she will say it. That I owe her for having helped me the day before. That she was the only one who tried—even the police wouldn't help me. But she doesn't say it, and I like her even better for it. She doesn't say another word. She just gets up and walks out of the room.

Finished with my packing, I have a brief conversation with McGee over the hotel's phone system. He wants me to take backup, either one of the other DCI agents or some local deputies in Johnson County. I explain there is no time—I'm leaving this minute. McGee reluctantly agrees to let me go but clearly isn't happy about it. I make him feel better by saying that I'm taking Oso, and that he will back me up. And I tell him I'll be back the next night, I hope. Thursday morning at the absolute latest, as that is when I'm due in federal court for the summary judgment hearing.

I tell Oso to heel, grimace as I sling the big pack over one shoulder, and walk out to the car. The old dog is almost dancing beside me with an excitement that this time I don't share.

I stop when I see the car. From the rear of it I can see a familiar ponytail in the passenger seat. When I open the driver's door, she says, "You can drag me out, but I'll make a scene and all those reporters by the pool will run over here. Besides," she tells me, finally playing the trump card, "you do owe me."

The hot wind whistles through the truck the entire ride to Buffalo. I keep the windows down so Oso can hang his massive head out and fling drool down the side of the Land Cruiser. We drive north past the ghost town of Bosler, then northeast through the jagged tear of Sybille Canyon. From the CD player I installed, the only modern convenience on the rattling old truck, howl the sounds of Blues Traveler and Blind Melon.

Rebecca's long hair wraps around her face until she uses a bandanna that she wears like a pirate to hold it down. From behind my sunglasses, which sit crooked on my swollen face, I admire the long runner's legs that extend from her shorts. She calls a brief halt as we pass the high fence of the wildlife refuge in the canyon. Beyond the gate, in a meadow cut down the center by a stream, stand a herd of elk. Rebecca climbs out of the truck and gazes at them without speaking. Oso shoves his head through the fence and stares beside her. After a moment he lets out a fierce bellow that startles the elk, causing them to turn and bound into the forest beyond the meadow. The beast looks at us for congratulations. Rebecca laughs and says to herself, "Wow. You're a long way from Denver, Dorothy."

We leave the canyon near Wheatland and meet up with the interstate highway. On it, the pitch of the wind in the car rises to a gale. There is no point in conversation in these conditions, so I simply turn up the music and press down the accelerator. One of the things I still enjoy about being a cop is my practical immunity from traffic tickets. We speed northward through the ranching towns of Douglas and Glenrock, then Wyoming's largest city, Casper, and then there is nothing but grass and sandstone and an ungodly wind that shakes the truck until we ascend up to the pine trees outside of Buffalo. Over the town and to the west I can see the snowcapped peaks of the Big Horn Mountains.

I point at them, finally feeling Oso's infectious excitement, and shout over the noise, "That's where we're going."

TWENTY

IN BUFFALO WE eat lunch on the patio of a small, funky café called the Moonbeam. It is the one place in town that isn't franchised fast food or a truck stop. We both order the special, some sort of couscous and tofu, and drink glass after glass of sweet mint tea. Besides us, there is only the proprietor. He is a thin, older man adorned with gold hoops in both ears and ribbons braided into his goatee. Without being asked, he brings Oso a bowl of cool water.

"This place belongs in Boulder," she says, referring to Denver's granola-ish suburb where I spent my graduate school years. "Or maybe even Ward. Did you ever go to Ward? I did an article on it last year, after the town elected a horse as their mayor."

I once dated a girl who lived there in the summertime and tell Rebecca about her. Her home was an old VW bus with a sun shower rigged on the roof. It was just one of many such homes in Ward. And across the road was the trailhead to the Indian Peaks Wilderness, where there are some of Colorado's finest and least-crowded mountaineering routes. I had liked the place. And I respected the people who had the good sense to elect a horse rather than a politician.

"Are you still dating her?" Rebecca asks, eyeing me with what I hope is more than casual interest. She looks good with the red bandanna tied over the top of her head. Her hair spills out from under it and has been twisted by the wind. Dressed like this she could be a local in the Moonbeam Café and she would fit right in in Ward. All she needs is a tie-dye instead of her black silk T-shirt.

"No. That was years ago. The last I heard she'd moved her van to the Valley. Yosemite."

"Tell me then, does Special Agent Burns have a love interest? My sources have confirmed that you've been spotted with a very tan blonde."

She certainly has good sources. That must have been Kristi, the DCI secretary. At least I hope no one spotted Lynn leaving my room early Saturday morning. As I ponder the safest way to answer her question, I realize that I don't mind the way the conversation is going. It gives me an excuse to ask about her situation.

I take a gamble. "If your sources are referring to a Mexican restaurant in Laramie, then no, that wasn't a love interest but a working dinner."

The gamble pays off—she looks satisfied with my answer.

"And how about you? What's your status?"

"I think in the Moonbeam Café you should be asking me my sign."

"Okay, what's your sign, then tell me your status."

"Aries. Dating, but nothing serious."

We watch each other for a moment, then at the same time we both look away. That makes her laugh.

"So why did you become a cop? With your background, you could have been a diplomat, a lawyer, or an Air Force officer like your father."

"I didn't want any more of the military life," I explain. "By growing up in it I put in my twenty years. And I'd lose my mind if I had to sit behind a desk all day. I don't have the attention span for that. I used to do some guiding in the summers, in Alaska, but that was boring too, short-roping clients up Denali. I thought carrying a badge and a gun would be more exciting. Going after drug dealers and child molesters. It sounded like fun."

"It's not?" she asks.

"Not anymore. Not since that thing in Cheyenne."

"Why don't you quit, do something else?"

"The problem is that it's a game. That's what's wrong with it—it shouldn't be a game. But it's a game I can't stand to lose. Every time I'm ready to quit, something like this comes up and I have to see it through." The thought of the Knapp brothers being put to death for a crime they didn't commit makes me angry. So does the thought of Heller, Karge, and Willis getting away with something, even profiting from it. A part of me feels not only righteously indignant but also competitive. I want to win.

After our food comes I begin to quiz her on the contents of the duffel bag that she's brought along. When she tells me, I shake my head in dismay, teasing her. It turns out that the things she brought aren't suitable for anything but car camping. And she finally admits that is the only kind of camping she has ever done. On a paper napkin I make a list of the things she will need. I feel like I'm starting a wonderful vacation rather than working on a murder investigation.

After paying an exorbitant bill for the healthy, flavorless meal, we drive a few miles outside of town to a small camping and mountaineering shop I know. I park the truck in the dirt parking lot outside the store. The only other car in the lot is a battered pickup, its back window and bumper plastered with stickers supporting environmental causes. Instead of telling Oso to stay, I invite him out of the truck. He bounds out too youthfully for his years and runs up on the porch. Rebecca looks at me, puzzled, as I hold the store's door open first for the beast, then her.

From inside come the sounds of squeals, shouts, and the clatter of merchandise being knocked over. It is a single cluttered room. Metal climbing devices hang from one wall; from another, sleeping bags are suspended; and from a third is an assortment of dehydrated food. On the floor there are tents both fully erected and half collapsed amid the racks of clothing. One rack is knocked over near a rapidly deflating tent. A middle-aged woman with long, stringy hair is yelling at Oso and two other dogs, the three of them leaping and wrestling in the tight spaces.

"Stop that, girls! Cut it out, Oso!" she says, then she turns to us at the door and yells at me too. "Goddamn it, Anton!"

I stand grinning. Despite the bruises and the aches, I'm feeling good. Relaxed. This place is another memory of better times.

The woman goes on yelling and the dogs scrambling and fighting until I grab Oso by the collar and drag him, with the two smaller females hanging on tenaciously, out through a small door at the back of the store which leads into a yard. When I come back in, the woman pushes her hair out of her face, then puts her hands on her hips, letting out a sigh of exasperation as she observes the mess. Then she turns to Rebecca.

"My name's Cecelia," she tells her.

"I'm Rebecca. I'm very sorry about Oso causing all this mess."

Cecelia glares at me. "Anton always does that. It scares the hell out of me. But my girls just love that monster of his."

I take Cecelia in my arms and kiss her cheek. Rebecca observes this critically, looking for signs of past or current intimacy, I guess.

Following the hug Cecelia pushes me out to arm's length and looks me over. "You look like shit," she tells me. She turns to Rebecca and asks, pointing at my face, "Did you do this to him? 'Cause he's been needing a woman to do that to him for a long time! I thought about it a few times myself."

Rebecca makes a denial, and I give a brief explanation about being jumped in the courthouse.

"I'd think you'd had enough excitement last year, Anton. When are you going to hang it up? Climbing's bad enough; you Burns boys act like you need risk in every part of your life." I think she sees my eyes harden involuntarily at the mention of my brother; she lets the subject drop. Rebecca is watching us both intently while she fingers the cams and ice screws hanging on one wall.

Instead I talk with Cecelia about mutual friends in the area. A Wyoming native, Cecelia's lived and climbed in the Big Horns all her life. She and her husband pioneered first ascents all through those loose and dangerous granite walls.

And a couple of years ago the probable finally happened to a couple who each possessed an insatiable Rat for isolated heights: a falling block of that stone they loved crushed her husband's spine. These days he only leaves the bed of their tiny cabin nearby in a wheelchair outfitted with mountain bike tires. Cecelia tells me he is still climbing from their bed, at least in his mind. He's writing a guidebook to the Big Horns. Rebecca wanders among the clothing but is still paying close attention. I wonder if she is thinking of doing another story.

While we talk I gather the items I had listed on the napkin for Rebecca. Fleece pants and jacket, sturdy boots, small backpack, sleeping bag, and an ensolite pad. She already has a Gore-Tex jacket, which is de rigueur for reporters and tourists in Wyoming this season.

While we help her try on boots, Cecelia winks at me when Rebecca can't see. She continues the pantomime by flashing me the okay sign, then shaking her hand as if she has touched something hot.

After we have talked about our mutual climbing friends, I tell her I'm working down in Laramie and ask if anyone from down that way has been around.

"Oh yeah," Cecelia answers. "That bad-ass Heller was in just yesterday morning with a couple of his latest protégés. He's been coming up here quite a bit, putting up new lines in the Horns, he says."

"Two guys were with him yesterday?"

"Yeah. Young guys, younger than you. What's this about? Are you a climber or a cop right now?"

"A little of both, Cece. I'll explain it all another time. Anyway, what were they buying?"

"Mainly beta," she says, meaning information on

the area. "Heller wanted to know the quickest trailhead and approach to Cloud Peak. Then just some food and pitons."

I kneel on the floor to help Cecelia reerect one of the collapsed tents. Absently I finger the cord that's used to anchor the tent to Velcro pads on the carpet. The cord is oddly soft. I look at it closer. It's pink with purple flecks. I drop it in surprise, then pick it up again.

"You sell a lot of this?" I ask.

"No. It's crap. Too soft to be trustworthy on the rock. And only French climbers like those colors. I ordered it by mistake a couple of years ago."

"Did Heller buy any of this?"

Cecelia shakes her head. "Not this trip—but he did maybe a year ago. Don't know what he wanted it for."

"Can you give me some of that? The cord?"

"Sure, Anton, whatever you need. When are you going to tell me what this is about?"

"Soon, Cece, real soon I hope."

She goes into the basement/storage room through a trapdoor behind the counter. Rebecca looks up from tying bootlaces and says, "This is great! Or terrible. I don't know anymore. This could be more proof that the Knapps didn't kill Kimberly Lee, right?"

"Right. What a clusterfuck, as our friend McGee would say."

Rebecca opens her purse and takes out a pad of paper and a pen. She makes some notes until I interrupt and get her to walk around in the boots in order to make sure they fit. I'm getting even more anxious to talk to Chris Braddock before Billy Heller gives him a loose belay.

Cecelia comes back and hands me a piece of thin pink cord that is flecked with purple. It looks the right color and size for the cord McGee had described as being used to tie and strangle Kimberly Lee. It also looks the right size for having caused the abrasions on Kate Danning's neck.

We pile the purchases onto the counter. Cecelia tallies it and Rebecca puts her Visa on the counter. Cecelia looks at me.

"The usual discount?" she asks.

Rebecca answers for me, "No discount. I'm going to expense it all to a major corporation."

Cecelia laughs and gives her a thumbs-up. "Stick it to the Man. I like this chick," she tells me.

I ask, "What trailhead did you send them to? Heller and his friends?"

"Hunter Corrals. But now that I think about it, there's a back road near Ant Hill that might be a little closer. Prettier too, although I don't think those boys were too interested in beauty. But taking a girl along that looks like Rebecca here, you just might..."

"Where do we park?"

Cecelia gives me complex directions. I have to borrow Rebecca's paper and pen to get it all down.

I retrieve Oso from the yard in back of the store, where he is still entangled with the two amorous husky bitches. When I walk back in I find Cecelia giving Rebecca a tight hug. Before she sees me, I hear her say, "Be good to him. He needs some goodness in his life."

Once Rebecca and Oso are situated in the truck, I start the engine. Then I turn to her and say, "I forgot something. I'll be right back." I leave the truck running and go back inside the store.

"Now what?" Cecelia asks with feigned exasperation.

I explain what I need and she just shakes her head.

"Mine's locked up as evidence in Laramie. C'mon, Cece, you know there's bears up there."

After a moment's consideration she bends behind the counter and hands me a snub-nosed .32 revolver with a scarred wooden grip. It's heavy in my hand, loaded with bullets. It is the first time I have held a loaded gun except on the pistol range in a year and a half. Giving it over, she says, "Bears, my ass. I hate this thing anyway. Don't bring it back." I slip it in a paper bag and give her another hug.

I follow Cecelia's directions until we are on an ancient and unsigned dirt road. The mountains are hidden from our view by low, rolling hills. After making the final turn, I press the button on the odometer and, as instructed, carefully gauge a distance of 6.8 miles to a small turnabout on the north side of the road.

The aspens at the eleven-thousand-foot trailhead have recently been stripped of their leaves. All that remains is their bone-colored bark mixed among the evergreens that lead up into the steep foothills. There are patches of early-season snow already on the ground. Despite the chilly afternoon wind, Rebecca is impressed by the scenery and says so. I don't reply. But I smile, secure in the knowledge that this is nothing compared to what is behind the hills.

I help her on with a small backpack and adjust it for her, enjoying the small intimacies as I move around her, sliding my hand behind her back and tugging on straps. My own pack is much larger and heavier. But I manage to swing it on without gasping as its weight presses down on the fresh bruises. She laughs when I pull black nylon saddlebags out of the truck and fit them across Oso's broad back.

"Everyone pulls his own weight," I tell her.

We climb a dirt and rock trail up and through the trees. I find myself excitedly running off at the mouth, telling her about the times I had come up here before with my dad and brother and later with friends and by myself. She doesn't understand my references to hairy pitches and off-width cracks, but she doesn't interrupt, not appearing to mind my babbling. I hope the stories will take her mind off the trail and the hot spots from the unfamiliar boots rubbing against her skin. Oso leads the way, obviously delighted, like I am, to be out of the city and out of the truck, back in our element.

A few hours later I can see she is sweating under her jacket as the afternoon sun presses down on the dark colors. She has pulled her hair into a ponytail beneath and behind the bandanna to keep its tangled weight off her neck. I pause at the top of a rise and set down my pack by a fallen tree. She gives me a grateful smile as she drops her own pack and digs in it for the water.

It is only when she stands back up to take a swig that she sees the tremendous wall before us. "My God," she says. "That thing's bigger than the Empire State Building!"

"Bigger. A lot bigger. It's called the East Face of Cloud Peak." I say it proudly, loving this mountain and all its siblings.

For another few hours we hop over fields of talus toward its base. There is no sign of another camp on the talus. Heller and his friends must already be on the wall, where chimneys and overhangs would hide them. Every so often I pause to point at features of the face and offer her descriptions from past climbs I've done there. Rebecca follows my finger and stares at the wall, and then questions me, apparently puzzled as to why anyone would want to try to climb its dark, vertical mass. I try to help her imagine what it's like: climbing free with nothing but space below you and a nylon thread as your only backup in case of a fall. Studying her as I talk, I wonder if this sort of thing appeals to her, if she would be willing to let me teach her. Hook her.

Nearer to the wall, I begin scanning it with binoculars. I search the summit first, then the broken upper face, the middle, and finally the maze of haphazard ledges toward its base. That is where I spot a tiny line of orange. It trails from a ledge low on the face, swinging limply in the cool wind. I pass the binoculars to Rebecca and direct her where to look. "It must have been Brad, Billy, or Chris who left that rope there. I can't imagine there would be any other parties back here this late in the year."

"Why would they want to leave a rope?"

"It's almost always a sign that something went wrong. No one would voluntarily leave a one-hundred-dollar rope."

I take back the binoculars and again search the wall without success. Could they already be up it? If they were at Cecelia's store on Monday morning, the earliest they could have started the wall was twenty-four hours ago, yesterday afternoon. And I don't think even Billy Heller can climb that fast on the dangerous face. Either they are on it, hidden from view by a ledge or a chimney, or they have come off, I decide. The latter would mean there has been an accident.

Rebecca says, "We aren't going up there, are we?" Her voice doesn't sound as if it is out of the question. Maybe she does have the disposition, genetic or acquired, for an adrenaline addiction.

I smile and shake my head. "Unfortunately, I didn't bring any gear for this trip. This is purely reconnaissance."

* * *

It is late in the afternoon when we are finally close to the wall. We have been in its shadow for a long time, but the sky above and around it is finally turning gray. From the summit of the wall thin-looking wisps of snow stream across the heavens far above our heads. They hadn't been there earlier. For me it is a telltale sign that the jet stream is lowering as the air pressure drops. It's likely a storm is coming.

Rebecca is clearly tired from our hike across the talus. She was all right when the scree was small and easy to walk across. But as it grew larger, when she had to leap from one uneven surface to the next, she began to falter. I'm impressed though that she has never once complained. Nor did she let me take her backpack when I offered.

I lead her to a small area of dried grass surrounded by piled rocks, and we drop our packs there. Instead of watching me or helping as I set up the tent, she fixes her eyes constantly up at the wall that looms above us like some monstrous wave. It seems to blot out the sky and threaten our existence.

Half the tent is rigid and the other half is fluttering in the breeze when we hear a whistling sound. It's high-pitched and alarming—it seems to be coming toward us. It sounds almost like the firecrackers called Piccolo Petes that I remember lighting as a child. "Rock," I tell her just as the whistling stops and we hear cracks like gunshots. The faint smell of cordite drifts over in the air. I smile grimly and touch the scar on my cheek. "I hate that sound."

I can see Rebecca is chilled by the time the tent is up and our gear is strewn inside. Although I encourage her to get in the tent, she can't take her eyes off the wall. Inside the tent I lay out three ensolite pads, two large sleeping bags, and a third that looks as if it has been cut in half. Oso promptly collapses on that one, which I had custom-made for him years ago. He is getting too old for these trips. He attempts to curl himself into a huge ball but his elderly bulk makes it impossible for him to jam his nose in his tail the way he did when he was younger. I'm saddened by the thought of leaving him behind on future trips, and then one day him leaving me behind altogether.

As I set up the stove on a rock outside, Rebecca finally ducks into the tent and changes into her new fleece tights. She slides into one of the sleeping bags and sits up Indian-style in the tent's open entrance, the hood of the bag pulled over her shoulders. The cold air and her exhaustion have drawn the white skin on her face tight against her cheek-bones. Taking the bandanna off her head, she shakes her hair free, then combs at it for a minute with her fingers before giving up. Once again I find it hard to stop looking at her in the increasing darkness.

"How do I look?" she asks, catching me.

I smile at her and try an understatement. "Fine. Just fine."

I find the leather bota in my pack, bite open the nipple, and take a long pull of the red wine inside. Its heat spreads through me like an electrical current. I feel so good it's hard to believe that we are alone in the wilderness with two or maybe three killers. It is more like a date that's going well. And I'm back to being the self-righteous, cocksure cop I was two years ago, made invulnerable by the badge and gun I carry. Then, as if to punish me, some brain cells flash to a memory of the shooting in Cheyenne. I almost lose the high. But I take control with another deep pull from the bag, which seems to drown the treacherous cells.

When I pass the bota to Rebecca she sputters at the leathery taste of the wine, then takes a second drink. Her teeth and the whites of her eyes flash at me.

I feed her rehydrated potato pasta with a thick red sauce and pan-fried turkey sausage. Oso rouses himself to eat a plate of his own, mixed with Purina, then licks the pot and bowls clean. It grows dark outside and the wind is increasing. I collapse the small stove and pull myself into the tent, where I light a small candle lantern and hang it from the tent's highest point. The nylon sides snap and the poles creak but the wind doesn't penetrate.

"I'm beginning to see why you do this."

"This is home," I say to her. "Maybe that comes from the way I grew up, always traveling. Except for my granddad's ranch, a tent was the most consistent home my family had."

"I've never been comfortable out in the wild, on the trips I took with my dad. But those were tame compared to this."

I tell her to close her eyes—that I'm going to change. She rolls to face Oso and pats his swollen belly. "If only it weren't so cold, or there was a hot tub."

I slide into my sleeping bag and ask her, "Are you cold?"

"A little."

I press my bag against hers, pinning her in the dead air space between the dog and myself. I can feel her hair on my face. She turns her head and kisses my nose. "Thanks," she says. Oso passes gas loudly and lets loose a jaw-popping yawn. She laughs, telling us both good night. I lie awake for a long time. My skin tingles where her lips had touched it.

TWENTY-ONE

I WAKE UP TO the familiar smell of my own day-old sweat, the gunpowderlike scent of cold granite, and the damp odor of mildew from the condensation on our sleeping bags. The walls of the tent are still. I don't move for a while, listening to the labored breathing of my elderly dog and the beautiful woman who lies between us. When I finally sit up, Oso lifts his head and stares at me expectantly. Then he folds back his ears in a smile. I unzip one wall of the tent and the beast slips out into the sunlight where I hear the jingle of his collar as he shakes off his dog-dreams.

Outside, the orange glow of the sunrise is seeping into the blackness of the great wall. The air is moist and heavy; there is a tension in it. Around the sun is a blurry haze that displays the unmistakable sign of an approaching storm. We won't be able to spend another night out. Not without skis or snowshoes. I know I have to get back anyway, for both the hearing Thursday afternoon in federal court and to try to get the sentencing of the Knapp brothers postponed.

I crawl out of my sleeping bag and the tent as quietly as I can, put on my parka, and fire up the stove. When I hear her moving in the tent, I pass in a mug of hot tea without a word.

"Thanks, Anton."

I stick my head in and surprise us both by kissing her sleep-swollen lips. After a moment she kisses back, then pushes me away. "I'm a mess," she tells me and lifts the errant strands of hair back from her face. "But God, that was nice."

Instead of replying I just smile.

When she comes out of the tent in her fleece and Gore-Tex shells, she finds me crouching over the stove brewing oatmeal. "I like a man who cooks," she says, examining our breakfast, "but I prefer lightly poached eggs and fresh-squeezed orange juice. Do you have any of that?"

"I'll make you all that the next time I wake up with you," I say.

She grins back and nods thoughtfully.

A half hour later I leave her half-in her sleeping bag, propped against a rock, with a full mug of tea and a paperback novel she brought in her pack. The binoculars lie within easy reach. We already discussed my opinion that Heller, Brad, and Chris are probably off the wall. If they were still anywhere on it, tucked out of sight, we would have heard them climbing by now. So either they have finished the climb and for some reason left the rope behind, or something has gone wrong.

Despite her comfortable position, Rebecca looks

worried. She comments on the fact that I am taking only a camera and my climbing slippers in a small hip pack.

"How are you going to get up to that rope without any ropes yourself?"

"Very carefully."

"What about the rockfall?"

I grimace and catch myself again touching my scarred cheek. "With any luck, that won't start till later, when the sun heats up the face." Unfortunately, I forgot to bring my helmet.

"This doesn't sound like a good idea, Anton. Why not come back with some other climbers?"

I don't reply other than to shrug. No time, with the sentencing in just two days. There is something wrong with that discarded rope high above and I need to know what it is. "Are you going to be okay here, all alone?"

"I think so. Are there any bears around here?"

"Only Oso. There shouldn't be any up this high. Not much to eat but marmots and the rare pretty journalist. But if it makes you feel any better, there's a gun in my pack."

It's her turn to grimace. "No thank you. Just be careful, please."

I smile at her again and start picking my way over the field of talus toward the wall. When I turn back to look at her, she has put down her book and is watching me intently. Every time I turn around her eyes are following my progress, her stare interrupted only to glance up at the rope that is hanging from the ledge several hundred feet up the face.

My progress up the wall is initially easy. It begins by simply scrambling up the slope of loose scree to where the more solid granite starts. From there I follow rising ledges back and forth, occasionally finding a dead end and having to seek out a new path. I can't see the dangling rope above, but I had roughly fixed its position in my mind, using the tent in the talus behind me as a guide.

One narrow, crumbling ledge leads me higher than the others. It isn't wide enough to walk on—it is scarcely wider than my feet. Instead I find myself moving sideways, searching for handholds in the rock. Half of the better holds come free in my hands. I toss them off the growing cliff beneath me to hear them crash onto the talus seconds later, far below. The ledge ends near a rotten chimney.

Studying its walls, I can make out faint marks of fresh chalk on obvious holds. I'm on the right track. I find a spot on the ledge that is wide enough for sitting and change into my sticky rubber slippers while taking care not to drop my boots into the void below. Once the shoes are tightly laced, I start bridging my way up the chimney.

My bruises burn when I move. I suppress a groan when I brace my back against one wall and push my legs against its opposite. The moves are relatively easy, but one place makes me sweat from more than just pain. A large boulder completely blocks the chimney like a marble in someone's throat. I am forced to lean out backward over the enormous space below and behind, shoving my fingers into the cool creases where the stone has wedged itself against the chimney's walls. I'm suspended like this by my fingertips, leaning out, searching for better holds, when the boulder shifts slightly. The air leaves my lungs in a single whoosh. I frantically claw my way on top of the rock, suddenly endowed with greater strength and perception as the familiar adrenaline floods my system. Just a little ways above, I can see the rope swaying as a gentle breeze begins to rise.

Sitting on the chockstone, letting my pulse and lungs slow in their work, I see the glint of the sun on the binoculars Rebecca holds. By the way the light flashes, it looks like she is shaking her head. Far beyond her Oso's large black form is in stalking mode on a small ridge above the talus valley, undoubtedly in pursuit of a fat marmot.

The chimney leads only thirty feet higher before it opens out on a broad ledge. The platform is littered with shattered stones. Three enormous ravens there give me dirty looks. They are standing on a red parka worn by a very dead young man. Chris Braddock, I presume. My hope for discovering what happened to Kate Danning that night in Vedauwoo.

He is lying on his back, arched across a boulder, his inverted face pointed at me. If he had been wearing sunglasses when he fell, they are missing. Along with his eyes. I find the glasses a few feet away where they have been carelessly discarded either by the fall or the birds. The ravens lift off the body at my approach. I stop ten feet from the corpse and stare at it, trying not to look at the face, but those empty sockets tug at my vision like a magnetic force. I can't help but think about how they have been emptied by the hard, pointed beaks. His mouth is open in horror at what the birds have done to him. But the horror is inexpressible, as the soft tongue is gone too.

There is some primal fear that arises when you are alone with a murdered corpse, and I admit that it grips me there on the ledge. Going near, I half expect his arms to clutch at me, sightlessly and wordlessly begging for help. I find myself muttering at this corpse.

"My name's Anton," I tell it. "I'm the one who's going to get the guys who did this to you."

I gently pat the hip and chest pockets of the parka but

feel no wallet. I don't expect to find one anyway—nobody climbs with his wallet. Most climbers I know prefer to climb without any ID whatsoever. It just seems like you will live a little longer if it takes more time to identify your corpse and notify your family and friends. When their tears begin, that's when you're dead.

The lead rope is still knotted to the harness on his limp body. From there it leads off the side of the ledge. I examine the knot and find that it is strangely loose in my fingers. If there had been any sort of a climbing fall where placed protection or the rope itself had failed, it should have been jerked tight by the attempt at belaying. I pull up the trail of loose line and see what I expect at the other end, fifty feet out. It isn't frayed from rubbing over a lip of rock and it isn't frazzled from a tension break. It's cut clean. The kind of cut only made by a knife. He was murdered and his missing tongue is nature's clue as to why—to keep from talking.

I loosen the harness buckle and carefully slide the harness off Chris's body, leaving the rope tied to it. Coiling the rope and attached harness, I sling them over my head and one shoulder. I take several photos of the body from different angles and then a few close-ups of the face. These I take without looking through the viewfinder—I just point and shoot, like the commercial says.

I don't notice any change in the weather until I'm done. The first wet sting of a snowflake brings it to my attention. The storm is moving in faster than I had expected. I look out and am barely able to spot the bright yellow walls of the tent through the swirling air, but can't see Rebecca. I hope she is warm inside. Oso too is nowhere to be seen.

I shimmy down to the chockstone and begin rigging an improvised rappel with the dead man's rope to get down and around the loose boulder. Halfway through the process,

I hear a sharp crack. For a fraction of a second I almost instinctively shout, "Rock!" But there was no whistle preceding the retort and there is no one to warn anyway. Strangely, I find myself hoping it was a falling rock. Then a second crack dashes my hope.

The shots echo off the wall, making it impossible to determine where they come from. They sound more like a bigger caliber than the borrowed .32 I had left in my pack.

I stand with my feet frozen on the precariously balanced chockstone. Twin worms of fear twist in my stomach. For a moment my organs feel loose and weak. The muscles in my thighs and back go soft too. Rebecca, I think. Oso. The fear rears up in my mind like a great wave. A cool, damp sweat pours out of my skin and soaks my fleece underclothes.

After rappelling off the boulder in what is really a barely controlled fall, the rest of my scramble down the wall goes by in a reckless blur. I tug my boots back on, indifferent to the danger of the tiny ledge, my fingers clumsy with the laces. There are no other sounds but that of the rocks kicked loose by my feet. I restrain myself from calling out their names. The snowflakes continue to fall, fatter and wetter. I am running and sliding once I hit the scree.

The tent is open and empty amidst the full force of the snowstorm. I crouch in the fresh snow, staring inside as the flakes blow in and wet the gear there. My breath is coming in short, harsh pants. I can't seem to catch it. After a long minute I finally move, open the top of my pack, and see that Cece's pistol is gone. Then I hear her quietly call to me.

"Anton?"

Spinning around, I see her emerge from a shelter of boulders with her damp sleeping bag pulled over her shoulders. The gun is shaking in her hand. Her eyes are wide and her lips are trembling with cold and fright.

"Rebecca. Are you all right?" I ask, stepping quickly toward her and putting my arms around her back.

"I'm okay. What's happening? Who's shooting?"

"I don't know. Where's Oso?"

"About the time you reached the wall, he started to growl and ran off."

"Fuck. Fuck. Which way did he go?"

She points in the direction of the ridge where I had seen him stalking from up high on the wall, but the storm impedes any vision more than one hundred feet away. I curse again.

"Listen, put on your warmest clothes right now. We're leaving everything else."

She does as she is told while I put a bottle of water and a few candy bars into my pack. The cut rope and harness I stuff in the pack as well. I slip the gun into my parka's front pocket, leaving it unzipped.

"We're going to get out of here. But first I've got to find Oso, and I can't leave you alone. So follow me, move as quietly as you can. Don't say anything. Okay? Not a word."

She nods.

I lead us into the swirling clouds of fat white flakes. They are quickly filling in the spaces between the rocks. Their wetness makes the talus slippery, and Rebecca falls again and again. I point for her to walk in my tracks. Through all her slips and trips she never makes a sound. I look back at her once and see her holding one wrist, the beginning of tears in her eyes.

A deeply ingrained lesson from my father to always be conscious of my surroundings and my remembered view from the wall brings us toward the small ridge above one side of the valley. Before stepping over each slick rock, I scan ahead and around as best I can, which isn't much. Visibility has dropped to maybe fifty feet and the storm is still closing in. I stop looking back each time I hear the sharp rasp of her nylon jacket on granite, not wanting to see the pain and fear in her eyes. She stays behind me, gamely not making a sound.

Coming on top of what I guess is the low rise I had seen from the wall, the boulders are more scattered and the ground more level. I spot a series of faint depressions that are being filled by the gathering snow. Maybe twenty minutes old. I scan 360 degrees around us, then kneel by the tracks, assessing their number and direction. I'm not surprised that there are two sets, walking together in a line toward the wall. And toward our tent. What is surprising is that we hadn't met the men who made the tracks on our way up the hill. We are very lucky. I silently lead Rebecca in the direction from which the tracks had come.

I stop again when I see the large black lump farther along the hillock. I stand still for a long, long time, staring at it, no longer feeling the wet flakes stinging my face. But I hear her gasp when she sees the dark mass and the bright cherry stain polluting the fresh snow around it.

"Oh God, Anton." She clutches my arm from behind.

I pull away from her, stepping forward quickly. Then I'm running toward the bloody shape. I kneel in the red snow and lower my head to press my face into the mane of fur at Oso's neck. The flakes keep falling. They sparkle like diamonds on the black fur. My hands lift my dog's shattered muzzle and I see his lips are locked in a snarl where a bullet hasn't torn them away. I press my forehead to his, love and grief and rage exploding like dynamite in my head.

When I finally stand and look at her, Rebecca looks

away. Something about my expression makes her do that. I try to swallow the fury. I open my mouth in an attempt to say something comforting, then shut it, my jaw clenched. My eyes stare through her and beyond her, back the way we came. She won't look at my face. She keeps her eyes on the bloody snow and walks around me to Oso's body. She kneels where I had knelt and rubs his still-steaming fur.

"Let's go." I pull her to her feet more roughly than I had intended.

"Where?"

"I'm taking you out of here. Come on."

"Shouldn't we bury him?"

I close my eyes for another long moment. "No, there's no time. They'll have found our tracks or tent by now." And this is the right way for him. His skin, muscle, blood, and bones would be absorbed into the stony ground and the mouths of animals, renourishing the Earth. His soul is gone, flashing somewhere through the snow and trees as he chases squirrels there. Oso is gone. I lead off again into the storm.

The wind rises until it begins to howl. There is nothing to see but the blinding white of the snowstorm and the images of revenge that play inside my mind. I can feel the crunch of Heller's nose as I smash my fist into his face. I'll cut out his heart. I'll piss in the hole. I stalk quickly over the rocks and deepening snow, dark fantasies reeling in my brain, slowing my pace only when I hear Rebecca fall and gasp again. She walks hunched over behind me, her face drawn behind the sunglasses I insist she wear to keep out the pelting flakes.

"The storm is good," I tell her after hours of stumbling over the talus, once the coals in my heart have been cooled a little by the blizzard. "It probably saved our lives. It's keeping us hidden." I don't tell her that her presence has saved Heller's and Brad's lives, at least for the time being.

"How much farther?"

"Not far now to the trail."

I have said that several times. Over a period of hours.

We work our way off the talus and into a forest of squat, wind-torn pines that I remember from the hike in when it was sunny and pleasant, another world. Now their lonely and forlorn shapes seem like demons arising out of the snow. At one point, when I look back at Rebecca, I notice the ice of tears frozen to her face. She is chilled to the bone, utterly exhausted, and I expect her shins and knees are as bruised as her palms from frequent falls. Crossing the scree, she had continually fallen through the whiteness between the rocks.

"We're on the trail," I tell her a little later.

Every little while I stop and hand her the bottle of water from my pack. I have mixed it with the last of the heavy wine. I make her drink but don't take any for myself. There isn't enough. Our hike through the storm goes on, into thicker and thicker pines. I can see that her reserves are almost gone. She follows blindly.

Finally I stop for good. I reach into the pack and take out my keys. Rebecca reaches out a mittened hand as if expecting me to hand her the water bottle once again. She doesn't realize she has long since drained it.

"Hey," I say as gently as I can amid the spinning flakes. "We're here. We're at the car. You made it."

Rebecca looks at me without intelligence behind her dark lenses. The snow has burned her pale skin red and it is stretched tight over her nose and cheekbones.

I brush at the mound of white in front of me, searching for the handle and lock. She climbs in without a word when

I open the door for her and hunches over in the seat, crying and holding her knees. I am overwhelmed with weariness too, but safe from the storm, the anger heats up until it is once again a dancing fire. The steering wheel is cold against my forehead when I rest it there. For just a moment I close my snow-stung eyes.

With the snow glittering in the headlights, I fight to keep the truck in the heavy powder between the parallel lines of pines. I inch our way down the unmarked road and drive past the turnoff that will take us back to Buffalo. I drive on to the Hunter Corrals trailhead, where Cecelia said she had told them to go instead of the shorter trail Rebecca and I had taken. There is one car there, buried under more than two feet of fresh snow. I pull up close to it, my headlights revealing the pristine and untracked accumulation around it. In my lap is Cecelia's pistol.

The car is a new-looking, souped-up van. The same van I saw at Heller's house. I slip the pistol back in my pocket and get out of the truck while opening a heavy folding knife. I shuffle around the van in the snow, driving the knife into all four tires. Then with the butt end of the knife, where the worn metal extends past the heel of my closed fist, I slam it down on the windshield. The windshield dissolves in a spider's web of cracked glass.

TWENTY-TWO

ON THE DRIVE back to Laramie, I force aside the grief and rage that is popping and crackling like a forest fire in my mind, replacing it with something more ancient, something colder and harder. Like the granite I'd gripped just hours earlier. The fury is stuffed in some dark hole in my brain as if it is an overlarge sleeping bag in a too-small stuff sack. The seams creak, threatening to burst, but I keep shoving. I will cry for my dog only when he is avenged.

As the Land Cruiser eats up the dark pavement, I use my cell phone to call the Johnson County Sheriff's Office. When I get the supervising sergeant on the phone, I tell him about the body he will find low on Cloud Peak's east face when the storm ends and he can get in there with a search-and-rescue team. I give him descriptions of Heller, Brad Karge, and their van, but I don't mention how I vandalized it.

"Christ," the sergeant says when I'm done, "we haven't had a murder in this county in ten years. Not since 'Fingers' Muletta was on the loose." I had heard about that case. A drifter who was camping in the Big Horns took too much LSD, then killed and partially ate a hitchhiking college student. When he was caught he still had the student's fingers in his pockets. "Snacks," he told the deputy who arrested him. After being found not guilty by reason of temporary insanity, Fingers spent about six months in an institution before being released. Supposedly he still lives in a cabin just outside of Sheridan.

"You DCI guys want to handle it?" the sergeant asks.

"I'm after those two for another murder in Albany County. And this has become a little personal, Sergeant. I'd like to run it myself."

"Lemme check with my boss before I make any promises, but yeah, that sounds good."

I also check my messages at the office up in Cody. There are only two. One is from McGee, who sounds typically surly, demanding to know why the hell have I taken Rebecca with me into the mountains. Not very subtly, he suggests that it's for some immoral purpose. He also reports that he is going back to Cheyenne for the night—his wife, "the old battle-ax," is ill. The second message is from a Captain Tobias of Colorado's Bureau of Investigation. I know from past multistate, joint-jurisdictional cases that CBI is Colorado's version of Wyoming's DCI. It is their statewide law enforcement agency. The captain sounds irate and says it's urgent that he speak with me. He doesn't say about what. It could be any number of cases, but something pokes at my mind in a warning. I think of Roberto.

*   *   *

It is eleven at night when I drive slowly through Laramie's dark streets back to our hotel. Rebecca has not spoken the entire ride, perhaps sensing my need for silence. Although somewhere around Wheatland she tilted back in the Land Cruiser's passenger seat, I don't think she has slept at all. I know from experience that the exertion, exhaustion, and dehydration can elevate your heart rate and blood pressure, making sleep desperately needed but impossible.

The sky in Laramie is clear and cold. Thousands of bright stars illuminate the night even though there is no moon. I am so tired that I fail to notice the patrol car sitting with its lights out at the far end of the lot, protected from the starlight by the shadows of a large elm.

I pull into a vacant spot near the building and turn off the engine. Rebecca doesn't move, but I can see that her eyes are open. Unable to risk the emotional burden of any conversation, I quickly walk around the car and open the door for her. When she gets out she steps right into my arms. Her tears begin anew.

"I'm so sorry, Anton. Sorry about Oso. Sorry about everything."

I stroke her dirty hair the way I had stroked Oso's pelt. There is nothing for me to say. I hold her tightly in the dark lot until my emotional dam threatens to crumble. Then I gently push her toward her room on the opposite end of the building from mine.

"Get some sleep, Rebecca. Drink some water and go to bed."

She looks back at me. "Do you want me to stay with you?"

"No. But thanks."

"You sure?"

"Yeah."

I watch her limp past the security lights and into the dimly lit hallway. More than anything, I wanted to tell her yes. But I'm feeling too weak, too brittle, and too cold. To have said yes would be to use her as a crutch. And I have a lot to do before the hearing in Cheyenne just fifteen hours away.

After she is gone I open the truck's back gate and drag out my pack. When I turn around, swinging the pack onto an aching shoulder, a beam of light from a powerful torch hits my face like a punch.

I squint and raise a hand to ward off the light, at the same time letting the pack drop off my shoulder and onto the pavement. I step back and quickly to the side, away from the tall figure holding the light. The police car I hadn't seen before now skids toward me from its hiding place with its roof-mounted gumballs ignited, the sirens off.

"Good-looking piece of ass," a voice says.

My sight is still devastated from the sudden light, but I recognize the voice. Bender. His comment about Rebecca prods me to the core.

"What do you want, Leroy?"

"For starters, you little half-spic, put your hands in the air. Unless you want to give me an excuse to cap your ass right here."

My vision is clearing despite the light that is still in my eyes. Bender's other hand holds his gun. It's pointed at my chest. I do as he says, seeing another deputy get out of the car with his hand on his holster. Deputy David Knight's young face looks scared in the revolving red and blue colors.

Bender shouts at Knight, "Cut the lights!"

Knight reaches in and flicks the switch. Bender keeps his torch on me.

He says, "Where's your piece?"

I can smell whiskey and tobacco on his breath. "In evidence. Remember, you booked it in after you let that gangbanger brain me with it." Sometime on the ride back to Laramie I had tucked Cecelia's .32 under the car seat.

"Right. Whoowee, now that was fun. Too bad it was unloaded. You've got to be a serious pussy to—"

I cut him off. "Leroy, do you have any idea what I'm going to do to you for this? For drawing on me in the middle of the night? Now get that fucking light out of my face before I go blind."

He laughs. I lower my arms and take a step toward him, ready to knock the flashlight away.

"Don't move! Up against the car," he shouts, the laughter abruptly cut off the second I moved. When I hesitate he drops the flashlight on the pavement and braces his gun hand with his free one. In the light from the stars and the hotel's low-watt security bulbs, I can see his finger on the trigger. "Move a muscle, QuickDraw, I'm gonna blow you away. Now turn around!"

Again I do as he says, almost choking with the fury that's flooding my head, and raise my hands once again above my shoulders. He shoves me toward the patrol car, where Knight stands as if frozen, not saying a word. Bender shoves me again with a hand on the back of my neck, propelling me roughly onto the car's hood. When my palms hit the warm metal his left hand is still on my neck. In his right he holds the barrel of his pistol pressed into the muscle on one side of my spine.

I allow myself to bounce off the hood. He is not expecting it when I come off and back, spinning. I knock his gun hand wide and see Bender's eyes go even wider with surprise. I drive my right fist straight into his face while his pistol arm is still outstretched. He starts to go down and I leap after him, ready to wrestle the gun away.

"Freeze! Freeze, Burns!" another voice is shouting.

Someone kicks me in the ribs, sending me off Bender and sprawling across the gravel. In my anger I had forgotten about Deputy Knight. He goes on screaming and repeating himself, his small automatic pointed at my head.

"Stay down! Stay the fuck down."

I watch, one cheek pressed against the ground, as Bender gets to his feet. He rubs his cheek thoughtfully. Then he takes two quick steps toward me and drives his boot between my ribs and my hip. A white light explodes in my head, a thousand times brighter than the beam of his torch. The kicks keep coming, but the white light is a little dimmer with each blow.

From a great distance I hear Knight's voice, pitched high with fright. "Stop it, Sarge! You'll kill him."

"Don't you tell me what to do, Dave," Bender snaps, breathing hard. But the force that propels his boots seems to diminish.

When he is finished kicking me, they work together to handcuff my hands behind my back. Even if I wanted to, I'm unable to help. Kneeling on the gravel with their hands lifting at my shoulders, I can't even raise my head. I try to retch but nothing comes up.

They haul me to the patrol car and toss me in the back like a duffel bag. At first the sandpaper texture of the rough, plastic bench seat feels cool on my face. It quickly becomes wet and sticky. I open an eye and see in the light of the car's dome that my own blood is staining it.

When Bender and Knight slam shut the doors it sounds

like a faraway echo. The engine starts and my head bounces on the plastic as we pull onto the street. Bender's voice comes from the same great distance.

He speaks to Knight. "Anyone taught you to make popcorn, boy?"

I don't hear Knight reply but I know what is coming. "Popcorn" is what makes a tough kernel of a suspect into a soft, fluffy, and edible meal for a cowboy cop.

"Got your seat belt on?"

Bender hits the brakes and I crash into the clear partition. Then he accelerates, throwing me back onto the bench seat. I can hear him laughing. He hits the brakes again. This goes on and on—the screech of the brakes, the smack of my body against the partition, the laughter, and the ricochet back onto the plastic seat. At some point I let myself enter a dream. In it I'm on an icy summit, the sun and the wind on my face, my ice tools hanging limply at my sides. I'm smiling, knowing that my big dog is waiting faithfully for me far below.

I come to my senses when they pull me out of the car and drag me by the arms into the Sheriff's Office through the underground garage. My knees and boots scuff along on the floor. Unlike the time I woke up in the hospital, now I'm fully alert. The rage cuts through all the mist.

They drop me on the floor in an interview room. It is like tens of others I have been in around the state, observing someone else handcuffed and scared. It is not much bigger than a closet and is furnished with a table, a couple of plastic chairs, an intercom box mounted on the wall, and a one-way mirror. The intercom and mirror would lead into a smaller room where a video camera or recording equipment is usually set up. There is an odor of fear and desperation in the room. So many times I have sat, protected and superior with my badge clipped to my shirt pocket, across the table or behind the mirror, watching a suspect sweat. Now I know a little of what they felt.

"I'm a little disappointed, QuickDraw," Bender says when I try to stagger to my feet despite having my hands cuffed behind my back. "You were supposed to be a tough guy. A cocky little son of a bitch. Now it just looks like you've been rode hard and put up wet." He pushes me back down onto the dirty carpet and sweeps my legs out of the way of the door.

"Let's go get the sheriff, Dave," he says to Knight as the door shuts and locks.

Left alone, I turn onto my back, then roll to my feet. The dizziness and pain come on so strong I almost go down again. With one foot I tug a chair out from under the table and barely make it into it. I want to put my head on the table's flat surface but I guess I'm being watched from beyond the mirror. So I sit up straight and stare into the glass.

The metallic sound of voices comes over the intercom after the sound of a door closing. The small-town idiots have left it on two-way transmit. Despite the pain, I almost grin when I realize that.

"Mean-looking fucker, ain't he?" It's Willis's voice.

"He's a pussy," Bender says.

Willis laughs. "You saying before or after you hooked him? Looks like he gave you a nice shiner."

There's silence for a moment.

"Look at him, glarin' at that mirror, like he can see us. Maybe he thinks he's still pretty," Bender says.

"Nathan won't be happy if he files a brutality complaint."

"Don't worry, Uncle Dan. It would be his word 'gainst Knight's and mine. Knight's a stand-up guy. And no one would believe a word that little spic has to say, 'specially as he's under investigation for aiding his brother's escape. Anyway, he ain't the type to do that. He likes to keep things personal. It'll be between him and me."

So Roberto has gone and done it. I should be worried, but I am strangely relieved to hear my brother has done what he threatened to do. His soul had been burning itself up while caged in that prison. He's better off with a short, wild run than a long death. And I don't believe he will let himself be caught. Not this time.

"The fucker's still staring at us. I'm gonna wipe that smirk off his face."

"Easy, boy. I want to talk to him first. Did he say anything 'bout his brother?"

"No, sir. I didn't say anything myself. I thought you'd want to bring that up."

"Good boy. Do the paperwork—charge him with obstruction and resisting. Assault on an officer too. That ought to get him held till Friday, even without those Colorado guys we got coming up. Nathan says it don't matter what we do with him after the sentencing. He'll be good as elected by then."

"What about his boss, that old guy with the beard?"

"Nathan says he'll take care of him."

The door opens and Sheriff Willis follows Bender into the room. A silver rodeo belt buckle holds up his big belly.

Instead of riding upright, facing out, the buckle reflects down to the snakeskin boots on his feet.

"I'm a little surprised to see you back in town, Agent."

"I'm a little surprised you haven't had a heart attack yet, Sheriff," I tell him, looking at his belly.

The sheriff sighs. "It sounds like you want to do this the hard way, boy."

"Sheriff, I don't think there's much that's hard about you."

The sheriff allows a chuckle, then slaps me across the mouth. My senses are too dulled from pain and exhaustion to see it coming. I gather my feet under me and start to stand, but Bender puts his hands on my shoulders and slams me back down in the chair. Again I can taste fresh blood in my mouth.

"You're already being charged with resisting and assault. You want to add to it? You're in a heap of trouble, boy. There's talk you may have helped your brother get out of Colorado last night."

I say, "Then you should call up to Johnson County, Sheriff. They'll tell you I was back there finding a body last night." I don't want to mention either Rebecca's or Cecelia's name to these two rednecks. "A boy named Chris Braddock, who the County Attorney's son dropped off a cliff just like he did Kate Danning."

The sheriff grunts. "I've been wanting to talk to you about that, find out exactly what kind of shit you're trying to pull with this Danning thing."

I spit a mouthful of blood on the carpet near his fancy boots and he dances back.

"I've been wanting to talk to you too, Sheriff. I want to know what you're going to say when it comes out that you told the coroner not to run a rape kit on her. I want to know what you're going to say when it comes out that you and Nathan Karge are protecting his son for her murder. I want to know what you're going to say when it comes out that nobody from your office investigated the similarities to the Lee killing. I want to know what you're going to do when I stick obstruction and assault charges up *your* fat ass. And I want to know how you're stupid enough to leave the intercom on."

The sheriff looks at the box on the wall, then behind me at Bender. His face blanches for a moment and the smile he gives Bender is not nice. He shakes his head, saying, "Leroy, sometimes you're dumber than pig shit."

"Somebody else must have left it on, Uncle Dan."

The sheriff shakes his head again, then brings his attention back down to me. "You're not gettin' it, are you, boy?"

Bender grabs both my wrists from behind and torques them high up behind my back. I'm jerked to my feet. Before I can bring my boot down hard on his instep, the sheriff steps forward and grabs me between the legs.

Whatever strength is left in me is gone in a second. Nausea floods my body and I feel the bile rise out of my stomach and into my throat. I want to vomit—to spew it all over the front of the sheriff's checked shirt and pearl buttons, but it won't come. My stomach is empty. I kick at the sheriff but my boot strikes his shin no harder than a kiss. Sounding as if it is coming from a long ways away, a groan escapes my lips.

The sheriff is talking. "Now you think anyone would believe you, boy? I don't think no one in this state would believe you if you said the wind might blow. You are what the lawyers call incredible, and I don't mean that in a good way. So you can forget about any charges 'gainst anyone but yourself. And you can forget anything you might have heard. So far we got you as a suspect in your spic brother's escape out of Colorado and for assault and resisting. You want to resist some more, boy?"

He grips me tighter and I think I might pass out.

"Now 'bout that Danning girl. I believe it's time for you to stop screwing around with that. Hell, you sign off on that little accident and I may even see my way fit to drop these charges against you. Course, I'm gonna have to hold you for a few days as a favor to our friends down south in Colorado. Those boys are lookin' forward to talking with you. So you behave, I might let you go, let's see..." He speaks over my head to Bender. "What time's that sentencing on Friday?"

"Nine o'clock, Uncle Dan."

"Then you behave and I might let you go on Friday night. Just think, son, you behave and you'll get to spend the weekend with that little reporter girl." He chuckles and squeezes me again. "But after this you might not be much good to her at playing hide the salami, if you know what I mean. My nephew here may have to show her a good time before then if you mess with us."

Then the door opens so fast it might have been kicked. My ears ring from the crash. Jones's massive form fills the doorway. He comes into the room without speaking a word. He is dressed in cotton pajama pants, ridiculously patterned with pictures of Mickey Mouse, and a tank top that reveals the enormous mounds of muscle. There are still the lines of a pillow on his face.

"What the hell," the sheriff says, releasing me and turning to him, "this ain't your shift, Sergeant. Now you get your black ass out—" Jones pushes him aside in what for him is a gentle nudge. The sheriff staggers against the metal table.

Jones reaches one arm past my head and puts his hand

across what I guess is Bender's throat. Grasping at Jones's wrists, Bender releases my handcuffs from where he'd been torquing them up high on my back. The sheriff is yelling at Jones now, but things are moving too quickly for me to understand.

The fury I had been stifling pops out of its hole like a jack-in-the-box. I twist in the small space between Bender and Jones, bent on attacking Bender with my teeth or my feet, and see that Jones has not grabbed his throat but his face. The parts of Bender's face that I can see between Jones's fingers are contorted under the pressure of those powerful digits.

With his free hand Jones takes one of my handcuffed arms and pushes me toward the door, but not before I bring my knee up hard between Bender's legs. Propelled across the room by another gentle push from Jones, I spin and drive my elbow hard into the sheriff's gut as I pass. I spill down onto the floor as the sheriff doubles over. I kick at his knee but miss. Then Jones drags me out of the room.

In the hallway he releases me for a second and leans back into the interview room. I hear him say, "Sheriff, you even think about retaliating or filing anything on me, I'll take you down. I got enough on you and your boys to bring in a federal corruption probe. Oh, by the way—I quit. Consider this my two weeks' notice."

TWENTY-THREE

IT'S DARK AND quiet on Ivinson Street when we get outside. From a few blocks away there is the faint pulse of music wafting from the downtown bars and the sound of drunken laughter. Jones only trusts to take my handcuffs off when we are standing by his low-slung Corvette. I rub at the deep cuts they left on my wrists, then pass my hands over my freshly swelling face. I feel like I'm ten feet tall and thin as a piece of paper. The lightest of breezes could knock me over. Thank God that for once the Wyoming wind is still.

"That girl called, that reporter friend of yours," Jones explains. "Said she saw from her room's window the cops taking you away in a car. She got the hotel to let her in your room, got your phone book, and started punching numbers. She remembered you saying how we were friends and woke me up to see if there was anything I could do. She sounded pretty worked up, man. You sure she's not your girlfriend?"

I don't answer the question. "Thanks, Jones. I owe you. In a big way."

"Shit yeah, in a very big way. But don't worry too much 'bout my job. Yesterday I got a letter from the FBI. I'm going to Quantico in four weeks."

"Congratulations. I hope you find a better class of cop there. I'm not too impressed with Laramie's."

"Yeah, fucking rednecks. I'm overdue for a little affirmative action. So, you want to stay at my place? Wife would love to see you, but she's still a little pissed about you taking me climbing the other day. She'll love that dog of yours."

The seams of my grief begin to part again but I somehow hold them together. I don't tell Jones what happened in the mountains—I can't bear to talk or even think about it yet. Instead I say, "No, the hotel is fine. I want to check on Rebecca and make sure those guys don't mess with her. Then I've got to be in Cheyenne for the hearing this afternoon. I'm going to have to figure out some way of making myself presentable."

"You show up looking and smelling like you do, the judge'll hold you in contempt. Watch your back, man. You need anything, just call."

He drops me off under the security lights of the parking lot by my truck. I pick up my pack from where it still rests on the pavement by my back bumper and get the .32 from under the seat. I slip it into my pocket. Jones maneuvers the Corvette so he can watch me limp down the exposed corridor to my room. I don't know which is Rebecca's and need to call the desk.

But she is in my room when I come through the door.

She sits at the small table by the window, hunched over with the phone to her ear, her unwashed hair tangled over her face. At the sound of the door swinging open she starts like a deer, then says, "He's here!" into the phone and comes to me, the receiver's cord stretched to the breaking point. "My God, what happened—"

"Who are you talking to?"

"McGee, on his cell. He's driving over."

I take the phone from her and say hello to my boss.

"What the hell is going on?" he roars.

I start to explain but he cuts me off. "I'm pulling off the highway—wait for me." Then he hangs up.

Rebecca is still in my arms, her lips pressed against my neck. I toss the dead phone onto the bed and hold her closer. I thank her again and again. This is the second time she has saved me with her courage and resourcefulness.

"What happened? I saw you being pulled into the police car...." She is crying now. "Your face...Ross said something about your brother...."

I quiet her by cupping her face in my hands and kissing her mouth, and tell her I will explain when McGee arrives. Her arms grip my bruised ribs so tight that I think I'll faint, but I don't want her to let go.

Even through the room's closed door I can hear the tap of his cane as he comes down the hallway in the late-night silence. I put Rebecca in a chair and go to the sink to wash my hands and face.

McGee comes in looking even more tired than usual. The lines that fan out from the corners of his eyes are so deep they look as if they were carved by an artist gripping a pencil in his fist. His beard is limp and ragged instead of its usual ferocious bristle. He weaves visibly on his feet as he comes into the room, breathing hard from the walk. As bad as he appears, I can see in the mirror that I look worse. Probably feel worse too. Anger is the only thing keeping me on my feet.

Once he is seated on the bed, I tell him about finding Chris Braddock's body in the Big Horns, and then tell them both about what Bender and Willis did to me and Karge's intention of keeping me locked away until after the sentencing. Gingerly lifting my blood- and sweat-encrusted shirt, I display the sharp bruises that are rising under my skin from the pointy toes of Sergeant Bender's boots.

After McGree growls out a long stream of his signature obscenities, he tells me of my brother's escape from Canon City. He doesn't yet know any of the circumstances— Colorado is playing it close to the vest. But for now I'm considered a suspect in aiding him, as I had just visited him for the first time three days earlier.

"I'm sure the sheriff was all too happy to tell them I was nowhere to be found," I say. "It gave them a great opportunity to tuck me away for a few days, until the Knapps get their ride on the gurney and Karge's election is all but assured."

Rebecca asks, "How can they think it won't come out after the sentencing?"

"For one, they think they...can easily discredit our young friend here," McGee explains. "They'll capitalize on his reputation as a rogue...and hope he doesn't have...an alibi for his brother's escape.... Second, they'll try to silence me...with a threat to my pension...or my health benefits...which God knows I need....And soon Karge will be in a position...to control any investigation, as the governor-elect....But I think these are desperate measures...not fully thought out."

"They're panicking," I say.

"They're fucking out of control," he growls. "There's more bad news, lad.... Talk of filing murder charges... against you again, for the Sureno shooting.... The Attorney General himself called... said they're thinking of suspending you... until a decision is reached.... Karge is cranking up the pressure."

We all sit silently for a few minutes; the only sound is McGee's ragged breath. I'm rocked back on my heels—they're going to take everything from me.

"I wish I could write about this, get it all before the public," Rebecca says angrily, breaking the spell. "Only my editor won't approve it until there's more solid evidence. What can you do from here?"

"I've got enough for a warrant now," I say. "For Heller and Brad Karge. I'm going to write it out now, get it to a judge. Once the word of their arrest is out, the County Attorney will have no choice but to postpone the sentencing."

"Run it down, lad.... What do you have?"

"Kate Danning's dead, with injuries inconsistent to a fall. I've got the bottle with Brad's fingerprints on it and Kate's blood type at the least. Witnesses that place Brad, Heller, and Chris at the scene. As circumstantial as that is, we've also got the fact that Chris is dead and the cut rope as evidence. Again, Heller and Brad were at that scene too in the Big Horns. That makes the inference that Kate was killed all the stronger—those two are taking care of the one witness we know was there when Kate died."

"You need probable cause to get a judge to sign the warrant, right? Is that enough?" Rebecca asks. We're silent for another moment.

McGee explains the concept of probable cause to her. In legalese, it requires facts and circumstances sufficient to cause a person of reasonable caution to believe that a crime has been committed and the person named in the warrant committed the crime. He concludes by saying, "It's very close, depends on the judge.... It's a lot stronger if we tie it in with Lee."

"The only connection we have with Lee right now is that she might have been about to turn in her drug suppliers," I say, "and Heller's a known and convicted dealer. And there's the cord, but of course the coroner threw out whatever was used on Danning. Anyway, no Albany County judge will be anxious to sign a warrant that casts doubts on the senior county judge's trial, especially when it's the trial of the century."

"Then take it to the judge in Johnson County... just get the fucking thing signed," McGee says.

After another moment's silence I say, "I need to get a search warrant for Heller's house too. See if that cord's there, the stuff Billy's been buying in Buffalo. But I don't have any proof that the cord's in his house, so a judge will never sign it. We have to find out if it's there, though. Then we'll know for sure if those guys did Lee and set up the Knapps." I say this looking straight at McGee, wondering how he will respond to my unspoken proposal of breaking into Heller's house. McGee spins his cane in his hands while his bright blue eyes stare back at me. I think I see him nod once, almost imperceptibly. That's enough for me.

Then he says, "What about a motive... something that ties it all together?"

For a few minutes we play the universal parlor entertainment of cops and prosecutors everywhere: the guessing game. Who did it is usually obvious. It is why he or she did it that is always the subject of much discussion and so hard for a jury to understand. So you pitch theories back and forth, trying to find one that makes sense. You look for one that gets you to nod and say to yourself, "Yeah, I can see it. I might've done that if I didn't have more control." And you take comfort in the fact that you have more control. We all have more or less the same urges; some are just taken to a more perverted degree. It is self-control that distinguishes the violent criminal from the law-abiding citizen.

My theory is little more than conjecture, but I feel it is true in my bones. Heller's getting older, losing his strength and skills, losing the idolatry of the young followers that surround him. He is seeking new ways to control them without having to risk his life to draw their awe on the rock. Control with drugs and rough group sex. And I think he's come to like it, this new method of manipulation he has developed. I think he likes degrading the youth he is jealous of—drugging them, choking them, penetrating them, and destroying them. He's found a new way to feed the Rat.

At some point Rebecca moves from the chair to curl up on the bed near where McGee hunches, leaning on his cane. The mental and physical exhaustion has reached a point that will finally allow her to rest. I feel the same—I'm near collapse. She asks in a sleepy voice, "What about the sheriff, Sergeant Bender, and Karge? They're obstructing your investigation. They falsely arrested Anton. Can't you charge them?"

I look at McGee. His face turns red anew with either embarrassment or anger. I hope the stress doesn't prove too much for him. "I've got to go to the fucking AG...the one who's already endorsed Karge for governor...before we do anything like that," he tells us. "And he's got to keep Karge happy...if he wants to keep his job....It's not very goddamn likely...he'll approve any charges like that...even if we can prove them."

"We'll worry about them later," I say, looking at the digital clock on the nightstand. "I'm going to shower, sleep a few hours, then get the warrants written up. And I've got to be in Cheyenne for the hearing at one-thirty this afternoon."

It's two in the morning when I finally get in the shower and try not to gasp as the hot water stings my bruises and open sores. When I come out ten minutes later McGee has gone back to his own room at the hotel. Rebecca is still curled on the bed in the clothes she has worn for the past two days. Her breath is soft and slow—she's asleep. I pull on a pair of shorts and lie down beside her, gently folding the comforter over her like a taco. It seems like I just closed my eyes when the phone blares beside my head.

"Burns," I say, putting my free arm across Rebecca's back to slow her attempt at bolting upright.

"I'm sorry, lad...but I just got the call...Sierra Calloway's been found dead...to the east of Buford in Laramie County...I'll pick you up in ten minutes." I recall that Laramie County is to the east of the town of Laramie and Albany County.

More asleep than awake, a thought rings through me like the crystal tone of a bell. "He's taking care of the witnesses, Ross."

"Appears so," he replies and hangs up.

I explain to Rebecca what's happening and get her to lie back down. "There's nothing you can do right now," I tell her. "The Laramie County sheriffs won't allow you near the scene. Just go back to sleep."

"This is a nightmare," I hear her murmur in an exhausted, frightened voice as I tug on a shirt and pants in the darkness.

* * *

A few minutes later, earlier than I expect, there's a soft knock on the door. I unlock it and pull it open while turning to take my wool jacket from the hook. When I turn back to the door it's not McGee waiting there but Lynn White.

"Hey man," she says softly, almost purring, "I figured the only way I'd get you back in bed is by—"

She stops when she sees my swollen face in the corridor lights and her eyes become wide. "What happened—"

Then her mouth drops open and she looks into the room past me when Rebecca says from the bed, "Anton?"

"Lynn, this isn't a good time..."

But she is already backing away from the door, looking small and angry in her baggy blue jeans and fleece jacket. Her brown eyes are as hard and smooth as river stones when she shoots me a final glare, then turns and runs past the pool, almost colliding with McGee as he shuffles down the hall.

I say to Rebecca, "I'll call you later." Then close the door. Despite everything, I see McGee has a sardonic grin on his evil face, the first I have seen in a long time, when he turns back to me after watching the girl flee down the hall and out of sight.

TWENTY-FOUR

HER TRAILER'S UP past Buford, in Laramie County.... The sheriff up there's asked us to assist... our crime scene techs are coming too...they'll be there in ninety minutes," McGee tells me as we get into his state-issued sedan. I know that Laramie County often works with DCI, especially since our office is based in Cheyenne, Laramie County's biggest town.

The car's interior is permanently stained with the odor of McGee's foul cigars. The smell penetrates even my swollen nose as I ease myself down into the passenger seat. When he's done wrestling his bulk behind the steering wheel, the amused look is gone from his face. We discuss what little he knows about Sierra Calloway's murder. He doesn't ask me for an explanation about the angry girl running down the hall and I don't offer one.

Stars still hang low over Happy Jack Mountains near

Vedauwoo as McGee drives me east on Grand Avenue out of town. The early-morning wind has swept the dark sky clean. A beautiful dawn is inevitable, but the circumstances will not allow me to contemplate it. I don't even turn my head to look at Vedauwoo as we drive past. My eyes are nearly swollen shut from the bruises and exhaustion. My ribs ache a little each time I inhale. A knifelike pain cuts across my stomach every few minutes, caused either by hunger or damage from the kicks I received. And I'm on my way to see the corpse of a girl who was probably killed for just talking with me.

It takes us thirty minutes to cross the county line due to McGee's cautious driving. Just before we reach the line, McGee points at a boarded-up saloon off to the side of the highway.

"I had a case from there once.... It used to be a strip joint...nearly twenty years back.... The place did a little prostitution on the side.... One morning a bunch of sheriff's deputies brought in five strippers for arraignment.... One of them was famous in those days...called herself 'Chris Colt and Her Twin .44s'.... The deputies had run an unapproved undercover sting...they said they had evidence of illegal touching for pay going on.... Turned out the evidence was a bunch of Polaroids taken by the bar's own photographer... each showing a grinning deputy holding the Twin .44s.... Apparently the boys were angry...they didn't get more than just a feel...so they arrested all the girls." McGee chuckles dryly and shakes his head. "I threw the charges out."

I ask out of habit, "Is there a point to that story, Boss?"

"Of course, lad.... One of the moronic young deputies...was named Daniel Willis.... He's moved up in the world since then...but he's still a vindictive piece of shit....I wonder if I still have that photo of him somewhere."

In the remaining moonlight that hangs over the prairie, I can see that Buford is not really a town at all, just a dark gas station with an attached diner, a few collapsing barns, and a couple of trailers. We turn onto a dirt road that parallels the highway.

A few miles past the insignificant town, a Laramie County Sheriff's Office SUV is parked with its lights off before another, smaller, unmarked dirt road. In the faint light, we can see that the road stretches south across the rolling plain toward the towering ice and granite of Rocky Mountain National Park and the 14,000-foot massif of Longs Peak. McGee pulls in behind the car and turns his lights off and on again. In their illumination the figure in the driver's seat makes a follow-me gesture and starts his car. We trail it down the unmarked road through the dust it kicks up. Our two-car caravan rocks up over a small rise, then drops into a broad depression that's a mile or more in circumference.

There's a long, battered trailer there among low shrub-like trees. A partially collapsed shed hunkers behind it and there's a dog run to the side. Two more SUVs bearing the emblem of the Laramie County Sheriff's Office are waiting with their lights turned on, pointing at the trailer. The barking of dogs penetrates the otherwise quiet night.

McGee pulls up alongside one and puts his car in park. I roll down my window and let McGee speak across me to the elderly man behind the wheel.

"Morning, McKittrick....I won't say it's a good one.... This is Special Agent Burns. He's DCI."

The sheriff nods at me, taking a minute to examine a little skeptically my two-day growth of beard and tired, beaten

face. He doesn't say it, but I can read what he's thinking—
Heard about you.

When the sheriff does speak, it's past me to McGee.
"Howdy, Ross. Good to see you, and thanks for coming out.
We've been waiting on you. Be careful now, there's some
dogs about. I think they're behind the trailer right now."

The man called McKittrick has a large head and a leathery face. Despite being parked, his weathered hands grip the
wheel at the ten-and-two positions. From what I can see of
him above the car's frame, he wears a sport coat with
Western-cut shoulders and lapels over a wool work shirt.
His face is clean-shaven except for a long mustache. On his
head he wears a smallish cowboy hat.

"What have you found?" I ask him, taking a legal pad
and pen from my briefcase.

"Girl lives there." He nods at the trailer. "She's the deceased. Works in town. Laramie. A friend of hers came out
to check on her a few hours ago and found her. We haven't
been in there yet. After we got the call, 'bout an hour ago,
one of my deputies and I just peeked inside with a torch.
She's clearly dead, bent over a chair or something. Then
those dogs came around. We've been sitting on our asses in
the cars ever since, waiting for y'all." Almost as an after-
thought, he adds, "There's a dog inside too. You'll hear him
in a minute."

As if on cue, there's a bellow that eclipses the other
barking. It's followed by a crash from inside the trailer. The
flimsy home shakes visibly on its foundations.

"Must be a big sucker," the sheriff comments. "We
think he's locked in a back room somewheres. The body's in
the front, just beyond the door."

"Who found her?" I ask.

"Pretty girl, name of Cindy Topper. Out of Laramie,

she says. She called it in from a cell phone 'bout two A.M. Said she came out here 'cause of some call she'd gotten herself—wouldn't say from who—but it scared her so she thought she'd just come on out and spend the night with her friend."

"Where's Topper now?" McGee asks. We are both thinking the same thing: she's undoubtedly next on Heller and Brad's hit list. Probably Lynn is high up on that list too. They are wiping out the whole Heller cult as if it were Jonestown.

"One of my boys picked her up. She's at the station right now, waiting to see if we've got any more questions."

"Hang on to her, Sheriff," I say. "I'm afraid I know who did this and I think she may be next."

McGee and I get out of the car. It's a small relief to feel the wind and smell the sagebrush after a half hour in McGee's rank sedan. The sheriff speaks a few words on his radio, then gets out in unison with two younger officers from the other two cars. They exchange nods with us in the blaze of the headlights. I hear some ragged barks and the sound of scampering paws and snapping twigs coming through the dry brush toward us.

A big German shepherd mix emerges from the night in a slow lope, coming at McGee and me where we stand in front of his sedan. The shepherd is tentatively followed by three smaller dogs, far less of a threat. The deputies have their guns out of their holsters but I yell at them not to shoot as the shepherd slows and comes at me, growling and baring his teeth. With a black coat and another one hundred pounds on his skinny frame he would look a bit like Oso.

I take a quick step toward him, waving the legal pad. "No," I tell him. "Cut it out! Bad dog." At first the dog just snarls louder, then finally lowers his volume as I continue to yell. The others keep up their yapping behind him. "Sit! Sit!" Grudgingly, the big dog half-lowers himself onto his hindquarters. "Sit!" I yell again and he finally lowers his butt into the dirt. "Good dog. Now stay." I walk past him, turning to keep my eyes locked on the dog's, and walk up three rickety wooden steps to the door of the trailer. The trailer shakes again as the dog inside bellows and hurls its weight against what I assume must be an interior door. McGee follows me up onto the porch, then the sheriff and one of the deputies. The other deputy stands behind us, covering our rear from the advancing dogs.

"Round up those mutts," the sheriff tells the surprised and alarmed deputy. "Start with the big 'un." The deputy looks like he wants to appeal that order but then turns away unhappily, already expecting to get bit.

"Whew. I hate that smell. . . . Seems like I've lived with it ever since Korea," McGee says to no one.

Even standing outside the door I can smell the sweet-sick scent of rotting meat. Adding to its offense is the sound of buzzing flies. My stomach turns, but it doesn't concern me—there's nothing in it to come up. Anger and loss and hunger and exhaustion have left me punch-drunk and cold as stone.

I take the flashlight from the deputy and examine the slightly open door. It's made of the same rusty aluminum as the trailer's body. A cheap brass lock is the only built-in security I can see. Someone has mounted the hinged steel of a padlock brace on the door to better secure the trailer from the outside. The padlock itself hangs open from the mounting on the side of the trailer.

The sheriff wipes his mustache with a rag and passes it to me. I sniff it and feel its scorch all the way to the back of my throat—gasoline to deaden our sense of smell. I wipe my own lips and nostrils and pass it on to McGee, my skin burning. With the toe of one hiking boot I ease the door open wider and probe the darkness with the flashlight as another bellow and crash shakes the trailer.

"Lord, that makes my hair stand on end," McKittrick says.

The beam of light is immediately drawn to the body that lies a few feet beyond the door. It's clearly a woman's, a girl's really, that's bent over a chair and facing away from the door. The pale, thin buttocks have been carefully posed to be the first thing anyone entering the trailer will see. A cloud of flies hangs in the darkness above the body. The strong beam of light shows carnivorous fire ants busily gorging themselves on the cold flesh. I hear the men behind me gasp and curse. I focus on the dead girl's thigh, and even from this angle I can see the long, familiar tattoo of a climber reaching nearly from knee to hip.

"It's Sierra. The hotel maid," I say out loud, without thinking. At the sound of my voice, or the dead girl's name, the trailer rocks again with another roar and crash from the rear of the trailer. The floor vibrates beneath my feet. I move the beam of light on, sweeping it steadily around the room.

Other than the body, the small room is orderly but for a single broken lamp. It lies on the floor not far from the corpse. The glass from the broken bulb is strewn on the tabletop. Its cord snakes across the floor to a socket in the wall. I suspect the naked wires that protrude from where the bulb had once been were used to get answers. Or to punish. A closer examination of the corpse will probably reveal tiny burn marks in painful places.

The windows are hung with tie-dyed sheets used as drapes. Other psychedelic art is tacked to the imitation-wood walls. One spells out the name of a band, "Phish," in bright, waving letters. Another features dancing bears and is a tribute to the Grateful Dead. As the light wavers on it, Sheriff McKittrick says from behind me, "I'd be gratefully dead too, someone done that to me." There are several other posters displaying climbers clinging tenaciously on wildly exposed rock. Cheap, mismatched glasses and dishes stand in formation on a shelf above the small sink and two-burner propane stove. Along the floor against one wall is a long line of various sized dog bowls.

With the sleeve of my coat pulled over my hand, I sweep my forearm against the inside wall, feeling for a light switch. Something catches the material at the right level and I flip it up. The room flickers into light, but loses none of its horror. If anything, the horror is intensified. Evil is one thing when cloaked in the dark, but it takes on an even more terrifying aspect in the light, when it becomes all too real.

I step cautiously around to the side of the body and wish I hadn't come. I could have told McGee I was just too tired. Or I could have left in my Land Cruiser after the first run-in with Dominic Torres's little brother and driven back up to Cody with Oso drooling out the windows. If I'd done that, two people and my dog would probably still be alive. Their relatively innocent lives were being exchanged for the more sullied lives of the Knapps. And unless something was done soon to halt the sentencing, the Knapps too would be sacrificed. And maybe others.

My knees feel weak as I stare at the long tattoo on Sierra Calloway's thigh. The hot taste of bile is in my mouth and I finally look away as I try to swallow it down. I swallow again and again, listening to the other men's obscenities and the howls and crashes from the rear of the trailer. I make myself step closer to the body and see the laughing skull on her neck, half hidden by lank blonde hair.

I ease down the narrow hallway to a bedroom door made of cheap wood that is splintering from the dog's repeated attacks. I brace my foot and hip against it, feeling the weight of the big dog on the other side. "Easy," I say through the door. But that only causes the dog to renew its baying and go at the door with greater force. I turn and see McGee and the sheriff behind me. The other deputy is still in the living room, transfixed by the corpse.

"Good thing he didn't get out. We wouldn't have a body left," McKittrick says.

I don't answer and don't bother to cover my hand when I turn the knob, my leg still bracing the door. I let it open toward me a few inches. A snarling muzzle protrudes, level with my stomach. The dog is gigantic—taller than even Oso, but much thinner. Some sort of mutated Great Dane. I push the door shut and reengage the latch.

"I guess we'll have to shoot the bastard," the sheriff advises a little sadly.

I shake my head. "Call the Game and Fish. Get them out here to tranquilize it."

"Already did, son. They said they don't do dogs."

"Then tell them it's a fucking wolf," McGee suggests. I recall his fondness for dogs and am thankful for that as well as his rough resourcefulness.

I continue to brace the door while the sheriff takes out a cell phone and a leather address book. Moving back down the hall, he dials a number and speaks for a few minutes over the noise. "She's coming," he finally says from the living room, stabbing a button to end the call.

I call for the nearly catatonic deputy to bring me one of the upright chairs from the table. The deputy awakens from his trance and lifts a chair, carefully staying as far away from the girl's body as he can. I brace the chair against the rear door's knob as added security. We all return to the living room where McGee and McKittrick crouch by the body, studying it. Soft pink cord binds her hands and ankles. They are the same unusual type and color of cord I'd been given by Cecelia up in Buffalo. I immediately recognize the knots that have been used to cinch and lock the line tight around her hands, ankles, and throat. Prusik knots, a climber's knot for ascending a rope.

I point them out to McGee and he says, "Same kind as was used on Lee."

"It's the same kind of cord Heller's been buying up in Buffalo," I tell him.

"You know her, Agent?" McKittrick asks, indicating the body before us.

"Yes, Sheriff, I do. She was a witness in an ongoing murder investigation. Two murders, actually, now three. Let's go outside until the lab guys get here," I say, my investigative instincts for preserving the evidence taking control. "Who touched what?"

"Nothing," both McGee and McKittrick respond.

"What about you?" I ask the deputy, observing his pale face, bulging eyes, and lips that are bloodless.

"Just the chair," he whispers.

Before I lead them through the front door, the sheriff pauses at a window, looking out into the yard. The sun has finally risen high enough to have its rays curve over the surface of eastern Wyoming and brush away the stars. Through the window's glass I see its light reaching the Snowy Range to the west, turning its glacial couloirs golden and its quartz and granite purple. I wish I were there, brewing tea on some snow-covered ledge.

The sheriff is looking down at the ground outside, shaking his head and grumbling to himself. I follow his gaze and see the deputy who was assigned the task of rounding up the dogs outside. He's holding a rope with a wide slipknot on one end, chasing the German shepherd out of sight around a corner. A moment later he runs back into view, the dog chasing him. I could laugh if I didn't feel so sick. For a moment I forget what I'm doing and rest my forehead against the trailer's cool aluminum wall.

Outside we stand on the porch for a few minutes while we wait for wildlife control and the DCI crime scene techs to show up. We watch the deputy, joined now by his colleague, pursuing and being pursued by the dogs. The dogs have turned it into a game. McGee sits on the steps and lights a cigar while the sheriff and I walk a circle around the trailer and shed, ignoring the play taking place around us. We can't find any broken windows or torn screens. I'm not surprised. I already know she was friends with her killers; she probably invited them in.

We spend a few minutes studying the dirt driveway. The ground is hard and rocky. We can't see any discernible tire marks.

I turn when I hear the sound of an engine coming down into the depression. It's a lime green pickup with the insignia of the Wyoming Game and Fish Department painted on its side. It pulls to a stop behind the other cars and a small woman gets out, pointedly ignoring us. From the back of the pickup she withdraws a long, flimsy pole with a wire noose on one end. The pole is as thin as a fly-fishing rod. We can still hear and feel the trailer shuddering as the Great Dane throws himself at the door. Beside me, the sheriff chuckles.

"That little lady don't know what she's in for." He

leaves my side and walks over to her while I join McGee on the steps.

We watch Sheriff McKittrick argue with the woman for a few minutes. He's telling her that the stick won't work, she has to tranquilize the damn wolf. And she says that she knows there isn't any damn wolf, and that the stick will work fine for a dog. Finally, after the sheriff has her observe the trailer rocking on its foundations from the force of the big dog's attacks on the door, she appears to give in and puts away the stick-and-noose. From behind the seat in the cab of the pickup she takes out a rifle bag and a smaller nylon case. She spreads them both on the hood of the truck and I hear her say as she unzips them, "I don't know what dose to use. Just how big is he?"

"Like an elk," McKittrick responds.

"Half an elk," McGee calls to them.

The woman snorts, disbelieving, and pops a cylinder of amber liquid into the chamber of the rifle.

The sheriff leads her onto the porch, where she gasps at the smell that even McGee's rancid cigar is unable to disguise. McKittrick explains to her what's inside before he opens the door. The wildlife officer turns a little white, but nods gamely when he tells her exactly what she should not look at. "We're just going to march straight down the hall, plug the dog, then leave. All right, honey?"

She nods again.

"Keep your eyes on me," I add.

The sheriff opens the door and steps inside quickly, in an attempt to shield the woman's eyes from the corpse. I back in after him, keeping my eyes on hers. "Follow me." She does as she was told and we quickly move down the hallway where the mutant Great Dane resumes its bellowing and attacks on the door.

I again brace my foot against the thin door and move the chair out of the way. The wildlife officer raises the rifle as I crack open the door. "Jesus," she says when the huge, snarling snout pushes through. She pushes the barrel of the gun through the crack above the dog's head and aims it down. With one eye shut and her tongue slightly protruding from between her teeth, she pulls the trigger.

From the gun comes a sharp hiss of escaping air. The dart imbeds itself just to one side of the brute's skinny spine. The dog lets out a high-pitched yelp that is surprisingly out of character for such a large canine. Then without any further warning it collapses onto one side.

The sheriff looks into the room past us. "Ma'am, I think you killed him," he deadpans. "Must not have been even half an elk. Maybe just an antelope." But then the Great Dane lets out a long groan. We can see its ribs rise and fall in slow motion. I'm glad for that—there's been more than enough death.

The sheriff and I escort the woman out of the trailer, again guarding her eyes. She walks straight to her truck and zips up her rifle. Without a word to anyone she climbs in the cab and slowly drives up and out of the depression. The sheriff and I work together to drag the Dane out by its front legs and carry it gently down the stairs below the porch. We leave it in the dog run with five out of the six dogs the deputies have caught so far.

McGee has abandoned his perch on the steps for the quieter and relatively less stinking sanctuary of the state's sedan. With the car's door open, McGee is sitting on the driver's seat with his feet in the dirt and his hands resting on the head of his cane. I walk over and stretch out on the car's dusty hood in the morning light. The sun, its rays now high enough to touch the earth directly, starts baking through my jacket. The warmth seeps through my clothes down to my battered skin, muscles, and bones.

"You meet her?" I finally ask.

"No, I was never . . . in the room when she came by."

"Heller and Brad killed her, Ross. Probably on Monday night, late or early in the morning. As they were leaving town with Chris, to kill him too. Somehow they found out she talked to me, or they thought she might have. She's the one who told me Chris wasn't so bad, that he was the one I should talk to. The weak link."

"Who knew that she talked to you?"

I try to think, but my brain is sluggish. "I told you in the hospital, right? And Rebecca. Who'd you talk to about it?"

"Karge's pal, the AG," he says. "No one else."

"Then he might have passed the word along to Karge."

"Much as I hate that self-righteous prig . . . the AG wouldn't have done it . . . if he knew this would be the re-sult. . . . And Karge sure as hell wouldn't . . . resort to mur-der. . . . He may be a typical politician . . . an ambitious cover-your-ass kind of guy . . . but he's not a frigging killer."

"Maybe not. But I think he's protecting his kid and Heller, trying to play Heller like a puppet. Doing it to save the Knapp trial, the election, and his son. He's assisting in this mess by passing along information that's getting every-one killed. Heller's nobody's puppet."

"More like a pet tiger on a leash . . . dragging Karge through all sorts of shit," McGee rasps. "Who's left?"

I think about it for a minute. "That girl you saw this morning in the hall, Lynn White. She was Heller's girlfriend at some point. But she told me she left early that night, be-fore Kate went off the cliff. Damn."

I have to find her, but I doubt now that she wants to be found by me, or will even be willing to listen. Not after this morning. I use my cell phone to call the climbing shop where she works in Laramie. The girl who answers tells me Lynn hasn't come in today and won't tell me where she is, even when I tell her it's an emergency. Finally I just leave an urgent message for her to call me along with my cell phone number. I leave a similar message on the anonymous recording that picks up when I call the number that I have for Lynn's house.

With my boss's nod of permission, I also call the duty officer at DCI. I request a BOLO on Heller and Brad Karge and describe Heller's van. The Be On the Lookout report will hopefully get them picked up for questioning. It's all I can do until I get a warrant written and signed.

A large black van comes bouncing down into the depression, going too fast for the poor condition of the unpaved road. The driver propels it like it's a vehicle owned by someone else. Which it is, even though its panels display no advertising. It skids to a halt behind the four cars gathered outside Sierra Calloway's trailer. Its approach sets the captured dogs to their manic barking again. By this time the young deputy sheriff, with the help of his colleague, has herded the last of them into the long dog run. Miraculously, neither of the deputies appears to have been bitten.

Dave Ruddick climbs out of the state vehicle followed by two of his assistants. With only a nod to McGee and me, the three slide open the van's side and slip orange jumpsuits over their clothing. I come out of my exhausted stupor slowly. I hesitate a long time, then slap my palms against the hood of McGee's car, letting the sting penetrate the fatigue, and roll up and off it in a single swift motion. Still thinking about how much I don't want to do this, don't want to go back inside that trailer, I walk over and select a pair of coveralls and gloves for myself.

The air inside becomes stifling as the sun rises in the sky, seeming to seek a better angle at which to increase the pressure of its heat on the tin-roofed trailer on the plain. The heat weakens us and makes the orange suits claustrophobic. I can manage the smell only with a liberal application of gasoline that scorches the skin of my upper lip and sears from my nostrils to the back of my throat. But there's no respite from the sound of a thousand flies buzzing, and there's no way to shield our eyes from the tasks we are required to perform before the body can be removed.

I come to a point when I've witnessed all I will need to in order to testify and I can't take another minute inside. I stagger out of the trailer, and although my sense of smell has long since been burned away, I know that my clothes must reek of sweat and death. Just the thought of it chokes me as does the sight of Sierra Calloway's body. I jerk the suit off and toss it in the dirt. I start walking through the chaparral with no purpose in mind other than to suck in the high plains air and let the rising wind cleanse my lungs. McGee watches me stalk away but doesn't yell after me.

A little later I hear Rebecca's voice calling my name. I look around me and find myself walking more or less parallel to the unpaved road, up and out of the depression in which the trailer sits. Squinting through the sunlight, I can see ten or more cars being held back at the rim by a Laramie deputy. The cars look cheap and American; I realize they are the rental cars of a town full of bored reporters.

She's walking through the dirt and brush toward me. Despite her clean shirt and blue jeans, she looks tired, as if she hasn't slept at all. But she's still impossibly beautiful. I hold up one hand as she approaches, and she stops ten or more feet from me.

"Stay back. I'm kind of a mess." I don't want her coming closer to the stench of my clothes and body. It's a smell that seems to penetrate all the way to my bones.

"Anton..." she says again, hesitating. "Are you all right?"

"That girl at the hotel," I say, "I dated her once. Not anymore, though. I want you to know that."

"I don't care, Anton," she says, her expression unreadable behind the sunglasses. I don't know if she means for me or about the fact that I had seen another girl. "Did they kill Sierra Calloway?"

"Yeah. They did, cords and all. For talking to me. That's what got her killed. Look, I'll call you later."

I turn and walk through the brush back into the depression on the plain.

When I return to the vicinity of the trailer, Dave Ruddick is heading toward me, smoking a cigarette. He still wears his orange crime scene suit but he has pulled the gloves off his hands. Sweat runs out of his hair and down his face.

"About finished?" I ask.

"Yep. The boys are bagging her right now."

"You got a TOD for me?"

Ruddick nods. "Looks like she was cooled sometime on Monday night. The parasites in her mouth, vagina, and anus—"

"That's all right," I tell him, "I don't want to hear about

that." The outside air has purified me to a fragile degree and I want to remember Sierra as she appeared when boldly propositioning me in my hotel room, not as the befouled corpse in a black bag that the other techs are dragging down the steps of the porch and across the dirt to the van. I want to walk over and order them to carry her gently but I don't. They deal with corpses all too often, and the only way they can cope is to treat their wards like pieces of meat. I remind myself that the body is nothing but a discarded husk.

"Does that time frame fit in with your perps?" Dave asks.

I nod. They could easily have stopped by on their way to the Big Horns. "Any prints?"

"Sure, lots of 'em. But I doubt your boys were dumb enough to do this bare-handed. We'll probably have better luck with hair and fiber."

I'm not so sure of that. "They've both been here a lot of times before. Unless we can tie it in to the actual killing, that's going to be a problem."

Dave shrugs, and then looks around before speaking again, as if to make sure we are alone. "Speaking of prints, I got a result on those unidentified ones. You know, on that bottle."

"Heller's?"

He shakes his head. "I'm not supposed to talk about it. Especially to you. When I IDed them, I went right to the AG. He ordered me to keep it under my hat." Now he makes a face. "But I've been thinking about what you said the other day, about politics and justice. So I'm going to tell you." He pauses to rethink his decision one last time then says, "To be thorough, I happened to run them through the state employee file. Surprise surprise, I got a hit. Nathan Karge, our next governor."

Dave is watching me closely for a reaction but I remain nonchalant. "His kid, Brad, could have taken the bottle from Dad's liquor cabinet. I used to do that when I was his age."

The techy looks disappointed. He was expecting to rock my world with his revelation. But instead my reaction to his information is outwardly innocuous. Inside, it's a little different. I try to soften the blow by telling him, "But thanks for telling me. I really mean that. What disturbs me more than the prints is that the AG would tell you to keep it quiet."

What the hell happened up there that night? I wonder.

TWENTY-FIVE

AN HOUR LATER McGee drives me back to the Holiday Inn. Then he turns around to head back up Third Street toward the courthouse. He's going to meet with Nathan Karge, to demand that Karge continue the Lee sentencing. The County Attorney will have no choice but to agree—if he doesn't, McGee will go to the judge with what we have learned. Although we have little in the way of actual evidence that could exonerate the Knapps—just the cord that might have been purchased by Heller and Brad Karge, and its use in the Calloway and Danning murders—it should be enough to ensure a continuance, or possibly even a mistrial, in order to allow the defense to look into it. Either way, Karge's aspirations to higher office will surely be affected. His rising star is about to become a black hole.

During the mostly silent ride I asked McGee if he wanted me to come along, but he told me no, that I need sleep, rest, food, and to suit up before the summary judgment hearing just hours away this afternoon in Cheyenne. He felt that my being there would just piss Karge off. I couldn't argue with that. But I want to piss him off. I want to pay him back for what Willis and Bender did to me in the interrogation room. I want to see his face as he realizes that it is all unfolding—that he will never be governor once the Lee trial blows up in his face and I arrest his son for multiple murders.

I stop before the door to my room and fumble in my pockets for the key. Even when I find it and slide it into the lock, I hesitate. I rub my face and push my hands through hair that is oily with sweat. Something is very wrong, I think, staring sightlessly at the blank orange door. It takes me a minute to realize what it is. Oso should be waiting for me on the other side of the door. The realization strikes me like a knee to the groin. After closing my eyes for a minute, willing myself to regain control, I turn the key in the lock and go in.

The room is neat inside, having been recently cleaned. Obviously someone's already covering for Sierra Calloway. How easily we are all replaced and forgotten. My eyes are caught by the angry flash of the message light on the telephone, then the dog bowls stacked beside a twenty-pound bag of Purina. I walk past it all like a zombie, straight to the bathroom, where I peel off my jeans and shirt and use the toilet before stepping into the shower. My urine comes out bright red, courtesy of Bender's boots.

The water blasts out of the cheap nozzle. It's so hot it turns my skin pink upon contact, but I don't feel its sting. I simply stand and let it wash over me. I sway involuntarily under the nozzle, rocking on my feet. Then, tearing upward from my stomach, the weakness overcomes me. First I crouch with my thighs against my chest and my palms on the shower floor. Then I roll back onto my buttocks and lean my back against the cool tile wall. Sounding as if it comes from a long ways away, I hear myself moan.

I step out of the shower naked, clean, and empty. The sink and mirror are outside the bathroom, in an alcove off the main room. There I lean my wet hips against the porcelain counter and stare at myself in the mirror. The slightly blurry image is of a man who is almost a stranger to me. It isn't the reflection that I grew up with, that I spent more than a decade of adulthood with. My eyes are laced with red and sunk deeper than ever. The bruises on my face have turned a sickly yellow and blue. As if it had just happened yesterday, the long scar from cheekbone to lip is vivid and fresh. The cords of my neck stand out like twin ropes. Between the muscles on my stomach are lines that could have been cut by a knife. The weakness comes again, ripping through my gut, and I lean forward to press my forehead against the cool mirror.

"Anton..."

I whirl around at the sound, pressing off the sink counter with my hands. It's Rebecca. She's sitting on my bed, wearing the jeans and white blouse she had on when I saw her earlier at Sierra Calloway's trailer. Next to her is a tray with a sandwich and a glass of milk on it. I say nothing but pull a towel off the rack and wrap it around my waist.

"Anton, I'm sorry, but I had to come. I'm worried about you. You look awful. I know you must feel awful too. You probably should see a doctor. Here, I brought you some food. You at least have to eat, and get some sleep." She rises as she speaks and comes toward me, her arms outstretched and her own tired eyes sad. I stand still as she wraps her arms around me, her shirt soaking up the water that still drips from my chest.

I feel my lungs constrict and my throat swell, as if again attempting to force tears out of my eyes. This simple kindness touches me more than grief, horror, outrage, or exhaustion. Just that, an act of compassion like a hug or the gift of food, almost overwhelms me.

"I'm so sorry about Oso."

I put my arms around her and pull her hard against me as I feel her humid breath and her tears warm on my shoulder. Her lips touch my skin and some current from our hearts passes between us. I hold her with one hand low on her back and the other high. Not too tightly, but just enough so that it feels as if her body is coming into mine. I draw strength from her.

When I finally let her go, I speak for the first time. "I'll be all right, Rebecca, but thank you. Thank you for everything. I'm going to eat this stuff you brought me and sleep now, just for a few hours anyway. Will you do me a favor and call me at noon? I've got to get up then and haul my tired ass to Cheyenne."

"It looked fine to me, Anton. Not too tired at all, just a little bruised," she says, smiling faintly. "I'll call."

I awake to the ringing of the phone. I try to ignore it with my head sunk deep into a pillow. But even after the phone stops ringing, I can see in my mind the incessant flashing red light of the message indicator. And besides that, despite the utter exhaustion and grief, I wake up angry. My pulse beats too fast in my veins and my jaw aches from unconscious clenching. More sleep will have to wait.

I had dreamt I was young and happy again, camping

with my brother in the Bitterroot Mountains near my parents' rented cabin. We spent the night stretched out on insulated pads above the hard crust of the late-spring snow. When we sat up in our down bags and rubbed the sleep from our faces, we saw the impossibly wide tracks in the snow all around us. They were enormous, far bigger than two hands together, the fingers stretched as wide as we could hold them. Grizzly tracks.

"Big sucker, *che*. Could have tried to eat us," Roberto said.

"Wonder why he didn't?"

" 'Cause we would've kicked his ass." He was grinning, excited that death had been so near.

"Yeah, right. The two of us would have been like a snack, *'mano*."

We studied the tracks, rearing up like caterpillars in our sleeping bags so as not to leave their warmth. Roberto pointed to where the tracks came right to the head of his sleeping bag. The massive grizzly had stood right over him and inhaled his scent. "Check it out, Ant," he said. "Bear probably kissed me in my sleep."

I could see in his eyes that he felt the bear had blessed him. And I was jealous there weren't any tracks by my head.

I sit up and feel the damp towel under the covers, still around my waist. Deliberately, I look at Oso's bowls and the short nylon leash that lies on the carpet beside them. It stokes the anger—it allows me to get up. I swing my feet out of the bed and pick up the phone to check my messages.

An automated woman's voice tells me that I have eleven new messages. Too many. I fight the temptation to simply hang up the phone, ignoring them all.

The first, the voice says, came in at ten thirty A.M. on Tuesday. I think back—that would have been shortly after I left for the Big Horn Mountains. I press the number 1 to hear the message. It is Lynn's voice. "Hey, Anton. Where you at, man? I've been looking for you for a couple of days now. Shit, you just love 'em and leave 'em or what?" She chuckles. "Sorry about the other message I left before, I was kind of pissed. Give me a call. There's something I need to talk to you about, dude. Call me." I press 7 to erase the message.

The second message was from later that same day and is also from Lynn. Her voice sounds strained. "Dude, where the fuck are you? Look, I really want to talk to you. Call me, please." I erase that message as well.

The third is from Kristi, made on Tuesday afternoon shortly after Lynn's second message. "Hey, Anton. Please give me a call. I'm really worried about you. We all heard what happened yesterday at the courthouse. I wanted to come over but Ross McGee wouldn't let me. The hospital says you left without checking out. That doesn't sound like a very good idea, buddy." There's a short pause. "And Anton, you should get away for a while. Maybe that's what you're doing. Anyway, my folks have a place in the mountains near Steamboat. No one's using it this weekend, and I wanted to see if you'd go with me. I guess I'm asking you out on a date." She laughs nervously. "Oh yeah, one other thing. That girl named Lynn White from Laramie keeps calling here, asking for you. Is she some competition or what? Anyway, give her a call too. She sounds worried, just like me." I erase that message too.

The fourth message came in Wednesday morning at seven A.M., according to the automated voice. About the time I found Chris Braddock's body on the ledge. It's an older man's voice, stiff and official, the same voice that left the message at my office and that I had retrieved on the drive back from the Big Horns. "This is Captain John Tobias of the Colorado Bureau of Investigation calling for Special Agent Antonio Burns. I was told by your office I could reach you at this number. It is absolutely urgent that I speak with you immediately. Call me back as soon as you get this message." He gives a number where he says he can be reached twenty-four hours a day. I write that down along with the man's name on the pad provided by Holiday Inn. Now I know roughly at what time Roberto escaped—sometime Tuesday night or in the early hours of Wednesday morning. I play the message again to be sure of the time and write that and the date as well.

The next message is again from Captain Tobias. "Agent Burns, do not ignore this message. It is imperative I speak to you immediately." He again leaves a Colorado number.

There are two more messages after that, both from Tobias, both even more insistent.

Then one from my mother, long-distance from my grandfather's ranch in Argentina. I can tell from her voice that she's trying hard to sound unconcerned and simply exasperated, but the deep worry carries through in the undertones. For many years she has been trying to give up on Roberto, but has never come close to succeeding. And since the trouble in Cheyenne, I have been as much a worry to her as him. "Antonio, what is happening in Colorado?" she asks in Spanish. "People from there keep calling me about Roberto. The people say he is missing from Canon City. Do you know what is happening? They will not hurt him, will they? Your office says they do not know where you are either."

The ninth message is from the Attorney General for the state of Wyoming, and he identifies himself as such, despite my knowing full well who he is and immediately recognizing his voice. With a terse tone he orders me to contact Captain Tobias of the Colorado Bureau of Investigation without delay. "Your brother," he says dryly, "apparently has decided to parole himself a little early."

And the next one is from the subject of all the fuss, the same reckless man who was thrilled after a seven-hundred-pound wild grizzly sniffed his hair. "*Che,* what's up? I called your work—they told me where to find you." He laughs. "Guess what? I'm on the loose. I blew the joint. Where do you think I'm at? Well, I'm not going to tell—I know you'd snitch me out. You're too straight for your own good, bro. But I bet you can guess where I'm heading. See you at Christmas! It's time to feed the Rat." He hoots. "Tell the boys from Colorado I'll be seeing them around. And keep your meat off the deck!" The message ends and I press 9 to save the message. Go, 'Berto, go, I think. A smile creeps across my swollen face.

The final message is another from Kristi. She asks, in a whispered voice, what's going on. "People are saying that you're about to be suspended, that you might've helped your brother escape, and that they're thinking again about filing murder charges. I'm worried about you, buddy. Oh yeah, that nice kid from the civil division, your attorney, keeps calling, sounding real upset. He wants to talk to you before the hearing today."

I hang up the phone and walk to the sink, the goose bumps my brother's voice had raised still on me. Bending over the counter, I put my head under the faucet and suck at the cold Wyoming water there. I let it run over my face and cool my burned lip and nostrils. The taste of gasoline is still in my throat.

Back at the phone I try to call Lynn but no one answers.

I let it ring and ring. Then there's a sharp knock on the door. If it were McGee or Rebecca, they would just come in.

I hang up the phone. "One minute," I call out as I drop the towel from around my waist and step into underwear and a pair of suit pants. As I'm pulling on a starched white shirt the knocking begins again, louder. It doesn't stop. I can feel the pressure of my blood rising, heating up my face with annoyance.

I walk over and kick the closed door hard with my bare forefoot. "I said one minute!" After that I stay still, not bothering to button the shirt. I will the anger to drain away.

"This is Captain Tobias of the Colorado Bureau of Investigation. Open this door!" a voice from beyond it orders.

I slowly exhale, then twist the handle and pull open the door. A short, middle-aged man with fierce eyes stands before me with one hand under his polyester suit jacket on the butt of his gun. The man's gray hair is buzzed short above his ears. It's a little longer on top and stands stiff like a brush. White walls, I remember it's called from my years as a military brat. He glares briefly at me, and then looks past me into the room. I don't move from where I'm holding the door open, partially blocking the little man's view.

"I'm Burns. I understand you want to talk to me."

"Agent Burns, I've been trying to reach you for two days. I'd like to hear an explanation."

I feel my pulse once again picking up its pace, the temperature of my blood rising. "I've been busy," I say rudely. "I'm investigating multiple murders."

"I'm afraid that's not good enough. Are you going to make me go over your head again?" he threatens. "Would you like me to call your Attorney General to find out why you've been ignoring my messages and now are evading my questions regarding your brother's escape?"

I've had enough. "Go ahead, Captain. I've had a rotten week and I really don't give a shit. It's been nice talking to you."

I begin to close the door in his face. With a quick motion Tobias presses one foot against the door and starts to push his way into the room with his free left hand.

The anger that's been simmering in my chest suddenly knocks the lid off the pot. In a grab equally quick, I snatch the wrist of the captain's gun hand where it's reaching across his chest to the shoulder holster and pull it out. It comes out without the gun. Using the captain's momentum as he tries to push forward through the door, I step out of the way, pull on the wrist with both hands, and neatly flip the captain over my hip. The small man's upper back thumps down hard on the unpadded carpet. Air escapes his lungs in a rush. Bending to him, I whip the gun out of its holster just as Tobias makes a long moan, trying to force air back into his chest. A moose call, I remember my brother calling it.

I feel a refreshing release.

With a malicious grin, I place the pistol high up on a shelf in the open closet where it will be out of the small man's reach. Then I sit on the bed, over Tobias, as the man rolls up into a kneeling position, then rests his forehead on the carpet. Slowly the air is coming back to him.

"You're under...arrest," he pants. "I'll...have... your badge....I'll...have your ass!"

"I'm not even going to ask how you're going to arrest me, Captain, seeing as how you're laying on my floor without a gun. Because a more important question is what are you going to arrest me for?"

"Assault on a peace...officer."

I laugh. "You must not have seen that sign as you were driving into town. About thirty miles back it says, 'Welcome to Wyoming.' You've got no jurisdiction here, asshole. You aren't a peace officer here and you can't arrest anyone."

When he looks up, his face is red. The look he gives me is meant to penetrate like a bullet, but I have taken far tougher blows lately.

"All right, Captain. You said you had questions. Go ahead and ask them."

After a long, embarrassed minute he gets up off the floor and sits in a chair. I can see he's struggling to keep himself under control.

"Where were you Tuesday night?"

"I was camping, in the Big Horn Mountains." I don't immediately explain further.

He smiles meanly, the hope that I'm un-alibied gleaming in his eyes. I let it build for a second, then dash his hopes. "You can call the Sheriff's Office there in Johnson County and verify that. Ask for Sergeant Sorrel. I found a body in the mountains and phoned it in. If you check around, you'll learn that I also had lunch at the Moonbeam Café and bought a bunch of stuff at a climbing shop."

My seesawing emotions waver again. I'm beginning to feel sorry for the captain. He has made countless phone calls in pursuit of me and driven all the way up from Colorado. Now he's been embarrassed and told his efforts were in vain. I, the missing brother, had probably been his only lead. In my weakened, exhausted state I momentarily feel bad for him. "Look, Captain, I did get a voice mail from Roberto. You tell me the details of his escape and I'll play it for you."

Wisely, Tobias doesn't tell me I have a duty to play the message for him. In clipped speech he explains that my brother somehow scaled a sheer, thirty-foot brick wall, then climbed a ten-foot fence topped with rolls of razor wire. They found chalk marks on a corner where the brick walls met, then tracked him through rolling hills of chaparral and cottonwoods to a highway. That was as far as they got.

I suspect Roberto had one of his many girlfriends pick him up, and say as much to Tobias. I also say that I don't believe they will catch him. As uncontrollable and impulsive as Roberto is, he's also very, very smart. And more than willing to take great risks. What I don't tell the captain is that my brother has property and a sizable trust in our ancestral home in Argentina. We each inherited one from our maternal grandfather, who was a cattle baron there, in a country from which Americans will not be extradited. By now Roberto is probably on a plane, never to return.

I pick up the phone and dial the numbers to retrieve my brother's message. Tobias listens intently, taking notes on a small leather-bound pad. He writes down the numbers on the outside of my phone as well, so he can subpoena the phone company for a tape of the message.

Then he asks suspiciously, "What does that mean, feed the Rat?"

"It means a sort of fix for adrenaline junkies like my brother. And about Christmas, I can't even guess. I haven't seen him over the holidays in nine or ten years." But I suspect Roberto had meant that he'll see me in Argentina, as I plan to see my parents there. He might have learned that in one of my mother's unanswered letters. "I don't think you'll be seeing Roberto again, Captain."

I reach up onto the high closet shelf and get Tobias's gun for him so he won't be further humiliated by having to ask or use a chair. Before I hand it over, I eject the clip and pop the round out of the chamber. I give those back to him separately, in another hand.

Before he leaves for his return trip to Colorado, the captain wants to talk to Ross, just as I do—I want to know the result of his meeting with Karge. So I call McGee's room and find that he's back from the meeting. I lead Tobias there, past the pool that's once again filled with splashing and tanning reporters. They're back from the murder scene in Buford, believing it's just another bizarre Wyoming tragedy, not connected with the sensational Lee case.

McGee has left the door unlatched. I push it wide and allow Tobias to enter ahead of me. Like a soldier, Tobias marches directly to where McGee slumps at the hotel's small desk. He's wearing a clear plastic oxygen mask, which he pulls off irritably with quaking hands. I should have knocked. There's an audible hiss from the steel bottle turned on high.

"Mr. McGee, my name is Captain John Tobias of the Colorado Bureau of Investigation. I want to file a complaint against Agent Burns. He assaulted me in his room just minutes ago. I ask that you relieve him of his duties immediately, pending an investigation and the filing of charges."

McGee's thick and grizzled eyebrows pinch together in either puzzlement or pain. He tries to turn on the hard seat to directly face the straight-backed captain but doesn't have the strength. "A big fucking pleasure . . . to meet you as well, Mr. Tobias. . . . What's this about, Anton?" A wet cough rumbles from his chest.

I step toward him in concern, then stop, remembering the indignant look he gave me on the courthouse stairs when I tried to take his arm. I shrug and say, "He pushed his way into my room uninvited. I took away his gun before he shot himself or me—"

The captain interrupts. "I really can't imagine why you'd allow a man such as this to be working as a law enforcement officer. He has a murderer for a brother, now an escaped convict no less, and may be one himself, as well as a history of excessive-force complaints and improper shootings. I've read up on him, you see."

Still coughing, McGee chokes out, "The complaints . . . were unsubstantiated . . . and the only thing improper . . . about the shootings . . . was the type . . . of ammunition used. . . . You must also have seen . . . that Agent Burns . . . is considered one of the finest . . . peace officers . . . in the state."

From where I stand, slightly behind Tobias, I roll my eyes at McGee. He's laying it on thick.

Tobias is red in the face again. Nothing is going as he planned. "Well, now he's a suspect in the escape of his brother."

McGee looks at the captain hard, then focuses on the obvious bulge near the captain's breast. "And you . . . Mr. Tobias, are a suspect . . . in the carrying of a concealed weapon. . . . Surely you realize your carry permit . . . is no good outside of Colorado?"

Good one, I think. I hadn't thought of that.

"I—" Tobias begins to sputter.

"Now you listen to me . . . you arrogant little prick," McGee says, dropping any pretense of civility. His voice is like a wounded lion's roar. "You don't come to me . . . and accuse one of my troops . . . of something like that . . . without some damn good evidence. . . . Now get the fuck out of my state."

Without a word the captain spins around and starts toward the door. He hits me with his shoulder as he passes. In the doorway he pauses and turns back to us. "Your Attorney General will be hearing from me. The governor too. And if either one of you ever sets foot in Colorado—" I shove the door shut in his face before he can finish.

"You seem to have a talent . . . for making friends, lad."

"People keep telling me that. Why don't I believe them?"

His coughing becomes uncontrollable again. "Ross, I'm going to call an ambulance. You need to be in the hospital."

McGee shakes his head angrily and ignores my suggestion. His hands are shaking so badly he has trouble reattaching the oxygen mask. I'm unsure what to do. I'm frightened for him—I honestly believe McGee's at Death's door. I know I should call an ambulance whether he likes it or not. But then this little giant of a man, who survived Korea and thirty or more years as an honest and respected prosecutor, deserves to call his own shots. I'm not going to take that away from him. If he wants to battle on his own I will let him. *Do not go gentle* . . . Dylan Thomas's poem comes unbidden into my mind.

After a few minutes he pulls the mask back down. "That's not a man to piss off lightly. . . . He's the third-in-command of . . . Colorado's state investigative agency. . . . I don't think . . . we'll be getting much cooperation . . . from them for a while."

"What happened with Karge?" I ask.

"He won't continue the sentencing. . . . He says I can't prove . . . he doesn't have the right killers. . . . He says the cord's . . . a bunch of bullshit. . . . He says he's got the Knapps' . . . fingerprints at the scene . . . and their confession to Sheriff Willis. . . . And he says he's got a conviction. . . . Then he threw me out of his office."

I'm stunned. I thought that game was up. Now Karge is playing chicken with us. "He's going to go ahead with the sentencing, even after learning we have exculpatory evidence, that we're going to get a warrant for his son?"

"It's his career, his future.... Our Nathan Karge... is an ambitious man.... The way he sees it... our jury said those boys... did it beyond a reasonable doubt... and the press believes it too.... I think he's gambling right now... betting he can get the AG to shut us up. ..."

"Well, we can't wait around to find out," I say. "I'm going to get a warrant. Today. As soon as I get back from court. I'll do everything I can to get Heller and Brad picked up tonight. Once they're in custody, the game will be over for Mr. Karge."

"And I'll be in court... in the morning... no matter what the office does.... Tell the judge everything.... She knows me, an old friend... trusts me.... She'll continue it... or declare a mistrial." He is again racked with a cough so fierce he nearly slides out of the chair.

There's a soft knock at the door, too soft for Tobias to be returning, and I open it. Rebecca stands outside, dressed in an expensive-looking cream-colored silk suit. She's looking down the corridor as if a stranger there had said something dirty. It turns out to be true—she'd passed Tobias, who was muttering profanities.

When she sees me she says, "There you are. I called your room like you asked but just got the answering service. Then I checked and you weren't there. I was worried..." Then she sees McGee at the small littered desk beyond me and rushes toward him.

"Oh, Ross," she says, kneeling by his chair. "You look horrible. Anton, we need to call an ambulance."

"I tried—he won't let me."

McGee is trying to pull the mask down again, his gray

skin turning red from a new fit of coughing. "No...don't... fucking...call! I'm...going...to your...hearing."

Rebecca looks at me, torn by the same indecision I feel.

"He's the boss," I tell her sadly.

"Then I'm coming too," she says. "I was going to anyway."

I pull the Land Cruiser as close as I can get it to McGee's room. After I load his oxygen and medical kit into the truck, he allows Rebecca and me to help him into the backseat. She sits there with him as we drive, Oso's hair quickly pasting itself to her light-colored clothes, and barely appears to listen to me as I fill her in on what McGee told me about his meeting with Karge. She's staring at him with soft eyes, and I feel my heart expand in my chest once again while my throat constricts.

TWENTY-SIX

MORRIS CASH FILED the suit on behalf of the three families just days after the shooting. Because it involves an alleged civil rights violation, the federal courts have jurisdiction. The plaintiffs claim that I killed the three young Hispanic men in cold blood. The original pleading, and the many amended pleadings that followed, boldly state that I lied when I said the gang members pulled their guns on me first, that I planted the weapons on their bodies after I shot them in cold blood. How else could I have come out of that ranch house alive?

The federal courthouse in Cheyenne is full of security. Obviously someone informed the federal marshals about the trouble with Sureno 13 earlier in the week at the Albany County courthouse. The local press has gotten the word too, and they're out in force. Although the case pales in comparison to the sensational Lee trial, its validity has been hotly debated in Wyoming since the shooting, and Monday's assault on me in Laramie's courthouse has increased the interest. A few national reporters have even shown up, eager for entertainment as they await the Lee sentencing.

One of the reporters there is Don Bradshaw, the *Cheyenne Observer* columnist who coined my nickname, QuickDraw. In his article he meant it sarcastically, as if it were impossible for me to have walked away alive from three armed gangbangers who intended to kill me. He ridiculed the notion that I could have fired five shots, taking the lives of three men, before they were able to put even a single bullet in me. Apparently he didn't believe in quick reflexes, a lifelong education in shooting from a father who commanded a Special Forces team, and a hell of a lot of luck.

QuickDraw, he had mocked. According to him I was a liar as well as a killer, and the people who believed me were fools who had seen too many *Rambo* movies. His columns railed at Wyoming law enforcement in general and me in particular, embarrassing state officers from the governor and Attorney General on down to the deputy sheriffs patrolling the streets. I had gotten away with murder and the state had allowed it by not prosecuting me.

Other columnists and commentators picked up on the theme. They openly discussed my brother and his manslaughter conviction, theorizing that we were cut from the same cloth. Devastated by the lives I'd taken and my brother's incarceration, I read the articles with a horror that finally culminated in a simple numb depression. For the last year and a half I had felt as if a low-pressure system, the kind so intense that it sucked tornadoes from across the plains, had settled over me. For a long time now I have fantasized about punching Don Bradshaw in the face and releasing the storm.

But when I pass him in the aisle of the packed courtroom, I repress the urge even though my anger is undiminished. I'm just too weary. So I hit him with my mouth instead of my fist.

"Hi, Don. Your boy out of rehab yet?" I ask. Even before I arrested him for dealing ecstasy, he had a juvenile conviction for sexual assault. Bradshaw's son was a stereotype for his generation: a selfish, narcissistic, spoiled young man. And he got a better deal than any other kid in his position simply because of the influence and fame of his journalist father. A deferred judgment would forever dismiss the case as long as he completed a rehabilitation program.

Bradshaw responds in kind. "Howdy, QuickDraw. Kill anyone lately?"

"Not lately. But who knows, maybe I'll have to come by your house with another arrest warrant sometime. . . ."

He blanches at the threat, and I immediately feel like an ass. McGee overheard the short exchange from where Rebecca seated him in the front of the courtroom. He whacks me across the ankle with his cane before pulling me down beside him with a quaking hand.

"Christ, Burns. . . . What are you trying to do . . . set back the reputation of . . . Wyoming law enforcement . . . fifty years?"

I roll my eyes. "If only they knew, Ross."

He grunts to silence me. The quiet ride from Laramie had improved his color. The coughing is still fierce but not as frequent. Rebecca sits close by him, holding his other heavy paw. I know this is a bad sign, just as was his allowing us to help him into the truck. That McGee is accepting support and pity means he is close to the edge.

My attorney approaches us. Clayton Wells looks about eighteen years old and now wears a pathetic goatee in an attempt to make himself look older, more masculine, more assured. But it's an obvious mask. No one looking at his nervous, unblemished face could mistake him for anything but a scared kid right out of law school. I've never asked him how many cases he's tried. I didn't really want to know, but I expect this is his first. I heard that none of the other civil trial attorneys in the AG's Office wanted to touch this case.

"You've been doing good, Agent," he tells me with a smile, attempting to be funny, to be one of the boys. "See if you can get them to attack you again in the courtroom here, in front of the judge."

I just stare at him until he looks away and busies himself with the papers on his desk. Young attorneys who work for the state or a local prosecutor's office are all too often frightened to take on the defendant, his attorneys, and a system of justice that is partial to everyone but the police. They're willing to sell their souls to avoid a trial. Once they become experienced and more cynical, they leave to make more money as defense or plaintiff's attorneys and take advantage of those they were once like.

"How come you never called me back?" he says, trying again at conversation as he shuffles nervously through his papers. "We might have been able to settle this. We still might be. The office has authorized me to offer up to fifty thousand to each of the families."

"Clayton, do you really think Mo Cash would take that? He stands to make more from the state just for his attorney's fees, even if he loses."

At the table just ten feet away sits Morris Cash, popularly known as Mo Cash, who represents the Torres, Lopez, and Gallegos families in their suit against the AG's Office and myself. He's a florid man, dressed sharply in a suit too fancy and stylish to have been bought in Wyoming. Armani, I guess. And Cash can afford it. It's rumored that in this case, like his others, he keeps forty percent of any damages as his contingency fee. And even if he loses, even if no money is awarded to his clients, a federal law allows him to recoup his attorney's fees from the state. He has quite a racket going, and he's said to be quite good at it.

Cash notices me looking at him and winks. That's his style. In court, on the record, he is both ferocious and contemptuous. But in person he can be as amusing a man as I have ever met. Once, in a simple distribution case where I testified as the arresting officer, he offered me the "services" of his client, who also worked as a stripper when she wasn't selling brown heroin. For that, all I had to do was change my testimony a little. At the time I laughed but knew he wasn't joking. She was standing next to him when he made the extraordinary offer, and she'd smiled at me.

The bailiff pounds the gavel and calls out, "Hearye, hearye, hearye. The United States District Court for the District of Wyoming is now in session, the Honorable Judge John S. Upton presiding. God save the United States and this honorable court!" I move up to the table and stand beside my attorney. The judge comes out and allows us to sit.

McGee has told me about Judge Upton. He was a corn-fed Wyoming cowboy, literally, before becoming a lawyer. Appointed to the bench by a liberal president who is despised across the state, the judge is unaffected by politics because unlike state judges, as a federal judge he's appointed for life. Rather than a former cowboy, he looks like a recently retired professional football player, easily six foot five and with a build to fit.

"Gentlemen, I've read the pleadings and the amended pleadings and the amended, amended pleadings." He shakes his head at the amount of paperwork he has been made to read. "Do you have anything *else* to add by way of oral argument? You first, Mr. Wells. It's your motion."

My attorney looks at me, his eyes wide in fear. The judge has just taken the bench and already things are moving too fast for him. I nod at him encouragingly, then finally poke his leg under the table with a pen. When he gets to his feet he is visibly shaking. He steps behind the podium and grips its upper edge until his knuckles turn white. When he begins to speak, his voice squeaks. Mo Cash catches my eye and again winks at me.

In a quavering voice, Clayton starts to repeat exactly what he wrote in the pleadings he filed with the court to support the motion for summary judgment. I suppress a groan. The judge displays his agitation, tapping his fingers on the bench before him, the sound amplified by the microphone, but my attorney is oblivious to it, caught up in his own nervousness. After a few more sentences the judge cuts him off.

"Mr. Wells, I told you I read the pleadings, amended pleadings, et cetera. If you don't have anything new to add, then sit down and shut up."

I want to slump lower in my seat. Not only is Mo Cash grinning at me, but so are his clients—the parents of the men who tried to kill me. Clayton apologizes to the court in a sudden rush and sits down. He doesn't look at me again.

"Mr. Cash, anything you want to add?"

Cash doesn't even bother to rise out of his chair. "No, your honor," he says smugly. Motions for summary judgment are only rarely granted. Only if there are absolutely no facts in dispute will the judge rule to dismiss the case.

I'm surprised and relieved to see Cash lose his grin when the judge tells him, "Good, because I have some questions for you. Exactly what evidence do you intend to present to show that Agent Burns here wasn't acting in self-defense?"

Now Cash rises. "Your honor, it's all there in the pleadings and in our answer to the defendant's motion."

"Exactly where, Counselor?"

Cash's face becomes shiny in the courtroom's fluorescent lights. He begins rifling through papers on his desk while the judge again impatiently taps his fingers near his microphone. Finally Cash stands erect again and proudly holds up a sheaf of paper. "In our answer to the defendant's motion, you can see on page thirty-two that I intend to call two friends of the victims. Both of them will testify that Dominic Torres, Luis Gallegos, and David Lopez had absolutely no intention of harming Agent Burns that evening. Their affidavits are attached at the end."

Cash has recovered his composure. But not for long.

"Tell me if I'm wrong," the judge asks, "but aren't your witnesses in prison?" He puts on a pair of glasses and reads, "Let's see, for robbery, sexual assault on a child, kidnapping, et cetera? Crimes that were committed the night of the shooting?"

Cash smiles weakly. "Unfortunately that's true, your honor."

McGee leans over from the first row of the spectator benches and hisses to my red-faced attorney, "It's also hearsay." I understand what he means—with a few limited exceptions, one witness cannot testify to the words or intentions of another. In this case they shouldn't be allowed to testify that the deceased did or did not intend to kill me.

But Clayton ignores McGee.

"Tell the judge that," I say to him, again poking him in the leg with my pen. He shakes his head and continues staring down at the legal pad in front of him.

I push back my chair and stand. "Excuse me, your honor, but I don't believe his witnesses can testify." The entire courtroom turns to stare at me. The judge's bailiff looks aghast that a nonlawyer would dare speak uninvited in her courtroom. Despite the judge's frown, I go on, "Their testimony would be hearsay." Exhaustion has emboldened me.

There's a long silence, then the judge says with a smile he tries to suppress, "Mr. Burns, you sit down too. You let your attorney speak for you, understand? Now, Mr. Wells, do you have something to tell me?"

Clayton gets unsteadily to his feet. He gives me a dirty look before saying, "Your honor, the testimony Mr. Cash is referring to would be hearsay."

"Good point, Counselor," the judge says. Clayton nearly collapses back in his chair with relief. "Mr. Cash, I believe defense counsel here has a point. How do you intend to admit this testimony of your felons?"

Cash looks beseechingly at the row of his paralegals that sit just behind the plaintiff's table. None of them will acknowledge his silent plea. I speculate that Cash has so many cases going on at any one moment that he lets his paralegals and junior associates handle everything but the trials, hearings, and public appearances. And his assistants don't look much older or much more experienced than my lawyer. "Well, Judge," he finally says, "I believe that some of the hearsay exceptions will apply."

"Oh? Which ones?"

Cash looks again to his paralegals unsuccessfully. I hear a couple of the reporters in the back of the room snicker and McGee begins to cough. Even Clayton raises his head from the legal pad and smiles. I don't, though. I know the judge will turn it back on us. The rare, good judges like Upton pride themselves on being tough but fair. What goes around will come back and slap us in the face. They are equal-opportunity punishers, brutal in their treatment of sneaky, pompous, or incompetent lawyers.

"Even if you are somehow able to get around the hearsay rule, Counselor, do you really expect a jury is going to buy the story of your two felons who kidnapped and raped an eight-year-old girl that very night?"

"There's also Agent Burns's testimony, your honor. I plan to cross-examine him."

"Oh? Hasn't Mr. Burns already testified under oath during the depositions that he acted in self-defense? How will that help your case?"

Cash is really grasping now. But instead of being amused, I hate him for what he says next. "I'll impeach his credibility, your honor."

"With what?"

"His brother is an escaped convicted killer—"

Even Clayton knows enough to leap to his feet and loudly object to that. But Cash goes on over Clayton's high-pitched voice, "And when he filled out his application to become a law enforcement officer, he signed an affidavit saying no one in his family had ever been convicted of a crime."

I hiss at Clayton, "I signed that two years before my brother was convicted!"

Clayton repeats it to the judge, "He signed that two years before my, excuse me, his brother was convicted, your honor."

The judge sighs and shakes his head at both attorneys. Then he speaks to Cash.

"Do you think you're going to have a Perry Mason moment as you cross-examine Mr. Burns? Do you think you're a brilliant enough interrogator that you'll break him up there on the stand? Mr. Burns doesn't look like he breaks easy, Counselor. Look at those bruises on his face—it appears somebody may have already tried that and failed. Now I know that you have a reputation as a hotshot litigator, although I've yet to see why, but I don't think anyone's that good except on TV. I'm tempted to find for the defense right now that there's no genuine issue of material fact. If I were you, I'd be talking settlement with Mr. Wells here."

Both the attorneys' confidence has turned around 180 degrees. Cash is red-faced and looks ill, although I know it won't last. Attorneys like him are shameless. Clayton Wells, on the other hand, is positively beaming. Hubris, I think. But for a moment even I'm hopeful. Then I wince when the judge turns his penetrating stare toward the defendant's table.

"Don't look so pleased, Mr. Wells. If a jury somehow were to believe Mr. Cash's witnesses, you could be in for the biggest wrongful death verdict in the history of Wyoming." I see Clayton visibly swallow. "And I can assure you, Counselor, that a verdict like that wouldn't look very good on your résumé. I suggest that you make Mr. Cash a generous offer. I'm going to recess for ten minutes. I expect that the two of you will have worked this out by then."

Fifteen minutes later Clayton comes out from a conference room alone. His face is whiter than normal, his skin glossy with sweat. He sits down at the table next to me and looks as though he might cry.

"I thought we had it," he says to me.

McGee had pulled off his oxygen mask when Clayton first sat down. He growls, "What the fuck happened?"

"I offered them everything, fifty grand per family, the maximum I was authorized to offer. Cash said he'd take it. I called the office to get the approval and was connected through to the Attorney General himself—the man's never said a word to me before. He said there's to be no offer. None. He said he wants it to go to trial; he wants you, Agent Burns, 'to sweat it out.' "

Only rarely have I heard anything like the haranguing the judge gives Clayton in chambers when Cash indignantly tells the judge his previous settlement offer has been revoked. It reminds me of the times my brother and I bicycled around the bases on which my father was stationed and listened to the drill sergeants abuse the new recruits. I feel truly sorry for my attorney. He has been pulled into a game that he was never schooled in, a game he doesn't even want to play. My pity is so great that I risk interrupting the judge to say just that.

Upton angrily demands to know what I mean.

McGee, who had hobbled into the judge's chambers after us clutching his oxygen bottle, answers for me. "There's a pissing contest going on," he rasps, "between Burns and the AG... about a case he's investigating... in Laramie."

The judge slams his massive hand on the desk and says to us all, "Then you tell the Attorney General to come across the street and see me. I want to hear from him by tomorrow afternoon. That's an order. I'm not going to be wasting my time and the taxpayers' on a case that's tried out of spite."

I wish I could be there to see the AG get reamed by the angry judge.

Back out in the judge's private hallway Morris Cash is lurking as I somewhat impatiently wait for McGee, who's a friend of the judge. I'm anxious to get back to Laramie and back to work. I intend to have an arrest warrant for Heller and Brad Karge drawn up within two hours.

Cash sticks out his hand and grins at me, but I ignore both the hand and the smile. He should never have brought my brother into it and he knows it.

"C'mon, Agent Burns," he says plaintively. "I got to do my job. Anyway, you got trouble with the office, you call me. We'll sue the shit out of them together."

I intend to respond with a simple "Fuck you," but the words don't leave my lips. Out of the corner of my eye I see McGee down the hall arguing hotly with someone in a suit. He looks as furious as I've ever seen him. McGee has both hands on the head of his cane, which is shaking like a rattlesnake's tail. His face is again a pasty white above his beard. The quiet force of the words he's speaking sends a spray of spittle into the air. I don't immediately recognize the man in the suit he's speaking to, but know he's familiar. Then it comes to me—he's the Assistant Attorney General, the office's second-in-command. He's also my boss's boss.

I walk away from Cash and toward the two.

The Assistant AG, seeing me, says somewhat nastily, "Ah, Mr. Burns. Just the man I've been looking for." Anyone in McGee's clique is automatically suspect in the administration's eyes.

"What can I do for you, sir?"

"You can start by giving me your badge. I have the unfortunate duty of informing you that as of now you're officially suspended, pending the filing of criminal charges for the deaths of Dominic Torres and two others."

I look to McGee in outrage. But he's staring fixedly at the Assistant's chest, his lips white, his cane beginning to whirl in ever-larger circles beneath his weight. His mouth is open but he has stopped breathing. Then he teeters to one side and starts to collapse.

"Ross!" I lunge toward him and catch his head and shoulders before they hit the ground.

"Get an ambulance!" I shout at the Assistant AG. He's standing frozen a little ways away from us, having taken several involuntary steps back. "Do it now!" I yell again to break his trance.

He comes to his senses and turns to go for a phone. As he turns away from us I swear I see him smile.

TWENTY-SEVEN

EARLY THAT EVENING I park my truck up high on the prairie. Although the road is paved, it's about the loneliest road I have ever come across. It leads from Laramie in a northeastern direction, angling toward the rocky hills that are the northern relatives of Vedauwoo. A few minutes before, I drove the road all the way to where it turned to dirt, twenty miles outside of town, up at the far end of a shallow limestone gorge called Roger's Canyon. Then I turned around and drove halfway back to this wide shoulder on the plain just before the canyon's entrance. Other than my Land Cruiser, the only traffic the road receives is quick crossings by a small herd of antelope and two jackrabbits.

NPR's *All Things Considered* is on the radio. There's a report from Laramie on the national program, mentioning that tomorrow the Knapp brothers will be sentenced for the sensational race-bias murder of University of Wyoming student Kimberly Lee. The death penalty is anticipated. And there's a brief mention about County Attorney Nathan Karge and how he's expected to assume the office of Wyoming governor immediately after the election, just weeks away now. The current governor, the announcer states, does not intend to remain in office during the traditional lame-duck period. I grimace, rolling down the windows to let the early-evening breeze cool the truck while I wait. Jones had told me that Deputy Sheriff David Knight often trains on this road at about this hour.

Ever since McGee collapsed I've been trying to think of a way to delay the sentencing without him. I could go to the court myself tomorrow, hope the judge will be willing to hear me out, and hope there is some way I can explain to her that she should postpone the sentencing or declare a mistrial based on a few similarities between Kimberly Lee's murder and those of Kate Danning and Sierra Calloway. A drug connection, a climbing connection, and some pink cord. But there are a number of problems with that plan. The evidence is flimsy at best, I'm suspended as a peace officer, and I'll have absolutely no credibility as the subject of a renewed multiple murder investigation. Karge will be aware of that—undoubtedly he engineered it—and will be sure to point it out.

During my hour and a half of driving, the exhaustion almost overtook me—I was tempted to just hang it up and let things take the course that more powerful people than I have directed. But the anger keeps returning. I'm enraged by the arrogance of these people. At Nathan Karge for thinking he can send innocent men to the death chamber in order to protect his family and his ambitions, for thinking he can shut me up and intimidate me by having my superiors suspend me and reraise the specter of murder charges. And at Heller's arrogance, for believing that he'll be protected in pursuing his thrills because he has made an accessory out of the County Attorney's own son. Then, when I think of Oso, my fingers grip the steering wheel as if I could crush it.

It has been just a little over two hours since I left Rebecca in the hallway of Cheyenne's large hospital. She was crying while she tapped away on her laptop computer with Kleenex awkwardly balled in both palms. Writing the story, she said, doing what she can. We both know it isn't ready for publication—there aren't enough hard facts, and there might never be unless I can find them. Her paper will want evidence in the form of affidavits and arrest warrants before they'll risk publishing a story critical of Wyoming law enforcement, from the future governor and current Attorney General to the Albany County Sheriff's Office. And tomorrow will be too late, when any investigation into the Lee case will be subverted and dismissed once the Knapps are sentenced and Nathan Karge takes up the reins of the governor's office.

Before I left the hospital a doctor spoke to us. McGee suffered a heart attack, he said, and was in critical condition. We could see for ourselves through the Critical Care Unit's small window that a respirator had been shoved down his throat and tubes were leaching drugs into his once powerful body. A hard life of stress, rich foods, potent liquor, and smoking had finally caught up to him. They were unsure if he would make it, the doctor told us. As unstable as his condition was one thing was certain: he wouldn't make court in the morning to delay the Knapps' sentencing. And I now lack both the official authority and the credibility to try to take his place.

Like Rebecca, I'm doing what I can to see that the wrong men aren't sentenced to death for a crime they didn't commit. Now, though, I can't write the necessary affidavits to get arrest warrants for Billy Heller and Bradley Karge. I'm suspended, under investigation for three supposed murders committed a year and a half ago. My options are to simply accept it—to step aside and wait for Sheriff McKittrick of Laramie County and the sergeant up in the Big Horns to get their own warrants, which could take weeks or even months—or to somehow learn enough about the Lee murder to convince the judge to delay the sentencing despite my discredited status. So I wait for Knight, hoping to penetrate the conscience of one of the junior officers involved in the arrest of the Knapps.

I managed to keep my badge, though. At least I still have the illusion of some authority. In the confusion created by McGee's collapse, when court security officers and paramedics rushed around us shouting, the Assistant Attorney General had slunk away, forgetting to take with him the symbol of the power I had held just minutes before. Perhaps it'll make a nice souvenir, I think. And I have Cecelia's .32 as well. My own office-issued gun is still in the custody of the Albany County sheriff as evidence.

I rise up in my seat as I catch sight of something moving on the road, coming fast out of Laramie. I turn off the radio and watch the figure approach, pedaling hard, wearing a colorful racing jersey and tights. When the figure is within a mile of me, I open the door and step out of the truck. I don't close the door, but simply stand by it at the edge of the road. The cyclist draws closer and I recognize the young, serious features, despite the helmet low on his forehead and the dark wraparound sunglasses. It's Knight.

I wave at him, then lean against my truck and wait, admiring the speed and grace with which the rookie deputy moves his bicycle. Powerful, circular strokes are delivered pistonlike by legs that are tan, muscular, and hairless. Incongruously, the arms that grip the handlebars are thin and still. Knight approaches fast, not slowing his pace at all. He doesn't even raise his fingers in greeting. And he doesn't touch the brakes.

I shout an obscenity as Knight rides by as if he hadn't seen me standing all alone on the empty prairie. I'm not going to fuck around anymore.

I hop into the driver's seat, twist the key, and spin the truck's rear in a fishtail across the dirt shoulder and onto the asphalt. Swinging into the left lane and starting to pass Knight, I ease the truck back over to the right, touching the brakes just a little. I hear a banging sound. In the right-side mirror I see Knight furiously slamming his fist against the truck's rear panel. Then he's off the road and into the dirt and sand. He launches into the air as if thrown by a horse, his skinny racing tires having sunk too deep in the soft earth.

I swerve back to the left and press the brakes hard so that I slow to almost a stop. I pull in front of where Knight lies half on the dirt, half in some dry brush. He's holding his elbow across his chest and rocking back and forth. Cursing. His helmet is sideways on his head. I step out of the truck and pick up the wraparound sunglasses that are crumpled at my feet. I walk over and hold them out to Knight.

"You asshole!" the younger man shouts, jerking the sunglasses from my hand.

"You break anything?"

"I easily could have! Are you fucking nuts?"

"Listen, Knight, I need you to talk to me. This whole

town, the whole state, is screwing with me and I need some straight answers."

"No way, Burns, I'm not talking to you about shit!"

I say nothing. I want to kick the young man in the head, beat the answers out of him. But I won't do it. I won't become like Willis and Bender. "Okay then, just listen to me. Get in the truck with me for ten minutes."

"Or else what?" Knight asks, twisting his arm to look at the lines of blood running down. They're already beginning to coagulate.

"Or else you're going to have a long walk back to town." I point at the bent front wheel of Knight's bicycle. Several spokes stick straight out like a porcupine's quills.

Knight looks at it almost sadly. He says, with most of the anger gone from his voice, "I can't be seen talking to you. I can't be seen listening to you."

"You won't."

I pick up the bicycle and put it through the open rear window of my truck. I hold the passenger door open for Knight and push my briefcase out of the way onto the floor. Knight looks up at me from where he's sitting on the dirt for a long moment without moving. I can see the wheels turning, a decision being reached. I imagine it's a decision far larger than simply whether to listen and maybe tell a few secrets. It will be a career-changing, possibly even a life-changing, conclusion, one that for a religious man could tip the balances between heaven and hell.

"Fuck it," Knight finally says as he pushes himself off the ground. "I'm quitting anyway. I'm going to go to Europe to race, try to get sponsored." He steps up into the truck.

I drive him up into Roger's Canyon. We bounce over a dirt trail into a cluster of dusty pines where I park. Taking the briefcase up from near Knight's feet, I pull out the various envelopes of photographs. I pinch open the metal stays on the one marked "Lee" and slide the photos out.

"You've seen these before, right? Kimberly Lee."

Knight doesn't reply, but looks at the first photo I hold before him.

"Note the marks on her wrists. Thin ligature marks. On her neck too, but deeper, where they cut off her air. Now look at this." I pass another photo. "Here are the cords you guys took off her. Pink with flecks of purple, soft nylon core. Remember? About five millimeters in diameter. This particular color and type is sold in only one place in Wyoming I can find. Up in Buffalo, where a lady remembers selling it to Billy Heller and Bradley Karge. Sold them a bunch of it. And look at the knots that were used. You're a Wyoming boy, aren't you, Knight? Fish, hunt, work outdoors?" Knight nods. "Have you ever seen a knot like that?" Knight shakes his head, then again when I ask if he's ever done any rock climbing. "That's called a prusik knot, used by climbers to ascend ropes. It can move one way but it clamps down the other. I can't think of any other use for it. Except maybe slowly strangling someone.

"Anyway," I continue, "you were in on the arrest of the Knapps for Kimberly's murder. You were there when you guys found the cut-off skin from her breast in the cab of their truck, the broken crank pipe with prints near Lee's body, and when one of the Knapps supposedly told Bender that the bitch had it coming, right?" Knight doesn't move; he just stares at the photos.

I take them back from him and open another envelope. This one's marked "K. Danning." I pass Knight a picture from the autopsy, a close-up of her face and neck. The color drains from his face and he looks a little ill as I point at it. "Look at that, that red line there across her throat. Not as deep as Kimberly Lee's, but just about as wide and it goes all the way around too. I don't have a close-up of her wrists, but look at this"—I pass another photo—"I think I can see another line there, on her left wrist. What about you?" Again Knight doesn't respond. "Your county coroner happened to throw away a cord he found around Kate's neck. There was also a contusion on the *back* of her head, one she couldn't have gotten from falling off a ledge because, remember, you told me she landed on her face. Someone hit her with something *before* she fell; hit her hard enough to fracture her skull.

"Now keep in mind that when Kate Danning died the Knapp boys were in jail, in the middle of their murder trial. I found a bottle up above the cliff Kate fell off. It had hair and blood on it, Kate's type, with DNA matches still pending, and Bradley Karge's fingerprints. His dad's too, by the way. What amazes me is those marks, so similar to Kimberly Lee's, and the fact that both girls were climbers and drug users who associated with Brad and Billy Heller. Some coincidences, huh?"

I open the third thick envelope. "Now check this out. Another young girl, climber, drug user, associate of Brad's and Billy's. Her name was Sierra Calloway until she was murdered Monday night. Look, her arms are behind her back, tied with that same pink cord. Same prusik knot as Kimberly Lee's. Now look at her neck. Same thing, right?" Now Knight gives the smallest of nods. "And those Knapp boys still in jail, now awaiting sentencing.

"There's been a fourth murder too. A kid named Chris Braddock, a good friend of both Billy's and Brad's. Kind of a hanger-on. He died in a fall while climbing with Brad and Billy in the Big Horns just two or three days ago. I found the body. Brad and Billy disappeared after they came looking for me and shot my dog.

"So now I have a hard time believing the Knapps killed all these people, since they were in jail for all three of them, and what I'm seeing, at least with the girls, is some sort of sex-thrill MO that exactly matches the murder of Lee. Now you and I both can see that it's pretty unlikely the Knapps even did Lee. But you were there for their arrest. What I want to know is how did the crank pipe with the Knapps' prints get into Lee's house? And how did that piece of her breast get into their truck?"

Knight sits silently, staring at the pines through the windshield without seeing them. I wait for a while, letting the pressure build, then ask quietly, "How come you became a cop, David?"

He just keeps staring and says nothing.

"Let me tell you about me then. I became a cop for three reasons. One, I thought it would be fun and exciting, getting to carry a gun and a badge and all. Two, I was pissed off about the drugs that ruined my brother's life and stole his future from him. And three, I wanted to do the right thing. I wanted to catch the cheaters—the people who don't follow the rules.

"I don't know your background—I don't know if you had a brother who got hooked or a relative who was murdered. But I'd be willing to bet that one and three apply to you too. I bet you like the power and authority and I bet you want to do the right thing. And so when you and the others found Kimberly Lee dead, then the Knapps opened fire on you in the middle of the night and there was a pretty good chance they were the perps, you thought the right thing was to make sure there was enough evidence to put them away permanently. You've seen that the courts all too often let bad guys go on technicalities, or just because a jury has their heads up their asses, so you think you'll improve the odds a little with some manufactured evidence.

"But David, I think you can see now that it was the *wrong* thing. The wrong guys are going to be put to death just so no one's embarrassed and Nathan Karge gets to move on to the governor's mansion, taking your sheriff with him. I'm asking you now to do the right thing."

I let him sit. I'm confident the decision the young deputy will make will be the right one. I can read it on his face. I can see it in his distressed eyes. After a while, Knight finally speaks.

"Let's go for a walk."

I nod and we both get out of the car.

"Are you recording this?"

I shake my head and say no.

Knight looks at me skeptically. So I peel off my suit jacket and lay it on the seat. Then I untuck my shirt and lift it high on my chest. I drop my pants to my knees and turn slowly around before tucking my shirt back into my pants.

"C'mon," I say, and we walk up the dirt trail.

"When Kimberly's body was found, I was one of the first ones there. I didn't see any crank pipe. Then, after the shoot-out with those fucking Knapp brothers, I went back as they were bagging up her body. The pipe was there, broken on the floor, almost underneath a couch. It was bright blue glass with a stem that looked like a flower. I realized I'd seen it before. I took it off one of the brothers when I arrested him a few months earlier, on a possession charge. I placed it into evidence. That case was eventually plea-bargained down to ten days plus probation, but the pipe stayed in evidence—to be destroyed, far as I knew. I told the sheriff I'd seen that pipe before. I told him as they were putting that girl in the bag. He didn't say anything, he just winked at me. After a little while that Nazi Sergeant Bender came over to me and told me I'd never seen that pipe before, to forget it."

"What about the girl's breast, found in the cab of the Knapps' truck? And the supposed confession?"

"I don't know about that. All I can tell you is that somebody had cut it off her when they killed her. But anyone could have put it in the truck."

"And the statement, that one of the Knapps supposedly made to Bender, that the chink bitch had it coming, that rape's all they're good for?"

"I don't know about that either. It might be bullshit, it might not. Those guys are racists. Someone could have told them the girl was dead and what happened to her. It was the sort of thing those fuckers would say. But I wasn't there for that."

That supposed confession was the cornerstone of Karge's case. It was the only piece of evidence that wasn't considered "circumstantial." Even though scientific proof such as fingerprints and DNA evidence is the most trustworthy and damning evidence there is, juries have been conditioned to treat it as suspect and instead weigh more heavily words people claim to have heard and things they claim to have seen.

"So you never considered that someone might be setting those boys up?"

Knight looks away, pained. "No," he says. "All I knew about for sure was the pipe. But there was enough evidence even without it, as far as I knew. It was just the cherry on top. That shit they wrote in blood on the walls, the racist stuff we found in their trailer, that they started shooting when cops just knocked on their door to question them. I thought they probably did it. I was sure they did it."

I stop and look at the young cop. I don't believe him. And Knight knows it too, the way he won't meet my eyes. He suspected all along there was a frame taking place, but he had said nothing. He was a part of it. By his silence, he played a role of sorts in the killings of another three young people. I feel sick again. It wasn't an intent to do harm that kept Knight silent. It was worse. Cowardice. Complacency. That resulted in three more murders.

I walk back to the Land Cruiser and Knight follows me, staring at the ground. I take Knight's broken bike out of the back of the truck and toss it in the dirt.

"I'm not going to drive you back to town. You can walk. Maybe someone will come along. It wouldn't be safe for you to be seen with me anyway."

Knight just nods without looking up.

"And watch your ass, Deputy Knight. Witnesses are getting whacked. You could be next."

TWENTY-EIGHT

AN HOUR LATER it is dark. With my headlights off, I drive slowly by Heller's dilapidated ranch house. The moon is bright enough that the droopy cottonwoods in his yard cast dark shadows beneath them. The unkempt lawn looks the same as when I saw it almost a week before. The broken-down pickup without wheels still rests on its axles. But the other car is gone. It takes me a few minutes of visualization to remember what kind of car it was. A Jeep Wrangler—I think I remember—dents, brown paint, and climbing stickers on the bumper.

There are no lights on in the house. For a moment I fantasize that Billy and Brad are hungry and cold, still trying to repair the damage I inflicted to Heller's van up at that remote trailhead in the Big Horns. Realistically, though, it would only have taken them a day or so to hike out and get a tow truck in. They could be anywhere by now.

My Land Cruiser's fat tires crunch up what once had been a gravel driveway, and I park in the moon-shade of a cottonwood. I take off my tie and tuck it in my pocket but leave on my navy wool suit jacket to hide my white shirt. Unfolding the jacket collar, I turn it up to cover the white cloth V that is bright beneath my neck. After a few minutes of sitting in the dark with the windows down, listening to the crickets and the wind in the leaves, I walk past the open garage that has been converted into a climbing gym and onto the sagging porch. No one answers my knock.

I feel a pang, something my mother calls *espirita.* A stab of conscience. But then I decide I'm not cheating since I'm no longer a cop. At least not one on active duty. I'm about to commit my first crime, and I'm going to do it as a private citizen. I'll accept the consequences.

With my penlight I quickly examine the lock and decide it would take me too long to try to pick it. I have never been very good at what some police officers consider an essential skill. There is a single-pane window next to the door that I'm tempted to simply kick my foot through. But a broken window might spawn allegations of planted evidence if what I hope to find inside is really there. So instead I circle the house, looking in all the likely spots for a hidden key and trying windows.

Illuminated by the moon is a second-floor window that I can see is obviously warped. Its stays look rotten and twisted, impossible to close properly. In the debris littering the yard I find the remains of a homemade pine ladder. I place it softly against the side of the house. The ladder is made of ancient gray wood and is missing several rungs. I shake it before I start up. The wood feels as if it is planting splinters in my palms with each grasp.

At the top of the dangerously creaking ladder I see that

I was right in believing the window is warped. Seeing it up close, I find it is not entirely shut on one side, while the other has more than a two-inch gap. I try to push it up and open and it gives just a little as the ladder groans beneath my feet. Pushing harder, it gives a little more. Then with a sharp snap the rung beneath my feet breaks away.

Somehow I slap at the sill with both palms and hold it. I hear the ladder collapse in the grass and leaves below. I hang with my face, hips, and toes pressed against the peeling paint of the side of the house. This is not going well. I always assumed that with my climbing skills I would make an excellent cat burglar. But I'm acting more like a clumsy heroin addict.

Just a few feet to the left of me a drainpipe runs down the side of the house. It looks as flimsy as the old ladder. With no other choice, I hook the toe of my left shoe into the gap between the pipe and the wall and torque it in tight. The pipe flexes outward, but holds. Fortunately someone has done a good job of bolting it to the wall. Still holding the sill with one hand, I work the other into the opening. Pushing up from my torqued toe, I'm able to generate enough upward thrust to rattle the window open. Breathing hard but relieved, I pull up on the sill and slide inside head-first.

Being alone in a stranger's house at night, wrongfully, illegally, and desperately, especially when it is the house of a killer, brings back forgotten childhood fears. The closed closet door, the dark space under the bed, the imagined shape behind the curtains. The cold sweat of those young, irrational fears oozes up out of my skin.

The high-plains stars cast a dim glow in the room. The door on the opposite wall is closed. Partially crumpled boxes litter the floor along with careless stacks of musty-smelling clothes. I crouch on the floor for a long minute, listening for any creaking of the pine floorboards. There isn't any.

Using my penlight, I begin to inspect the contents of the boxes. Several hold piles of papers that appear to be everything from ancient bills to out-of-date catalogs. A couple are full of empty Sudafed containers, a prime ingredient in the cooking of methamphetamine. The clothes appear to be ratty castoffs. No matter how softly I try to move, my leather-soled courtroom shoes scrape and clunk on the rotting floor.

Outside the room a hallway runs across the upstairs portion of the house. I find another bedroom in similar disarray, the bed just a mattress on the floor covered with funky sheets. Pictures torn from magazines are taped to the walls. Most are of naked women exposing their breasts, genitals, and buttocks. Others have been ripped out of climbing magazines. Looking at them closely using the penlight, I recognize Billy as the star. The floor of this bedroom too is littered with *Hustler, Climbing, Rock and Ice,* and assorted catalogs.

The other upstairs bedroom is both neater and cleaner. Its walls are unadorned. Not a single picture or poster is tacked to the white walls. A cinderblock-and-pine-board bookshelf is the only furniture other than the bed. The shelves are lined with a library full of climbing books and guides. Billy's room, I'm sure. I check the four corner posts of the bed for marks that could have been made by cords, hoping for at least a small indication of his preference for rough, controlling sex, but find none.

The small bathroom hasn't been cleaned in a long time. Empty toilet paper rolls cover the floor and there is an ashtray near the toilet filled with the dead ends of joints.

Roaches, they are called, and that is just what they resemble. I make myself sniff them and smell the sweet odor of burnt marijuana along with a slightly harsher chemical smell. Cocoa puffs. Marijuana cigarettes dipped in liquid cocaine or meth.

The stairs leading down to the first floor creak in agony as I move across them. I try to walk with one shoulder brushing the wall, hoping they'll be steadier there. They aren't. They end in a small entryway opposite the front door. I can see more than a few days' worth of mail in a pile beneath the slot.

With the exception of Heller's bedroom, the downstairs is as dirty as the floor above. Everywhere is climbing gear, strewn across the floor. An old TV with a lop-eared antenna perches precariously on a pile of old phone books. The kitchen is the worst. Just standing inside it makes me want to throw a bucket of bleach across the counters.

I find a half-door to the cellar stairs concealed inside a small coat-closet off the kitchen. The door is locked with a large padlock. I study the lock's mounting with my penlight. Someone simply screwed a cheap aluminum mount to both the door and the wood siding on the wall. Two screws out of the eight have fallen out and the others are poorly driven. I make a mental note not to ever hire Heller for his carpentry skills. With the screwdriver on the utility tool attached to my key chain, I have the mounting off in about two minutes.

I push the short door open and initially see little but blackness. When I probe it with the tiny flashlight I see that half of the stairs seem to be broken or missing. Looking into the depths I feel an ominous presence. I don't know where it comes from, whether it is a lingering odor in the air down there or an electric current of fear that travels out of that darkness. The hairs on my arms rise, though.

Using the penlight, which is growing dimmer by the minute as the batteries wear down, I navigate the stairs as carefully as if I'm descending an avalanche-prone couloir. Both my arms are raised, fingers just below my eyes, like a boxer in a defensive pose, the miniature light clenched in one fist. I left Cecelia's gun in the car—if I'm caught in here with a weapon, the sentence I will receive for burglary will only be aggravated. The broken stairs squeal beneath my feet.

A large pale shape lies just beyond the fading beam of light. Trying hard to control my breathing and heart rate, I move down and closer, jiggling the flashlight and hoping for a resurgence of power. The shape is a bare, semen-stained mattress on the dirt floor. Rotted two-by-fours cross the area above and around the mattress. Numerous limp cords hang from them. I try to look at them closely in the tiny beam of light. The light dies like a candle being snuffed. The darkness closes in, pushing the air out of my chest.

I shake the pen hard and a little of its beam returns. Pink cord, woven through with purple thread. I run my unsteady fingers over it. This is all the evidence I need, once I figure out a way to get it properly retrieved by officers with warrants. With this and what Deputy Knight has admitted, there is no longer any doubt that Heller and Brad Karge killed Kimberly Lee.

At the edge of my field of vision a small glint in the dark draws my attention. At first I assume it's just the tiny flashlight's reflection off an exposed nail. But the flashlight dims again and the reflection is still there. I don't turn to face it right away. I try to control my breath and study the glint without moving my head or the diminishing beam of my flashlight toward it. There are really two glints, I can tell, close together. Like eyes in the dark. Like the red eyes of people in photographs, surprised by a flashbulb. My breath begins to come shallow and fast, my lungs accelerating their rhythm. Someone is crouching there, my senses shout.

The eyes come from down low near the floor in the expanse of darkness to my left. I try to slow my own breathing so that I can listen for another's, but I can hear nothing over my own rising panic, the blood beginning to roar through my veins. I'm afraid to point the light, afraid of what's there watching me.

Fight or flight, I think. Finally I move. I spin to the left, take two quick steps, and kick hard with my shoe. I thrust my leg, toe first, right between those two small lights. I feel it crunch through something and strike a firmness beyond. The flashlight flickers brighter with the motion, and I see a head of dark hair and skin, but that is all there is. A crushed mannequin's head on a low shelf, turned toward whatever depravity might have happened on the bed. Around its neck the renewed beam of the torch reveals more pink cords.

TWENTY-NINE

RATTLING ALONG THE back roads of Vedauwoo, I have never felt so tired and alone. I have only missed one full night of sleep, but the tension, exertion, and bruises make it feel like a week.

Around the turns my headlights sweep across the white trunks of nearly leafless aspens and random granite boulders. They all remind me of headstones, and the place looks like a cemetery. I feel as if I'm just another spirit in the night moving through it, lonely and unable to communicate with mortals but desperately needing to.

After leaving Heller's house I again called the hospital from my cell phone. The duty nurse told me there had been no change in McGee's condition. I decided to not have her wake up Rebecca, who according to the nurse was sleeping on a waiting room couch. Then I drove to the address Kristi had given me for Lynn White. The decrepit cottage was dark and still. Her pickup truck was gone.

I drove around Laramie for half an hour, checking the bars and coffee shops, remembering the furious look on Lynn's face when she saw Rebecca in the hotel room's bed. She would be going back to Heller, I knew. Sierra Calloway had told me she was Billy's frolicsome Titania who used other men as pawns in some private game they played. From the look Lynn gave me, I can bet she isn't used to having her pawns defect to take another queen into their beds. So she would go back to her king—a dangerous emperor who is in the process of eliminating his entire court.

It was at ten o'clock when I decided to look for her at Vedauwoo. I remembered thinking on the day I had climbed with her that the place seemed like her backyard, like her spiritual home. She is the Fairy Queen who rules the stone and trees there. Although I haven't admitted it to myself before, it is obvious she knows more than she has said about what happened to Kate Danning up there. Maybe about Kimberly Lee too. If I can find her, tell her what has happened to Sierra Calloway and Chris Braddock, convince her that she and Cindy Topper are surely next, maybe I can get her to open up. Besides, I have nothing else to do.

Because of my suspension I don't have the authority to make arrests or write affidavits for others to make the arrests. I can't even get a warrant to enter Heller's house, because I found the cords there illegally. I would be charged with breaking and entering, and worse, the evidence that he was a killer would never see the light of a courtroom. It would be suppressed due to the illegal search.

If I can find Lynn, I think maybe she can tell Sheriff McKittrick in Laramie County about the night Kate Danning died. And there is every chance she knows something about Kimberly Lee's murder. As Heller's sometime girlfriend, maybe she has seen the cords in the basement and around the mannequin's head. Maybe she has even been a participant in whatever games were played there. Her testimony, if I can bring her before the court, along with the evidence I have gathered so far, might be enough to convince the judge to delay the sentencing.

Only one thing is certain: if I don't find some way of halting the Knapps' sentencing in the morning, there's a fair chance they will die for a crime they didn't commit.

I hit the brakes and skid in the dirt. Throwing my truck into reverse, I spin the tires backward, cranking the wheel, letting the headlights cut across a section of the forest. There, alone in a small hollow of trees and rocks, is Lynn's beat-up truck. I bounce over the rough trail behind it and park.

The hood is cool when I put my hand on its flaking paint, as is the rusty exhaust pipe. When I look through the windows of the cab all I see in the moonlight are littered papers and coffee cups. So I stand in the night listening to the wind in the trees and the clicks of my own engine cooling, trying to figure out where I am and where she could be.

The hollow seems vaguely familiar—there is the white trunk of a fallen aspen lying on the ground near my truck. I remember sitting on that trunk, studying the guidebook while Jones talked sarcastically about starving in the wilderness. This is where we turned around after I got us lost just a week ago.

I start moving along a trail. My courtroom shoes skitter on small stones and sharp branches tug at my suit. The trail crosses a dirt road, near where I parked that day with Jones, and begins winding its way toward the base of the formation where Kate Danning died. Several times I stop to listen but hear only the increasing wind. Finally, I hop awkwardly up the last few boulders to the rocks beneath the wall, where Danning's blood soaked the ground.

There is no way I'm going to climb the cliff in my battered condition without at least my climbing slippers and preferably a rope. Some internal warning keeps me from calling out—it is a feeling so strong that I can't imagine breaking the night with a shout. So I start circling the tower, remembering the narrow ledges and granite slabs I saw before that looked as if they led up the back side.

On the other side the formation begins with a steep slab, about fifty feet high, which looks as though it rises up to a series of parallel ledges high on the formation. In the moon's light the ledges appear to be separated by only short walls ten feet high or so that are broken with cracks and shadows. The slab will be the tricky part. It is shaped like a great rising wave, scooped out in the middle. The initial twenty feet are low-angled before the slab steadily steepens to near vertical.

I try to smear my dress shoes on the granite, but the smooth leather soles just slide off its hard surface. Pulling them off along with my socks, I lay them at the slab's base where I hope I can find them again in the dark if I don't find an easier way down. If Lynn is up there in the cave she will surely have a rope, and we can rappel off the other side. Just climbing up this untested slab will be hard enough in the dark.

Before starting up, I kick my feet in the dust to dry the sweat. My bare soles stick well enough to the stone until it begins to steepen. Then I'm forced to feel for small edges with my fingers and toes. I'm so exhausted that I climb without thinking and without fear, totally absorbed by the search for holds and the tearing pain I feel in my ribs when I'm forced to suspend much weight from my hands.

Abruptly it all changes. I'm nearly to the top of the slab, fifty feet off a forest floor that is strewn with sharp-edged boulders, when my feet slip out from under me. My right forefoot had been smeared on an edge no larger than a quarter and my left foot reaching for a small toehold when it happened. All my weight suddenly came onto the fingertips of both my hands where they are crimping small quartz crystals protruding from the granite. I almost yelp from the sharp pain that feels as if it is separating my ribs. I make the mistake of looking down to frantically try and spot the footholds again.

The dark ground seems to swell at me and for a moment I'm sure I'm falling. But then the agony in my fingers' tendons alerts me that I'm not—yet. With my bare feet I pedal at the rock while fear soaks my suit with sweat. Somehow I find marginal toeholds and am able to relieve some of the pain in my fingers and ribs. A small rain of pebbles rattles past as I startle a bird or a mouse somewhere above.

I finally pull over the top of the slab, gasping for air and shaking with fright. Several minutes go by before I come to the realization that someone is standing on the ledge with me.

Brad Karge is grinning at me from where he stands in the moon-shadow of an overhang just fifteen feet away. "Never seen a dude climb in a monkey suit before," he says quietly. His blond dreadlocks look like light-colored snakes in the night, and they are writhing in the wind. There is something squat and heavy in his hand, pointed at me.

It takes me a minute to find my voice. "That the gun

you used to kill my dog, Brad?" I manage after I calm myself.

He laughs, his voice pitched high with the fever of methamphetamine. "Oh yeah, man. We blasted that sucker when we were looking for you up in the Horns. It was Billy pulling the trigger, though."

A gust of wind rises up behind him and blows the links of his hair straight out from his head. I feel it sweep through me too, fanning the carefully tended anger within me.

"Where's Billy now, Brad?"

"Gone climbing. He's taking Lynn on her last climb, he says. Dude's psychic or something—he said you'd be coming up here tonight, just like she would. So this is your last climb too. Hope it was fun, dude."

Heller has left him here to kill me, knowing I would come up to look for Lynn. The man does seem psychic, or at least perceptive and very smart. But there is a madness in his actions. He has nothing to gain anymore by killing me. The Sheriff's Office in Johnson County will still seek him for Chris Braddock's murder on the east face of Cloud Peak. Sheriff McKittrick will still hunt him for Sierra Calloway's murder even if the state office tries to let it go. I can sense that he has recognized me as the enemy from the start, just as I have recognized him. Even that first night at the bar there was a competitiveness between us, a need to dominate and destroy. I have always suspected Brad is just another of his disposable pawns, but a valuable one because of his paternity. And I think it is cowardice that made him leave Brad here to ambush me. I can't help but take some satisfaction in believing Heller's afraid to do it himself. The worst part, though, the part that makes me want to scream, is that he is going to succeed—Cecelia's .32 revolver is still under the seat in the truck and Brad is out of reach, fifteen feet away on the narrow ledge.

"Where did he take her?" I ask. "In whose car? Yours?"

"Yeah, they took my ride. But where? I dunno, dude. Somewhere insane I bet. Her last climb'll be really something, not a shitty little slab like yours. Billy has a sense of style when it comes to that," he says admiringly.

"This is yours, too, Brad," I tell him as I get to my feet so I can at least die fighting. "There's enough evidence now to nail you for three murders: Kate Danning, Sierra Calloway, and Chris Braddock. My office knows about all of it. Tomorrow morning they're going to stop the Knapps' sentencing too and arrest your dad for obstruction of justice, malicious prosecution, and anything else they can think of. And they're going to take you down for Kimberly Lee. Make that four murders, Brad. You're the one who's going to be strapped to the gurney. You and your hero Billy."

"That's bullshit, man. You can't prove anything, and you can't fuck with my dad. He's the next governor—your boss!" He laughs.

I shake my head sadly at him, my eyes fixed on his, ignoring the gun in his hand but trying to think of a way to get it from him. I talk as if I'm the one holding the gun, not the one having it pointed at me. "You're wrong. Karge is history as of tomorrow," I lie. "And I've got the rope you used to cut down Chris. We know about the cords you and Heller bought in Buffalo. We know about the cords in Heller's basement. The same cords that were used on them all: Kimberly, Kate, and Sierra—"

He is starting to jitter a little in the shadows when he interrupts, "No, man, no. I didn't do any of that. Heller did them by himself, I just waited outside."

"Your prints on the bottle, Brad. Along with Kate's blood. You hit her on the back of the head with it."

"You got that wrong, Agent. My *dad* smacked her with it. That's right, the future governor of Wyoming. He came up here that night wanting to talk with me about some shit he learned during the trial of those Knapp brothers. When he was looking at the Knapps' past convictions, he figured out the pipe'd come from the evidence locker. That the sheriffs planted that piece of shit to make their case a little better, and probably made up the confession too. Dad was starting to think maybe I'd had a part in it. So he came up where you just did and snuck up on us. Saw Billy and me with Kate. And Lynn, your little friend, fucked-up and screaming at Billy like a banshee. Man, she didn't like it one bit! But good old solid, straight-arrow Pop is the one who really freaked out, started spitting and swinging at us as we were workin' on her. Kate jumped up to get out of the way when he grabbed my bottle to hit Billy—he missed, smacked her on the head, and knocked her off the fucking cliff!"

So Lynn was there. She lied to me. I can understand why, although I can't understand why she'd go back to Heller. But all the rest of it makes sense. I remember Dave Ruddick telling me about Nathan's fingerprints on the bottle, and then I think of Sierra Calloway's comment that Billy had been talking at Kate's funeral about how he owned the cops and the County Attorney. That he was untouchable. It all fits. Billy is the one who carefully stuck the bottle in the recess in the hidden cave. His own Get Out of Jail Free card.

"Even if you didn't directly participate in the killings, it doesn't matter. All we have to do is prove that you knew about them and assisted before, after, or during. Then you're toast. And killing me's just going to up the dosage, Brad. Killing a cop is an automatic ride. You put the gun down and cooperate with me in stopping Heller, I'll do all I can to keep you off the gurney, see that you live."

He hesitates and the gun slowly lowers until it's pointing at my legs. But then he raises it again with a smile, aiming at my head. I've overplayed my hand.

"Fuck it, dude," he says. "I'm not ratting Billy out. I'll take my chances on the lope if it comes to that. Better to die than fade away."

I close my eyes for a minute and think of all the things left undone. Saving Lynn, stopping Heller, seeing Karge's downfall, avenging Oso, making love to Rebecca...the list is endless. I feel another gust of cool wind on my face and wait for the bullet to split my flesh and tumble me off the rock. Bending my knees, I ready myself to launch at him and with any luck take him over the edge with me.

Rather than a gunshot, a voice from behind and above Brad breaks the silence. A dark silhouette is poised on a ledge over our heads. "You pull that trigger, you're going to die a real slow death, kid." The shadow turns and hangs one-handed from the rock, pushing off the short, overhanging wall with the other, then drops as softly as a spider on an invisible silken thread onto the tiny, flat space behind Brad. I recognize the voice and feel a thrill come over me. My brother.

Brad starts to turn toward him with the gun and I step forward. Before I get more than a step, though, he somehow sees my movement and whirls back to me. I can't imagine what Roberto's wraithlike appearance is doing to Brad's mind, scrambled with crank.

"Who the fuck are you!" Brad shouts. "Come closer and I'll shoot the cop!"

Roberto doesn't even slow. He comes along the narrow ledge behind Brad with a predatory grace. Talking while he moves, his voice is hypnotic in the night, even to me. "You think Heller's a badass, you little punk? You don't know what bad is. I beat men to death with my hands, not little girls. I've ripped a full-grown man's throat open with just a piece of glass and my fingers. I tore away his face with my teeth. I've leaned farther out over the edge than anything you can imagine. I've jumped off it a hundred times and always floated back. I can eat you and your pal Heller whole, kid. Bones, skin, muscle, and blood. I can chew you up and spit you out."

Brad's hand is shaking violently as he grips the pistol and struggles to keep it pointed at me.

Still talking softly, Roberto comes up right behind him but doesn't touch him. My brother keeps talking with his lips almost against the back of Brad's throat, his voice now a whisper that the wind whips away before I can decipher the words. Brad's rattling so hard he is in danger of coming apart. Behind him I see my brother lift his powerful arm like a matador's short sword, then drive it into the side of Brad's neck as if he were plunging it home. Brad is slammed into the wall. My brother almost gently catches him before he bounces right off into the night. He sets him on the ledge. The gun in Brad's hand slides over the side and clatters down the slab.

"Jesus, bro," I say.

Roberto shrugs as if to lift the menace from his shoulders. But it doesn't work. Violence surrounds him like a dark cloak. "No worries, Ant. It's just yard talk, you know? Something you got to learn in the can to survive."

I move toward them carefully and put my fingers to

Brad's throat, where he is slumped on the ground. I feel a fast pulse. "I hope you didn't break his neck. How long have you been up here?"

"Ever since I split out of Canon City. I remembered you saying that you were doing some climbing up here at the 'Voo and figured it'd be a good place to hang until the heat's off and I can get down to Argentina. I hoped to spot you up here and blow your mind," he says, chuckling. "You know, write you a letter and say I saw you or something. Instead I've just been watching these freaks dope up and talk about killing you."

"I need a rope to get him off of the ledge. Did you see one by the cave?"

"Be right back, Ant."

Spiderlike, he effortlessly ascends the wall, moving up the short vertical sections between the ledges with a sure- and soft-footed elegance that awes me. His hands and feet seem to barely touch the rock as he glides up, somehow finding holds in the darkness. He disappears up into the night without a sound.

While he is gone I pull my folded tie from my pocket and cinch it tight around Brad's slack wrists. By the time I'm done Roberto is already returning, floating down the wall with the same elegance. In the moonlight I can see a bright rope coiled and draped over his head and one shoulder. He helps me loop it over a thick, scrubby pine that juts out of a crack over our heads. I tie one end around Brad's waist, then set up a body belay with the other part of the rope that hangs from the tree. Unceremoniously, Roberto kicks Brad off the ledge and I start lowering his limp and jackknifed body to the ground. His feet and head strike first and I hear him moan.

While I wrap the rope around my own body to rappel

to the ground, Roberto down-climbs the scooped-out slab I nearly died on. He reaches the ground before I do.

I manage to find my shoes and socks after feeling around in the dirt. I find the heavy pistol Brad dropped too. For a few moments I balance it in my hand, feeling Roberto's hard blue eyes on me. Finally I make a decision. "Want it?" I ask, holding it out to him. "You earned it."

He laughs and says, "You've stepped off the edge, 'mano. Offering an escaped murderer a gun!" Then he *tsks* his tongue against the roof of his mouth the way our mother used to do. "No thanks. I won't be needing it. Sometime tomorrow I'm catching a ride to the airport and a flight south. I'm going to do some climbing, take a stab at the clean life."

He throws Brad over his shoulder as lightly as if he were a coat. As we walk through the dark trees I'm fascinated, as always, by the way Roberto moves through the forest. Normally I feel at home in the backcountry, but I'm a clumsy foreigner compared to my brother. Even with a man's weight on his back he moves effortlessly. Roberto has always been at home in his body and with the environment around him. Utterly unself-conscious, he is a part of the earth rather than just a tourist. He moves with such grace that one wouldn't be surprised to see him walk through walls and rocks. Despite his insatiable appetites and urges, his cells are somehow more directly related to the dirt, the wind, and the trees. Once again, I feel a childhood envy. When we reach the truck I open the back door and Roberto dumps his load inside. I find my handcuffs under the seat and lock the unconscious young man's hands together, taking back my tie.

Roberto flashes a grin at me in the darkness and holds out his own hands, palms upturned and wrists close together.

"Sorry. I only have one set of cuffs," I tell him.

I put my arms around him to say goodbye and feel the thick slabs of prison muscle on his back. A vision of Ross McGee enters my mind for some reason and I recite his mantra to my brother: "Do the right thing, bro—don't fuck around." But the words sound corny from my mouth.

Roberto pushes his hands through my hair playfully, amused, and disappears into the blowing trees as if he had never been there at all.

I need somewhere to stash Bradley Karge, and the Albany County jail is definitely out of the question. As is DCI's holding facility in Cheyenne. I have him handcuffed and gagged with a wool sock and some duct tape I found among Oso's shedded hair under the seat. We sit quietly in the Land Cruiser while I think. Brad's waking up; he attempts to cough as strands from my dead dog's thick hair scratch his throat. I half hope he will choke on them. That would be justice of a sort.

Finally I put the truck in gear and begin bouncing over the dirt roads. I head north, winding among the granite towers that are hidden by the night. After twenty minutes we hit the Happy Jack Road that meanders through the mountains separating Laramie and Cheyenne. Every now and then I stop to study a map from the glove box, check to make sure I can reach Laramie County and Sheriff McKittrick without straying back over the Albany County line. I don't want to drive through that jurisdiction with this particular passenger.

THIRTY

NOT KNOWING WHERE else to go, I return to the Holiday Inn from Laramie County. Sheriff McKittrick had been happy enough to hold on to Brad, and he still had Cindy Topper in protective custody. He told me that she was at home with his wife. "Sweet girl," he said. "She's scared shitless that the same guys are going to come for her." With good reason, I agreed, but wasn't so sure about the sweet part.

I think he was delighted that I was doing all his work for him in catching the murderers of Sierra Calloway, even letting him have the credit of holding Brad in his Cheyenne jail rather than the cells nearby at DCI. And I think he was surprised I brought Brad in alive. "Your reputation's slipping, Agent QuickDraw Burns," he said. "Maybe you ain't a killer." He promised to keep the news of the arrest quiet until the next morning. I asked him to do that more out of fear that my suspended authority would be disclosed than to keep the media at bay.

I call Kristi's home. Her voice is anxious when she answers the phone. "Anton, what's going on? Ross is in the hospital, and everyone's saying you've been suspended, that they're talking of filing those charges again."

"I need some serious help, Kristi. And I can't explain all the reasons why right now. Just that they're trying to screw with me so I can't do anything to postpone the Knapps' sentencing tomorrow morning. The Knapps didn't do it, by the way. They didn't kill that girl. A guy named Billy Heller did with some help from the Karges."

"Those guys you had me pull the records on?"

"Right. They set the Knapp brothers up, and the sheriff and County Attorney went along with it. And they've killed or had a role in the killing of three other people that I know of since then, trying to shut them up. They're about to do a fourth. What I need is help, a BOLO out on a tan Jeep Wrangler registered in Wyoming to Bradley Karge. There's a good chance it's at a climbing area somewhere within a hundred miles or so of Laramie. Either in eastern Wyoming or maybe northern Colorado."

There is a long pause on the other end of the phone. Finally Kristi says, "Anton, I don't know if I can do that, with you being suspended and all. I'd lose my job. I'm sorry, buddy."

After another long moment I ask, "How do you know I'm suspended?"

"Everybody knows it. Everybody's been talking about it."

"But do you know *officially*?"

"You mean, like, have they sent out an e-mail or a memo or something. No, nothing like that."

"Then I'm telling you what you've heard is just rumor, okay? I'm not suspended. You can tell anyone who asks that I told you that. I still have my badge." Since DCI has someone at a communications desk twenty-four hours a day to assist the agents in the field, I ask who is working the desk tonight.

"A guy named Ted," she says, her voice getting excited once again, "and he's got a serious crush on me. He's been trying to get in my pants for months."

"Get him to put out the BOLO. No one will even know about it till morning, and then you guys can just say I lied to you about my status. Okay? Will you do it?"

"Okay, buddy, you got it. But you owe me. I can already think of a few ways I'll make you pay. . . ."

A little while later the phone rings.

"We got a confirmation," a man's voice over the phone says. Ted. "Tan Jeep Wrangler, Wyoming plate number 7–528. At Longs Peak trailhead. That's outside Estes, Colorado, Agent. It's a national park. The ranger on duty said the Jeep's been there all day."

"Did he check the climber's log?" I ask. When the voice at DCI headquarters doesn't immediately respond, I quickly explain, "There's a sign-in book at the trailhead where climbers write their name and intended route."

"Hang on, I've got the ranger on the other line."

There is a click and music begins to play over the phone. I listen in annoyance to an instrumental version of Creedence Clearwater Revival's "Bad Moon Rising." The song seems a little too appropriate. I look out the window and see the turquoise water of the swimming pool. In the lu-minescence of the underwater lights I can see that the wind is whipping up small wavelets. If the pool were just a little larger, there'd be whitecaps. I turn out the lights in my room and look out past the curtains again, up at the sky. The stars and planets are clear, but there is an ominous, hazy ring like a halo around the moon. A sure indicator that a serious storm is brewing. I flip the inside lights back on and curse to myself.

With the phone gripped between my ear and shoulder, I lift the lids off the crates of climbing gear that are still pushed against one wall. I kick off my pants and begin to tug on a pair of fleece tights.

The music clicks off and the voice returns.

"The ranger checked. There's a William Heller and Lynn White with 'King of Swords' written after it. Do you know what that means? The ranger said it was the name of a climb."

I curse again, out loud this time. King of Swords is a legend. Not only is it known as one of the hardest alpine routes in North America, it's also one of the longest and at the highest altitude. Thousands of years ago a glacier cut away half the 14,255-foot mountain now called Longs Peak. The grinding tear resulted in a vertical to overhanging 2,000-foot face of granite that rises to the highest point on the mountain. The face is called the Diamond because of its vague resemblance to a square turned on one corner. And King of Swords, I recall from photos I have seen, leads straight up the middle. I had shaken my head at the audacity and grade of the route.

"Yeah, I know what it means. I've heard of it." For a moment I wonder why Heller would've signed the guide-book, but then realize he'd signed it so if there were questions about Lynn's death he could just call it an accident. I shake the camping gear out of my pack and begin shoving climbing gear into it. A rope. A helmet. A pair of ice tools. Crampons. A small rack of cams, nuts, and a harness. "Listen, get the ranger to call out the park's search-and-rescue team. Get them to the trailhead. Get them there now, tonight."

"Why search-and-rescue? Is someone hurt?"

"Not yet, if we're lucky. But someone's going to get hurt."

The big Land Cruiser rocks on its axles as I take the canyon turns far too fast. Racing up Big Thompson Canyon toward Estes, I keep my hazard lights on and my finger poised on the switch that controls the high beams. Again and again I come up on motor homes creeping up the inclines at far below the speed limit. I angrily flip the beams on and off, honking the horn. I grind my teeth when the campers reluctantly pull over, their drivers displaying annoyance, moving out of the way as slowly as possible. I have to struggle to keep my free hand from beating the steering wheel in frustration.

I curse anew when I roar past a local police car concealed beyond a bend with its lights out. My headlights catch a surprised patrolman in mid-sip from a paper coffee cup, and then I'm past. A few moments later I see the inevitable revolving red and blue lights in my rearview mirror but I keep my foot on the accelerator.

With one hand I lift the cell phone off the console and punch in the numbers to the twenty-four-hour desk at DCI. Unexpectedly the call goes through, the digital connection somehow being made over the canyon walls.

The same voice answers brusquely, "DCI."

"Ted, this is Agent Burns. I'm in Colorado now.

Larimer County, I think. Call the Sheriff's Office here, tell them to get the patrolman off my ass in Big Thompson Canyon. I'm in my personal car, a red Land Cruiser, Wyoming plates." I pause, trying to remember what the numbers are, but can't. "Tell them it's an emergency. I'm meeting Colorado law enforcement and a park search-and-rescue team on Highway 7 at the Longs Peak trailhead."

"Gotcha, Burns. Do you want to hold?"

I hit the end button and toss the phone onto the passenger seat.

The patrol car pulls within feet of the Land Cruiser's rear bumper. The flashing lights seem to be all around me, reflecting off the canyon walls. Then a spot beam comes on, lighting up the interior of my truck with a ten-thousand-watt beam. It's a blinding ray. Furiously, I swipe at my rearview mirror to turn it away from the beam. Instead I knock it off its windshield mount. I can hear over the rumble of my burdened eight cylinders a voice shouting into the night through a loudspeaker. Not slowing, I fish in my fleece jacket's pocket and come up with my badge wallet. I hold it open up where the mirror had been and see it illuminated by the beam. It blazes gold. Switching it to the other hand, I roll down the window and hold it out there too, into the wind.

The spotlight abruptly goes out. Relieved, I can see the police car backing off a little. Then it swings wide out into the left-hand lane and leaps forward like a startled deer. Within seconds it roars past me, engine pitched high, and abruptly cuts back into my lane. "Shit," I almost shout, anticipating that the patrol car will hit its brakes to stop me. But instead the car keeps on accelerating with its red and blue lights flashing. I feel a rush of gratitude as the patrol car sets out to clear a path for me.

*   *   *

I'm almost to the town of Estes when my phone chimes the Mexican Hat Dance from the seat beside me.

"Burns," I say sharply as I swing too fast into another curve.

"This is Captain Tobias of the Colorado Bureau of Investigation. What the hell do you think you're doing?"

"Trying to stop a murder. And catch a killer. Guess what, Captain, I need your help." I need to placate him, to get him to help expedite the search-and-rescue team.

There is a laugh on the other end of the line. It isn't a pleasant laugh. "You bet your ass you do. Remember what I told you about coming into my state? What you're going to do right now is stop whatever it is you're doing. I know where you are, Burns, and you better pull over and stop right now."

"Captain, there's a man who's killed four people in Wyoming. Now he's about to kill another up on Longs Peak, if he hasn't done it al—"

"Stop right now! And shut your goddamn mouth!" Tobias interrupts. "You don't come down here out of your jurisdiction without official permission—"

The man isn't listening. And he isn't going to listen. I hit the end button and try to focus on the road.

After a few minutes the patrol car that's been escorting me suddenly begins to slow. In the glow of my headlights I can see the patrolman in the car raising both hands into the air in a dramatic shrug or "what-the-hell" gesture. Tobias must have reached him on his radio. I slow with him for a moment, then shove my foot on the gas pedal and spin the wheel to the left as I shoot by the confused patrolman. Past him, I flick my own lights on and off once, knowing the brake lights would flicker on and off too, in the trucker's gesture of "thank you." The phone next to me keeps playing the Mexican Hat Dance until I find the thumbnail button that shuts it off.

Another patrol car, this one a U.S. Park Services SUV, is lighting up the night at the entrance to the trailhead parking lot. Parked behind it is a Larimer County sheriff's car. I skid past both and don't slow until I reach the small ranger's cabin at the end of the lot. My headlights reveal six or seven men and women standing in the darkness around a camper that has a Search and Rescue insignia on its side. The S & R team is dressed like I am, in Gore-Tex and fleece. They have aluminum mugs of coffee in their hands. Loose leaves blow among them and I notice the pine trees beyond are bending. The storm is picking up.

I get out of the Land Cruiser, pull my climbing pack from the rear, and step through the informally assembled group, nodding at them in a rushed greeting. They are a random assortment of climbers, long-haired and short-, doctors, lawyers, construction workers, and bums. They train many hours a week, several weekends a month, for the unpaid privilege of rescuing one of their own. The positive energy of that radiates from their concerned faces and makes me feel embarrassed when I return to my truck and slip Cecelia's gun into my pocket.

Several of them ask me questions that I barely hear over the wind.

"Two climbers on the Diamond," I say quickly, moving toward the cabin, "on a route called King of Swords."

"In this fucking storm? Lunatics!" one says. But he grins like the others. The idea of going on up the highest alpine wall in the continental United States in the middle of a gale appeals to them. They are amped.

I walk quickly to the door of the ranger's cabin, rap it twice with my knuckles, and push it open.

Three men turn to stare at me from inside the small building. Tobias is there, a phone to his ear, his face immediately coloring at the sight of me. Even his ridiculously outdated military haircut seems to bristle. One of the other two is a man I've never met but I've seen before in climbing magazines, honored for the rescues he performs. I remember his position as that of the highest-ranking ranger in one of the country's busiest national parks. The third man is a total stranger.

The one from the magazines is older, probably in his early sixties, and wearing a Park Service uniform below a lean, weatherworn face. His lantern jaw reaches far over the collar of the stiff, green uniform, and the look in his eyes is as strong as the jaw and the starch.

The other man, the stranger, is almost the ranger's opposite. He is small and thick with a chin that recesses instead of jutting. He wears a cheap blue suit, much of its polyester lining hanging below the hem of the jacket. The fat jowls of his sweaty face rise above his version of a uniform. Despite his obvious dishevelment, his small dark eyes are probing, assessing. Cop's eyes. The small man looks from me to Tobias as if awaiting a command. I peg him as Tobias's toady.

I nod at the ranger. Before either of us can speak, Tobias starts in.

"I warned you, Burns. I warned you not to come into my state. Now I'm going to have you up on charges. Reckless driving, eluding a police officer, even accessory to escape, if I can make it stick. You're not going to—"

I ignore him and speak to the ranger, holding out my no-longer-official badge and hoping Tobias hasn't heard of my suspension. "As you've probably heard, my name's Antonio Burns. A man I believe is responsible for several recent murders in Wyoming is on the Diamond with an essential witness. He's going to drop her. He's done it before."

The ranger too ignores Tobias's harangue and looks hard at my eyes as I speak. It looks as though he has already spent enough time with the captain of CBI to assess his character.

"I will not be ignored!" Tobias tries to shout over me as I continue talking. "Burns, you are under arrest!"

His underling again looks from Tobias to me, still awaiting an order.

The ranger asks, "Can you document any of this?"

I nod, but then hesitate. "My briefcase, reports, and the photos are in my hotel room in Laramie ... and there is some other stuff at the DCI lab in Cheyenne ..." But then I remember that I'm suspended, that I don't want him calling the office. And Ross McGee's in the hospital. "You can call Sheriff Don McKittrick of Laramie County. He's got one of the suspects in custody. He'll vouch for me."

Tobias is still shouting as I speak. A slight foam is gathering in the corners of his mouth. He points at his heavy underling and says, "Arrest him. Now!" just as the ranger asks what I want done. The captain is afraid to come near me himself, it appears. He must remember being thrown to the floor in the hotel room.

His toady moves toward me, reaching around his heavy waist for the handcuffs he keeps on his belt. I keep my eyes locked on the ranger's, knowing the man is about to make a decision.

"What do you want?" he asks, staring back.

"Helicopter your S & R team and me to the summit. The sight of the copter alone may be enough to save the witness. When we're over the summit, we can rappel or sling off the copter—" Tobias's toady tries to take one of my arms, but I shrug him off.

The ranger holds his hand up to the heavy man as if he is an unruly child. "Stop it. No one's getting arrested here."

The underling stops and looks again to Tobias. I can see the captain is losing it. The foam at his mouth has grown. His face is as red as a fire engine and his eyes have taken on a crazed look. The captain reaches into his own jacket and puts his hand again on the butt of his gun. I feel my own knees bend slightly, preparing to spring.

The ranger sees it too and quickly steps between Tobias and me. With an icy look he freezes Tobias's hand as it withdraws the gun. "Captain Tobias," he says sharply, "you aren't arresting anyone. This is a national park; this land belongs to the federal government, sir—you have no authority here."

I almost smile when I see the fight go out of Tobias's eyes at the same time the blood drains from his face. Twice in two days the man's been caught outside his jurisdiction.

"Now sit down while we work this out! If there's any truth to what Agent Burns is telling us, he's of far more value here than he would be in your jail."

A twisted smile creeps to the captain's lips. He slowly lowers himself on a hard bench and shoots me with a look of pure hate.

The ranger turns to me and says, "Now I'm responsible for law enforcement and public safety in the park. But what you're talking about, a murder suspect and a potential kidnap victim up there on the wall, is way outside my league. And it's way outside my team's training. Most of them aren't even in law enforcement. What I'm going to do right now is make a call to the FBI."

"There's no time," I argue. "The girl already may be dead, or he may be about to drop her."

"Agent Burns, surely you noticed that the winds are gusting thirty to forty miles an hour down here." Now the ranger's a little annoyed with me. "How hard do you think it's blowing up on the Diamond, nearly five thousand feet higher? There's no way I can send a helicopter anywhere right now. The boys and girls out there aren't going anywhere either," he says, indicating the S & R team with a finger pointed at the door. "In fact, this storm may have already killed anyone who's on that wall tonight." He walks to a desk and pulls a thin phone book out of a drawer. Turning his back to me, he picks up the phone and dials a number.

As the ranger talks into the receiver, I spot a large, hand-drawn map of the Diamond posted on a wall and stand before it. I find the route called King of Swords and mark it with a red pen I take off another desk. I trace it upward, from where it begins a third of the way up the wall on a ledge called Broadway. The Broadway Ledge itself is more than five hundred feet off the ground, above a small glacier. According to the map it can be accessed either by a circuitous couloir far to the south of the face or by a more direct, and more difficult, chimney that rises off the glacier. It looks as if King of Swords begins in a corner to the right of a prominent buttress, and then follows a series of wide, off-width cracks for a few hundred feet until a fist crack leads through a steep roof. More cracks lead onward and upward, through more small roofs, until, after a single crackless pitch of tiny holds, the route reaches a long platform known as Table Ledge. Again, more wide cracks lead from there to the top of the climb, just to the right of the highest point on the Diamond and the 14,255-foot summit of Longs Peak.

I stare at the topo, memorizing all the detail I can of the seven roughly 150-foot pitches, not even including the three to four easier ones beneath the Broadway Ledge, until I hear the ranger put down the phone.

"They're waking up the Special Agent in Charge at the Denver office. Apparently someone from the Wyoming AG's Office already has been trying to call, Agent Burns. The FBI will call us once they are briefed."

I suppress a groan. I don't have much time before it is discovered that I'm suspended. I point at the topo and say, "I know you're used to rescues. Say you had someone hurt on that wall tonight, how would you go about getting them off?"

The ranger stands beside me at the topo and studies it too, rubbing the coarse shadow on his anvil jaw. "Heli sling-out or heli to the top and rap are out of the question tonight, at least for now. The wind's coming out of the west, probably blowing over the summit at a hundred to a hundred twenty miles per hour. A helicopter is not an option in this wind, especially at night. But the Diamond has at least a little protection from the wind, since it faces east. It'll still be gusting eighty to ninety on the wall, though. The only way to do a rescue is either to wait out the storm or go up from the bottom, maybe on an easier route like Kieners or the Notch," he says, referring to more moderate routes to the left of the face, "and rappel laterally from below the summit." He pauses for a minute, then shakes his head as he notices the red tracing I've done next to King of Swords. "But if you're talking someone on Swords, when we don't even know where they are on the route, you can't do anything but wait it out. You can't rappel that route—too many roofs and no permanent anchors. See, you would have to go all the way up it to find them in the dark. And there are only a handful of climbers in the country who can get up that route, and that's when it's in good condition."

The phone rings again and the ranger answers it. "I'll be right back," I say to the ranger, who doesn't hear me. Tobias looks pale and confused as I swing my pack over one shoulder and push open the cabin's door. I step out into the night.

I can hear them inside as I pause, buckling the hip belt. The wind is holding the door open.

"Where's he going?" the ranger asks Tobias and his underling.

"He took his pack outside," the toady says.

"Shit!" I hear Tobias yell in realization.

I'm already a little ways up the trail, moving fast and disappearing into the darkness of the swaying pines, when I hear Tobias shouting at the S & R team gathered outside the cabin.

"Where'd he go?"

"Dude just ran up the trail," one of the team members answers.

THIRTY-ONE

I DON'T USE MY headlamp as I run up the rocky trail through the pines. My eyes adjust quickly to the light of the moon and I run without stumbling, trying to move as my brother would, at one with the gusting wind and the stones beneath my feet. The gear inside the heavy pack I wear jangles out a rhythm. The switchbacks take me higher and higher until the pines grow smaller, stunted by lack of oxygen at this elevation.

Coming out of the trees, I can see a vast, starless obstruction in the sky to the west. The Diamond. It looks like what astronomers call a black hole, sucking in all the space around it, big enough and yawning wide enough to swallow the Earth. I pause for a moment, gulping some water from a bottle, transfixed by the size of the absolute darkness. Fear freezes me for a moment, then a stinging rain of wind-blown gravel slaps my face. At this altitude there are no more trees to protect me. I run on, against the wind, toward the huge sucking hole.

The trail keeps rising, along a broad ridge above empty fields of talus, before it traverses the side of a small mountain. At one point I'm halted by a fat patch of ice that drools down across the trail and into the deep valley below. Its hard gray surface angles slightly toward the abyss. Without removing my pack, I reach up and behind me to unclip one of the ice tools. I don't take the time to put on my crampons. I move gingerly over the ice, both hands on the ax, the pick always buried deeply in the frozen water, trying not to think of how a slip will lead to a 500-foot tumble into the gorge.

I've long since sweated through my fleece. I'm jogging along the trail now, the hip belt of my pack blistering my sides through the damp pile. Lactic acid burns ferociously in my legs. My throat is hot and dry from an hour of panting. Just when I feel the rigid grip of exhaustion seizing my muscles, I let the stifled anger leach back through me like the gentle turn of a pressure valve.

The trail rises onto a wide field of broken rocks. Over the howl of the wind, I can hear the soft gurgling of water running over them. I splash through the tiny streams of icy water and remember this place from the ranger's map. I look for and spot the small, deserted rescue cabin that crouches under a boulder-strewn slope.

I lose the trail amid the shallow water, but know it lies somewhere above the cabin. Scrambling up the slope, I pull myself over the walls of irregular truck-size blocks until I reach another plateau. Here, in a wide depression, the moonlight streaks crazy yellow shapes over the surface of a glacial lake. Small waves sweep up and over the ice that rims the water's edge. I find the trail again and follow it at a run around the lake. The vast black shape looms up above me, leaning over, ready to crash down on the lake and everything around it.

The foot of the dark wall is shod in white. The hard glacial snow runs hundreds of feet down from the Diamond's lower reaches. I pause again to study it, my hands on my knees, my breath coming in harsh gasps, my head arched all the way back. The glacier resembles a white hand pushing against the base of the wall. There are two ways to reach Broadway Ledge a third of the way up the face, where the King of Swords begins. One way I can see to my left; a low-angled couloir called Lamb's Slide rising diagonally left, up, and slightly away from the face. If the snowfield is a right hand, then the couloir looks like the outstretched thumb. A slow, safe, circuitous route. The other, more difficult but more direct, route is the North Chimney. Far steeper, its narrow line of snow leads up directly above me, like an extended middle finger, until it disappears in darkness a few hundred feet up the wall.

Speed is my priority, I decide. If it were safety, I wouldn't be here in the first place. I dump my pack in the scree at the edge of the snowfield, tug on my harness, and snap the crampons onto my boots. I tie one end of the skinny, eight-millimeter rope to the harness and drape the rest in coils over my head and one shoulder. Over the other shoulder, I lift a small rack of cams and wired chocks. I jam the second ax through a harness loop and with the other I prod the firm snow. Like a magician's trick, my now unweighted pack is stolen by the wind and vanishes into the night.

At first the glacier isn't steep enough to force me onto my crampon's front points. I'm able to place my feet flat on the snow, sideways, so that all the lower points in the crampons are engaged. This is painful on my bent ankles, which are flexed to the side 30 degrees or more to keep me upright, but it saves my tired calves from the exertion of front pointing. I traverse in this awkward manner, known as the French Technique, for twenty steps up and to the right, turn, then twenty up and in the other direction. I grip my long ice tool in my uphill hand and firmly plant the spike in the snow with each step.

Within twenty minutes I reach the top of the glacier and the beginning of what had looked like an extended middle finger from the glacier below. Up close, it looks to me more like a narrow white tongue lolling out of some dark recess. The North Chimney. The tongue is much steeper than the slope below. I move up it without hesitation, front-pointing now. I pull my second tool from my harness as I climb and use the two in tandem, my gloved palms wrapped around their steel heads. After every two steps, I pull the axes out of the snow one at a time and replant them into the snow ahead, shoving them in the way one would plunge a dagger into another man's belly.

Close to the top of the tongue, I pause to look up at a starless expanse of darkness. The sky has turned to black stone. Despite the fear that expands within me, I feel a familiar thrill.

The hard snow drools out of the chimney's three-sided space. The opening is as broad as an elevator shaft, but its concave walls close in tighter farther back. The rear of the chimney is just two and a half feet wide. The temperature drops at least twenty degrees in the dark, high chamber. The wind rumbles down the shaft like a train. Without having touched the stone walls yet, I can feel their chill through my gloves. I feel it on my skin, in my muscles, down to my tired bones. The cold seems to grip at my chest, choking me.

I lift the coil of rope off my shoulder and drop it on a small depression I stamp out at the very top of the snow tongue. Gently passing it through my gloves, I uncoil it and feel for any knots that could catch on the chimney's many cracks and edges. I let my leashed tools dangle free from my wrists as I press myself into the shaft and begin stemming upward, the line trailing out beneath me from where one end is tied to my harness.

It takes a half hour of hard climbing, the sort that would be easy without the cold and darkness, before I reach the Broadway Ledge. Up the entire North Chimney route the rope hung loosely from my harness. I never felt unsteady enough to need to slow my progress by placing protection in the rock or ice and tying in. But standing on the narrow ledge, when the wind staggers me slightly, I'm glad I brought the rope. I look up at the dank wall that leans over me and know I will need it.

The ledge slopes disturbingly down toward the edge. But as I move north, the bench broadens until it is almost ten feet wide. Rock debris litters its surface. At one point I have to move gingerly around the base of a massive buttress that projects from the wall. In the recess on the pillar's far side, I remember from the ranger's map, begins the route known as the King of Swords. If Lynn and Billy are somewhere on it, I hope they are riding out the storm on some higher ledge. I hope that at least Lynn is still alive.

I find a wide, vertical crack in a corner of the recess that must be the route's start. I'm tempted to turn on my head-lamp to inspect the fissure for chalk marks, any sign of recent passage, but am afraid the light could be seen from above. Hesitating, I pull off my gloves and stare upward, trying to recall a Catholic prayer my mother taught my brother and me. Something about being weak, cold, and scared, asking the Lord to give me strength and courage as I strap on my sword and shield to go into battle. But my mind can't find it, or God isn't with me on this wall.

Instead other images rise within me: Billy Heller raging at me on his porch; Oso's snarling and shattered muzzle as his blood drains out on the snow; Sierra Calloway's bound corpse and the faint burn marks on her back from the broken lamp; and Ross McGee collapsing on the marble floor as the Assistant AG asks for my badge. I open the pressure valve all the way, letting the fury out in an enormous torrent. Then I put my hands in the crack and start climbing.

An hour later there is no way to tell how much higher the wall reaches above my position clinging flat against it. The blackness beneath me is also impossible to measure. I'm almost overcome by doubts—maybe Heller has already thrown Lynn off, then finished the route or rapped off. Maybe the Jeep at the trailhead and the note in the climber's log were just decoys, and they are really somewhere else, on another route.

At a small stance I set two mechanical cams in a crack and wearily tie the rope to them. For the sixth time I rappel the skinny 50-meter line, picking out the pieces of protection I left when I climbed up the rock, remove the anchor I built at the lowest point, then knot slings into ascension knots and jug back up the rope while swinging free in the wind. In this cumbersome way, having to climb each pitch twice, I have progressed six rope lengths above Broadway Ledge.

Back at the stance where I tied the highest anchor, I feel for the crack to reach higher but can't find it. My frozen hands slide across the dark, vertical surface and find nothing but small edges. Then I remember the topo map in the ranger's cabin. I must be at the pitch below Table Ledge, not too far from the summit. The drawing showed the crack I've followed for over six hundred feet ending and the hundred feet above devoid of all but the smallest holds.

I slot another cam into the very top of the crack and secure it to the other pieces of protection that provide my anchor. I know this is just a pretense of greater security—there's unlikely to be much in the way of further placements until Table Ledge, which I guess is a hundred feet higher. The act of strengthening the anchor is futile. I know my single skinny rope won't hold much of a fall if I come off.

After what feels like eighty feet of crimping and edging on tiny holds, I find a small, horizontal crack into which I can fit a small cam. I punch it in frantically, finally achieving some protection when I snap the rope through its carabiner. I risk hanging off the single piece to rest for a minute, spinning on the rope and seeing a pink glow on the horizon at my back. The first blush of dawn. The Knapps' sentencing will be starting just hours from now in Laramie, a hundred miles to the north. The thought of it gets me started again.

After only a few moves beyond the cam I pause again, listening.

Not far above, over the bay of the wind that roars in my ears, I hear the soft flapping of nylon. There's a voice somewhere too, a man's monotone, and then a chuckle and a slap. Reaching up, I grip a solid edge. I pull myself up on it with both my torn, frozen hands and discover Table Ledge just as the sun's first curving rays paint the wall from black to a dark gray.

The ledge is a small, cavelike platform that extends back into the face only five feet or so. The length is no more than fifteen feet from where I cling at the left-most end. To the right of me a tiny blue bivouac tent snaps in the wind, nestled back against the rock. From it comes the man's low voice.

Hesitating before crawling up, I look into the grayness beneath me and try to remember where I placed my last piece of protection—that insignificant little cam. Twenty feet below? There's no way to tell. I note with a mixture of relief and wariness the safety cord that the tent's occupants have stretched low across the back of the ledge.

I slide up and stand on the first real horizontal surface I have felt in what seems like forever. As I do, the gear and axes that hang from me jingle against the rock. The voice I heard from the tent is suddenly silent. Hurrying now, I take a long piece of webbing that's attached to my harness and clip it to the safety line. When the carabiner snaps shut, the tent's door rips open with a zipper's shriek.

"Heller! Billy Heller!" I call over the howl of a sudden gust that staggers me on the ledge.

A ponytailed head shoves through the opening in the faint predawn light. The face splits into a grin as easily as the tent's fly had parted. He looks absolutely satanic.

"My, my. I wasn't expecting company," he shouts to me. There's laughter in his voice. "You gonna serve a warrant on me, Agent Burns? Here?"

"I just want Lynn."

"The little bitch who ran off and banged you, then came crawling back to me? Sure, hang on a sec." He says it casually, as if I'd knocked on his screen door and Lynn was watching TV somewhere inside.

Heller's face disappears for a moment. Then it returns and he parts the opening with his massive shoulders and crawls halfway out of the tent. With a meaty fist he pulls a

handful of blonde hair after him, onto the small space between us. It's Lynn. She's only wearing polypropylene underwear, the bottoms pushed down around her knees.
There's a harness still around her waist with the leg loops
undone but I can't see any rope or cord attached to it. Her
eyes are swollen almost shut by deep bruises, her mouth is
open, and her head is lolling on the cold stone.

"Anton?" I think I hear her say. But the wind's too loud
and her voice barely a whisper. I can't be sure if she spoke at
all.

"This little darling was just fixing to see if she could fly.
You might give it a try yourself, Agent," Heller shouts, the
laughter still in his voice. He's squatting next to her now by
the tent's entrance. In the early-morning light I can see that
he's wearing a harness too. A long, loose length of cord
snakes to the safety line.

I take a step toward them but stop when he nudges
Lynn so that she's almost at the edge.

"Don't do it, Billy! Even if she's not around to testify,
there's more than enough evidence to nail you for the murders of Kimberly, Kate, Chris, and Sierra. You don't need to
hurt her."

"Kate? I think you got that one wrong, cowboy. I didn't
kill Kate. Sure, I did the others, Kim, Chris, and Sierra. But
not Kate, not that tasty little piece of ass. Tell him, sweet-
heart."

I see Lynn's head nod. Her mouth moves and she says
one word, "Karge."

"I already know about that. But you and Brad are ac-
cessories, at the least. I've already got Brad in a cell in
Laramie County. It's over, Billy. Let her go."

"So you've got me, Agent? What are you going to do,
handcuff me? And I don't see any gun." He smiles. "That's

right, I hear you don't carry one. A climbing cop without a gun." He shakes his head, his voice full of mirth. "It doesn't look like you thought this one through, Agent. Now this is really getting fun. More fun than banging young broads, then whacking them. You ought to try it, Agent. Combine it with climbing and you've got one powerful fucking brew."

"It's over," I say again. "Let her clip to me; I'll take her out of here. Do that, I can promise you life, not a ride on a gurney. Okay? Life—I swear." I usually know just the right thing to say, the right thing to do, but I'm unsure how to play this. My exhaustion and his obvious confidence combine to have me rattled. All I know for sure is that I have to get Lynn away from the edge.

The weight of Cecelia's pistol is heavy in my jacket pocket. I want to slip it out, point it between his eyes, blast him away into the dawn. But I can't. With one hand he could push her off in half a second. Despite my ridiculous nickname, there's no way I can draw that fast.

"I'll tell you about life, Agent. *This is life!* And it's getting better and better," he says, his voice fast and excited like a preacher's. "When I first did that bitch Kim, she was about to go to the cops and tell them about my selling a little meth. I just meant to kill her, make it look like those stupid Knapps did it by throwing some piece of her meat in their truck and writing some shit on the wall. But when I had her all tied up, I just couldn't resist giving her one last fuck for old times' sake. God, that felt good!" He stares right through my eyes and licks his lips. "Tightening that cord around the bitch's neck as I gave her one last hurrah. I couldn't wait to do it again."

I find myself almost mesmerized by his words. It's the passion in his voice that's so enthralling, despite the ugliness of his words and deeds. For the first time I can see why the young climbers worship him. He's sick, I think, like a rabid dog, but I feel no pity. The wind reels up to deliver another blow and I sway on the ledge.

"Kate was my second taste. She was about to go to the cops too. Brad, that dumb kid, even helped me out with that one, after I told him how good it'd been with Kim. Then his father showed up, right in the fucking middle of things. Came out of nowhere, yelling like a maniac and coming at me." He rumbles with laughter, one hand sliding over Lynn's unmoving buttock and tucking between her legs. "I couldn't believe it when he missed me with Brad's bottle of bourbon and nailed the bitch. You should've heard her scream as she went over the edge!"

My mouth's too dry to spit, so I just say, "Shut the fuck up and let her come over, Heller. You aren't going to convert me." But he's not listening.

"Man, I'm telling you, it's just like climbing. Once you get that first little taste, that first fucking thrill, there's no going back. It's the Rat, man. Killing, God, that's milk and honey! Don't talk to me about life until you've tasted it." His face is lit up by one of the widest grins I've ever seen. And the most perverse. His eyes are shining as if he's in the midst of some religious ecstasy. At one point he starts to raise his hands to more forcefully show his emotion, but he's too cunning to move them far from Lynn's still form.

"Anyway, where was I? Oh yeah, sweet Sierra. My third slice of pie. After I heard she talked to you, I took my time with her, man, and I almost got it just right. Then when I got worried about young Chris spilling the beans, he was next in line. Man, the look he gave me when I cut the rope! I was God to him. He's there looking up at me, coming up the pitch while I'm belaying, totally psyched to be out with me. It was like God playing a little joke."

He pauses for a minute and goes back to stroking Lynn's bare legs. The wind roars again across us but he doesn't appear to notice. He's too caught up in reliving his triumphs. I'm standing just seven or eight feet away, my hands loose at my sides, ready to go for the pistol if he so much as turns his head.

"You were next. I was watching you through binoculars that morning in the Horns, watching you solo up toward Chris. Brad and I were heading down the valley to have some fun with that piece of ass you'd brought along when your dog came at us. Man, what a brute! At first we thought he was a bear. I popped him one in the face, damn near tore his nose off, but he didn't stop till I blew a .45 caliber hole right in his fucking heart. I shit you not, I didn't think that dog was ever going down! If it hadn't been for that storm, I'd of nailed you then."

The heat rises so fast within me that it feels like my hair might catch fire. The frozen numbness in my ragged hands melts away with a single surge of blood. So strong is the urge to reach for the pistol that I feel my hands tremble. The moment I get a sure, safe shot, I'm going to kill this man. I'm going to unload all six rounds into his head and paint the rock red.

"What you did to my van wasn't funny, though." His heavy brow drops down over his eyes as he frowns. We share a moment of hate that's like a bolt of lightning between us. Then he brightens with another smile. His voice is so soft the wind almost carries it away when he says, "But you've given me so many more reasons to kill you, Agent Burns."

"Let her clip to me. Then you can go. Go wherever you want," I lie, trying to mask my rage and work a scared plea into my words.

Heller chuckles. "Sorry, but Lynn's a little tied up right now, if you know what I mean." He tips her a little to one side, away from the edge. For the first time I see that her hands are bound with the familiar pink cord. "I got it perfect with her, man—climbing and fucking, then dying. I didn't think it could get any better, then you show up." He grins again. "You ready to fly?"

Just then a gust of wind fills the tent, billowing its nylon walls with a sudden *whoomff*. Heller whips his head around and half turns his torso. The wind bounces me off the wall and it knocks Heller in the same direction, out of his crouch. As his hands slap the granite for balance, I slip one hand inside my anorak and come out with the gun I'd borrowed in Buffalo. I try to point it at Heller's head but another gust stings my eyes with blowing spindrift.

Then in a blink Heller's gone. He's ducked back into the tent.

Not knowing what else to do, but with only the fear of ricochets keeping me from filling the nylon with holes, I step forward quickly and grab Lynn's shirt. I need both my hands to pull her away from the edge. The gun goes back in my pocket for just a moment. I crouch between the tent and Lynn, my left shoulder to the abyss, and as fast as I can I clip a sling of webbing from the harness Lynn wears over bare legs to mine. At least now she's tied to me. And through me to the safety line Heller had run along the wall side of the ledge.

When the carabiner snaps shut I stand and turn toward the tent while fumbling in my pocket with numb fingers for the gun.

The tent fly erupts as if a bull is charging through it. His speed and power are unreal as he hurtles along the narrow ledge toward me. The gun is caught on some fabric—it won't come free. I've just enough time to take a step forward and lean in.

Heller comes at me, bellowing like a berserker, with an upraised ax in one hand. He rears up and drives into me with his hip and churning knees. I plant my arms against his chest and shove forward to keep from being blown back off the edge. With the ax Heller chops—but not at me. The ax comes down on the safety line, parting it with a single stroke. With a mental jolt as powerful as the impact of Heller's body, I realize Lynn and I are now tied to the wall only through the skinny rope I'd used to ascend. And that rope is only connected to the rock twenty feet down where I'd placed the single cam. I have no idea what Heller is tied to, or if he's tied to anything at all.

For a moment we're caught in a snarling embrace on the narrow ledge. I push forward with all the strength in my legs but I'm no match for Heller's muscle and weight. I feel myself being forced back over Lynn, back over the edge. He's going to throw us off. *Fuck. Fuck. Fuck.* The adrenaline rips through me—I try to bite his throat but can't get my teeth through his parka.

Then a thought comes to me as I'm forced a step back, my rear foot just inches from the edge. The thought is so simple. So clean. It's like a revelation. *Try it,* a voice whispers from somewhere inside me. *Try it. You'll be dead anyway—why not have some fun?*

Still shoving forward with all my strength, I wrap my arms all the way around the big man. The Rat in my chest shrieks with delight as I suddenly shift my weight. I throw myself backward, off the edge, letting Heller's momentum drive him with me. I pray he's not tied in to anything but the cut safety line. I pray that my single skinny rope will hold my fall. I pray that God might listen.

For a moment we float in the sky as Lynn's dragging weight slows the drop, then begin to plummet as she slides over after us. I see us fall past the small cam I'd placed twenty feet down. It looks ridiculously small and fragile. And the rope whipping through it looks as soft and delicate as wet spaghetti.

Heller's body is jerked out of my arms, upward, when his own unseen rope catches him. The big man is yanked back up into the dark sky as if he's a yo-yo on a string. Then my teeth snap together as my own rope finally pulls tight on the cam. That one tiny cam halts my plummet. Miraculously, the rope doesn't break. A fraction of a second later I scream soundlessly as Lynn's weight hits the webbing by which she's tied to the back of my harness. It feels as if I'm being cut in half.

Because of the overhang beneath the ledge, I'm floating out more than six feet from the wall. Looking down, I can see her hanging limply, a body length below me. Her back is arched at a sharp angle, her bare belly pointed toward me. When I look up I see Heller's massive form swinging just ten feet above. A moan is squeezed from my lungs by the weight on my harness. I hear Heller's answering groan, which turns into a choked laugh.

There's a flash of motion above me. Dimly I see the arc of the ax still in Heller's hand. "You fly...like shit...the two of you....Better try again." I watch, transfixed with pain, as Heller, who is hanging free like some terrible spider, takes the taut line of my rope in one of his hands. He pulls it toward him. The glint of the ax in his other hand slashes toward it. He misses with the first strike; only the ax handle bounces off the line. Not the sharp point. It's awkward for him to chop at the rope as he spins in the wind.

With another involuntary groan, I slap at my jacket.

The pistol is still there, hanging halfway out of the pocket, caught by the trigger guard. I grab at it with both hands, trying to find the grip, as my vision begins to grow dim around the edges. I can't breathe—Lynn's weight is strangling me, cutting off my air.

I see the flash of metal above a second time. Again the ax handle bounces off my rope. I see Heller's white teeth for a moment and then the back-and-forth sawing motion of one of his hands. He's using the tiny serrated edges that droop from the pick to saw through the rope. I find the gun's butt, lift it out, hear its roar and see its flash break the dawn wide open.

For a long time I simply hang, fighting to breathe. It feels as if I'm pinned to a wall by a truck, its bumper pressing into my damaged waist and ribs while some demon presses on the gas pedal. I feel a stream of liquid spray across my face and head. It stops for a second and then comes again in a sort of regular rhythm. It runs down the back of my neck, hot and viscous, like oil. When I look up, it splashes my face. In the faint light the fluid is a cherry red. Heller hangs limply, head down, just a few feet above me.

I let my head drop again to where Lynn sways below me, stretched out in the wind. The pistol slides out of my hand on its own and simply disappears beyond her without a sound. Her cutting weight persists in the small of my back and leaves me without strength, without will.

So I let the wind and the dawn take me. The warm stream from above spills on me as I swing, as if I'm penduluming back and forth under a waterspout. A bright light seems to envelop me. Brighter than the sun. The spindrift no longer stings my face—it starts to feel more like the warm caress of a kind hand. I can hear nothing but a smooth, steady heartbeat that grows closer and closer, coming for me.

All those times I've cheated Death—that I've felt him climbing just beneath me in his swirling black robe—that I've laughed and kicked him in his face as he's reached up with bony fingers to grab at my ankles—and now he's just swooping in, surprisingly tender, to finally carry me away.

THIRTY-TWO

NOTHING IS AS I expect. I had imagined soothing light and quiet, then a slow fade into blackness. I'd expected my soul to be drawn out of my battered shell of a body as gently as silk from a spider's belly. Instead there is a tremendous vibrating noise. And the sound of men shouting. My body, sensed only vaguely, is pummeled, pulled, and dragged. The realization comes to me slowly, at first in the form of a question. *Rescue?*

I lapse in and out of consciousness on the short helicopter flight to the Estes hospital. The medics of the Search-and-Rescue team have bundled me in coarse wool blankets. After checking my pulse and respiration, they ignore me. They must realize the blood that covers me belongs to someone else. Instead they hover around Heller's huge form, pressing, shouting, injecting. Lynn's blonde hair is sprayed out on the cargo bay floor not far from me. One of the men is bent low over her, monitoring her breathing.

Trying to figure out what happened, I dimly recall the beat of that giant heart coming closer in the bath of a light far brighter than the sun. It had been poised somewhere above me, and then a phantom shadow came soaring out from beyond the light. The phantom thudded against the wall above me and flew away again. Then it came back, and I thought I heard a curse. There was a violent tug on my rope but I was beyond feeling pain. There was the sound of a stranger barking commands. The phantom moved down the ropes, then gripped my harness. It shouted something in my face before it moved down past me.

The phantom climbed back up using my ankle, my clothes, and my shoulders as hand- and footholds. Suddenly I was flying again, soaring out off the wall, back into the dawn. The cutting weight falling from my back as I took my first deep breath. The next thing I felt was a multitude of arms grabbing me, dragging me up, into that giant beating heart.

Pondering all this, I slide away again.

"QuickDraw, you seem to spend way too much time screwing around in hospital beds." Jefferson Jones looms over me. "They say you're gonna live, but you sure don't look like it. Again. You're better off than Heller anyway—they say you killed the son of a bitch. Winged him in the neck—remind me to take you out to the range sometime, teach you to shoot. Anyway, he bled out. On you, the way it looks."

"Lynn, the girl," I say, my throat raw and my teeth chattering. "Is she going to be all right?"

"I talked to the doctor who was with her a little while

ago. Said that little pixie should be up and about before long. She was hypothermic and had a concussion, is all. Heller probably punched her around pretty good before you showed up. There were some minor rope burns to her neck, wrists, and ankles. Sound familiar?"

"How about me? Am I going to be all right?"

"Hypothermia, exhaustion, and a concussion, the doc says. That makes two concussions in a week, QuickDraw. You've probably lost whatever mind you had."

I nod and feel the muscles spasm in my neck. "How did you get here?"

"Your reporter girlfriend woke me up again, worrying about you. Tell her to leave me alone from now on, let me sleep. I can't spend every night chasing after your sorry ass. Anyway, I checked the hotel and the jail, then called your office and heard from the desk that you were screwing around down here in Colorado." He shrugs and smiles. "Figured since I was already awake, I might as well see what you were up to, so I drove down here at dawn. I don't have to work that sentencing today, since I quit."

"How did I get here?"

"Some stern-looking guy, the head ranger or something, brought you in on a helicopter a couple of hours ago. I met them here. A Search-and-Rescue team dragged you off some mountain."

My brain is sluggish, but I process what he's telling me item by item. Heller's dead. Rebecca's worried about me. Lynn's going to be okay. The sentencing...

"What time is it? The sentencing—I've got to get to Laramie!"

"Ten o'clock, but it's too late, QuickDraw." He points at the TV in the corner of the hospital room. On its screen a pretty woman is standing in front of the Albany County

Courthouse talking into a microphone. Either the sound is too low or the buzz that hums in my ears and the chattering of my teeth is too loud for me to tell what she's saying. "According to that, the prosecution already started calling witnesses this morning," Jones explains.

I get up out of the bed, gritting my teeth against the pain that racks every inch of my body. I nearly collapse before I even get my feet on the cool linoleum floor. But I fight the sensation of a swirling room and I bat weakly at Jones's arms when he tries to push me back into the bed. Inside a grocery sack at the foot of the bed are some of my clothes, still filthy but neatly folded. I grunt and groan and start pulling on the fleece pants.

Jones tries to argue with me. He tells me to get my ass back in the bed but I ignore him. "If they're still on the witnesses, we can make it," I tell him. "What is it, a ninety-minute drive?"

My friend is frowning. "Maybe in your piece-of-shit truck. It doesn't matter, though, it'll all be over before we get there. And even if we made it in time, no one's going to listen to you or me, Ant."

My back feels as if every muscle, every sinew, has been twisted and torn when I bend over to tie the laces. I fumble at the laces with swollen, bloody fingers. "I have to try. I couldn't live with myself if I didn't try."

Jones grunts, unconvinced.

"Wouldn't it be something to blow Willis and Karge out of the water in front of all those cameras? You could leave Wyoming in style, Jeff. Payback for your wasted years there."

I stand, giving up on the laces, stagger once, and look at him. Jones's usually frowning mouth curls up at the ends.

"You remember me making fun of your car, and you

telling me sometimes you just feel the need for speed?" I ask. "Well, my friend, I need it now. I'm feeling the need. How about it?"

He shakes his head and grins at me. "I guess I've got nothing else to do."

The rest of my clothes we find in a second grocery sack in a cabinet. My shirt and jacket are stiff with Billy Heller's blood. The same stiffness is in my hair. It smells faintly of a metal like copper or iron. When I step out into the hallway, the imposing ranger is waiting along with two other men in suits.

"Thank you, sir," I tell him as I try to hurry past the group. "There's no way I can thank you enough. But I've got to move now—I'll call you later and tell you what's going on."

"Hey, where do you think you're going?" one of the suits asks as he puts a hand on my chest. I look down at his arm, feeling too weak and dizzy to swat it away, and see that he has FBI credentials clipped to his coat pocket. He and his partner stand before us, blocking our passage, eyeing Jones's now glowering face nervously.

I ignore them and speak again to the ranger, knowing that he has no real authority over the federal agents except for the kind that comes from his powerful charisma. "You checked up on me, right?"

He nods. "I called Sheriff McKittrick up in Laramie County. But then I got a call from your office. They said you were suspended."

"McKittrick must have told you what I'm doing—what I'm trying to do. If I don't get up to Laramie with that girl right now, some innocent men are going to be sentenced to death. The Lee case. That dead man you brought off the Diamond, Billy Heller, he was the killer, not the Knapps.

Let me have a few hours and I promise you I'll answer everyone's questions this afternoon."

He studies me for a long time with his hard gray eyes. It feels like several minutes. "Let him go," the ranger finally tells the agents. "He's already done the impossible, soloing up King of Swords at night, in a storm. The boy's used up all his luck. Give him a little slack now—he'll either hang himself or come out clean."

One of the agents shakes his head. "He's not going anywhere."

The ranger's eyes turn to granite. He steps in front of the agent who spoke. "On what charges are you going to hold him? You can't detain him unless you're going to charge him."

The agent takes a step back. "He shot a man—"

"In self-defense. Do you have probable cause to believe it was otherwise?"

"But the CBI guy, Tobias—"

"Mr. Tobias isn't here. And he has no such evidence either. I brought this man and the girl off that mountain. They're in my custody. Any crime that was committed occurred in the park—my jurisdiction. Do you understand that? If I want to allow him to go to Wyoming, then he's going." The ranger's voice is low in the corridor but still his words have a visible impact on the agent's face.

He hesitates a moment, then takes a cell phone out of his pocket. "We'd better talk to someone," he says to his colleague. They step into a room, leaving Jones and me alone with the tall ranger.

"You sure you want to join the FBI?" I ask Jones.

"The girl's in there," the ranger says, pointing at a different door. "You'd better get moving. Take the stairs and go out through the emergency exit—your friend Tobias has more state officers in the lobby with him. He may not be as easy to confuse as our federal agents."

I thank him again quickly and promise to call him in the afternoon.

Lynn smiles weakly when we enter the room. She lies under the starched white sheets in the hospital bed. The tan is gone from her face and has been replaced by deep yellow and blue bruises.

"This is Jefferson Jones," I tell her. "He was a sergeant up in Laramie. Still is, I guess."

"For about another week and a half. At least they're paying me for that, since I gave 'em two weeks' notice," Jones says.

Lynn gives him a shy, girlish smile that I know is at odds with her personality.

I tell her to get dressed, which she begins to do without asking why, and without apparent modesty. While she pulls on her own blood-encrusted clothes, I start asking her questions. She answers as if Jones weren't there.

Lynn explains that after she found Rebecca in my room, she was really pissed off. "Must be a fine piece of ass, you prefer her to me," she comments bitterly. She tells me that Billy found her moping up at Vedauwoo and told her to come climbing with him. She went without giving it a second thought. Her way to get back at me, she explains. Two thirds of the way up the wall, when they settled in for the night to wait out the storm, Billy abruptly told her she'd talked too much, fucked around too much. He punched her a few times. She became sick and dizzy. After beating her some more, forcing himself upon her, he tied her hands and feet. Then I showed up.

I ask about Heller's denial of killing Kate.

"I was there, man. It wasn't Billy. He didn't do Kate.

Well, he was fucking her, yeah. With Brad. They were doing this asphyxiation thing on her, like to make a better orgasm. Then Brad's dad showed up. All of a sudden. Don't know how that old dude got up there. He just stepped out, you know? He was screaming some shit, seeing his son and Billy on Kate, her all tied up with that funky pink cord Billy keeps in his basement. Anyway, I guess you can't blame Brad's dad. Billy got off her just as the old guy grabbed a bottle Brad'd been drinking from and came in swinging. Dad dragged Brad off her about then. Kate started to get up, get out of the way, and Dad took another swing at Heller but hit her with the bottle instead. Knocked her right off the fucking edge, man."

As she talks and dresses I'm watching Jones's face. It's the first time I've ever seen the big man speechless. He appears utterly stunned by the words coming out of this young, pretty girl's mouth. There's something rotten within her lithe frame. When his eyes meet mine they are wide.

"What about Kimberly Lee?" I ask. "Did Billy and Brad kill her?"

"I don't know. They joked about it a lot. You know, saying what a bitch she was, how she'd threatened to tell the cops they were dealing, how the Knapps were trying to cut in on their action, stuff like that. They'd just say that shit and laugh. Like she got what she had coming, like she went out in style."

I ask the next question as softly as I can. It's the one thing I still don't understand. "Lynn, why did you keep going back to Billy? You had to know what he was capable of. I heard that he attacked you before, when you first moved to Laramie."

Lynn's eyes seem to become a little unfocused. "That guy's magnetic, you know? He's so big, his energy, his power, and his body. Like a planet. Gravity. Just pulls you in. Look into the eyes of a grizzly bear, man. You'll want to walk right up and give him a big fucking hug. You won't care if he puts his mouth over your head. Besides," she says with a small smile that makes me feel a chill, "sometimes you've got to stand at the edge."

THIRTY-THREE

T HE CROWD THAT swarms on the grass outside the sandstone courthouse has multiplied over the last week, as if it were reproducing with a rabbitlike intensity while awaiting this day. It swells out onto the sidewalk, and even into the street at certain places. The people huddle together against the incoming storm's cold wind. The blow is finally reaching Laramie, after dropping seven thousand vertical feet from the Rocky Mountains' highest peaks onto the plain. Grim-faced sheriff's deputies are posted on the curb every ten yards. Oddly, they're not scanning the impassioned crowd but the street.

"Looking for you," Jones says from the driver's seat.

He pulls the car into the only available spot—in front of a fire hydrant between two satellite-roofed media vans, and cracks his darkly tinted window a few inches. A human roar fills the car. Listening, I can discern some of the shouts.

ACLU protesters, anti–death penalty advocates, Catholic nuns, and bizarrely, the pathetic Klansmen, all chanting that the state has no right to do God's work. Concurrently, some church groups, Asian activists, and victims' rights zealots scream for blood.

"How you plannin' to get through *that*?" Jones asks.

"We need a diversion. Some sort of commotion," I tell him, thinking. I glimpse patches of browning grass among the crowd. "That grass is looking a little dry. Do you know how to turn on the sprinklers?"

Jones gives me an evil flash of white teeth from beneath his sunglasses before unfolding himself from the low-slung Corvette. Some of the watchful deputies look at him, surprised to see him, as he gets out. He merely nods at them, then disappears into the crowd toward the courthouse.

While we wait, Lynn asks from her cramped position in the tiny rear space, "Why not just go in? This car is getting way too tight and my ass is asleep. What are they gonna do, man, shoot us?"

"They just might."

Jones's cell phone rings. I stab the talk button and say, "Burns."

A whispered voice, barely audible, says, "Where are you?"

"We're outside the courthouse, Rebecca, trying to figure out how to get in. There are Albany County deputies all around, looking for me."

"Get in here now, Anton!" she hisses. "The jury's taking their seats!" We had called her from the car an hour earlier as we sped out of Estes, having left the hospital through an emergency exit with the alarm blaring behind us, and learned that the attorneys' arguments were finished. The jury had retired to deliberate their two options—life or death. Everyone knew the decision was preordained.

A minute later Jones is jogging down the middle of the street, weaving through barely moving traffic. He looks at his watch as he runs, then lifts a finger above his head and circles it in the air.

"Get ready!" I say to Lynn.

Just as the words leave my lips there's a surprised cry from the crowd. And in a sudden, mass movement the throng of people propels itself forward, overrunning the deputies' positions and flooding into the street. The cars that have been creeping along begin honking, adding to the swelling din. The crowd keeps spilling off the lawn, until the angry, wet mass surrounds even Jones's car across the street from the courthouse.

I shove my door open, striking demonstrators' legs and hips, just as Jones yanks open the driver's side and plucks Lynn from the backseat. With her tucked under one arm, he half carries her as he charges across the street like the football star he once was. I put my forehead between his massive shoulder blades and churn my legs behind him.

We're up the steps and almost to the courthouse doors before there is a shout from the deputies that penetrates the mayhem. I turn my head and see several brown uniforms pointing in our direction, fighting their way toward us.

Jones crashes the door open into the faces of startled security officers. One of them actually slaps his holster before Jones freezes his hand with a cold glance.

"Don't fuck with me right now, Sam," Jones tells him, then jerks his head at Lynn and me and says, "they're with me."

We're running down the empty hallway, past the metal detectors and the guards with their mouths hanging slack.

"Touchdown!" Jones says, finally releasing Lynn outside the courtroom's entrance. There's a clattering of footsteps and gun belts behind us in the hallway, but the deputies are too late. I grab Lynn's sinewy arm and pull her through the swinging doors.

"Your honor," I shout, "my name is Special Agent Antonio Burns. I have information for the court!" A roar of whispered voices swells and a hundred faces turn to stare at me in my bloodstained jacket. The judge's bulldog jaw juts forward as she beats her gavel on the bench.

Willis and Bender are already on their feet, coming down the aisle toward us. Almost in unison, they reach behind them and unclip handcuffs from their belts. I see Deputy Knight off to one side, standing near the defendants' tables. His head is turned, staring at me. He is stone-faced.

They're almost to me when the door at my back bursts open, striking me hard in my battered ribs. Jones steps through it, arguing with the deputies in the hallway. He pauses for just a second and takes stock of the judge's angry stare and the determined approach of Willis and Bender. "I can vouch for this man," he says quietly, his deep bass penetrating through the shocked murmurs in the courtroom. He looms over me from behind. Some of the determination leaves Willis's face. Both his and Bender's strides falter a little.

"Stop, Sheriff," the judge says. "Jefferson Jones, you've served this court well for several years now. For the life of me I cannot imagine why you would interrupt these proceedings in such a dramatic manner as this, but based on your good service, I'm going to grant you and this young man a brief audience of five minutes. All of you, come back into my chambers. The court will be in recess until then."

* * *

We march past the stunned reporters and jurors, down the aisle, through the well and through a small door to one side of the bench. The judge sits behind her desk. Lynn and I stand before it. Bender moves until he is just behind me and to one side, his face menacingly close to mine. I feel his to-bacco-flavored breath on my cheek and neck. Within seconds the oak-paneled room is packed with people. Nathan Karge and the defendants' puzzled lawyers have followed, along with Jones and Sheriff Willis and the court reporter and all the judge's curious staff.

I can smell the sweat from the hours on the wall emanating from my ragged clothes. Along with the coppery smell of blood. "I'd like to have Deputy David Knight and Rebecca Hersh of the *Denver Post* join us, your honor."

"Deputy Knight may, but I won't have a reporter in here," she says, glaring at me.

Jones struggles through us toward the door. "I'll get him."

"So just what information do you have that's worth disturbing these proceedings, Agent Burns?"

Before I can say a word, Nathan Karge is speaking. "Judge, I object—" His face is white, striped with the same red streaks I saw the day I interviewed Brad at the hotel. But his voice is calm, as if he's tranquilized by the fact that he's staring into the pit. "Mr. Burns is a rogue agent and a murderer, your honor. He is currently under suspension from the AG's Office pending the investigation of murder charges—"

"Because of you," I remind him.

"This is a violent man with no credibility, your honor.

He's even believed to have helped his brother, also a murderer, escape from a prison in Colorado—"

I look back to the judge, my voice hoarse as I try to speak over Karge. "There's a lot of political shit, excuse me, maneuvering, going on right now, Judge. Ross McGee was supposed to be here, but he had a heart attack last night just as I was suspended to keep me from investigating further into—"

"Be quiet, both of you!" she shouts at us. Her eyes pierce first me, then Karge. "Mr. Karge, your objection is noted. What do you want to tell me, Mr. Burns? Make it fast."

"Your honor!" Karge shouts, outraged. "You cannot—"

The fierce little woman in the black robes fixes him with a stare. I can almost see icy darts shooting from her eyes. "Mr. Karge, you aren't governor yet. And until you are, hell, even when you are, don't you ever try to tell me what to do in my own chambers! Now Mr. Burns...speak."

Karge slumps back against the wall, his eyes wide with indignation and fear. When I start to speak he slowly closes them.

And so I begin my tale, starting with the murder of Kimberly Lee and the pipe planted by Sheriff Willis and Sergeant Bender to make the case stronger against the Knapps. I tell her about Kate Danning and the strange contusion on the back of her head and the rope burns on her neck and wrists. About how it led me to find the bottle smeared with her blood up at Vedauwoo. About how the DCI crime lab found both Brad and Nathan Karge's fingerprints on it. About how the Surenos were sicced on me when I started looking into it. About Chris Braddock's fatal fall in the Big Horns. About the shooting of my dog. About my false arrest and beating in the Albany County jail. About Sierra Calloway's murder and the pink cords that bound her tortured body. And finally, about both Brad's and Heller's admissions the night before. Lynn is surprisingly docile at my side, but she nods her affirmation when it is required, as does David Knight.

"Your honor," I finish, my voice raw and scratchy, "the Knapps didn't kill Kimberly Lee. Nathan Karge learned that his son was one of the real killers sometime during the trial and went looking for him up at Vedauwoo. During the scuffle Kate Danning was knocked off a cliff. To save his career and his son, he tried to cover it up. All the rest of it, the murders of Chris Braddock and Sierra Calloway, was an attempt by Billy Heller and Brad Karge, with the possible collusion of the sheriff and the County Attorney, to cover up evidence that could exculpate the Knapps. They were trying to save their asses, excuse me, their political futures, your honor."

I turn my head for a moment and see Karge and Willis standing together against the wall by the door. Bender has moved away from me at some point in my narrative and edged toward them, so the three stand together in a guilty row. For a moment I fear they'll try to slip out of the room. But then Jones smiles at me and steps back to plant his broad back firmly against the door.

When I turn back to the judge, her lean jaw is jutting out farther than ever. I'm reminded of how I once thought it resembled the brush guard on my truck. Now it looks like the pick of my ice ax. She stares at me with hard eyes for a long, silent moment. I meet her gaze, summoning up all the integrity in my heart and trying to wear it on my face.

"Can you prove all of this, Mr. Burns?"

I answer slowly, for the first time trying to put it all

together in my head as an investigator should. "I can prove Heller and Bradley Karge were the real killers of Kimberly Lee, as well as Chris Braddock and Sierra Calloway." I can testify that both of them confessed to me. In addition, I have Lynn's corroboration and the cord the police will find when they search Heller's basement.

"I can prove Nathan Karge was up at Vedauwoo the night Kate Danning fell and that it was his swing with the bottle that knocked her to her death." Again, I have the confessions of Brad and Heller, along with Lynn's corroboration, and the bottle with the fingerprints.

"I can prove Sheriff Willis manufactured evidence against the Knapps in this trial." Deputy Knight nods again beside me. He looks stronger now, more sure of himself since everything's come out in the open. He must realize he's done the right thing in talking to me. I feel a moment's guilt for having wrecked his bike and then left him on the plains to walk back to Laramie.

"And I can prove Nathan Karge and Sheriff Willis knew of some exculpatory evidence in this trial and failed to share it with the Knapps' attorneys." McGee, if he survives, will back me up.

After a moment's thought I add lamely, "And I may be able to prove a lot more, your honor, once I've had the time to sort this all out."

She keeps staring. I'm reminded of the way McGee analyzed me after my run-in with the Surenos, as if he were trying to weigh what was in my mind and in my heart. The thought of McGee makes me stand straighter. But I still worry I'll collapse under the judge's gaze if she keeps this up.

Slowly she turns her head and looks at the Knapps' lawyers. "Gentlemen, do you have a motion for me?" Her voice is almost sad.

The lead attorney quickly says, with a broad, twitching smile on his lips that it looks like he's trying hard to contain, "We move for a mistrial, your honor!"

"So granted. Mr. Jones, I believe you have probable cause to make some arrests."

THIRTY-FOUR

ALL AFTERNOON AND evening I'm interrogated by a swarm of attorneys from the AG's Office, as well as some federal prosecutors whom the judge had notified of the potential civil rights violations committed by Albany County's elected officials. It's after eight o'clock at night when I finally sneak out past the reporters who have besieged both the courthouse and the Sheriff's Office. I'm exhausted to the point of near-unconsciousness. It has been more than forty-eight hours since I last had any serious sleep. My battered body and psyche are shutting down. Two federal agents, the same ones who were in the hospital in Estes that morning, escort me back to the hotel.

News of the arrests of County Attorney Nathan Karge and Sheriff Daniel Willis has created a sensation that eclipses anything the state of Wyoming has ever seen. Between meetings I caught part of a newscast, one that had interrupted the afternoon's regular programming. A reporter whose carefully coiffed hair had been spoiled by the wind shouted out the publicly known details into the camera from amid the turmoil of the courthouse lawn. The Knapp brothers were expected to be released within hours, he yelled, the charges against them dismissed.

Someone told me that the Albany County Commissioners had convened an emergency session, during which they appointed Jefferson Jones as interim sheriff. Apparently he had put his plans for Quantico on hold. He's now Wyoming's first black sheriff, temporarily at least. I had to smile at that—my friend's ambition has been fulfilled.

Back in my room at the hotel, I strip off my filthy clothes, shower, and collapse into my bed. The lights are off and my body desperately craves rest, but my pulse still races. In the faint light from the corridor that penetrates the heavy curtains, Oso's water bowl gleams at me from against the wall. I lie with my head propped on a pillow and stare at it. My heart and my body ache unremittingly, despite having swallowed the four remaining pills in my old bottle of Tylenol-codeine. I long for sleep to embrace me, to pull me down into the mattress and anesthetize me. Just when the exhaustion and the gentle numbness of the pills finally begin to overtake me, I hear the delicate snick of a key sliding into my door's lock.

With that slight noise, my mind accelerates out of its stupor. I twitch in the bed as if I've been shocked. A sudden realization grips me. I am the only one who can put it all together. Although the state prosecutors I spoke with today have granted Lynn White, Leroy Bender, and David Knight immunity in return for their testimony against Nathan Karge and Daniel Willis, I am the only one who wasn't involved to some degree. Even Lynn, a victim herself and the least culpable, will not be much use. The corruption of her spirit is too obvious whenever she opens her mouth. Only I can put it all together and lock the County Attorney and Sheriff Willis in prison for a long, long time. If I am dead, they will be released from the holding cells and walk out, their reputations irreversibly tarnished but their bodies free.

The key is turning in the lock when I lunge halfway off the bed; the door is starting to swing open. I dive naked onto the floor. My hands skim the carpet and the rumpled clothes I discarded there, trying to find the jacket pocket and Cecelia's small pistol. Then I remember. I remember it falling; falling soundlessly into the void beneath the Diamond. I'm defenseless.

Overpowering the terror is a feeling of humiliation. I'm going to die, I think, slapping uselessly at the filthy clothes on the hotel's carpet, my bare ass in the air. Shot through the butt. I twist my body toward the doorway with dread.

Rebecca stands framed in the corridor's lights. Her mouth is slightly open and her eyes are bright and wide. She starts to smile.

"Sorry, Anton," she says, her smile broadening into a laugh. "I probably should have knocked."

I collapse on the carpet, roll onto my back, and groan. As the adrenaline subsides, the pain returns. Still laughing, she kneels beside me. For a moment I think she's going to give me CPR. Her hair sweeps across my bare chest and neck as she lowers her lips to mine. A kind of CPR, anyway. The Breath of Life.

Within minutes, with barely another word, she's naked in my arms and tangled in the sheets, her white skin like silk, her lips locked cool and smooth against my mouth. I gasp in delight rather than pain when her thin weight presses against my hips and her arms encircle my back. While the moment lasts, the bruises, sprains, and twinges are all magically healed.

The phone rings. Even though the hotel's voice-mail system keeps cutting it off, a few seconds later it starts again. Finally I scoop it up off the nightstand and answer with a breathless grunt of "Burns."

"Caught you with your knickers down, eh?"

"Ross! How are you feeling?"

"Better, lad. They might let me out...of this hellhole tomorrow. I just had a visit from the AG...things are wild at the office...the Torres suit has settled...the murder investigation's been dropped....You're reinstated, God help us all."

"That's great! Whatever you did, thank you."

"It's not my work, it's the frigging media...they're all over the place trying to figure out...just how deep the shit's piled....The office is going to be kissing your ass for a long time...hoping like hell you won't point your finger at them....Now where's my girl Rebecca?...Is that young vixen with you?"

"Yeah, but she's indisposed at the moment." With her palm Rebecca smacks me gently on the back. I gasp as the bruises there flare for a few seconds. Rebecca murmurs an apology.

"Ah well...to the victor...go the spoils," he says, chuckling. "And good job, lad....Sorry I let you down."

I hang up the phone. Rebecca and I slowly begin to finish what we started.

* * *

A little later she's still pressed against me but her breath is finally slowing. There's a sensation as if love is blowing gently on my skin. Feeling like Oso, a wounded and abused animal suddenly in the presence of kindness and affection, I magnify it and reflect it back a hundred times. I lie with my head deep in the pillow, letting her warmth envelop me and carry me on. Like this I drift away.

Two days later I'm allowed by the office's attorneys and the federal authorities to return to my former office-of-exile in Cody. Rather than suspended, I'm now merely "on leave." It's standard procedure after any duty-related shooting.

"Consider it a paid vacation," the Assistant Attorney General told me with an oily smile, the same sort of grin I had seen on his face when McGee collapsed. "Take as long as you like."

"I will," I told him, stepping close. "And by the way, go fuck yourself."

His smile never faltered. The office is now willing to do anything to keep me happy, to keep me from talking about their complicity in the attempts to silence me prior to the sentencing. Apparently my suspension was never official. An administrative mistake, one of the junior attorneys there told me. It happens sometimes. The office is anxious to get me out of town and away from the swarming reporters.

Rebecca has been as busy as me. Her articles have been picked up by papers across the country. She told me she's received job offers from New York, Chicago, and Washington. Already there's talk about the possibility of a journalistic award. Pulitzer, she mouthed to me one evening with her face just inches above mine, not speaking the word for fear of jinxing herself. I see her only late at night, when she slips through my room's door without knocking.

I will be seeing a lot more of her, though. She's going to take a vacation too, once the developments on what is known as the Laramie Scandal have died down and she's milked it for all she can. In anticipation, I liberated a small portion of my grandfather's trust from a bank in Argentina and bought two first-class tickets to South America.

We're going to Torres del Paine National Park in Patagonia. There I plan to introduce her to mountains of ice and granite that dwarf even Cloud Peak, which had impressed her so much. Maybe I'll be able to interest her in putting on a rope. Like any true addict, I would like nothing better than to hook another on the adrenaline surge that comes from having a thousand feet of empty space beneath your heels.

I drive back up over the plains, where the chaparral is still dusted with the storm's debris, to my rented cabin and my office in Cody. There's an enormous hole in my heart because no beast is grinning and drooling out the backseat window. I picture him at Vedauwoo, that afternoon ten days ago when I first arrived, hunched beneath a cliff and gazing up at me. His gold eyes glisten with devotion. As my tires hum across the asphalt that cuts through the prairie like an open vein, I finally cry for him.

I'm going twenty or thirty miles an hour faster than the bullet-holed, near-invisible sign states is allowable as I enter Cody's city limits. I blow right through the speed trap, one that anyone who has been through Cody before knows is always manned. It's the town's way of generating revenue from midwestern tourists in their motor homes. Racing past the screen of pines concealing the ever present patrol car, I turn my head and observe the deputy there relieving himself on one tire. My speed visibly startles him. Then he recognizes my truck in time to release himself and pantomime the gunslinger's move of drawing a pistol from each hip. QuickDraw. Despite having lived in Cody for eighteen months, I hadn't realized before that people here might like me. My depression made me entirely too self-absorbed.

I drive down the main street, past the ramshackle buildings, looking at the ranchers in their cowboy hats and pointed boots intermingling with the hippies and climbers wearing shorts and Tevas. Everyone nods politely to one another as they pass on the street. This is a nice town, I think, a lot like Laramie. A good place. At the top of a small hill, I park outside the small post office to retrieve my mail.

The florid matron behind the counter smiles when I walk in. "Been reading about you," she says with a wink. "Good stuff, these days. What're you going to do for an encore, Agent?"

"I think I'm done fighting crime. I'm going back to fighting gravity," I tell her.

My words surprise me. Up until this very second I hadn't thought much about the future. Just the trip south with Rebecca, and then the inevitable weeks of testimony that will be required to convict both the Karges and Sheriff Willis. But I'm done with law enforcement, I realize. I'm done playing the Game. The decision feels invigorating, as if I kicked over the table, declared the other players cheats, and walked away with all the cash.

I unlock my box and take out the tight sheaf of mail stuffed into the small metal compartment. I sit in my truck and let the wind gently rock it as I sort through the junk. A bent postcard slips out from the pages of a climbing catalog that I'd tossed on the passenger seat to be thrown away.

The picture on the wrinkled front is of Los Angeles International Airport. It's a photograph of a plane roaring off the runway and into a sunset swirling with color. Flipping the card over, I see there's no text other than my name and address spelled in block letters. There is simply a drawing. It's well done, as if the artist had spent a lot of time practicing and dreaming. What else is there to do in prison? The picture is of a sleek and well-muscled rat. The creature is fitting sharp teeth around a hunk of what appears to be Swiss cheese in the shape of a jagged peak. Smiling, I tuck the card back into the catalog and toss it in the first trash can I drive by. But the wind tugs the card free before the catalog drops. I watch the wind suck it straight up into the sky, then send it soaring over the stores and pine trees toward the mountains.

Maybe I will take Rebecca by the ranch for Christmas. To see my parents and whoever else is there.

ABOUT THE AUTHOR

CLINTON McKINZIE is the acclaimed author of THE EDGE OF JUSTICE. His second book, POINT OF LAW, is forthcoming from Dell. He was raised in Santa Monica and now lives in Colorado with his wife, son, and dog. Prior to becoming a writer, he worked as a peace officer and deputy district attorney in Denver. His passion is climbing alpine walls. Visit his website at www.clintonmckinzie.com.

Don't miss the new Antonio Burns novel,

POINT OF LAW,

the exciting prequel to

THE EDGE
OF JUSTICE.

On sale May 2003 from Dell.

Please turn the page to read a preview.

"Watch me. Keep it tight."

My father's calm voice belies his precarious position. He clings to the vertical granite forty feet above where I sway in my harness, another one hundred and fifty feet above the canyon floor. Although my vision is slightly blurred by the waves of early-morning heat the sun is generating off the cliff's face, I can see where his right hand grips a tiny edge barely thicker than a pencil. His left hand sorts through the rack of protective gear slung around one burly shoulder. The toes of the old man's climbing slippers are splayed on nubbins of quartz that look as if they could pop off the sandstone wall at any moment. But there's no quiver in his muscles, no panic in his voice. I glance at that last piece of protection my father had clipped to the rope twenty feet beneath him and feel a familiar admiration swelling in my chest.

"You say you want slack?" I shout up, pretending to have misunderstood. My hands shuffle over the belay device—a slotted piece of cold-forged steel appropriately called an Air Traffic Controller—and take in the few inches of loose rope between us.

My father drops down a hard look before he returns to the task of finding a cam to fit in the narrow crack above his head. From the look I guess he isn't in a humorous mood. My mother had warned me about this: in recent months his tolerance for frivolity has suffered a dramatic decline. Resolving to remain silent and simply focus on my job, I study the forty feet of vertical space between us.

The rock is a combination of sandstone, gneiss, and pinkish pegmatite. Its texture is sometimes smooth and sometimes coarse under my fingertips. The entire five-hundred-foot canyon wall overhangs slightly from where it's been carved out of ancient bedrock by thousands of years of rushing water and tumbling boulders. The distance between my father and me appears almost featureless but for where a single recess mars the wall—a short and flaring horizontal fissure, the only opportunity for him to have placed some gear to protect against a fall. Above his head begins the comfort of the deep vertical crack into which he's working the spring-loaded camming device.

According to my father's tattered guidebook that describes the route, called "Big Balls and a Puckered Ass" (the route's name could just as easily describe my father), and which credits him with the route's first ascent, this second pitch is the toughest of the four rope-lengths up the cliff. I had led the easier first one hundred and fifty feet or so and had expected that this crux pitch would be mine as well. Dad hasn't been cimbing much lately and the years have to be taking their toll. But the old man insisted on keeping the crux for himself, taking what is known as the "sharp end" of the rope from me rather than being safely belayed from above, where a fall could be measured in inches rather than feet or broken limbs.

Dad has something to prove today, I realize. It is the last time he'll be able to climb here at the scene of his glory days thirty years ago. And this is the hardest single pitch of the numerous routes he'd pioneered on the isolated canyon's walls, when climbs of this level were only rarely attempted and the land around the canyon and the entire Wild Fire Valley region was believed to be forever in the public trust. It must pain him to know that in just weeks this land—his land—will become private property and climbing will be forbidden.

The narrow gorge is sacred to me, too, because of a sort of mythology I'd invented about the place when I was a child. Although my brother and I had never been to the canyon, we grew up listening to stories told by our parents' friends about Dad's long-ago exploits here. For me in my childhood this was Mount Olympus, where the gods frolicked in ancient times.

For a moment I try to image my father in the old days, before my birth and before the war that turned him into a career soldier. I can see him laughing and joking with equally loose-jointed and tight-muscled young partners, clad in felt-soled boots while trusting their lives to primitive gear, made delirious by the heights and the virgin risks they faced. At night they camped around bonfires up in the broader valley where the canyon walls begin their deep cut through the red and gold sandstone. There they drank cheap wine from jugs and relived each day's thrills in a sort of Olympian bacchanal. They would wake in the morning, groggy and heavy-headed in the damp meadow grass, but ready to lay it all on the line once again. If the stories were true, Dad must have been a far more effusive man back then. The tales his friends told my brother and me made him sound wild-ass crazy and larger than life, not at all like the somber, cautious man above me now.

Refocusing on the present and the expanse of steep rock between us, I can see that there's good reason for caution. If he slips, he'll be looking at more than a forty-foot fall before the rope locked in my belay device can catch him. And that's only if the one lousy piece of protection he'd placed twenty feet beneath his heels doesn't fail him. If it blows, then the rope will catch on the anchor I hang from. An eighty-foot fall for Dad. A serious whipper for any man; one that few could walk away from unscathed. I take a quick look at the boulder-strewn ground well over a hundred feet below me and reassure myself that at least he won't deck out. As long as the rope and my anchor hold, he might shatter his bones on the cliff face but he won't hit the ground. Then I look at the three pieces of gear that compose the anchor in front of me, suspending me from the wall, and wish I'd done a better job of positioning them.

My father gingerly slots the mechanical cam in the crack over his head. A good fit. He finally calls for slack in that same terse, unconcerned voice. I give him a few feet so that he can clip the rope to the cam's nylon runner. My lungs release an unconsciously retained breath as the carabiner's gate snaps shut.

"Want to rest?" I yell up, unable to restrain myself.

He doesn't even bother to give me a look this time. My question had been meant as another joke, but as far as I can tell he never even smiles. Either he climbs or he falls—Dad never hangs on a rope. But he does spit out a brown glob of tobacco juice that I watch float down toward me then past, barely missing my arm. After a few seconds I hear its soft smack on the boulders below. Above me he resumes his deliberate crawl into the sky.

I start to shift in my harness, trying to ease where the nylon straps are cutting into my crotch. But after a quick glance at the sketchy anchor, I resolve to stop squirming and simply endure it. If the anchor fails, I will plummet, pulling Dad off with me. It isn't the danger that concerns me, as in all likelihood the cam he's just placed will hold us both on our separate ends of the rope, but the shame that will result. Above me my father continues upward with apparent ease although I know his forearms and calves must be burning, his shoulders pumped with lactic acid. *Christ. Closing in on sixty and the old man's still an animal.*

By the time he pulls over a small roof and disappears from sight, I'm beginning to wonder if I'll ever be able to have children of my own. My harness's crotch loop feels as if it's attempting to sterilize me with a cutting pressure. With great relief I hear his deep voice call out, "Off belay!" There are two sharp tugs on the rope.

"Nice work, Colonel," I shout up into the sky. "You've still got it!"

I feel another two tugs on the rope, signaling that he's anchored and it's my turn to be belayed. I disassemble the anchor, wipe my sweaty hands on my shorts, dip them in the pouch of chalk that hangs just below my butt, and ease onto the hot rock.

After pulling over the short, difficult roof, I find my father comfortably belaying me from a wide ledge. He sits with his back propped by the sandstone wall and his legs spread before him. He's removed his shoes; his bare feet and ankles protrude off the edge and into space. His eyes are half-closed against the sunlight. I step to the anchor he's built out of two hexes stuffed deep in a constricting crack and clip a bight of rope to the carabiners connecting them. I shake the anchor a little and try to make another joke.

"Jesus, Dad, whatever happened to not trusting just two pieces? Remember the way you used to yell at 'Berto and me for that?"

His eyes remain half-closed but I can sense a sudden heat in them. Even his bald, sun-freckled scalp turns a little pink at the mention of my brother's name. For a moment I want to stuff a stinking climbing slipper in my mouth, thinking I've spoken the name too soon. But then I remind myself that Roberto is the reason we're here. The primary reason, anyway. This trip is supposed to be an intervention with Roberto, my drug-addicted brother, as well as a holiday in which our father can relive his glory days and say goodbye to a remote piece of Colorado that's soon slated to become a part of a massive ski resort. Roberto will arrive this afternoon or maybe the next day, and it's time for Dad and me to get some things out in the open.

So I slump down next to my father. I offer him the bottle of warm water that I've carried dangling from my harness. He speaks first, and I suppose he's trying to head me off from the direction he must know I'm traveling.

He asks without looking at me, "So, how are you liking this cop stuff?"

His tone sounds vaguely condescending, as it does every time I see him and he asks this same question. He has to know the response this will provoke from me.

And I can't resist falling into the trap. "I'm not really a cop, Dad. I'm an agent," I explain as I always do. I try to keep the annoyance and defensiveness out of my voice. "I don't wear a uniform, I don't write speeding tickets, and I don't eat donuts. I investigate drug crimes—mostly meth—and that's it. Anyway, I like it. I run my own ops and I make my own hours."

This last part is something I add in a juvenile attempt to make my father appreciate my job. His dead-ending career is as an Air Force officer in command of an elite Special Forces unit known as the Pararescue Corps, or PJs. Being harnessed to a rigid chain of command, he never runs his own ops or makes his own hours. And he seldom takes a leave that isn't interrupted. We've had this discussion a hundred times.

With a self-deprecating smile, I add, "And I get to take vacations like this whenever I manage to get myself suspended."

That almost makes Dad chuckle. I can see the lines around his mouth deepen for just an instant. I've been suspended twice in my three years as a special narcotics agent for Wyoming's Division of Criminal Investigations, a part of the state Attorney General's Office. The first time had been the result of an officer-involved shooting. Any time a law enforcement officer is forced by circumstances to pull a trigger, especially if he or she manages to put a bullet in someone, there is a mandatory period of suspension during which the shooting is investigated by the office's version of Internal Affairs and ruled either justifiable or not. These bureaucratic inquiries take a long, long time. During the investigation the officer is supposed to seek counseling in order to alleviate the guilt and grief of having shot some scumbag who'd been trying to kill him. I hadn't felt the need for any counseling, but then I didn't kill anyone. I just winged the bastard. And the only thing I felt even a little guilty about was my lousy aim and the terrific amount of climbing I'd gotten in during the prolonged period of suspension-with-pay.

My current suspension is for three months without pay. It's part of a negotiated plea agreement to avoid having criminal charges pressed against me for assaulting a fellow peace officer. The charges would have embarrassed both my office and the local sheriff's department the so-called "victim" was a member of. I've accepted three months without pay, an official reprimand, and been forced to make a half-assed apology. Kind of like with the prior suspension, the only guilt I feel is for not having hit the deputy harder.

Instead of continuing our usual subtle but tense banter in which my father will attempt to degrade my career choice and voice his preference for something more "professional," I'm surprised when he tries a new tack, mentioning Roberto for the first time himself.

"Do your bosses know about your brother, *Agent* Burns?"

"They know I've got one, but they don't know about any of the trouble. It probably wouldn't do my career much good if they found out."

This is something my father knows about firsthand. Just a few years ago he'd been on the verge of becoming one of the youngest generals in the Air Force. Then the crimes of his eldest son had come to the attention of the military. Dad ended up being denied further advancement. You don't become a general, the ultimate leader of men, when you've sired a felon. Fortunately for me, though, the Wyoming AG's Office doesn't concern itself much with background checks on family members prior to promotion. I make a mental note to mention this additional benefit the next time we argue on the career subject, but don't want to bring it up now that we're finally talking about Roberto.

"Do you know what he's using these days?"

"Not for sure. He's banging—injecting—I know that much."

My father nods. Even in magazine photographs, the tracks of scabby pinpricks on my brother's arms are hard to miss.

"So that leads me to guess it's either crank or heroin," I say. After a moment I add quietly, "There's not much out there that's worse, Dad. At least we don't have to worry anymore about him turning to harder drugs."

My father doesn't say anything for a while. He just takes a few short pulls from my water bottle and stares up the canyon.

The ledge is narrow where I'm slumped next to him. My feet and calves dangle over more than two hundred feet of space. I lean over and look down for the large black shape of my dog. Oso lies under the shade of a green-leafed cottonwood, staring straight up at us with his red tongue parting sharp, white teeth. The dog is the cause of my current suspension—the deputy I supposedly assaulted had been trying to spear him with a shovel. I wave my hand at him and see the ears twitch forward.

Taking back the water bottle from my father, I notice that one of his thick fists still holds the rope locked tight through his belay device.

"By the way, Dad, I tied in. I'm off belay."

He nods. "Waiting for you to say it, son. Belay off," Finally he releases his grip. I'm annoyed and embarrassed. I've violated one of his cardinal rules by failing to announce my status, but at least he's too preoccupied to comment further.

"Do you have a strategy for dealing with your brother when or if he shows up?" he asks.

I take a deep breath. This is something I've been

thinking about for weeks, ever since my suspension and the news about the pending development of Wild Fire Valley as a part of a Forest Service land swap. I'd convinced my father to fly in from the Pentagon to meet Roberto and me for a last climb here together—and an attempt to save my brother's life. Despite a lot of mental effort, I'm still uncertain what our plan should be. A hard-core user like Roberto needs confinement and careful medication, something he's not likely to submit to voluntarily. One thing I know for sure is that my father's unconcealed animosity, born out of the impending termination of his career, won't help things. Nor will my own distaste for the hard drugs I've devoted my professional life to combating. Persuading Roberto to swerve away from the path of self-destruction he's speeding down won't be easy, and there's no place in any strategy for anger and recrimination.

Climbing has always been the Burns family's first drug of choice. *La llamada del salvaje,* as my mother describes it. The call of the wild. According to her it's a sort of genetic flaw on my father's side that has descended to Roberto and me. It's a hunger we learned to feed by getting lethal amounts of air beneath our heels. The fear you feel free-climbing, hundreds or thousands of feet off the deck, and with just a skinny rope as backup, is like an illicit substance—once ingested it makes the sweet stuff called noradrenaline just ooze out from the adrenal glands. It blows through all the panic that comes from deadly heights, replacing it with a tingly sensation. Ecstasy. Exaltation. Rapture. The negative side effect is that it's a little harder to replicate that feeling after each session. You have to push it a little further. Dad and I have learned to control our addiction—we've learned that there's pleasure in just crawling up into the heights without needing to lay it all on the line for that hormonal surge. Roberto hasn't.

He reached for something even stronger. Starting in his early twenties he turned to pharmaceuticals to pump up the volume. He began with pot, mushrooms, and acid, then moved on to methamphetamine, cocaine, and heroin. He was chasing the dragon, looking for a better and louder amp. On the frequent climbing trips we used to take together in my college days, he would sometimes offer me some. I'd never been interested. Even then, before having really seen the damage those drugs could do, I preferred a natural high, although I had occasionally smoked marijuana with him in my teenage years (something I still consider no more dangerous than beer). Roberto once told me he'd discovered that cocaine mixed with heroin—a speedball— could push him beyond climbing's natural rush. It could take him places far further than the thrill of fighting ordinary gravity.

"It's just an ice cream habit," he'd explained when I'd given him a hard time about the hard drugs. "I got it under control, bro."

Right.

But it isn't just the drugs, although they've become the center of Roberto's life. It's the way he interacts with people, the way he thinks, even the way he climbs. Roberto has become addicted to living on the very edge. If he isn't climbing, he's slamming a needle deep into a vein. If he isn't surrounded by the circle of fast-living friends who worship him as the fastest of them all, then he's brawling with anyone he perceives as having done something unjust. And if he isn't utterly free, then he's caged in a county jail somewhere. Recently there had even been a brief stint in a federal prison. Roberto has happily danced so far out on the edge and for so long that it's a miracle the void hasn't yet sucked him in.

Do I really believe we can change that? It would require almost a repolarization of my brother's soul. I know, even now, that this is simply a last hurrah before the odds catch up with him. There's no chance in hell he'll ever become an ordinary citizen, responsible with his life and his future, and constrained by the rules that civilization demands.

So I say to my father, "No strategy, Dad. Just show him that we love him, that if he keeps this up we'll be the ones who suffer."

My father shakes his head and uncharacteristically expresses some emotion in his voice while looking at the red and gold stone of the canyon's opposite wall. "Shit, Anton, it'd be hard to suffer much more. It'd be a relief if he were dead."

You'd think a son would be shocked to hear his father talk about his brother like that. But I'm not. In my darkest moments I often think the same thing. I'm tired of waiting for the telephone to ring late in the night; waiting for the quiet voice of some Colorado police officer to tell me that my brother's dead.

There isn't much more to say than that.

I close my eyes and recall a scene from this morning, just a few hours ago, when my father and I sped on the highway out of the seemingly endless suburbs of Tomichi in the predawn blackness, on our way to the valley. I'd been glancing over at my father's deeply lined face while we talked, noticing how old it looked in the glow of the dashboard's light. His mouth opened suddenly. His eyes narrowed. I snapped my own eyes forward to the road. A big coyote was braced facing us in the middle of the lane. His eyes burned with green fire in the reflected heat of the headlights. The silver-tipped ruff of fur around his neck and shoulders was standing straight up. I swung the wheel hard to the left, onto the wrong side of the road, mashing the brake and throwing my big dog in the backseat across the truck. The coyote never even flinched.

That coyote was just like Roberto. Totally defiant in the face of law and civilization, even when it's coming at him seventy miles per hour in the form of three thousand pounds of rusty Japanese steel. Utterly audacious, reckless, and not long for this world. But beautiful all the same.

I realize that my brother's luck must soon run out, that the world won't swerve away much longer. And that Roberto's nuclear-powered élan combined with whatever sort of shit he likes to spike in his veins will vastly magnify the force of the inevitable collision. What I don't yet realize is just how many lives are about to be lost in the crash.

Opening my eyes to the blue sky, I take up the sling of gear my father has laid between us. Without a word I add the pieces from the anchor I'd pulled below and slip it clanking over my head and one shoulder. Standing, I arch my neck upward and try to plot the course that will take me another rope length into the sky. My skin touches the warm, rough rock as I slide my fingers over the lip of a small contour above my head. The familiar texture of it for the first time in my life fails to give me a small thrill. For a moment I'm caught off balance, experiencing a sense of vertigo and dread I've never experienced before. This is a mistake, I tell myself, as I will the web of well-conditioned muscles in my forearms to grip with my fingers and hold me on the ledge. Something bad is going to happen. A cold sweat seeps out of my skin. I glance at my father and see him looking back curiously. Concerned.

"Locked and loaded?" I ask, trying to reassure myself

with the start of the short litany he'd drilled into Roberto and me as children. We examine the harness buckles and knots at each other's waist.

"Tight and right," Dad responds, his voice puzzled.

"On belay?"

"Belay on."

"Climbing."